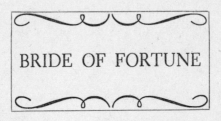

BRIDE OF FORTUNE

Bride of Fortune

A NOVEL BASED ON THE LIFE OF
MRS. JEFFERSON DAVIS

BY HARNETT T. KANE

DOUBLEDAY & COMPANY, INC.

GARDEN CITY, NEW YORK, 1948

Dear wife, this is not the fate to which I invited you when the future was rose-colored to us both. But I know you will bear it even better than myself, and that of us two, I alone will ever look back reproachfully on my past career. Farewell, my dear; there may be better things in store for us than are now in view. But my love is all that I have to offer, and that has the value of a thing long possessed, and sure not to be lost.

—*Jefferson Davis*

It is surely not the fate to which you invited me in brighter days. But you must remember that you did not invite me to a great hero's home but to that of a plain farmer, have shared all your triumphs, been the only beneficiary of them. Now I am but claiming the privilege for the first time of being all to you, now these pleasures have passed for us. God bless you, and keep you . . . I believe He will restore us to happiness.

—*Varina Davis*

Acknowledgments

TEN YEARS AGO I FIRST BEGAN TO GATHER MATERIAL REGARDING Varina Howell Davis. From time to time I have stayed in practically every locality in which she lived. Then, two years or so ago, I started the intensive writing of this book. Many persons in many places have assisted me.

My primary sources have been the two-volume *Memoir* of her husband, published in 1890, by Mrs. Davis; and her own letters, written over a period of seventy years or so. I have also drawn heavily upon letters by her husband, her friends, and connections. Varina Davis's own letters have been especially voluminous and give information that cannot be found anywhere else.

I have also talked with many descendants of those who participated in the events that occur in these pages; looked over memoirs, published and unpublished, letters and other data. Jefferson Davis's own writings, including *Rise and Fall of the Confederate Government*, have been helpful, as have been the memoirs of other Confederate leaders, their autobiographies and similar volumes. There have been occasional discrepancies in the many accounts of the happenings of the era. Sometimes Varina Davis herself has been in error; in one amusing instance she has given the wrong date (by a full year) for the birth of one of the children. In the main, however, I have found her writings remarkably precise and accurate, and I have followed them for the most part.

My thanks, therefore, to Mrs. Richard F. Goldsborough of New York City; Mrs. J. Harvey Jones of Spring Hill, Alabama; Mr. Trist Wood, New Orleans; Mrs. Edith L'Hote, New Orleans;

Mr. Howell Morgan, Shreveport, Louisiana; Mr. Cecil Morgan, Baton Rouge, Louisiana; Mrs. John G. O'Kelley, Pass Christian, Mississippi; Mr. Stamps Farrar, New Orleans; Mrs. Fullerton Weaver, New York City; Mrs. Livingston R. Schuyler, New York City; Dr. Robert D. Meade, Lynchburg, Virginia; Mr. Jefferson Hayes Davis, Colorado Springs, Colorado; the late Mrs. Winifred Kittredge, New York City.

To Dr. W. A. Evans of Aberdeen, Mississippi, who has been a lifelong student of Jefferson Davis; to Miss Zoe Posey of New Orleans, who has collected a wide range of Davis materials.

To Dr. William McCain, director of the Mississippi Department of Archives and History; to Miss Charlotte Capers, his assistant, and Mrs. Laura Harrell, formerly of the staff.

To Mrs. Dunbar Rowland of Jackson, Mississippi, a long-time admirer and student of the Davises.

To Miss India Thomas of the Confederate Museum of Richmond, and Miss Dorothy Brockenbrough of the museum.

To Dr. Garland Taylor, librarian of the Howard-Tilton Memorial Library of Tulane University, and to Miss Marguerite D. Renshaw, Mrs. Mary Bell Herndon, Mrs. Margaret Hughes, and the late Mrs. Elizabeth Shannon, formerly of the staff, and to John M. Dawson, formerly assistant librarian.

To Dr. Wendell H. Stephenson, chairman of the History Department and professor of Southern history, Tulane University, and Dr. Fred Cole, dean of the College of Arts and Sciences, Tulane University, and Dr. Gerald Capers and Dr. William R. Hogan of the History Department.

To Mr. John Hall Jacobs, librarian of the New Orleans Public Library; Mr. George King Logan, assistant librarian; Miss Margaret Ruckert, Miss Gladys Peyronnin, and others of the staff. To Mr. Stanley C. Arthur, executive director of the Louisiana State Museum, and Miss Josie Cerf, librarian; Miss Essae M. Culver, executive secretary of the Louisiana Library Commission; Miss Katrina Perrault of the Fisk Public Library of Natchez, and Miss Lily Carson of the staff.

To Mrs. William Winans Wall, owner of The Briers, the Natchez home of the Howells, for her hospitality and generous assistance.

To Miss Marguerite Fortier, curator of the Confederate Memorial Hall, New Orleans, and General Allison Owen, president of the board.

To Dr. Douglas Southall Freeman of Richmond for his courteous help; Dr. H. J. Eckenrode; Mr. and Mrs. Clifford Dowdey of that city; Mr. Clayton Torrence, director of the Virginia Historical Society; Mrs. Ralph Catterall of the Valentine Museum, Miss Meredith Dietz, Miss Sally Archer Anderson, Mrs. Eudora Ramsey Richardson, Miss Ellen Bagby, Miss Julia G. Moore, and Miss Margaret Dashiel, all of Richmond.

To Mrs. Edith Wyatt Moore, Mrs. Katherine Miller, Miss Courtney Winchester, and Miss Inez Montgomery, all of Natchez.

To Mr. Luther Evans, librarian of the Library of Congress; Mr. John C. L. Andreassen, acting director of administrative services at the library; Mr. David C. Mearns, director of the reference department; Mr. St. George L. Sioussat, chief of the division of manuscripts.

To Mr. G. R. Lyle, director of libraries of Louisiana State University, and Miss Ruth Campbell, curator of the Louisiana Room, Hill Memorial Library, Louisiana State University.

To Mr. Paul North Rice, chief of the reference department of the New York Public Library; Dr. Solon J. Buck, Archivist of the United States, Washington, D.C.; Mr. Harold F. Hutzhorn, manuscript division, New York Historical Society Library; Mr. Stanley Pargellis, librarian, Newberry Library; Mr. Joseph C. Wolf, head of the department of genealogy and local history, Newberry Library; Mr. Francis L. Berkeley, Jr., curator of manuscripts, Alderman Library, University of Virginia, Charlottesville; Dr. J. G. de Roulhac Hamilton, Southern Historical Collection, University of North Carolina Library, Chapel Hill, and Mrs. J. T. Watters of the staff; Miss Marie B. Owen, director of the Alabama Department of Archives and History; Miss Carolina W. Hiatt, curator of manuscripts, Princeton University; Miss Helen H. Salls, assistant in the manuscript department, Duke University Library; Miss Ruth Blair of the Atlanta Historical Society.

To Mrs. W. M. Newman, Vicksburg; Mr. Robert McElroy, Baltimore; Mrs. Paula Coad, Savannah, Georgia, and Wymberley W. DeRenne, Athens, Georgia; to Jean Selby, Vicksburg; Mrs. Lillian Kimbrough, V. Blane Russell, Mrs. Julia Arnold, Mrs. E. M. Durham, all of Vicksburg; Mrs. Jeanne Sully Smyth of New

Orleans and Miss Julia Sully of Richmond; Dr. Robert G. Stephens, Washington, Georgia; Mrs. C. D. Burchenal, Brooklyn, New York; Mr. Kenneth Vander Hulse, Auburndale, Florida.

To Miss Mary Railey, New Orleans; Mrs. Janie Cook Selby, Hattiesburg; Miss Nannie-Mayes Crump, Washington, D.C.; Mrs. Ida H. Louque, New Orleans; Mrs. Rene H. Himel, Franklin, Louisiana; Mr. Max Baird, New Orleans; Mr. F. P. Hagaman, New York; Mr. Hobart Huson, Refugio, Texas; Mrs. S. E. McClendon, New Orleans; Mrs. W. O. Bingham, Greenwood, Mississippi; Mrs. Henry P. Hughes, Longbeach, Mississippi.

Mrs. Lucy Stillman, San Francisco; Miss Josephine Balfour Payne, Church Hill, Mississippi; Dr. Holman Hamilton, Fort Wayne, Indiana; Mrs. C. S. Pierce, Tallulah, Louisiana; Mrs. Will Whitaker, Baton Rouge; Mr. Paul Veith, New Orleans; Miss Anne Siewers, Chicago; Mrs. Martha Adams, Lynchburg; Miss Bayliss McShane, Greenwood, Mississippi; Mrs. Mede Ferguson, Vicksburg; Thomas M. Wade, III, Tallulah; Mr. Thomas M. Wade, Jr., St. Joseph.

To Mrs. Mary Emerson Sanders, Covington, Louisiana; Mrs. Aubrey E. Orr, Beaumont, Texas; Mrs. R. F. Whitfield, Jackson, Mississippi; Mrs. H. P. Hughes, Memphis; Miss Merrill Parish Hudson, Memphis; Miss Lillian C. Young, Stuttgart, Arkansas; Dr. George Bolling Lee, New York; Mrs. George Janvier, New Orleans; Mrs. Denzil Price Marshall, Jonesboro, Arkansas; Mrs. Thomas Stone Howell, Alexandria, Louisiana; Mrs. Thomas Dickson, Sewanee, Tennessee.

Dr. Pierce Butler of Natchez; Miss Peytona L. Howell, New Orleans; Mrs. Charles T. Colseon, Jackson, Mississippi; Mrs. H. Herbert Hawkins, Vicksburg; Miss Edith H. Wiggs, North Hollywood, California; Miss Virginia Westbrook, New Orleans; Miss Carrie Freret, New Orleans; Mrs. Eli Landry, Jr., St. Francisville, Louisiana; Mrs. Emily Hosmer, Covington, Louisiana; Mrs. Mary Patterson Fisher, Chapel Hill, North Carolina; Miss Mary Field Mounger, Hattiesburg, Mississippi; Miss Louise Crawford, Bay St. Louis, Mississippi; Mrs. William H. King, New Orleans; Mrs. Catherine Worsley, New Orleans; Mrs. Earle Rowe Glenn of Port Gibson, Mississippi; Mrs. George E. Mixon, Hattiesburg, Mississippi; Miss Nannie Gillis, McComb, Mississippi.

Mrs. Alice Walworth Graham, Mrs. Frances Bryson Moore, and Mrs. Burdette Huggins of New Orleans.

Mrs. Wesley Mackie, Aberdeen, Mississippi; Mrs. Rosa D. Leatherbury, Clarksdale, Mississippi; Miss Estelle Lake, Memphis; Dr. Rudolph Matas, New Orleans; former Governor Dennis Murphree, Jackson, Mississippi; Mrs. George Bowyer Young, Arrowhead Ranch, Norwood, California; Mrs. Undine F. Mc-Caleb, Byrnmore plantation, Mississippi; Mrs. Lucinda Ballard, New York City; Mrs. Elizabeth Messick Houk and Mrs. R. O. Johnston, Memphis; Mrs. R. F. Whitfield, Jackson, Mississippi; Mrs. F. F. Litchliter, Picayune, Mississippi; Mrs. Malcolm J. Triche, Baton Rouge; Mrs. Alice Crisman, Dallas, Texas.

To the Misses Maude and Fanny Walthall, Jackson, Mississippi.

To Mrs. Maud O'Bryan Ronstrom, Columnist and Want-Ad Reporter for the *Times Picayune*—New Orleans States, who helped me in locating numerous Davis items.

Contents

Part One

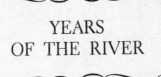

YEARS
OF THE RIVER

Chapter 1

OUT OF THE SHELTERING DIMNESS OF THE DEEP-SUNKEN ROAD THAT was the Natchez Trace, the carriages rolled toward the wide white house atop a rise in the uneven earth. In the dusk The Briers glowed like an ornamented cake, brightly lighted, against an irregularly hung background of green. Over the edge of the nearby cliff, concealed by the upheld arms of cedars and walnuts and mossy, fern-grown oaks, the Mississippi glided slowly southward toward New Orleans and its union with the Gulf.

In the candlelight of the arched central doorway a tall, dark-haired girl stood temporarily alone. Behind her, figures passed in a swirl, skirts rustling to the scrape of fiddles, servants maneuvering in and out with trays of wine punch, men leading partners across the hall. Many of the guests, from their seats along the walls, watched the quick-moving Varina Howell to see how she was behaving as she helped receive at her first grown-up party.

She knew what they were doing and why, and her full bright lips widened in amusement. Let the old hens stare and cackle among themselves! She wanted to be over there among the dancers; she didn't intend to simper and curtsy all night. A poised hand reached up to the sleek black coiffure with its precise central part, the hair drawn to a roll at the back of the neck; then abruptly it fell. Varina Howell's dark brown eyes, the color of the Spanish sherry in the glasses, brightened as a robust new figure filled the doorway:

"Of course! You're Jules Amant! We used to play together along the bayou."

The handsome boy responded promptly, his gaze darting over Varina's cream-white skin, her short round nose, the firm breasts, the half-exposed shoulders over the dress of unrelieved white that had been caught tightly at the waist. Heads in the dowagers' line twisted for a better view, and some with daughters who were also seventeen observed uneasily how, at such moments, Varina took on a new, yet more warming beauty. There was nothing languid in the look she turned to young Mr. Amant.

"And do you remember"—his nose wrinkled—"the day you pushed me down the bank, and I turned and spanked you?"

"Don't I? I felt it for days!" She rubbed her backside, and a pair of neighbors, arriving at the door, cleared their throats in disapproval. The boy bowed himself reluctantly away; Varina bit her lip and showed her relief as her mother rejoined her. But at her first glimpse of the soft, still comely face with its tight brown curls she realized that as usual Margaret Howell had missed very little. Her plump hands folded firmly; her round lips set.

"Please, dear." Margaret gave her daughter's arm a tap that was half affection, half reprimand. "Watch your tongue. You promised, you know." The smile made her words more an appeal than a rebuke.

Behind her Varina heard the echo of a murmur or two:

"A bad example, that girl. Headstrong, pampered . . ."

"Just because she's gone to school so much . . ."

By this time her mother had shifted her attention to the candle-lights at the door. Her gesture was nervous, overemphasized. Margaret, Varina told herself with a sigh, seemed always in a hurry, trying to catch up with one of her hundred duties.

Three butlers—two borrowed for the occasion—moved gingerly by with a heavy nougat on a platter, brought up a few hours earlier by a fast New Orleans steamboat. Her father had insisted on it; Varina sensed rather than heard her mother's groan. And after she'd worked so hard over the month's expenses! Margaret had had a great deal of "arranging" to do this year of 1843. Varina wondered if the day would ever arrive when they would not have a debt suspended over them. Absently she waved to the line of her brothers and sisters peering down over the stairway. Then she smiled as her older brother danced by with his arm around one of the Surget girls and winked at her. If only Father . . .

A few feet away she heard one of the gossips, staring toward young Mr. Amant: "Three hundred slaves when his father dies!"

"You don't have to say it," Varina said to her mother, and laughed. "Everybody's sure he's a catch."

"You can joke, Varina, but——"

Her mother did not finish her sentence. A gap opened in the crowd across the room, and both of them looked toward a man with irregular, pleasing features and a smile that seldom went away. His yellowish hair hung down over guileless brown eyes that appeared to like everything they saw. Just now he was bending his lean frame forward and shaking a finger at a young friend beside the brandy table.

"Giving advice again!" Varina told her mother with a chuckle. Her tone was affectionate. Hardly anybody in the world disliked William Howell; he was always ready to do something for someone else, this man who could never quite manage his own affairs.

Yet, Varina reflected, hadn't William Howell been called a catch in his day? His father had been a Revolutionary fighter, eight times governor of New Jersey. In the War of 1812 William had won commendations for gallantry, almost losing his life on several occasions. Then he had heard of Natchez, the emerging cotton capital of the lower Mississippi. Everybody was going to Natchez to get rich. Varina, tilting her head a little, made out William Howell's favorite remarks on his favorite subject.

"Why, young fellow, we were the West then, the frontier. Every man had a chance, a fair share. Just get a little capital, a parcel of blacks, and go to work. In three years, maybe four, with any luck at all, you had a fortune." Now William was telling how first one great plantation, then another sprang up; how a tight little society began to thrive—a small world of opulence on the bluff across from the steaming green Louisiana flatlands. And, Varina reminded herself, William Howell had come here under the happiest of circumstances: a good name, entree to the best drawing rooms.

Soon, at Kempton Plantation, he met the Kempes, who had brought their wealth and their coat of arms from Virginia. Margaret Kempe waltzed with him several times that first night, and then again. A little later they were married, and to the union Margaret contributed two plantations, several lots of slaves.

William Howell had made a start of his own, but now his fate caught up with him. It seemed that bad fortune hunted out the young couple—a flood, sudden collapse of the cotton market, always something worse. Or was it William's own inexpertness? Had anyone else used the word, Varina would have lashed out; even when she said it to herself, as she did now, she felt a sense of guilt. In the years of their marriage the Howells had made one move and then another, in Louisiana and Mississippi.

One of Varina's first sharp memories was of the morning Margaret walked in on her at play and all at once, unaccountably, threw her arms about her and broke into sobs. Not knowing why, Varina had also cried. From time to time after that she had seen her plump young mother huddled at her desk with that same blurring of her features, that look of hurt about her tiny pink mouth. Usually, afterward, there occurred a change in their ménage. With fresh capital, help from relatives or friends, William made a new start; and then Margaret went to work to "manage," struggling over economies, making things fit.

No matter what happened, they kept the finely carved old rosewood furnishings that had come to her from the Kempes. Tonight Varina's glance went from one to another—the great sofa on which eight could sit, the high bookcases that lined the hall, the sideboards and the row of precise, feminine-looking chairs. The curtains might be worn—her eyes passed over patched spots—but they kept their elegance, their good appearance. And the Howells had never lost the hundred and thirty-seven pieces to the main china set!

Margaret Howell, Varina assured herself, could get along anywhere, in any society. She had watched her mother alter her setting, gradually, deftly. Margaret, she suspected, could make herself like anything. "Do I have the same ability?" she inquired as she caught sight of her white figure in the mirror. "Maybe. When I want to I can get on with anybody—when I want to. But why should I go around all the time that way, fitting myself to things? Let them fit to me!"

Poor Margaret. She showed the effects of these recent years. Married early, she was still only thirty-eight, and she retained most of her full-blown handsomeness. Yet Varina detected lines about the mouth far deeper than they should have been, markings below the eyes that resembled those of a woman of fifty. There she went now, moving to the doorway and back with her nervous step, her eyes constantly darting about the room.

Some years ago Grandpa Kempe had made this house, The

Briers, available to them. Natchez had many more pretentious establishments than this white wooden building, but it was big and airy and it had an air of simple good taste. It stood two and a half stories high, with a gallery along the whole width, a long row of windows and doors at the front, and a deep roof. There was a series of side buildings clustered around the main dwelling. A short time ago when Grandpa Kempe died he left a sizable inheritance for Margaret, but when it was gone there would be no reserve on which to draw, and Varina and Margaret understood it well.

Varina's wide-spaced eyes darkened, and she lifted her chin in a favorite movement of defiance. She'd never let herself get married to anybody but a rich man! She knew how she wanted things— just the way the Surgets had them. Natchez's most affluent family enjoyed its acres of land, with parties nearly every night or so, trips to Europe whenever you looked around for them, jaunts up to the Virginia springs. Economy was all right, but not too much of it. . . .

She wheeled about to find she was alone again. Margaret Howell had crossed the room to her husband's side. There she stood now with an expression close to worship that she seldom lost when they were together. In spite of everything, Varina realized again, Margaret Howell was happy. "Well, that wouldn't be enough for me. I haven't any intention——"

A rumbling voice, a beloved one, called her back to the present. Judge George Winchester, her tutor, black-bearded, barrel-shaped, called her name as he passed with a cousin on his arm: "Don't forget, child, your lessons tomorrow as usual!"

She wished he hadn't reminded her, or the others on the gossip row. She heard snatches of disapproval: "Still being educated!" . . . "Why, even for a boy . . ."

When she was hardly six, Varina's tutor, much impressed with her showing, had called the family aside. After that they had watched her advance more rapidly than any of the others around her. For a while the family had sent her up to Philadelphia, to Madame Greenland's "select school." Her nose lifted in disdain. She would have collapsed if she had to work at "gentility" for another term. She didn't want to be that kind of lady, and she had insisted on returning.

Years earlier the generous Judge Winchester had taken over

supervision of her training, and now he resumed his work. "You know a lot, my dear," he told her. "Pretty soon you'll have all I'm able to teach you." The end of her courses was approaching, yet she was far from happy about it.

From the next room, as he moved beneath the chandelier with his partner, Jules Amant made a signal to her. Should she be offended? The books of conduct said, of course, that such a thing was ungentlemanly. If he wanted a dance he'd certainly be coming over with a bow and a proper request. But, in spite of all that, she found herself smiling to him. Ashamed, she faced away and almost bumped into General John Quitman.

The big man snapped his heels together and bent over her hand. Some didn't like the imposing, erratic, trouble-hunting fellow, but Varina's family did. He was supposed to be the hottest-blooded Southerner in the South, and he came from New York. Now he hated the North with a consuming passion. His profuse beard and mustaches bristling, he beamed down at her. "My dear, I once held you on this knee . . ." And he was off on a monologue. What was it her mother had said of Quitman? He had everything needed for a great man—courage, brawn, an imposing face—everything except a first-class brain.

Somehow, though she had not followed him, he had worked his talk around to politics and Mr. Calhoun. Varina's long fingers tensed, and her full black brows narrowed in annoyance. "Mr. Calhoun, missy, that's the man who'll save our South. He'll unify us against the Yankees, give us our chance——"

"Our chance to commit suicide?" The words were out before she could help it. As a good Whig, she had heard a great deal about that wild Democrat Calhoun. Quitman, taken by surprise, flushed and spluttered, as he always did when confused. For a moment Varina felt sorry for him. But here, across the room, relief approached—young Jules Amant. He stepped forward a little proudly, a hint of challenge in his face, and with it a calm appraisal that stirred her pulse.

She danced away, leaving General Quitman with her now unhappy brother. Jules Amant had a faunlike face, with a delicately tapered nose, a sheen of hair that reminded her of the pelt of a freshly curried animal. Already certain of the girls were tossing themselves at him; the gossips had been talking of an exploit of his among the tosspots Under the Hill, the water-front hell spot of Natchez. Perhaps it should make her feel a revulsion; she remembered the sight of the gamblers and the blowzy, red-lipped women from her last ride to the river. Oddly, however, it seemed to make Jules much more interesting.

For a while she enjoyed his brisk banter. He had just come back from school in the East, and they had a lot to talk over. Though she was considered tall, her pert nose reached only to his shoulder. She was aware of his searching scrutiny of her rounded cheeks, of her half-veiled brown eyes. Her lips had parted in the excitement of the hour. A moment before she had caught up a deep red rose and thrust it against the blue-black hair behind her ear. As she danced with him, wide skirts swaying, the flower a splash of stain against dark hair and white skin, she nodded her replies to his questions.

"Yes, it's a wonderful evening," she murmured, her words a happy sigh. She liked crowds, excitement, the hum of music, the lowering and lifting of the candle flames whenever the doors opened, the smells of perfume and spiced dishes on the trays.

Jules asked her about her studies, and when he learned she had not yet finished them he said: "Why are you keeping all that up?"

"I like it. I may make use of it someday."

"So?" Jules glanced disdainfully about him. "I don't suppose you've gotten as far as Ovid."

"Finished it two years ago. It was simple."

That made it worse. His narrow face, half averted, had darkened; he looked like a spoiled child. For once Varina, who could always think of something to say, found herself speechless. This was far from the exchange she had planned for them. She felt the perspiration gathering in her palms as she danced on miserably with this man who might as well be miles away. And she had been so certain of herself, of the poise they said she had. Almost sick, she looked over the other girls tossing their curls, blinking like ninnies. So this was what she got for having "her own mind."

At last, with a flourish of the bows, the music halted. To her surprise she found that Jules's hand still held hers. He had regained his good humor; his eyes had the dancing light she had first seen in them. "Can't we go outside?" he whispered. Before she replied he had opened the paneled door and led her to the half-enclosed rear gallery.

A rush of wind lifted the strands of her black hair. Holding hands, they passed the group seated at the edge of the porch. Some would chatter over it, but what did she care? Along the outside brick walk one or two couples (engaged, of course) were strolling. Jules took her quickly away from them toward one of the side buildings. The boy had a good memory from his childhood days at The Briers. She grew alarmed; this would hardly be allowed.

"I don't——"

She did not finish. By now they were in the shadows of the schoolhouse, and his arms had gone around her, quickly, expertly. Her lips evaded his. Then, with a sense of surprise and delight, she relaxed. He kissed her once more, and she returned it. A narrow edge of moonlight cut its way downward across a well-remembered wall thick with vines. Her upturned face was clearly outlined, and also the beginning of her throat.

The hand he held behind her trembled, and she felt his breath against her cheek. "No," she told him. "We'd better go."

He came closer again, his fingers passing from her face to her bare neck. She pulled away, her voice angry. "Stop it. I didn't mean——"

"You didn't!" Jules gave a muffled laugh, and as he moved he blotted out the line of moonlight, leaving them in blackness. "Why'd you come out here, then? To recite your Latin?"

Before she quite realized what she was doing she had slapped him. The sound echoed across the yard; in a panic she wondered if the people on the gallery had heard. Now Jules guffawed. "Why, you are a bluestocking!"

Quivering in her uncertainty, she remained as if tied there. "You——" The words would not issue. She could only conclude lamely: "You bore me!"

He had turned into the moonlight again, and she could make out the grin on his lips. "Oh no, Miss Naïve. You weren't bored just now."

From a nearby cabin there arose a chuckle. Then one of the servants had heard; tomorrow it would be all around. The ripple of amusement followed her as she darted ahead and up the stairs. Inside, as she took a glass of punch and plied her fan, she tried to quiet herself.

Naïve, indeed! It was what she might have expected from a simpleton like that, and one who'd been to Harvard, the Yankee.

Yet even Harvard wouldn't make a Yankee; and anyway, hadn't her father lived in the North?

The rose, picked up so confidently a short time ago, slipped from her hair; she let it fall. What did it matter? Her evening was ruined. Margaret Howell was watching her with a curious expression. Perhaps her mother was right about her "attitude." You didn't get a husband by being strong-minded!

Early the next afternoon Varina sat in silence at the bluff's edge, in the wild luxuriance of the vines that tangled the overhanging oaks and cedars. Above, the clouds drifted toward the blue-green haze of the Louisiana flat country; below, over the jagged outline of the broken red earth, the river slipped lake-like toward the south. Her younger sister Maggie, a towheaded child with a bridge of freckles across her face, had asked to join her, but this time Varina wanted to escape the interruptions of the family.

For the fiftieth time she was asking herself why she didn't feel more at ease with people of her own age. Was it because she had been too often in the company of her elders, her teachers, the Howells' friends? The gossips might be right when they muttered that she had been brought up too differently, given her own head in too many things. The Fall of Rome dropped from her hands, and her eyes followed the river's twistings to the cluster of faded shacks on the opposite bank near the bend. She broke off a twig and sent it spinning over the bluff. Was she going to be an old maid like the three sad Galt sisters down the road?

The bush rustled, and the maid appeared. "Miss Marg'ret say can you come?" Automatically she put out her hand to help Varina up. There was an odd gleam in the girl's eye, and Varina knew at once that it had been Tildy who heard the previous night. Her cleft chin rose; she wouldn't give her the satisfaction. . . .

Varina found her mother working over her sewing, her small plump hands moving tirelessly about a hill of cloth. Thrusting a hairpin back into the brown waves of her high-piled hair, Margaret spoke at once, running on at her usual breathless pace.

"Dear, you remember last Christmas when Mr. Joe Davis asked you for a visit up in the country? You were too young then. Now he's written again, and we think you ought to go."

Margaret was looking intently at her. "Well . . ." Varina

hesitated. Joseph Emory Davis, the big bluff planter up near Vicksburg . . . She had seen "Uncle Joe" off and on for most of her life. She remembered the way her father talked of him; Joe Davis had taken the younger man under his wing during William Howell's first years at Natchez, when Joe was a lawyer in the town. Mr. Davis eventually had purchased a long low stretch of land at the river's edge, in a remote bend that had never been cultivated, and he had asked William Howell to join him in planting it.

"I went there," her father always said. "But it looked too low, too fevery to me. Rich enough, I thought, but sickly, and too far off from things. So," he would conclude with a laugh that was wry, "so I lost a fortune." "Uncle Joe" Davis had gone on to become one of the richest planters on the river, yet a remote figure by Natchez's standards. Varina had never met him at her friends' parties, and she never heard the Natchezians talk about him. She hadn't thought much about it; now she asked: "Mother, just who are the Davises?"

Margaret, with one of her nervous gestures, put her sewing down. "They're simpler folk than some in Natchez. Still, they're good people, as good as any I know. You understand Natchez, don't you? If you don't live within ten miles of this town you're nothing!" Varina reflected; until she made her trip up to Pennsylvania she had thought that too. Picking up one of her husband's ruffled shirts, Margaret began to take in the tucks. "It's Joe that runs the family— and runs it well." She seemed about to say more, then changed her mind.

A step sounded outside, and William Howell ambled in, hands in the baggy pockets of his broadcloth trousers, his ruddy face creased by his ever-present smile. "The field hands are doing all right by themselves." He yawned. "Thought I'd spend a little time with my family." It was his usual explanation when he left his duties. His light hair fell over his brow as he bent down to kiss them. Then, rather too casually, he, too, went to the subject of the invitation from the Davises. "You'll go, won't you, dear?" His small brown eyes were more earnest than usual.

Resentment stirred within Varina. It would be dull out there among the bumpkins, and she thought of the dozen of Christmas-season affairs she would miss in Natchez. The Marshalls were plan-ing an eggnog party; the Quitmans were inviting seventy-five couples to their Monmouth. She let out a long breath. "But you've said yourself that it's wild country, nothing but swamp!"

"That was a mistake I made, child." Her father's eyes lowered, and for once he did not tell the story with a smile.

Margaret Howell turned a sharp look in his direction, then busied herself with her needle. "It won't be as—as wild as you think, dear," she said, as if speaking to herself.

"Oh well." Varina lifted a slim shoulder and ran her fingers through her hair. "If you want it. But what shall I wear?"

"I thought of that." Margaret's round lips puckered wisely. "I'm getting seamstresses from town to help us. You'll have five new gowns, hats and all." Varina's eyes took on a new sparkle. "Crazy about clothes . . ." She was aware that Natchezians said it about her, and she didn't mind.

She knew what became her; she understood how to produce an effect, and from Margaret Howell she had learned how to produce it with the least expense. There were usually whispers among the old maids about the way Varina, for all the Howells' problems, managed to dress better than practically anybody of her age in Natchez. It took a little ingenuity on her part as well as Margaret's, and ingenuity meant the difference between a passing glance and a long, approving one. She wanted the latter, whether from man or woman.

Her eyes fell on a pile of material at her mother's side. She lifted the dark-red taffeta and saw the rich material take the light, shining in her hands. "Grandma's best party dress," her mother murmured. "I'm going to cut it down for you."

Varina's face showed how impressed she was. This visit to "Uncle Joe's" would be quite an occasion, then. She held the gown against her slim young form. "Mm . . . I'm lucky. Grandma was wider than me, everywhere."

That brought back an unhappy memory. Dropping the cloth, she went quickly to her father. "Papa, am I—naïve?"

William Howell's heavy brows shot up, and his brown eyes widened. "What a word, child. No." Then the lines at the corners of his eyes deepened, and he went on more slowly. "No. Not more than anybody else of seventeen!" This was hardly the reply she wanted, and she walked swiftly out.

Chapter 2

A LIGHT KNOCK AWAKENED VARINA. RISING ON ONE ELBOW, SHE stared at the unfamiliar canopy above her head and asked herself where she was. Then it came back—this was the house of one of Joe Davis's daughters, Mrs. Florida McCaleb. All the previous day she had ridden up the chilly river on the *Magnolia* with her escort for part of the trip, Judge Winchester. Late last night the black crewmen, holding lighted torches, had guided her across the gangplank to the soggy shore, where several of the Davis family waited.

To get to the Joe Davis place was even more difficult than she had realized. It lay in a turn of the Mississippi, where the stream had dropped countless acres of rich soil through the years. Davis Bend, she already knew, was a rough peninsula with a difficult landing. They had debarked at the most accessible spot, an outlying family holding. It was a pleasant house, the McCalebs', about the size of The Briers in Natchez, larger than she had expected.

Young Mrs. McCaleb looked hardly older than Varina herself, and she had welcomed her in easy, friendly style. "Father's talked about you over and over," she had confided, "especially since you've —you've grown up." At that she looked embarrassed, as if she had said a wrong thing, and Varina smiled to show that she did not mind. It had been late, and she had gone wearily to bed.

When Varina replied to the morning knock a heavy-framed black woman entered with a portable tin tub of warm water and, a moment later, the usual river-country eye opener, a tiny cup of steaming black coffee. Gratefully she sipped it. Then she swung her long white legs over the edge of the bed, dropped her beribboned silk nightdress, and, as the girl held out her hand to help, sank quickly into the welcome water. It was a chilly morning; she had seen signs of frost in the garden outside her window. She was out of the tub more promptly than usual, and the Negro woman used one towel to dry her while Varina applied the other.

So far, so good, she mused. No question that the McCalebs were prosperous; her quick glance at the mahogany pieces, well rubbed, and the rich curtains had told her that. (No patches such as the Howells had, she had noticed. Somehow, whenever she entered a house these days she seemed to peer first of all for unobtrusive patches.) Yet she had not lost her slight dread of Joe Davis's own place—so remote, out among the far swamps. Would it be a barn-like hut in the wilderness?

A few minutes later she had donned the dress Margaret Howell finished only an hour before she left. The costume, a brilliant brown velvet, braided at the small waist and wide collar, emphasized the whiteness of her skin. "Uh-huh," said the maid, adding her approval. As she combed her long straight hair—this morning she wanted to do it herself—Varina stared at her face.

"I hope I look just a little more than seventeen," she told herself. She turned her head to get the effect of the soft roll of hair at the back of her neck. That cleft in her firm chin—she was glad she had it now, though she had been teased enough about it as a child. As she attached the brooch at the collar she wondered if her lips could take a touch of coloring. Then she shook her head; they didn't need it.

"Anyt'ing more, miss?" As she waved her dismissal Varina's glance fell to Jules Amant's letter she had left on the table. Just before she left Natchez it had been brought to the house; she had opened it on the way. Could she, he asked, forgive his "poor behavior" and see him again? That, she had told herself with a nod, put an entirely new view on things; indeed it did. Yes, she would see Mr. Amant. . . . Her mind shifted to those three hundred slaves the boy would inherit, then jumped, abashed, to other matters.

Setting her last comb in place, Varina reached over to write her reply. "I'll be forgiving," she assured herself. "Forgiving, yet very definite. No more such behavior." From below she heard a beat of horse's hoofs, and quickly afterward the maid rapped, this time apologetically. "Mistis, she back lookin' after sick in the

horspital. Mister Jeff Davis, he say can he see you instead?"
Puzzled, Varina dropped the pen and, taking her skirts in her hand,
followed the girl. She'd never heard that name Jeff among the
Davises.

At the bottom of the stairs stood an erect man, nearly six feet
tall and extremely lean, gazing upward with a touch of curiosity in
his blue-gray eyes. Clearly he was the rider; he wore boots, dark
gray trousers that encased slim legs, a light, loose-hung coat with a
casually arranged stock at his throat. Those intent eyes were passing
over her face and figure with evident approval, but he stayed silent.

Then all at once, remembering himself, he said: "Miss Howell?
I'm Joseph's brother. He asked me to stop on my way past and say
they'll be over for you before long." The low, melodic voice made
her look harder. It was Southern, yet slightly changed; he pronounced the end of each word with care, and there was a richness,
a cultivation in his deep baritone.

As he accompanied her into the parlor she found him talking
about Natchez. He knew quite a little about her. Yet he addressed
her with reserve; she had an impression of cautiousness, almost of
withdrawal. For a moment the voice seemed almost too controlled.

"Oh yes," he answered her. "I live near here, a couple of miles
from Brother Joe." He avoided her name, as if uncertain how to
address her.

As he spoke she studied him. The face had an earnest, rather—
she groped for the word—rather an ascetic look: slightly sunken
cheeks beneath high cheekbones that appeared to touch the eyes;
a high forehead that ended in heavy brown eyebrows, a long jaw
line. The nose was sharp, regular, with a high bridge, and pleasing.
He wore his medium-dark hair rather long, parted far to one side.
The thin, firm lips—these seemed to dominate the face, giving it
tone and feeling. The skin, drawn tightly over the smooth-shaven
cheeks, had a bronzed look; at least of late this man had spent much
time in the open. For all its gauntness, she would call it a handsome
face.

Still there was an air of tension, as if he had been through a
strain. Had this Mr. Jeff Davis been ill for a time? She emerged
from her musing; she had missed the question he asked. He smiled
fleetingly, but in that moment she saw another person. For his own
good he should smile more often. He picked up the thread of his

remark: "The women, Joe's daughters and the rest, are making a great deal of preparation for you. A great deal."

Varina bridled at the hint of disapproval in his tone. Her fingers tugged angrily at the braid of her dress.

"Not so much that they're going to regret it, I hope!" she said quickly.

Jeff Davis's narrow lips compressed. So he had a temper too, did he? However, he checked himself. "I'm sorry. I didn't mean to imply that." There followed an awkward pause. As she worked at her cuffs, face averted, she sensed the searching observation he was giving her. When he spoke again his tone had changed. "I hope you'll like our place and us—Varina." He was asking for her friendship, and when he smiled she joined him. Tactfully she asked him about himself.

"I'm one of ten children," he told her easily, and she began to notice something close to courtliness in his manner. "They christened me Thomas Jefferson Davis, you know, but we soon dropped the Thomas. Oh no, I wasn't born down here, but in Kentucky. Father moved several times. I was about three, I guess, when we went to Louisiana, and then Mississippi." She had heard vaguely that the older Davis was a small farmer.

"Still"—her curiosity had grown—"still I've never seen you in Natchez, even with Uncle Joe."

"I've been away a lot—a Catholic college in Kentucky, Jefferson in Mississippi, and Transylvania University in Kentucky again. Then West Point." It was an impressive list; the schools accounted for his fine speech and also, she reflected, for that slight air of a scholar. And West Point, that explained the almost rigid bearing. "Then I went to the Northwest for six years—border duty, watching Indians." His long face had brightened; his words were beginning to come quickly and spontaneously. Then suddenly the light went out of his eyes and he stopped.

"After that I went home," he said in a flat voice. "I haven't gone about much since."

A curtain had dropped between them. There was something odd about this change. Varina could only ask: "What are you doing now?"

"I farm." He was examining his palms, and she saw that they were callused. Student or not, Mr. Jeff Davis worked with his hands. "Lately," he added, "I've been going out a little in politics. That's what brings me here today."

"You're a Whig, of course." She made the remark automatically.

"Of course not! I'm a Democrat. I don't favor oligarchies or combinations of power. We're the party of liberty, opportunity——"

"And ruin!" She thought scornfully of the warlike Quitman of Natchez, with his sulphuric talk of that wild man Calhoun. She had been oversharp with Quitman that last time, she realized, but now she could not force herself to be quiet. Jefferson Davis was going on as if he spoke biblical truth!

His light eyes darkened until there was no trace of gray in them. "Of course, Miss Varina"—so she had become Miss!—"these are subjects——"

"Subjects I have a right to think about, like anybody else."

For the first time he noticed the "Whig brooch" she wore, a shell cameo showing a strongbox, symbol of the fight against "dangerous tendencies." As he recognized it Jeff Davis's manner became even colder. "In any event, I think I'm due to resume my trip." He clasped her hand quite formally and left.

As he sprang nimbly to the saddle and rode off she watched from the window. What a superb horseman he was, what command! Her annoyance at him had begun to subside. Had she needed to be so—well, so self-assertive?

She was remembering their long conversation. What made this man act as he did? What was the story? That there was a "story" she did not doubt for a moment. As soon as horse and rider had disappeared she hurried upstairs to her room, sat down, and, with her thoughts still whirling, began a letter to her mother:

I do not know whether this Mr. Jefferson Davis is old or young. He looks both at times, but I believe he is old, for from what I hear he is only about two years younger than you are. He impresses me as a remarkable kind of man but of uncertain temper and has a way of taking for granted that everybody agrees with him when he expresses an opinion, which offends me; yet he is most agreeable and has a peculiarly sweet voice and a winning manner of asserting himself. The fact is, he is the kind of person I should expect to rescue me from a mad dog at any risk but to insist upon a stoical indifference to fright afterward. I do not believe I shall ever like him as I do his brother Joe. Would you believe it, he is refined and cultivated, and yet he is a Democrat!

As she read it over her elbow touched the note she had begun to Mr. Amant of Natchez. It lay there forgotten.

The country road, thick with moist leaves, appeared to be interminable. Florida McCaleb, the bright young daughter of Joe Davis, chatted easily as they rode on. "Didn't you realize how big our land is? Two miles across where it joins the mainland, yes, but to get around it a steamboat goes nineteen miles!" The dark-haired younger girl, who had ridden over that morning to escort her, spoke more somberly: "They say that the river's going to cut right across the neck of land one day and make this all an island. . . ." Mary Bradford, Joe Davis's niece, looked away at the curtain of moss-piled oaks and giant pecan trees that lined the road.

Varina stared at the back of Mary's head. The girl was obviously reserving judgment, sizing her up, listening for undertones in her remarks. She had made fun of the number of boxes of hats and costumes Varina had brought and that now filled the high-swung carriage behind them. "Oh well." Varina shrugged. "I can take care of myself, I think." She didn't merely think it; she knew she could.

"How many brothers and sisters——" She stopped in the middle of a sentence. The road had curved, and there, through a pair of high brick pillars, beyond a winding path, waited Joe Davis's house, The Hurricane. "Why, why—it's so big!" Her high voice had risen yet higher. It stood boldly there, all three stories of it, a great irregular brick-and-wood pile, with high front gallery, heavily pillared side ones, gables, soaring chimneys, kitchens, and other side structures. It gave the effect of two or three houses coupled with their outlying units. She had hardly anticipated anything like this; Natchez had more elegant, more graceful ones, but hardly more ponderous.

At the door was a tall, thickset figure, the beaming Joseph Davis, surrounded by more than a dozen men and women of all ages. At the sight of Varina's mount he hurried forth, black beard flying in the wind, voice booming, and caught her before she could slip from the sidesaddle. His sharp nose lifted, and his small piercing eyes that were never still moved rapidly over her. "Varina, my child!" his voice rumbled, and he reached over to envelop her in his arms. "We're ready for you, all of us!"

At that, as if awaiting a signal, the rest of them joined them. His heavy hand about her waist, he introduced her to them one by one, though it would be some time before she could distinguish them in her mind. "My brother Sam . . . Mrs. Stamps, my sister; Dr. Ben Davis from down in the Feliciana country; and these are the Ike Davises, and this is Amanda." Some smiled; others looked at her with unconcealed curiosity. The men's eyes lingered over her ripe lips, her blooming figure; the women made other appraisals. One or two, she told herself, were like the niece, Mary Bradford. They were waiting to see. They all had a certain family manner, a concentration of expression, and the high-bridged nose that she already recognized as a Davis mark.

Meanwhile "Uncle Joe" was throwing out compliments with an expansive hand: "Handsomest girl in Mississippi . . . Belle of Natchez, they say." She glanced around for Jeff and found him absent. Then, above her at the foot of the main gallery, she suddenly saw a woman, fragile-faced, small-framed, who had appeared quietly after Varina's arrival. There was an air of self-containment about this woman, as if she had learned to live within herself.

At once Joe Davis's deep voice dropped, and with an unexpectedly gentle expression he whispered to Varina: "Eliza, my wife."

They went together to her side, and Eliza extended a thin pink hand. She spoke in a low, curiously appealing tone. "My child, you're everything they said. Everything." The oval face widened in a smile, and the warm green eyes twinkled. Her hair might once have been red, Varina thought; now it had whitened prematurely. Somehow Varina sensed that, of all who came under Joe Davis's influence, it was his wife who was least dominated by him.

Moved by a sudden impulse, she leaned forward to kiss Eliza Davis's pale cheek. The older woman gave her a grateful look. "Whenever you can, dear, come to my room. We'll have a long talk. I'm generally there; I don't get out often." Now, though dressed in a heavy blue coat, she began to shiver, and Joe Davis whispered, "You're feeling the chill, Eliza."

With a firm gesture she quieted her big husband. "We want you to enjoy yourself here, Varina. We're comfortable, though we are a little out of the way of things." There was a suggestion of a break in the weary voice. "I'm from New Orleans, you know——" A pause, and then, "Originally." And Varina realized what a lonely life Eliza Davis had lived on this island plantation, far from the gay city of her youth. Eliza murmured something about her ill health, pressed Varina's hand again in the same affectionate way, and, summoning her maid, went inside.

Joe Davis now resumed his control of the situation. The others moved around him, and he took over the entire conversation. "So you've met Jeff!" he said to Varina. His sharp eyes studied her face. "What did you think of him? No," he interrupted himself, "wait until you've seen more of him." Varina's head rose in annoyance; this Mr. Jeff was certainly supposed to be somebody very important, wasn't he? Her vexation increased when Joe Davis added: "Supper's delayed a little. We hope Jeff will be back from Vicksburg." Before she could say anything he had given her his arm to conduct her around the estate. Varina looked back, expecting the others to follow, but she and Joe Davis walked on alone and she was certain he wanted it that way.

He took her through the wide hallway that was a room in itself, pointing out on the right the drawing room and the tea room— on the other side he indicated a bedroom and office. Each floor was arranged the same way, with a hallway and four great rooms. Everything came large here, and her woman's eye noticed a lack of finish by Natchez's standards. The ground floor was bricked; the walls looked almost unnecessarily thick, the windows overly small. Yet it had, above all, comfort and a certain heavy grandeur. The furniture—and she noticed quantities of it—was of rosewood and mahogany, carefully polished, much ornamented.

"And now, over here . . ." He led her through halls and side passages to the newer buildings, higher-ceilinged, rather more delicate. One had two rooms forty feet by twenty-five, a dining room, and an arched-ceiling music room with a harp and piano and a stage for games. Varina felt utterly lost.

They stopped before a portrait of a man with light hair and pale eyes, obviously a Davis. "Our father, Sam." Joe nodded. Varina's eyes narrowed; many would have thought the face plain and dismissed it. But no, there was something in that face, an expression of endless determination. He would never have given up; he would have died before he bent his head. It was the same look, she realized all at once, that she had found in the two brothers. Would Jeff Davis someday have that tight-eyed, almost violent firmness?

"Mother's still alive, in her eighties, down in Louisiana," Joe added. "We'd hoped she would come for Christmas, but it's too long a trip." He paused. "Someday I hope you'll meet her." Varina had a sense of disappointment; she would have liked to see the mother of such strong-minded sons.

"Let's go outside," Joe Davis rumbled, opening a door. Varina walked out into the almost endless garden as Joe proudly called out the names of the flowers and shrubs. It was the duty of the gardeners to see that five or six kinds of blooms splashed pinks and yellows and reds against these walls through most of the winter. Joe Davis pointed to the front. "Forty acres of live oaks." She blinked; she had been so intent on the house that she had missed the majesty of the great trees that guarded the approach. In the afternoon five servants worked in the groves; from the precise rows rose the musty smell of upturned earth. Rich soil it was, black and oily. . . . Suppose her father had come here, after all, when Joe Davis offered him the opportunity?

Joe Davis led her to a beautifully carved bench. He nodded a little moodily toward the cotton fields in the distance. "It's all fine now. It wasn't at first. One of my other brothers, with me at the beginning, saw the wind and water tear this land to pieces. People were killed or maimed; one child never fully recovered. That's how it got its name, The Hurricane. My brother left; I stayed on and I won.

"Still, there's a lot I've missed." He tugged at his dark beard, and the small light eyes had dulled. "I've been too busy growing my crops, handling my business, to do half what I hoped to do." He paused, rubbing his thick fingers along the seam of his trousers. Then he turned his head quickly and stared at her. "That's where Jeff fits in."

Varina's interest heightened; perhaps she was to learn more about the attractive but irritating younger brother. "He's the coming man of the family, Varina. He needs guidance, though, if he's to realize his chances." There was no question that Joe Davis meant to see to that both now and later.

The deep voice boomed on: "By the time he was eight or nine, Varina, I decided that, with his mind, the boy had the world before him. Father died, and I got to be a sort of parent in his place. It was I who talked him into going to West Point. He'd wanted to keep on with his classes at college up in Virginia." Joe Davis's lips twitched in contempt. "Well, I persuaded him to try West Point, for a year, anyway. After that he didn't want to leave the Army, ever!" A fleeting thought came to Varina: Suppose Jeff Davis had objected strongly to this course; would Joe have seen that he followed it anyway?

"Well, they sent him West as a lieutenant. He was a robust, plump-faced boy then, handsome as you could find. Some people thought he wasn't well fitted for the frontier, too educated. Jeff showed 'em! He's never been the kind to go around slapping backs, but he got along fine. The French settlers out there liked him, and so did the other soldiers, even the Indians. They called him Little Chief."

Joe Davis touched his beard with a hesitant motion, and now he was coming to something for which Varina had been waiting. "Affairs went well until his"—the plump fingers passed over the white vest—"his troubles with Colonel Taylor."

Varina had heard vaguely of Zachary Taylor, who had a plantation along the river and visited there when he was away from Army service. Joe had resumed: "I'm not sure what it was, maybe a little disagreement at the beginning. Taylor's a homespun sort, not much taken with West Point, they say. I guess he and Jeff are both hotheads, one as much as the other. Once, they tell me, Jeff wanted to fight a duel with him." His gaze had shifted to the horizon, where the tall trees nudged the sky. "Anyway, it came to a head about Taylor's daughter Knox."

So a woman had been mixed up in this! Varina could not analyze the feeling that came over her, but she knew she was disturbed. "She and Jeff fell in love. Taylor didn't like it; for whatever the cause, he sent Jeff off, four hundred miles in the wilderness." Joe wandered a little: "She was a small thing, hardly half your size." Varina's dark eyebrows met in a frown; she could not tell whether that was a compliment or a reproach. Like most tall women, she felt sensitive about her height. Joe Davis blinked in thought. "But not so pretty." At that Varina brightened.

"Well, Knox and Jeff decided to get married anyway. She told her father she intended to marry Jeff. They didn't elope, the way the gossips made it out at the time. She told the colonel good-by, Jeff left the Army, and they were married at the house of her relatives. That was nearly nine years ago."

Varina sat up. Were Jeff and the girl still married? Her heartbeat had quickened. Joe looked down, his eyes softening. "They were happy together, mighty happy. I gave Jeff nine hundred acres over there and helped him get a start. They were there about three months. Then the fever season came, and neither was acclimated. They moved to our first family homestead down the river, but it was too late. Both of them were taken. She died; Jeff hung on, but for a while I think he wanted to go too."

Haltingly the older brother told of the months when Jeff lay listless, his life in ruin around him. Haggard, emaciated, he took scant interest in his surroundings. He made one or two trips, then slowly he improved and went back to running his plantation. After all these years he still seemed a different man from the easygoing lieutenant of the border days. "Ever since she died, Varina, he's been a recluse, barely leaving his place for months at a time, living by the dull routine of plantation life. For a long time I saw my hopes for his future gone, and I wondered if Jeff would ever be more than a tired wreck."

Joe Davis's manner altered, and his voice quickened. "Lately, though, he's begun to come out of himself. All these years he and I have talked over public affairs. A while back he agreed to attend meetings. He got up at one of them and said what he thought, and the papers were quite extravagant in praising him. Since then he's been speaking more and more."

Varina wondered: Could this be Joe's own great ambition, politics? In Jeff, whom he wanted to guide, he might have someone to carry out his own hopes. A sharp look at the older man, and she realized she was correct. "That's what he's doing now in Vicksburg!" the brother finished.

"I wish we'd gone to hear him," Varina said quickly, and realized immediately that she should not have shown quite so much interest in a man she had barely met.

"Well, Jeff asked us not to go," Joe answered imperturbably. "It's the first time he's been in front of a big crowd, and he's pretty nervous. He's been working in the library here for weeks, scarcely sleeping because he's been so anxious. I suppose you don't know who's opposing him today?"

She shook her head.

"Mr. Seargent Prentiss."

So Jeff was competing against the golden-tongued Mr. Prentiss, idol of the Whigs, a crippled man with a gleaming dome of a forehead and a flow of magic words that made people cry and laugh and shout. Varina had heard him once and had never forgotten it. A sudden feeling of sympathy for Jeff Davis swept over her. How could an amateur speaker hold up against Mr. Prentiss, the man whom many thought the greatest orator in America? No wonder Jeff had appeared nervous when he saw her.

Joe Davis stroked his heavy jaw, and she saw that he was more upset than he wanted her to perceive. "I asked Jeff not to take this on. It's too hard a test. But he insisted. It may settle everything —the wrong way."

In the silence that followed, Varina noticed that dusk was creeping up on them. Here and there a leaf rustled in the brisk air, but otherwise it was very still in the garden.

"I'm worried, Varina," Joe said at last—and now he was taking her completely into his confidence. "If only we can keep him interested—not only in politics." He seemed to be asking for her help, and now she sensed that he had thought over his words a long time before uttering them. She turned on the bench to face him; then, against the red arc of the sun, she made out two horsemen riding swiftly toward the house.

Joe suppressed an exclamation, jumped to his feet, and hurried toward the gallery, forgetting Varina completely. By the time he had taken ten steps she was almost at his side. At the gallery the riders reined in, one a grinning stranger, the other the lean-faced Jeff, worn, disheveled, his wet clothes clinging to his body. Drops of perspiration were rolling down his cheeks. The stranger shouted: "It was wonderful, magnificent! Jeff held his own, all right. My God, the best show in years. They expected him to be slaughtered, and he gave back as much as he got. It was a draw!"

All at once Jeff Davis looked ten years younger than when she had seen him before. He was enjoying his new triumph, the thing he had achieved. The smooth, sunburned countenance, with its sharply cut features, appeared handsomer than ever.

The stranger's voice bubbled on: "People, thousands from all over the state, standing in the broiling sun, leaning on their wagons, lying in the grass, chawing, spitting, snapping their galluses when they liked what was said. Yelling, screaming, clapping——"

"Fighting, too." Jeff spoke quietly. "Five fist fights stopped, and a couple of duels."

Varina suppressed a shudder. This was not politics as she had imagined it. As she stood aside the family crowded about Jeff— the McCalebs, Davises, Smiths, and the rest. Joe Davis clapped his hands for drinks. Of them all, however, it was Varina who saw that Jeff was beginning to shiver. She called out to them angrily: "Look, this poor man is nearly dead! Let's get him inside and let him rest. Uncle Joe, you help!"

The womenfolk stared in amazement; the men darted looks at the patriarch. It was always Joe Davis who made the suggestions here and gave the orders. But Joe contented himself with a laugh. "You're exactly right, Varina. In with us!" He continued to smile to himself as he saw that Jeff had taken Varina's arm and that she was gazing up at the younger brother with a new look in her eyes.

Chapter 3

LATER THAT EVENING—AFTER A TEDIOUS DINNER AT WHICH JOE presided and Jeff looked mainly at the food on his plate—the younger Davises escorted Varina to the music room. There she soon found out, with some annoyance, that she was expected to take part in a very elementary game of charades.

Down the hall, during a lull, she heard the echo of a familiar voice, warm and persuasive: "However we believe, we feel . . ." Whatever Jeff was saying, it had a heavy roll, a fine conviction. How superb a public speaker he must be. Slowly she got up, whispering to the dark Mary Bradford: "I have a headache; I think I'll lie down." Mary frowned sympathetically. "Oh, that's too bad." But Varina detected a sparkle of suspicion in Mary's eyes. The girl was still withholding her opinion of the newcomer.

Varina walked deliberately past that other doorway down the hall. As she crossed the thin band of light from the lamp inside a recollection came to her and she chuckled. Her father had once said: "When Varina wants a thing, neither God nor the Mississippi can stop her." Well, she'd see. She tried to appear surprised when a hand touched her arm. Jeff was beside her in the passage.

"You've left the young ones?"

"They're so young!" She smiled, her eyes dark and wide, her nose disdainful.

He stared down at her and suddenly grinned. "We'd thought of asking you to join us, but——"

"You thought it would be beyond me?" She held her head tilted a little, looking half amused and half angered. Before Jeff could reply she turned to go toward her room, and, as she had expected, he again touched her arm. In the dim light his strong face was less earnest than usual. There was even a coaxing note in his voice as he said: "Come on, Varina. I want you to come in here for a few minutes."

Joe Davis faced about with a flicker of surprise, put aside his cigar, and pulled out a chair. "Jeff and I have been meeting this way in the library every night for years," he told her, speaking cordially, expansively. "We read together, talk about crops, law, anything that pops up." Out of the light, seated so inconspicuously that Varina had missed her at first, was Eliza Davis. Despite the warmth of the room, Eliza was swathed in a woolen shawl; her green eyes were shadowed and tired. She reached over and gave Varina's hand a gentle squeeze.

While Jeff went on reading out loud Varina's eyes ranged over the well-packed shelves: Macaulay, British law cases, Tennyson, thick piles of journals, the Richmond *Enquirer*, the Charleston *Mercury*. The room had an air of comfort, seclusion, and considerable use. So it was here, during the long years of his withdrawal from the world, that Jeff had developed much of the philosophy that carried him on. Had he thought at such times of the dead girl who had been his wife?

She caught words and phrases: "States' rights, the basis of our Constitution . . . Federal government—what is it except the agency of the states, to do only what they wish?" Jeff talked of "this new South, these farmers of our land." She found herself half persuaded. Why, he didn't sound at all like a wild Democrat!

Jeff Davis, in fact, had turned out to be unlike anything she might have expected. He looked as polished as anybody in Natchez: he had better manners than most of the sons of the rich plantation owners, including Jules Amant. At the thought of Jules she felt suddenly ashamed, for she had neglected to answer him. Then she forgot all about Jules as her thoughts went back to Jeff.

He had paused to rest his eyes. Automatically Varina reached out for the book and began reading where Jeff had left off. Above his beard Joe Davis's blue eyes widened, but Eliza looked encouragingly at her. "Please go on, child." Varina, a little abashed by now, was nevertheless determined to go on if she hanged for it. Was she supposed to sit back like a dolt because she was a woman?

For a few minutes she read smoothly; then she reached a mis-

print. She corrected it calmly: "That should be mala prohibita."
Jeff Davis, his eyebrows lifting, nodded in his brother's direction,
and he continued to watch her, increased respect in his expression.

When she came to the passage: " 'To these lordly ones, who
hold to themselves in archaic splendor; these elegant planters,
great Whigs——' " Varina stopped in annoyance.

She became aware that both Davis brothers were looking at her
quizzically. "Ah, I almost forgot." Joe fingered his whiskers. "We
have a lady Whig here."

"Well, don't say the word as if it meant snake!" Varina's brown
eyes had turned almost black, and her face was crimson. Well,
she'd trapped herself, hadn't she? She saw out of the corner of her
eye that Eliza Davis had grown alarmed; the older woman's veined
hand was quivering, and abruptly Varina began to regret her outburst. Often Judge Winchester had toned down her impulsiveness
with a quiet word: "Now, Varina—too much heat, too little light."

Meanwhile Jeff, his blue-gray eyes sympathetic, leaned forward.
"Varina, we're not such shoeless jackanapes as your friends may
think."

"Oh," she replied, somewhat mollified. "But you and Uncle
Joe, you're different. You're not like the other Democrats at all!
Certainly not like General Quitman."

Joe Davis slapped his knee and guffawed, but his brother, the
kindness increasing in his face, leaned toward her. "No, we've
never thought we were like John Quitman. He's a well-intentioned
man. But——" The curve at the side of his lips left no doubt what
he thought of the tempestuous Yankee-hater of Natchez. With that
Jeff took up the journal and resumed in a less controversial section.
After a time his eyes lifted to Varina's and their gaze held for
several moments. Then with some embarrassment they both
looked away.

Suddenly she discovered that she was trembling and her head
felt curiously light. She glanced shyly at Jeff's stern face. For the
first time she realized that she was falling in love. So this was what
it was like—this feeling of confusion, the way her heart thumped
so that the others must be able to hear.

Jeff read steadily on. Joe, his dark chin in his hand, had his face
turned toward the logs that glowed in the fireplace. Only Eliza
Davis was looking at her, and in an illuminating second Varina

perceived that the older woman understood. Her gaze was a shining, steadily confronting one.

Joe Davis, scratching at his sideburns, yawned, and Eliza rose. After they had said good night Jeff elaborately put away the book and turned toward Varina. An hour ago she would have looked forward happily to a tête-à-tête with him. Now she wanted only to be by herself. She hastily made an excuse and ran upstairs. Late that night she was still sitting by the window, her head against the damask curtain of the darkened chamber. Did he care anything about her? Did she have any real reason to think he would? A man old enough to be . . . She checked herself. No, Jeff was only thirty-five, and he looked younger than that. What did age matter anyway?

In the moonlight, at the edge of the clearing below her, she made out a tall figure. It was Jeff, his hands clasped behind him, his face outlined clearly against the velvety blackness of the trees. He appeared disturbed, uncertain, his anxieties apparent in every movement. As he strode slowly up and down, a thing her mother had said returned to her: "Now and then there's a strain of pessimism in the Davises. They're rigid people, most of them, and they can be grim and dour."

How different life must seem to Jeff. To have known happiness and then to have seen it destroyed and now to be emerging into the world of affairs once more. She turned from the window, feeling as if she were peering into the man's mind. For a few minutes she continued to hear the crunch of earth beneath his feet, and then silence fell.

Christmas began early at The Hurricane. Dawn had hardly broken when the noises from the Negro quarters—running feet, half-suppressed giggles—aroused Varina. Eliza Davis knocked to remind her of the ceremony to take place within an hour—Christmas bounty for the blacks. While she waited for the bath water Varina suffered a pang of homesickness. What were they doing now at home—Margaret and William Howell, her brothers and sisters, especially her favorite, Maggie of the blond locks and freckles?

Then Annabelle, the maid assigned to her, called out that her bath was ready, and the girl's husky voice put everything else out of her mind. Annabelle was some six or seven years older than Varina, with slow, wise yellow-brown eyes, a pugnacious nose, and an expression that shifted from sharp severity to easy good humor. Across the left side of her broad face, from ear to mouth, there was a deep zigzag scar. Varina had heard whispers among the Davis servants of a "love fight" from which Annabelle had emerged victorious, if somewhat damaged.

Despite her bulk, Annabelle moved with a speed that amazed. She had calmly taken over Varina and her affairs, becoming daily more competent. There was hardly a thing concerning the Davises that Annabelle did not know and was only too glad to tell. Once or twice, embarrassed, Varina had asked her to gossip no more about the relations of Joe Davis and his many dependents.

As Annabelle poured the warm water over her shoulders Varina mused over the situation in which she found herself. Only now did she comprehend what a powerful person Joe Davis had become. Over a period of years he had bought out most of the small growers in the vicinity; the land for miles around belonged to him, and on it lived his daughters, sons-in-law, nieces, nephews, brothers, and sisters. Most of them were obligated to him for gifts of land and even financial help. There were many outward signs of family affection on all sides and much talk of "Brother Joe" and "Uncle." And yet Varina thought she observed a little element of uneasy awe. It was a small kingdom with an undisputed king.

From the beginning she had sensed another thing: Joe Davis wanted it known that his actions, his decisions were his alone. "I do as I think best for us," she had heard him say. His voice did not emphasize the second "I," but his facial expression did. His attitude toward her seemed puzzling. He was admiring, amused—and determined, as always, to be master. Her opinion of him had changed several times since her arrival. He was a more complex individual than she had suspected. What her final attitude would be she could not guess. . . .

"How long you gonna wait to git married, Miss Rina?"

Varina came back to the present as Annabelle waddled over with Varina's outside petticoat. She waited a little too casually for her question to be answered.

Disconcerted, Varina pretended to study her straight black hair in the mirror. "I don't know, girl. I haven't been asked yet."

"Don' believe *dat!*" Annabelle's shrewd eyes were looking at her now. "Don' know, neider, why people waits like you do. At yo' age, I had me two childs. I'm a widder now, but don' intend to stay long." Receiving no encouragement, Annabelle peered over, stout hands on overflowing hips. "Nobody kin say you hafta worry, anyhow. I see how some folks cain't keep eyes off you——"

"That's fine, Annabelle. I'm finished now." Spots of color on her cheeks, Varina packed the maid off. Annabelle had meant, of course, Jeff Davis. He had been over six times during the past week for dinner, rides, and picnics when the afternoons were bright. Usually his mood was easy, now and then gay; clearly he enjoyed being with Varina. One thing she noticed again and again: he never talked down, the way some men did to women, presuming they were flutter-headed and would not understand more profound remarks. Jeff treated her as an equal; she was pleased and also flattered.

Yet it was not all so simple. Sometimes, in the middle of a merry group, a change would come over him and he would sit there, remote from the rest of them, his face set in unhappy lines, his mind far away. A casual word had started a chain of reflections, touched a sad chord from the past. When she spoke to him at such moments she saw that he was trying to respond, but there was a look of withdrawal in his eyes which she could not drive away.

Certainly he was interested in her. But how much? As she examined herself in the mirror, discouragement momentarily took possession of her. Would it amount to nothing, after all? The eyes that stared back at her seemed almost black in their determination. "If I've got anything to do with it, it will come to something!"

She must be late. She raced to tie the green ribbons at the front of her dress and at the sleeves. She had picked this one with care —the best of all her gowns, a brown wool with corded waist and narrow velvet-trimmed sleeves. The skirt did not billow out quite as she had hoped; at the last Margaret Howell had had to economize. But it would do well. As she picked up the rich green hat with its heavy feathers she saw that the costume did all she had expected it to do.

She reached the front gallery just as the festivities started. The slaves on the grass below clustered around the steps, jostling and laughing. Eliza Davis, her tiny hands crossed as she sat in her chair, called out a greeting. Joe, beard bristling, flushed with the excitement of the occasion, raised his hand, and the brothers and sisters and cousins and nieces moved back to give her a place in the center of the gallery. She heard a step at her side and there was Jeff. The green cloth of his new trousers clung to his lean flanks; the dark coat was well cut, approaching the elegant, and he had a neat black stock at his throat. His light eyes were serene; he looked more rested, more refreshed than she had ever seen him. "I think I'm going to enjoy this day," she whispered, and he nodded brightly.

Annabelle advanced toward them holding a tray with two large cups of coffee. Catching Varina's eye, she began to grin. With a little chuckle she passed the coffee to Jeff and Varina. Spying the cups, Joe reached down beside him for a decanter. "Wait! You two need something to perk you up, and this is it!" Varina saw that her first suspicion of a moment ago had been correct; Joe had been sipping for some time.

The first swallow of the coffee heavily laced with whisky made her choke, but she had to finish the fiery stuff. From then on she saw the celebration through a rosy haze.

"All right, Big Jim!" Joe Davis tossed up a heavy green sweater. Jumping forward, Big Jim grabbed it and donned it then and there. The laugh that went up was drowned out as Joe called, "Dilcy!" The girl had produced twins, and her gifts were numerous—two dresses, a hat, and three sides of meat. An old woman shouted: "Well, watch Julia next year, gal! She workin' hard to beat you!" Warmed by the strong drink she'd had, Varina enjoyed the raucous show which at home might have been considered a trifle broad. Although Varina smiled, Eliza Davis was clearly taken aback at one or two comments.

One by one the slaves moved up, some shy, others shouting with delight, a few skylarking, prancing about with their presents. Then as Joe cried out a last name—"Harry!"—she noticed the stir it caused. A massive brown man with clearly marked features walked slowly forward. He started to take the hat, then dropped his hand. "Don' wan' it." The voice, firm and clear, could be heard by everyone. A muttered oath broke from Joe Davis, and he slammed his big hand against the banister. "Nigger, you take it!"

The two men eyed each other, and the Negro, unfaltering, shook his head. Varina studied the face, the long wide nose, the heavily set lips. What had he, or his father, been in Africa—a warrior, a leader of some kind?

"So you won't have it," Davis was saying slowly. "Then, damn it, I'll make you wish you had!"

There was an awkward pause, and Varina heard Joe say: "That's gratitude. After all I do. . . ." And then, receiving no answer from the Negro, he lost control of himself completely. Varina had never seen a man so beside himself. Whirling around, he yelled directions, and four Negroes stepped forward and laid hands on Harry. A bitter struggle resulted which the white people on the gallery saw only in blurred flashes. Varina saw an occasional brown arm, heard the thud of a fist and once a groan. Then suddenly it was all over and Harry lay on the brick walk.

Varina stared, her hands clenched. What had the man done to deserve such treatment? He was lying with his arms and legs pinned down, the blood spurting from a cut over his eye, his lips torn. Still he was unconquered. Joe Davis bent forward, his face livid. "All right, now take him and——"

The other slaves fell back, and a low murmur of protest broke out. "On Chris'mas!" That made the patriarch only the more furious. Eliza Davis rose unsteadily, a look of dull pain on her face, which had turned as white as her hair. For a moment Varina thought she was going to say something. Then, as if realizing it would be hopeless, she dropped her arms and went quickly into the house. As the door slammed Varina wondered how many such explosions of wrath Eliza had beheld during her years at The Hurricane.

One of the Davis girls—Florida McCaleb, with whom she had stayed that first night—was explaining to her: "That Harry Mounger's been acting badly; he's a new one, and discontented as they come!" Varina, barely listening, could not take her eyes from the Negro. Arms pinioned, helpless, he still retained his dignity. As they started to drag him off Varina suddenly came to life and called angrily to Joe Davis: "Please, I don't think——"

Before she had finished her sentence Jeff stepped in front of her and began to argue in a low voice. "Let me take him to my place. I'll trade you one of my men." Joe glared at him, jaw protruding, heavy beard standing out in all directions. Varina hesitated and then moved back. This was Jeff's affair, not hers, and she saw that he was already beginning to gain control of the situation. As she followed Eliza inside she noticed that the slaves had quickly slipped away, and the rest of the family, constraint in their voices and their faces, were leaving the gallery as fast as possible. In the parlor two of the married cousins tried to help matters by chattering nervously. "Do you know who's coming to dinner, Varina?" "There'll be forty-five people. . . ." But all of them, as they spoke, were listening to the two men on the gallery.

Finally they heard a heavy step up the stairs, and then Jeff joined them. "Joe's going to lie down awhile," he whispered to Varina. "Don't worry. Things are all right."

Then he called to the family: "Carriages are ready outside. You all ready for church?" As he helped Varina into her green velvet coat she felt his hand shake a little. His bluish eyes showed the agitation of the past few minutes, yet in them there was also a quiet satisfaction. This, Varina speculated, must be one of the few times he had stood up against his brother. The effort had cost him something, but, judging by his expression, it had been worth it.

On the way to church, as she sat next to Jeff in the front seat, Varina spoke brightly, for her mood had lifted. December in the river country could be bland. The air carried a perfumed caress, and the evergreen branches brushed lightly against the top of the carriage as they passed. However, as she watched, Jeff's spirits slowly began to decline. After a time he only nodded; on his thin features there settled a look of withdrawal, of reserve. So, she nodded, he was paying a price for standing up to Joe.

Until then she had thought of Jeff as a man under a single shadow, the memory of that first marriage. Now she asked herself: Was he also haunted by something else, the domination of Joe Davis? True, he owed a great deal to Joe, and he showed he knew it. Yet wasn't there a danger in too great a dependence on this older man, on any man? In everything she had seen during this past week, Joe's hand had made itself felt—sometimes gently, or easily, but always there. . . . The ride ended in an awkward silence, only the creaking of the wagon wheels breaking the morning stillness.

They stopped before a small whitewashed building, the interior almost as bare as the outer walls, for it was a Baptist church. The

Howells were Episcopalians, and this was the first time Varina had attended Baptist services.

Arriving late, they hurried in, to the turning of dozens of heads. Varina saw that she was being scrutinized from the top of her feathered hat to the bottoms of her neat brown shoes. After a while she realized that most of the congregation were of the class described in Natchez as "very plain." They were not dressed with the style she had been accustomed to see in the pews of Trinity with its fashionable location on the hill. Why, she had no reason to be wasting this new . . . She lowered her eyes. She would say an extra prayer tonight for forgiveness.

The service over, men and women crowded together at the rear of the church. A lank country man in a shiny blue suit took her hand. "You a Howell, ain't you? I once saw your maw on the street in Natchez." His wife, a gingham bonnet flapping about her face, was just behind him. "She was the purtiest thing ever walked in two shoes, I says then and I says now . . ." For a moment Varina hesitated, puzzled; she didn't know people like this. Then she caught herself. Was she behaving the way those journals in the Davis library had described the "arrogant Whigs"? These were good people, going out of their way to be friendly to her, a stranger.

She smiled and put out her hand. At that Eliza Davis, who, as Varina was soon aware, saw everything that happened, came over quickly and helped by making introductions. Varina, now completely at ease, laughed and talked about Natchez, the river steamboats, and also Jeff Davis.

"He's the comin' man, miss," one of the farmers told her. "We'll all be hearin' of 'im, you'll see."

"I can tell that already." Varina nodded. "Hasn't he made a fine start?"

She glanced over at Jeff. To her surprise, though he was among people whom he had known for a long time, he looked stiff and embarrassed. Why couldn't he unbend? He was certainly making a poor impression. A second later she felt not irritated but sorry for him. She signaled him over to her side and set out to draw him out of himself. She joked about the way Jeff had handled the great orator Prentiss a week before. "And, do you know, he nearly talked himself into a collapse," she told the farm wife at her elbow.

At that Jeff began to laugh and tell his own version of the debate. The circle about them widened. Jeff was now the center of the crowd, his face shining with new color, his voice carrying to more and more eager listeners. This was the kind of Jeff Davis she wanted to see.

He was in the middle of a funny story when their eyes met, and their laughter rang out together. Eliza, just behind her, leaned forward to whisper: "It's the first time he's laughed that way since, since . . ." Her voice trailed off, and Varina thought again, as she had so often, of that girl who had died.

They had finished the Christmas dinner, a meal gargantuan in scope, splendid in country-style succulence. Varina, who had not touched the last four courses, sat back limply, surveying it all—the remains of white-fleshed fish, broiled in butter, covered with tender shrimp; squab buried in a thick brown covering; the master-sized ham piled high with vegetables; wild ducks and geese, each bursting with stuffing; a platter of turkeys so huge that three men had been needed to carry it; the flaming pudding; the fruit-filled cakes. Joe Davis, his composure well restored, gave the sign that dinner was over and the company rose. He called out to the men, "Gentlemen, we will enjoy our cigars and whisky when the ladies have left us."

At the door Varina halted. Jeff was walking uncertainly toward the window. For the second time that day his gaiety had deserted him. Through the meal he had sat silent, and from a remark he had made to young Mary Bradford she understood he was planning to return to his plantation.

"Jeff," she said quietly, and even in the tumult of the large room he heard her and turned to meet her eyes.

"Yes, Varina."

"Jeff," she went on wildly, "what about that ride you promised me?"

She saw him start in surprise, for he knew as well as she did that no ride had ever been suggested. But even if he was startled he was quick to fall in with her plan, telling her he'd wait in the hallway while she went upstairs.

"I'll change in a minute," she called back.

With Annabelle's excited help she got into another dress more quickly than she had thought possible. She was afraid he might not be there when she got down. Annabelle, silent for once, worked as nervously as Varina herself. Shortly afterward Varina was riding with Jeff along the road that twisted with the river. In the window Annabelle watched until they were out of sight, then went back to the quarters. "I done my bit," she said to herself. "Now it's up to dem two!"

The day had further brightened. It was perfect Christmas weather for the river region, snowless, almost windless, with a warm sun that lit up long stretches of grass and hanging greens. From the sleeping earth there rose a soft fragrance with a hint of the spring that was soon to come.

Their horses were evenly matched. Varina spurred on her steed, a slim filly with a lovely sorrel coat, and at once they were in a race. For ten, nearly fifteen, minutes they rode nose to nose, straining forward in their saddles as they bent low to avoid the down-reaching branches of the trees that lined the narrow road. Then gradually Jeff edged ahead and the air was filled with dirt from his horse's hoofs.

"Jeff! Jeff, I've had enough!" she panted.

He slowed his horse to a walk and returned to where she waited under a vast oak that stood in a little clearing beside the road. He swung easily to the ground, and as he helped her down she felt the strength of his lean arms. As she smoothed her dress her fingers touched the old "Whig brooch" at her throat, which she had put on earlier without thinking. She unclasped it deftly and covered it in her palm. There was a moment of embarrassed silence and then, because she realized she must be the one to do it, Varina took the lead. "What do you plan to do with yourself, Jeff?"

His eyes clouded. "Oh, I guess I'll be a farmer."

"But what about the start you've made in these campaigns?"

"Oh, that." He looked away. "I don't know that I'm fitted for politics. Suspicions, backbiting, uncertainties. Even now they're trying to twist my words. I don't want to be a demagogue."

She wondered: Was this man too sensitive, too finely wrought for public life? Then she remembered Eliza Davis's words, and Joe's, and she faced him.

"No, Jeff, you don't have to be a demagogue. You've shown what you can do against Mr. Prentiss, haven't you? All you'll ever have to do is tell people what you think and let them decide!"

"I don't know if it's as simple as that, Varina."

Suppose he drifted back to those years of withdrawal . . . A frown creased her brow, and her full lips tightened. Not if she could help it!

For a flying moment her mind went back to the still unanswered letter in her room. Jules Amant, three hundred slaves, a place in fashionable Natchez—no, it seemed too unreal. Over the trees she could see the roof of Jeff's plantation house which he had pointed out to her before. It was not a large roof and it did not look too heavy. It occurred to her that if she married Jeff she might some-times know the same uncertainty that her mother had known— a husband who might not provide her with all the pleasant things she wanted. She still held the Whig pin, symbol of Natchez and its aristocracy.

Then her eyes shifted to Jeff's fine and sensitive face. Nothing mattered except this man. Her voice faltered as she said: "Jeff! What about us?"

For almost a minute he stared at her. Then he reached out, his hand trembling a little, and pulled her against him. Her hands opened as her arms went up and around his neck. The brooch slipped into the grass, forgotten.

Chapter 4

MORE THAN A YEAR HAD GONE BY SINCE THAT CHRISTMAS DAY RIDE, and now Varina Davis was going home to her husband's house for the first time.

Jeff Davis's Brierfield was a small cat-and-clayed house, a story and a half high, roughly thrown together, in the middle of a cluster of thick trees. As they approached it Varina realized there was something odd about it. It resembled a blockhouse; the windows were nearly breast-high, the doors six feet wide! Opening a door, she reflected, would reveal the interior of the whole house. Her nose wrinkled as she tried to hide her merriment. "Well," Jeff apologized, "I designed it, and I suppose I made a few miscalculations." Then he joined in her laughter.

Her eyes swept the grove of superb oaks and the rows of fig trees. Already that clear spring morning it was changing before her eyes, changing as she would change it. Her hand sought her husband's. "It's ours, dear," she told him. "It's beautiful. And we'll be alone in it."

Only then did she see the group of twenty or more Negroes waiting beside the house. From that group came a very dark Negro with slightly grizzled hair and a still powerful body. Stepping forward, Jeff put out his hand. The Negro calmly took it, and Varina caught the gleam of affection that came into the bright eyes.

"How have you been, James?" Jeff inquired.

"Very well. And you, sir?"

"The same, James."

Varina blinked. Here was little of the feeling of command and humble obedience to which she had grown accustomed. It was as if two fellow planters were meeting.

"Varina"—Jeff went to her side—"this is my friend and manager, James Pemberton. We've been together since we were boys."

James Pemberton extended his hand slowly. Varina returned his smile, then all at once she realized that she was supposed to shake hands with him. She reached out swiftly and touched his hand. It was—yes, it was the first time. She had been nursed, cradled, and fed by Negroes; but handshaking—that was different. Nervously she let Jeff lead her forward as he greeted the other Negroes.

"William, you're well? . . . Cora. How's the child?"

Jeff was at his best with these black people, good-humored, easy-mannered. Toward Varina the servants—most of them field hands—remained polite, carefully so. In the faces, intelligent or stolid, she read their questions. She was the newcomer, they the long-time residents who would have to get on with her. Or was it the other way? Must she adjust herself to them? Some had been here, certainly, when that other girl, the dainty Knox Taylor, had come. Had they liked Knox a great deal, and would they hold that against Varina?

At the end of the line she saw a man with a vaguely familiar face. She remembered now that Christmas morning a year and more ago and the Negro who had refused to accept a present from Joe Davis. Yes, it was the same man, Harry Mounger. He stood there motionless, earnest, but after a few minutes he grinned and she sensed that a considerable change had taken place in him.

"Well, Varina . . ." Jeff murmured. They stepped up to the slightly raised brick gallery, with latticework at the side to make it a cool summer retreat. She paused at the thick door. Would Jeff carry her across the threshold? She hoped he would; to judge by their covert gestures, the Negroes also anticipated something of the sort. But as he took her arm she realized it had not occurred to him.

Inside their Brierfield house she forgot everything else. It was dark and gloomy, and also cluttered. Most of the furniture was rough oak and massive mahogany, though there were also two or three pieces of good Sheraton arranged rather ostentatiously. It all shone as if rag and brush had passed over it hardly an hour before. The recent cleaning, however, had not been very thorough. She sniffed—strong tobacco fumes, and also the smell of dogs. She would have to change some routines here, she assured herself.

"Is everything all right?" Jeff was watching her, apprehensive.

"Oh yes, dear." She smiled. Better wait a bit to launch the new regime.

Through a door in the rear of the hall came a well-known, bulky figure holding a tray of cakes and a coffeepot. It was the large and irrepressible Annabelle, whom she thought was still on Joe Davis's plantation. "Yes'm. Dat's me!" Annabelle exuded her pleasure. "You don' seem to git rid of me, does you?"

Varina's look told her how pleased she was. Some might resent Annabelle's manner as "familiar," yet her grin removed any offense; and it would be good to have a friendly face near her during the months to follow. Varina's first sip told her the coffee was made right—strong and full of flavor. But with a quick sampling of the soggy cake she perceived that she had further work set out for her.

Dusting off the crumbs, she jumped up. "Jeff, could you call in one or two of the men?" As Jeff watched, cup in hand, she gave directions: "That sofa, put it at the window. The armoire—no, anywhere but that corner. And, Annabelle—look in the attic and bring down whatever looks like a curtain." In an hour she had the furniture on the ground floor rearranged and she and Jeff were alone at last in their own living room.

"We've forgotten one thing, Jeff," she said, raising her lips to his.

In the next room Annabelle nodded to herself. "Dat's startin' things right!"

That night Jeff had to see a plantation owner up the road, and while he was gone Varina mused over the year that had gone by. She and Jeff had wanted a marriage without delay. Margaret Howell had been unshakable—they must wait twelve months, no less. At Varina's urging Jeff had accepted a chance to run as an elector in the national campaign of 1844 and he had won. Then, almost a month ago, Jeff had arrived in Natchez for the ceremony. At the last minute the anxious-eyed Margaret had called Varina aside.

"Child, this won't be altogether easy for you." She ran the words together at her usual breathless rate. "He's older, and he has a strong will. I suppose we've all been a little lenient with you. You're headstrong—and impatient. Promise me you'll fit yourself to his ways?"

"Yes." Varina nodded, but her tone was dubious. "That doesn't mean I can't try to influence him—when I think it's best?"

With an uncertain gesture Margaret brushed back the curls from her own plump cheeks. "Perhaps. But don't go too far. You ought to be glad to have a husband who's able to"—she paused—"who's settled in his life." It was the closest to a complaint against her own fate that Margaret Howell had ever uttered. With a brief "Bless you," she had hurried away.

Three weeks ago, late in the morning, the couple had stood together in the drawing room of the Natchez house to exchange their vows. There followed a late breakfast, and the whole party, Howells and Davises and their guests, had ridden down to the river to see Varina and Jeff off on a steamboat. At dusk, in their flower-decorated suite, Jeff moved toward the unlighted lamp on the wall; then he dropped his hand and turned toward his bride.

A day later they disembarked at Bayou Sara, his sister's place in Louisiana, the home to which Jeff and Zachary Taylor's daughter had once gone. He took Varina about the small white house, to the chamber where Knox had been ill. "I was in the next room," he told her, his voice low. "I was stricken myself, and they'd left me alone for a few minutes. I heard her thin voice singing an old song, one of our favorites. I got up and forced myself across the threshold to her bed." The last words came in a whisper. "She died there in my arms."

Jeff remained there, staring at the bed, and Varina slipped away. A little later he went upstairs and found her weeping, her head buried in a pillow. Brokenly she asked him if he would ever love her as he had that other wife. "Don't," Jeff pleaded. "That's over. Let the past go."

After a while she got up. "May I see the grave?" Together they walked to the family cemetery in the moss-hung woods. There, on a rise in a sun-splashed clearing, she spied the weathered slab. From an unseen bayou, water trickled over a log; a single redbird swung upward toward the clouds, and they were alone in the silence.

While Jeff knelt before the grave Varina wandered off and brought back a handful of wild flowers. After that they started slowly along a path that curved toward the house. As they neared it Jeff stopped to kiss her gratefully, and then warmly.

There followed a few days at the original Davis home at Woodville, Mississippi, a neat weatherboarded house of an earlier day. Here waited the mother she had missed at the Christmas party, a pink-faced old woman who lifted her arms and wept at the sight of Jeff. At eighty-five Jane Davis was seeing her son for the first time in many months. She could not leave her chair, and he dropped to his knees beside her. She looked up and held out her hand to Varina.

"Child, child! So many years between us. But we both have him, haven't we?" As Varina clung to her hand she began to talk of the way Jeff had been taken from her at seven to ride far away to school; he had returned, then gone away again. "I've never really had him very much," she sighed. Despite time's markings, Varina saw something of Jeff in the old face with its high cheekbones and forehead and its gentle sweetness. There was even more of him, however, in the face of the man whose picture hung on the wall at The Hurricane. When they left later that week, Jane Davis caught Varina against her, and her final words were a simple compliment: "My boy did well, dear!"

And now tonight in their upstairs room at Brierfield, Varina awaited her husband's return. Annabelle had gone to her room in the quarters. In the March evening the budding spring came close. A shower of pale peach blossoms sprinkled the gallery roof before her as she lifted her eyes to the racing clouds in the distance. The night was calling.

By five the next morning they were up. "You can sleep till later," Jeff told her when he rose first. But as she kissed him she shook her head. "We'll follow your old schedule." Long before this she had made up her mind to do what she could to help Jeff with the plantation. While Jeff bathed and dressed she went down to give Annabelle her first lesson in cooking.

Later in the sitting room she and Jeff met Jeff's manager, James Pemberton, who had a sheaf of papers in his hand. Jeff pulled a chair into place. "Sit down, James." Varina excused herself to work with Annabelle in the next room, sorting household supplies. She heard them talking about crops, fences, assignments. Jeff took out a box of cigars, and the two men smoked together. After a time the Negro told Jeff quietly: "That old packing shed—it collapsed last month."

"How did it happen?" Jeff inquired.

"I rather think from my neglect." The answer was prompt, in a clear voice, and the words were those of a respected associate. "I rather think . . ." Varina smiled to herself. It was one of Jeff's favorite expressions.

When James left, Jeff called for their horses and together they made an inspection of the property. "That's the chicken yard. And the gin. At first it was only a shack; now—well, you can see." He took a great deal of pride in the place, as Varina could tell from his expression. How well he looked this morning, less intent, his features softened by the early morning sunlight. As they jogged along he told her of the way he operated Brierfield.

"I run it myself, with James as right-hand man. When I'm away he has charge. It's unusual, I know, not to have a white overseer. But it's worked." She nodded and he went on:

"I've always insisted that the people get good treatment. I won't have beatings as punishment, except in very rare cases." Varina remembered certain Natchez planters who claimed that one good whipping a week was necessary to "keep them in line." She was glad there were no such practices here.

"Whenever there's anything wrong," Jeff resumed, "I like to have the Negroes handle it themselves. I've shown them how to set up a jury and hold a trial, with their own people to judge. I keep one power—the pardon. Sometimes they're harsh, and I step in."

Varina pondered his last remark. "I see. Still, wouldn't it give them more—more responsibility, if you didn't step in?"

He shrugged. "Everything won't come in a day." Slackening his hold on the reins, he looked away. "Joe and I have pretty much the same system. But Joe—you know, he's inclined to let his temper get in the way." Varina, her eyes on the irregular road, sat her horse without making any comment. It would not be wise to express her opinion on that matter, at least for the time being. He went on: "You've noticed I didn't call John and Margaret 'Johnnie' or "Maggie'? They've got a right to their real names, and I think they ought to be called anything they pick." Here were more surprises.

"What about James Pemberton?" she asked.

"He knows me as well as anybody on earth." He was speaking quickly, as if happy to explain the man. "They gave him to me for a body servant just before I went into the Army. We moved together into free territory, and James could've freed himself whenever he desired. He preferred to stay with me. He's saved my life more than once, nursed me back when I nearly died in the Northwest. James is one of my best friends."

"You've freed him, of course?" Her question was casual.

"Why, no." Jeff looked surprised. "There's no need for it."

"Suppose something happens to you?"

Her husband smiled. "We needn't worry about that for a long time." He was waving his hand; they had arrived at the slave quarters, a double row of wooden cabins. A dozen or so children who were playing in the road came running to cluster around their horses. Varina patted the nearest ones and talked to the withered grandmother who had them in charge. They dismounted before the "hospital," the cabin in which four or five sick men were being cared for. Expertly Jeff questioned the patients, examined tongues and eyes, and ordered medicine. He murmured in an aside to Varina: "To grow cotton you have to be a doctor, a businessman, a lawyer, practically everything."

Varina nodded. It all looked neat and pleasant. Jeff, on his comparatively small acreage, was closer to the slaves than were most of the bigger growers. Yet even under these conditions . . . She was recalling something that Grandma Kempe of Virginia had told them years ago. "Slavery's got to go. Maybe it'll be hard for a lot of us. Still, it's going to happen." The old woman had shaken her head. "The founders allowed it because they had to; they made all sorts of compromises to get a government started. Most of them, though, expected it to die away—a declining evil." And Varina remembered Virginia relatives and connections who had freed their slaves. . . .

As they mounted again and started she asked Jeff: "What's going to happen to slavery?"

He hesitated, his pale eyes on the horizon. "It'll end slowly, naturally. It will take time, a lot of time—and preparation."

Tossing back her head, she said: "Still, we're not teaching ours to read and write, and——"

"I don't mean that kind of preparation. I mean work with the hands!" His tone was sharp.

"How can a man learn to care for himself if he can't cipher?" In her intensity her cheeks had flushed a deep pink.

Jeff ran his tongue thoughtfully over his lips. "Some of them are beginning to stand on their own feet. Let me show you something." He took her to one of the cabins. Inside an elderly Negro looked up at them. "Alfred, Mrs. Davis would like to buy thread," Jeff told him, and handed over a coin. Varina looked around her: against the four walls were rows of shelves containing jars of sweets, boxes of nails, ropes, and a dozen other articles. "Alfred sells to everybody in the quarter, and when I'm out of things I buy from him too," Jeff explained.

Outside he continued: "Any slave can try to benefit himself. If he returns me the value of a day's work he can take the time for himself. Last year one earned a couple of thousand dollars. All of them"—he pointed to several small gardens—"can keep garden plots and sell to me or anybody else on the river."

Yet Varina still wondered. Only the previous week Jeff had been telling happily how slavery was multiplying through all the lower South. But she must wait for another occasion to ask him about that. To please Jeff she smiled and said: "Well, you've done well with Harry Mounger."

Jeff brightened. "I talked to him that first day and found out about the trouble. Harry'd been through hell on his previous plantation. He had a wife and four children. The owner changed; they took his wife away and sold two of the children separately." Jeff's thin nostrils quivered; it was a part of slavery he found hard to defend. "I tried to find out what became of them and buy them. But there wasn't much chance. In cases like that . . ."

Varina took her husband's hand, pride in her eyes. Not many men would have made such an effort.

That same day she saw how Jeff's jury system operated. As they returned to the house James Pemberton met them. "The people are a mite upset." He frowned. "You know, I told you about the hog that's missing? They swear they've traced it to George—the one with the big stomach."

Varina heard a buzz of voices; the jury was assembling.

"Mayn't I go?" Her dark eyes pleaded.

"I'm afraid not," he said sternly. "I never do."

But Varina could watch from a distance. Standing on the gallery, her hand shielding her eyes, she strained to make out the jurors under a tree, the judge for the day in a chair opposite them, and a row of agitated witnesses. Occasionally muffled words came to her:

"Not a bit of truf' in it!"

"Smelt dat hog myse'f."

Eventually James Pemberton walked over to the house with the glutton, a large fellow in a broken purple shirt and tentlike trousers. James addressed Jeff: "Three of 'em swear they can prove that others helped George. But he wants to talk to you first."

James withdrew to the side, his arms folded. George spoke hoarsely, with an apprehensive side glance at Varina. "Yessir, I admits it. De fact is, dey all tellin' lies dat says folks he'p me. I stole it all alone and et prett' near de whole hawg."

Jeff chuckled and motioned to James Pemberton. "George's confessed! He's been punished aplenty already. I adjourn court."

James, his heavy face carefully expressionless, nodded. A minute or two later, when Jeff's action was announced, Varina heard from a distance the loud complaints: "We'd a-cotch de whole lot of 'em." . . . "A real shame, yes!" Jeff cocked an eyebrow at her and smiled, and she laughed with him. However, as they started back into the house she asked herself: Mightn't it have been better not to interfere, to let them decide the case as they saw fit?

After supper they went to the small library where she had already begun rearranging the books. A pile of newspapers had accumulated, and together they plunged into them. "Did you see this—about Mr. Calhoun?" she asked. A little later she passed him another newspaper which contained an article detailing the position of the Texas republic and its relations with Mexico. For an hour or so he read, partly to her, partly to himself. Then his vision gave him trouble. She brought warm water and cloths, and while he rested his eyes she read on. But while she was reading, hoofbeats sounded on the road outside. Jeff went to the door, then returned. "Messenger from Vicksburg. My friends over there want to know where I stand on certain political issues. They want a reply tonight." Wearily he moved toward the desk, but Varina intercepted him. "Close your eyes again and dictate to me." By the time he had seated himself she had pen and paper ready. When he finished she skimmed over the message, suggested a change, copied it, and took it out to the messenger.

An hour later, in the middle of a sentence she was reading, Varina's voice trailed off. Jeff pulled the cloth from one eye and saw that she was fast asleep. He smiled, softly lowered the lamp, slipped his arms beneath her, and carried her out of the room. At the threshold she waked. Then her arms tightened about his shoulders, and she lifted her face to his.

Only after she had lived at Brierfield for a month did she realize how completely isolated it was. Theirs was a tiny village in the middle of the rich green land with nothing but the fields, the sky, and the river beyond the mound of the levee. Wild birds passed in endless flights, their shadows moving across the land. Geese came over them and landed on the fields to fatten on waste corn. On some days their honking cries and the rush of their wings were the only sounds in the stillness. There was water all about them, in the low spots in the fields where the wild cane rose stiffly, in the marshes which lay between their land and the delta.

"You see why we called the place Brierfield," Jeff said.

A short way from the house wild iris turned some of the hollows into blooming purple gardens. Goldenrod grew waist-high, and its stalks and blooms made a green-and-yellow hedge along the roads. Cranes stood on one leg in the lagoons among lily pads the size of platters.

For days, except when they visited Joe Davis's place a few miles away, they met no one except their own Negroes. But sometimes Varina could make out the distant smoke of a steamboat, and it occurred to her that in a few hours the vessel would be passing Natchez and the Howells, too, might be watching it. At such moments a wave of homesickness would come over her, but soon it would disappear.

She had scant time for idle thoughts. For her, as for Jeff, nearly every waking hour was filled with the running of Brierfield. Morning, afternoon, evening, the work of the plantation consumed their thoughts. "How's the chopping going? . . . Did the gangs miss much yesterday?" The plantation bell rang at four o'clock, long before dawn, and Jeff reached the fields almost as soon as the slaves. He was back at noon and left again immediately after the noon meal. Jeff, she saw, was a man of detail, and such things as the full use of surplus fats, the supply of corn for the animals, and the repair of outbuildings occupied his full attention.

When they met during the day he was warm and appreciative, his hand clasping hers for a moment, his grayish eyes looking into hers with deep affection. Then he was off again, protesting that the fields were calling. At first she felt hurt that he could be so preoccupied. Then she realized that Jeff had determined to make a success of the plantation if he killed himself in the process. If anyone "worked like a nigger," as the haughty Natchezians would have said, it was her husband, and also, in these days, Varina as well. She had never applied herself as she did now, and she was glorying in it.

She soon had the household in order, for she had not watched her mother in Natchez for nothing. She husbanded her supply of foodstuff until Jeff occasionally made fun of her. "Don't tell me you've found something else to do with that little bit of pig?" he would say. She missed no chance to use whatever game was available. The Negroes brought her great loads of canvasbacks, mallards, and wild geese. Varina labored with Annabelle to devise new dishes, and she served game stewed, smothered, and jellied, even game soup.

Annabelle, fat hands on hips, admitted her astonishment at Varina's economies. "Save dis too? Over at Mister Joe's, we trow it away."

"Yes." Varina was firm. "That, and the wings too. I never heard that they spoiled a stew."

Her one extravagance, Jeff told her with a grin, was the matter of her clothes. She still kept her Natchez "dress box," the bank in which she dropped every spare dollar she saved. When he saw the money accumulate he gave her a quizzical look. "All that for clothes out in the country?"

She nodded. "I'm not going to go to seed out here. I'll have just as many dresses as I used to. I'll use them, sometime if not now."

She sent orders by steamboat to Natchez and New Orleans, and she and Annabelle worked for hours over the materials. One night when Jeff sat down to supper she appeared at the doorway in a soft pink party dress. Jeff chuckled. "That's Natchez pride if I ever heard of it." But he was not displeased. Varina had found out long ago that no man objected to seeing a woman in a handsome costume, especially if she was not ugly. She tilted her head to the side. Perhaps that, too, was Natchez pride. . . .

For most of the day Annabelle was Varina's only companion. The girl had been only a minor servant at the Joe Davis house; now she was learning rapidly, acquiring new skills. From this colored woman, in turn, Varina received a quiet guidance of another kind. Whenever Varina stepped out of the kitchen, hair awry, streaks over her face, Annabelle directed her promptly to the washstand and mirror. "You a sight!" she would advise. "You nineteen and you look twenty-nine. Mister Jeff, he work hard, too, but he don' hafta please no manfolk, like you do!"

One afternoon, when Jeff had finished early and wanted Varina to ride down the road with him, she was inclined to refuse. "The jelly's still in the kettle, Jeff. But, oh, I guess I can go." Annabelle brought her the towel and warm water. Too low for Jeff to hear, just loud enough for Varina, she grumbled: "Hm. What come firs', blackberry or husbing?"

One thing Varina noticed with dismay was the absence of flowers around the house, for Jeff's bachelor household had never needed them. She wrote home for seeds and cuts, and Margaret Howell responded with a wide assortment. Moreover, Eliza Davis, always a good neighbor, sent over fresh shoots.

Laboring one morning in the garden, Varina saw that Harry Mounger was watching her closely.

"What is it?" She smiled.

Embarrassment made him hesitate. "Well, seems to me like you ain' plantin' de roses right."

"No?"

"Uh-uh. Like dis." He dug deftly; he fingered the plants with a delicate hand. His constraint was vanishing. "Dis ain' de best time, you know. And over dere—oughta be a lil wider out. Likes air and sun, dose." For nearly an hour Varina watched while Harry replanted her roses.

That night Varina talked to Jeff; the next morning they sent for Harry. "From now on I want you to look after the garden," Jeff told him. Harry seemed happier than she had ever seen him. He brought out a small bush wrapped in a sack. "I been raisin' it by my cabin. It's a gif'," he explained. She thanked him, more touched than she would admit as she watched him plant it beside the house.

Suppose matters had developed only a little differently for Harry? Suppose Jeff had not been there that Christmas morning when Harry dared to defy Joe Davis. . . . She heard him whistling now as he bent over the bush. Presently Annabelle, somewhat over-casual in her manner, asked Varina: "Dat big feller Harry—he gon' be around here much?"

When Varina nodded Annabelle's face became expressionless. But Varina saw that Annabelle was taking frequent opportunities to pass Harry in the garden. When the girl brought him a glass of milk Varina knew that a new interest had come into Annabelle's life. Harry went quietly about his work. "He ain' a talkin' man," said Annabelle. But from her tone it was clear that, articulate or inarticulate, he pleased her.

Everywhere at Brierfield things were going well, Varina reflected. The servants were beginning to like her; of that she could be certain. It was Annabelle, however, who reminded her how fortunate she was in the main thing, the love of her husband. "Don' hafta tell me you happy, Miss Rina! Dat man, he got his horse hitch' to one pos'!" Jeff's quick warm glance when she hurried downstairs to greet him, the way he turned toward her as she left—she needed no other signs of his feeling. And when he was gone only a little while she still listened for his steps and tingled at his approach.

He had started to call her by a pet name—"Winnie." After a while she chose one for him—"Banny." How she had thought of it she was never sure, but she used it whenever they were alone. Whereas Jeff called her "Winnie" most of the time, she could not bring herself to call him "Banny" except when they were alone. It was a private thing.

Yet even now she felt she did not fully understand him. There remained that tendency to moodiness. Frequently she found him dour, almost melancholy. "What's the matter?" she would ask. With an effort he would smile and tell her: "Nothing, child. Nothing at all," and after a time she would usually succeed in joking him out of it. She had discovered that he could be strangely oversensitive, injured by a word, a gesture. Much of it, she knew, was part of his unusual shyness. Hadn't it been Joe Davis who said that his brother would never be one to slap men's backs, to pretend an affability he did not feel? For the most part he managed to conceal his sensitivity, and people who misunderstood said he was cold and overproud.

She admitted to herself that Jeff was not someone who could see many sides to an argument. When he spoke he had usually thought out the subject with care; he had come to a conclusion, to him the right conclusion. Those who differed were wrong. "Why, it can't be," he once told her. "I've worked this thing through. Listen . . ." Carefully he repeated each step of his argument. "Can anything else be right?" For a moment she agreed, but later she wondered. If you accepted Jeff's premise, yes. If not . . . it seemed almost as if Jeff placed too high a value on logic. Once her tutor, Judge Winchester, had cautioned her: "There's more to life, Varina, than logical thought. Much more."

Occasionally, when she watched Jeff with callers at Brierfield, she felt baffled. He sat there, distant, rather chill; he found it hard to relax, to unburden himself. If the man were one of the lesser white farmers, another obstacle raised itself. She was sure that Jeff did not quite understand such men and their troubles. Yet she herself, in spite of her past training, had little difficulty in such cases.

Whenever she could, she joined Jeff and his guests and tried to make them feel at home, to draw her husband out. Jeff, she thought, did not quite realize what she was doing, until one day when they walked back into the house he took her cleft chin and shook it playfully. "You can be arrogant when you want, ma'am, but what a politician you've become!"

"Why, Banny"—she looked very innocent—"I can't imagine what you mean." Then they both laughed. On the rear porch Annabelle and Harry exchanged nods. . . . If only, Varina thought, if only others could see Jeff as he was now, completely at ease, his warm humor changing the features that were sometimes too rigid. But she alone knew that he had a great deal of sympathy for people. She had seen him struggle day after day to save an elderly hand who had been with them for years but who now lay desperately ill. She had studied him as he listened to the complicated problems of the Negroes. "No matter what happens, I want them to know they have a chance to tell their side," he told her. When one day he spoke brusquely to a field worker who upset some elaborate computations he was making, he soon tossed aside his records and hunted up the man in the cotton field. Varina could not hear, but she knew that Jeff was apologizing to the slave.

Afterward, in the dusk, he told her of an earlier episode. He had taken part in the arrest and transfer of Black Hawk, the celebrated Indian chief, during his Northwest days. Jeff was to bring him part of the way East, and the warrior was then to be taken to Fortress Monroe in Virginia. The chief, bitter and sorrowing, managed to bear up; but along the route crowds gathered to inspect the fallen hero, to point and gibe. Quickly Jeff gave the order that this had to stop. Black Hawk was to be protected from such humiliations. "Even a captured enemy has rights," he told Varina. "When I saw the expression in his face, Winnie, that he tried his best to hide, I knew I had to step in." His head lowered, and she touched his hand.

Late that same evening, as she lay beside her husband and listened to his slow breathing, she asked herself: Was this to be their life, this Brierfield? She was content; she would be happy if the years brought her nothing else. What of the ambition that had rushed through her only a little while ago? She didn't know, she didn't care. This was what she wanted; let the world go its own way.

Until now she had never been one for the quiet life; she had liked parties, social affairs, bright talk. Margaret Howell had lamented: "Varina, you're too spirited. You dash around; you don't sit there in your place like the other girls." Now here she was, a housewife, buried on a plantation in the country and thoroughly liking it.

As for Jeff . . . Now and then in these past months she had been asking herself: Was he not, after all, best suited for the plantation work that he enjoyed so much? A public career was scarcely the thing for a man who suffered so much in the presence of strangers, who had difficulty in understanding the thoughts and ways of others. Yet several times in the past Jeff had been on the verge of embarking on just such a career.

The next morning she said to him: "Have you ever thought,

Banny, that planting would be enough for us? It would be——"

"Yes," he interrupted. "Yes, but we'll have to find how it works out." He hesitated, and then she realized that the same thing had been in his mind.

"By the way," he continued, "yesterday I saw Brother Joe down the road. He was a little upset that we go over there so seldom. He's anxious for us to come tonight."

"Of course. I've been thoughtless." As she spoke she wondered if Jeff, too, guessed that there might be some connection between a visit to Joe Davis and their plans for the future.

Joe appeared pleased when they arrived, but as he led them upstairs she thought she detected a restraint in his manner, and with it, oddly enough, a trace of excitement. As they passed his wife's room Varina saw that Eliza was sitting up in bed, a cap over her white curls. "Just a chest cold," Joe murmured. Varina hurried in to greet her.

"And you're entirely satisfied here after Natchez?" Eliza's faded green eyes had a look of sympathy.

"As satisfied as I could be."

They talked of the New Orleans that Eliza still missed, of the new fashions, the routine at Brierfield. Varina heard a step on the threshold, and Joe Davis stood in the doorway, tugging at his whiskers, a frown on his face. "I wish you'd come to the library with us, Varina."

Eliza's wrinkled face clouded. "We've had our visit, Joseph. Varina's just leaving."

Irked by his manner, Varina merely shifted a little in her chair. "I'll be there presently, thank you." Joe waited a minute or two, then lumbered away.

When Varina entered the library at last, Jeff looked up quickly, plainly worried. "Brother Joe says he has a surprise, Winnie. He's waited for you."

There followed an awkward pause. "I'm sorry," Varina began. "I really hadn't realized——"

"It's just this." Joe Davis leaned against the fireplace, a touch of the dramatic in his manner. "Some of our party want to back Jeff for Congress."

Jeff sat forward, his blue-gray eyes widening. Varina felt frozen to her chair. "Congress—in Washington City?" she asked foolishly.

"Of course!" Joe's glance conveyed his scorn.

She said slowly: "That would mean we'd be away from Brier-field for long months at a time?"

No answer was necessary. Joe shrugged and looked at his brother. Jeff was rubbing at his chin. "Of course, we've just gotten the plantation well under way. I don't—I don't know . . ."

Joe Davis's heavy head came up, and when he spoke his voice had an edge to it. "We've worked for years for just this sort of op-portunity for Jeff!" His eyes went from Jeff to Varina. "Don't you see? It's his chance."

In the silence a light wind lifted a curtain. Rising, Varina went to the window. Her mind was racing ahead, her heart beating loudly. Her husband's opportunity . . . She remembered his face that day when he had done well against the great Mr. Prentiss; she thought of the predictions at the church on Christmas morning, that Jeff would be "heard from someday."

She couldn't hold him back; and now, suddenly, she realized that she didn't want to. Brierfield would have to wait, and so, too, their tranquil, happy life together. She was still Varina Howell and she knew that before them lay their great adventure, if she but had the courage now. . . . She faced her husband. She knew what she was going to say, and she knew what the result would be.

Chapter 5

THE DAY'S ROUND OF PLANTATION TASKS HAD REACHED AN END.
A late afternoon somnolence had settled over Brierfield in its lush
green setting. The blue light of dusk drew nearer down the road.
This, Varina decided, was her favorite hour; beside her on the
latticed gallery Jeff stirred and shifted his position on the sofa. The
expected nomination for Congress was very close, but she tried not
to think about it.

In the distance a haze of dust lifted toward the sky. Jeff's eyes
narrowed, and he got to his feet. "Something tells me, Winnie,
it's Brother Joe."

Almost before his horse had halted Joe Davis was on the ground.
He dashed up the steps to the porch, his coattails flying, a newspaper in his hand. Joe's face was livid with rage. "There's hell to
pay!" he cried, handing them the paper.

It developed that an anonymous letter writer had revived an old
issue. Years earlier Jeff's party had taken a stand for the repudiation
of bonds issued during a boom. Jeff had always differed from other
party members on this point. Now one of the main figures behind
the scenes had let it be known that he would back no one opposed
to repudiation. "But I've told all my friends that I'm against it,"
Jeff observed quietly.

"That's just it!" Joe slammed his cigar to the floor. "You can
wreck your career here and now."

Jeff clenched the fingers of his right hand. "I'm not going to give
way. I'll stand for what I believe, no matter what anybody says
about it."

With a discouraged sigh Joe rose and walked to his horse. "Think it over!" he called back over his shoulder, and galloped off while Jeff ran his hand nervously over his face. The lines along his mouth were deeper than ever and his eyes looked tired. "Well, we'll just have to see . . ." he said, his voice trailing off. Until then Varina had sat silent, her dark eyes bright with pride in her husband. He was going to tell the politicians to go to hell! But something else, her ambition for him, had been stirred.

"Don't wait, Banny. Hit back! See that they understand what you think about the whole thing. When's the nominating meeting?"

"Five days from now," Jeff told her falteringly.

Varina's face was alight; she hurried inside, took out paper and pencil, and called over her shoulder: "I'll take down what you say. Begin right now."

He started slowly. Then the words rolled out in the rich baritone she knew so well. After a while she proposed changes: "That's not quite what you mean, is it? . . . Banny, they wouldn't be able to twist it if you put it that way. Or could they?" It was hours before they finished. When they read it together over cups of coffee it seemed to say the right things. Afterward, as Jeff tossed anxiously in bed, she tried to comfort him. He finally went to sleep with her arm around him, but she lay awake for a long time.

In the morning she was up before the four o'clock bell rang to see that Annabelle hurried with the breakfast and Harry had the horse ready. She woke Jeff and said as soon as he had rubbed the sleep from his eyes: "You've just got time to get to Vicksburg." As they ate a hasty breakfast she made the suggestions she had been mulling over for hours. "Why don't you hunt out this Mr. Big who has all the control? Let him know where you do stand. And this statement, couldn't you get it printed and hand it around so that everybody has it in black and white?" She watched his face. "Of course the decisions are yours to make." She had learned by this time that with her husband tact would accomplish more than anything else.

He listened quietly and then he nodded, and now, with a brisk final kiss, she sent him off. It would be their first separation since their marriage, and for the first time at Brierfield she felt lonely.

Ten days later Jeff rode back, with Joe Davis beside him. "He made it!" the brother yelled as they approached. "They just had to take him." With that he rushed ahead into the house, crying to Annabelle to bring a bottle and glasses for a celebration.

Alone with Varina on the gallery, Jeff took her quickly into his arms. After a moment he said: "It was close, very close, Winnie. If it hadn't been—if you hadn't——" She put her finger across his mouth, but he went on: "It's going to be a hard race, though, and a long one. I have a lot of opponents for the office, and I've got to start in a day or so."

She pulled away, her lips quivering. She hadn't thought of that! Blinking back her tears, she hurried off with an excuse: "I have to get some food for you." In the kitchen anger got the better of her. She picked up a plate for the cake, and before she quite realized it she had sent it crashing to the brick floor. The noise sobered her, and she stood staring at the pieces.

Almost at once Jeff was beside her. "Come here, child." He put his hand under her trembling chin. "I wouldn't want it this way, either, if I could help it. You know that. It won't be forever." She summoned up a thin smile. In the next room Joe Davis was shouting for them to come and help him celebrate.

Sometimes it did feel like forever. Varina followed her duties mechanically, wondering, waiting. She visited the hospital cabin; she prescribed for the colds and stomach pains of the children in the quarter; she listened to James Pemberton's careful reports. But with Jeff gone it was all dull and pointless.

One evening as she struggled over her sewing Annabelle came toward her, grinning. "Ef you don' min', me and Harry—kin we git married?"

Varina looked up and smiled. "Of course you can. And I'm happy; Harry's a good man. It will be fine for both of you." That other wife—Harry would never find her again, and this would be a good match. She remembered Annabelle's announcement that Christmas morning at The Hurricane; she hadn't intended to stay a widow for long. It had taken rather more time than Annabelle planned, but she had managed it.

As the girl headed for the door she gave Varina a curious, searching look. "Miss Rina. Er—is you expectin'?"

Varina had to blush. "No." She, too, had been wondering why she was not yet pregnant. It was what she wanted now as much as anything in the world. Nearly a year had passed since her arrival at Brierfield, and still no sign. Annabelle went on: "Chirren, they a protection. Man won' roam so easy; an' ef anythin' happen to 'im, you got somethin'. Ain' dat right?"

These were thoughts that Varina had not expressed even to herself. She hoped for babies to share with Jeff, a pledge to the future. Then why hadn't they come? Whenever she saw Jeff with children —her young brothers and sisters in Natchez, or the younger ones at The Hurricane—she realized how much he loved them. . . . Resentment welled up within her; she thrust the needle savagely into her scarf, and her eyes filled with tears. She looked up to find Annabelle looming over her, compassion in her round dark face. "Don' fret. Hit'll happen when de time come right. Don' fret."

The next week or two was enlivened by preparation for Annabelle's wedding. Varina provided the ingredients for the cakes, punch, and candies, over which two of Annabelle's friends and also Annabelle herself labored for hours; she gave Annabelle the material she had bought for a white dress for herself, then supervised the making of the gown. Where it didn't cover all of Annabelle, they filled in with insets of a bright green material which Annabelle admired even more than the white.

When the wedding day came Varina took charge of the proceedings. She saw to it that the ceremony itself was held in the master's parlor. The Negroes crowded in, a little awkward in the surroundings, until Varina signaled the minister and proposed toasts to the bride and groom. With that the spirits of the guests lifted; singing broke out, and jigging and skylarking. A minstrel jumped up with a song composed for the occasion about Annabelle and the long line of offspring that she and Harry would undoubtedly produce. "Who know—maybe a hundred?" he ended. To shouts and backslapping, Annabelle sighed: "Who know? Who know?" Harry looked shy and said nothing at all.

After that the singer rose with a song, more circumspect, more restrained, but broadly flattering, about Jeff and Varina and Brierfield. They were the "bes' mas'ers in de worl'. De whol' worl' for true." Mister Jeff the "bes' man on all de river." Varina's thoughts went to Jeff. Where was he tonight? How was he making out? She found it hard to smile, and eventually when the wedding party left, she stood for a long time at the door, then crept upstairs to her empty room.

James Pemberton puzzled her. From the start she had been curious about this Negro who for years had been as close to her husband as any other human being. At the beginning she had thought she detected an indication of wariness in the calm, intelligent eyes. Did he resent her? She had watched carefully and she had done everything she could to assure him of her good will. He continued polite, respectful, but she still could not tell what he thought of her.

She had often heard Jeff laughing with him, and there were things to which they both made oblique references, matters from which she was shut out. Would she ever learn more about this man who was so much a part of the plantation life?

She tried to talk with him. "How're your children, James?"

"Fine, Miss Varina. Fine." He volunteered nothing more.

"And your wife? Wasn't she sick last week?"

"Some trifling thing." He shrugged. "Nothing to worry your head about."

That was all. She wondered what James felt about his role as a slave. Did he ask himself how it would be to enjoy freedom? Did he feel badly because Jeff had not granted him the privilege of freedom? Walking alone one day, she came upon him as he sat on a fence, a paper in his hand, frowning and figuring. She was certain he was having trouble with his computation.

When she stopped he stepped down at once. Would he tell her about the problem? She glanced purposely at the paper in his hand, but he talked of other things—the crop, the season's change. She tried another tack: "James, can't I help you sometimes with your figures?"

"Maybe so, Miss Varina. I'll let you know." There was politeness here and not much else. "I'll sure do it," he repeated. The dark face still told her nothing. With a nod she left him.

One day Varina's mother wrote from Natchez: "We've been wondering why you don't visit us for a while." Margaret Howell's clear handwriting had much of her own nervous strength. The note ran on: "When will it be? Soon, we hope, because everybody asks about you, and we tell them . . ." Well, why not? she thought. With Jeff away for another two months at best, this would be an ideal time to visit her family. By the next week she had written Jeff and secured his permission by return post and was on her way back to Natchez.

The sight of the wide white house with the columns across the front and the dormers like a row of eyes on the roof brought a sudden lump to her throat. As her carriage rolled out of the tunnel-like sunken road she saw the whole family lined up on the gallery. In a few minutes, standing before the fireplace in the room where she had been married, she realized how little anything had changed here—her older brother grinning broadly; the blond sister, Maggie, with even more freckles than usual; the line of other children, a little in awe of her now; and, of course, her mother, as competent as she had ever been, and as busy with her duties. And, finally, William Howell, tall, bland, his innocent eyes smiling from the pink face with its crisscrossings of tiny lines.

"Do we have to wait till your husband leaves you before we see you again?" William Howell demanded with a laugh.

Before Varina had time to reply Margaret Howell had led her to the sofa. "Are you well? Are you really comfortable way out there? How's Eliza Davis, still sick? What do you think . . ."

In a few minutes William Howell, impatient to chat with her, was sitting beside her too. "Everybody's talking about Jeff these days. Some people in Natchez say he's a good man even if he is a Democrat!"

She started to say: "Why, the Democrats are the coming men of the South, and—and——" Then she saw that her father was having a joke at her expense, and she threw her arms around him and laughed too. And this was Varina, the fiery little Whig of only two years ago!

Margaret Howell, who had little time for fun, said impatiently: "William Howell, you'd best get back to your crops; and you, Varina, as soon as you can change, you're going calling with me on all the people who've been hinting that it's time you showed your face in Natchez again. If I hear another remark about your retreating into the woods . . ." Varina got up, thinking how nice it was to take orders for a change.

As their carriage turned into the Esplanade along the Natchez bluff, a handsome young man at the curb, his silk waistcoat gleaming in the sun, lifted his tall hat to them.

"What a surprise!" Varina cried. "Jules Amant." He came to the side of their carriage and after greeting Varina warmly talked with them about the social season, the Philadelphia opera troupe that was there this week, the reception that was spoiled by the rain. He mentioned names and goings on, the Hunts and Surgets and picnics and parties and charades. Once she would have asked a dozen questions; now she was content to nod. She felt old and remote, removed from it all. How narrow the Natchez circle had grown for her!

Her mind wandered to those kisses in the shadows near her house. This elegant young man, his face still characterless and unformed, had had the impertinence to call her naïve! He was asking something—"Your husband, Mr. Jefferson, what does he do?"

"Mr. Davis," she told him, her eyes widening in irritation. "He grows cotton, and he's going to be our next representative in the Congress!"

"So?" The thin eyebrow lifted, and the young man nodded absently. Jules Amant bowed and the carriage started.

After they were out of earshot Margaret Howell said casually: "If I'm not mistaken, Varina, you once liked that young man."

"Did I? I don't know what I could have seen in that jack-on-a-string!"

It was late afternoon when their carriage came to a halt again before the Howells' gallery. She had gone halfway up the stairs when her ears caught the hoofbeats of a galloping horse. Instinctively she ran back to the gallery. Yes, she had guessed right. It was Jeff.

But as soon as he tossed the reins aside and took her in his arms she cried out: "You're sick. Something's wrong, Banny!" His skin was flushed; the sweat ran down his cheeks, which were more heavily sunken than ever before. One eye looked badly inflamed. To her questions he murmured answers she could barely hear. Margaret Howell, after her first quick inspection, ordered him to an upstairs bedroom.

There, with curtains lowered, he spoke in broken sentences. "I was supposed to speak down at Woodville—my mother's town, you know. I—I wanted her to hear me. Once, anyway." A pause followed. "When I got there the family was waiting. She died—a few hours too soon. I went to the funeral, and then I—I had to see you." He shuddered, and Varina held his head in her arms. Her only meeting with the white-haired old woman had been too brief; she had hoped to visit with her again. . . . And so Jane Davis, whose son had been taken from her many times before, had missed him for the last time.

He became quieter and Varina sat beside him, bathing his fevered face with cool cloths, stroking his hands. Margaret Howell, tiptoeing in, made a diagnosis: "It's his malaria come back. Riding in the sun for hours like that will bring it back every time." But then Jeff stirred and pushed himself up. "I've got to be there again for the speaking," he said.

Varina tried to make him lie down again. "Banny, do you want to kill yourself? Banny, please." He frowned wearily, and then he looked up at Margaret and called out a list of medicines. "I've had to dose this disease before; I know what I need." Margaret Howell brought him several bottles. He took some medicine from one, wrapped up the rest to take with him, and forced himself to his feet. His face still looked hot, but otherwise he was improved by his brief rest. "Don't worry," he whispered to Varina. "My time with you was what I needed most. I'll manage now."

At the doorway Varina waved good-by again; for the first time she understood how truly determined a man her husband was. Could he survive the rest of this grueling summer?

Tense, frightened, she returned to Brierfield for the last nerve-racking months. It was there at Brierfield, early in the morning, that she received a scrawled note from Joe Davis. The steamboat had halted the night before with the great news. Jeff was the winner; he would be home the next night!

For hours Varina worked with Annabelle over a meal for the home-coming. "No economy today," Varina ordered, and they gathered things that appealed especially to him: a thick soup, broiled chicken, fruit pudding, a sharp cheese. By dark the table was set, the candles made ready, and Varina told Annabelle: "You don't have to wait; go on to Harry." Donning a low-cut white crepe that clung the way a dress was not supposed to cling, Varina sat alone at the doorway, her eyes fixed on the lightly waving branches at the bend in the road, on the lavender of the wisteria that hung like a shawl over the latticework of the gallery.

In the quarters silence had fallen. Somewhere in the distance a dog barked, then fell asleep again. It was hard to believe that she was not alone in a dreaming world. Then she heard hoofbeats, and at the turn of the road a horseman rode forward in the moonlight.

In one motion Jeff was on the ground and racing toward her. The supper went untouched, and the candles melted slowly until they guttered to nothing in their dripping holders.

Jeff peered up from his mail the morning after his return with a look of excitement. "John Calhoun's passing through Vicksburg—and they've asked me to introduce him!" The honor meant more to him than anything that had happened.

John Calhoun . . . For years she had been taught to think of him as little short of a monster—a crafty politician who would try any scheme to get to the White House. "Jeff," she ventured, "wasn't it Mr. Calhoun and his fanatics in South Carolina who tried to nullify what Congress did some years back?"

Jeff's eyes were serious. "Yes, and Joe and I have never been nullificationists. You can't stay in a union and say you won't obey its laws. Mr. Calhoun was wrong there, but it was one of the few times in his life. He's a patriot, Winnie; he's the South's best advocate. And he's our greatest authority on the Constitution—on strict construction, states' rights. He sent my name to West Point, and I met him some years ago. Wait till you hear him . . ." Jeff went on until she grew more confused than before. She had persuaded herself to accept nearly everything Jeff thought. But Calhoun!

Jeff's speech—he would make it on their way to the North—became their main concern. For most of a week he sat beside her, drawing out the phrases that he would use. Together they reworded, rephrased, elaborated words for her to set down. "It's wonderful, Jeff," she finally burst out. "Poor Mr. Calhoun. It'll make him sound weak." Jeff laughed; yet the address to her was superb, packed with unusual imagery and sound rhetoric. It lapsed occasionally into poetry, and at the end the Ship of State tossed on a stormy sea while the great Calhoun labored to bring it "safe into port." (Jeff, of course, had him bring it in.)

Putting the many pages of notes into Jeff's inner pocket, Varina finished the packing. While Jeff conferred with James Pemberton she walked from room to room, shoving a chair into place, touching a vase. When Annabelle sniffed, Varina almost cried, too, and hurried to apply rice powder to her cheeks. Jeff mustn't know how she felt. Her last sight of Brierfield was of Annabelle and Harry at the door, and James Pemberton waving slowly from the side of the gallery. She strained her eyes to take in every detail: the roses they had planted, the latticework, Jeff's homemade windows that were too high.

It was her house, and she was leaving it.

At Vicksburg, the river town on the high bluff, they rode quickly along the streets that followed the line of the Mississippi, with the lights of the steamboats forming a panorama in the river below. At the meeting hall they found that Calhoun's vessel had been delayed. They waited together nervously while hundreds of people around them voiced their impatience. Then suddenly a whistle blew, the band began to play, and in the middle of a pushing, screaming crowd the evening's hero appeared.

He was a tall, stooped man with a harsh face, frowning and intent. The head was long, with ears set low, a short forehead, and eyes of a peculiar yellow-brown that gleamed in their sockets. The wide mouth was held as straight as a piece of string, and everything about the man looked rigid. Here was an individual, she sensed, who would die for what he thought right—but might also condemn others to death for differing with him.

Jeff arose and Varina's heart thumped. It was a great moment and the first time she had heard him make a formal address. Before getting up he whispered, "Please don't look at me. It will make me more nervous than I am." Hands in her lap, eyes on the floor, she listened for his first words. He faltered and she knew he was trying to remember the words they had written down. Then his voice grew stronger, deeper, and the audience fell silent. But the words sounded unfamiliar, for Jeff was departing completely from the eloquent speech they had planned. Then she realized that it was better the new way. Gone were the elaborate similes, the pompous phrases. Only at the end did Jeff return to the original speech to hail the Ship of State sailing neatly in to port.

He sat down. Let Calhoun equal that! thought Varina as the

great Southern orator came striding to the front of the platform. His opening remarks shocked her, for his voice was almost flat, his language so plain it was like conversation, his delivery so fast it was hard to follow. The man spoke nervously, without gestures, without appeal to the emotions. He reminded her of a professor of mathematics!

Then all at once, like everyone else, she found herself becoming absorbed in what he was saying. It was as if Calhoun were speaking individually to her and to everyone in the audience, taking it for granted that only the unintelligent would disagree with him. To her astonishment Varina agreed with practically every word he said. She could see now how this man, as Secretary of War, Vice-President, and senator, had changed American history.

He ended to shouts and applause. While the crowd pushed about them she heard Mr. Calhoun thank Jeff: "A fine address, and a generous one, sir. Of course I remember our meeting. . . . You'll be in Congress. I'm back in the Senate this year, you know. I'll expect you to call on me." The crowd swept him away, and Jeff at last made his way to Varina's side. His hand, holding hers, trembled slightly. He was deeply moved by the occasion, while Varina, watching Calhoun's figure disappearing in the distance, wondered what part he would play in their lives in Washington.

That same night they started on their way up the Mississippi. At the juncture with the Ohio they changed to a smaller boat and found that the weather had become much chillier. Once or twice Varina went on deck, to retreat at once, her nose red with cold, her eyes running. On each occasion she noticed more ice in the river and she was not surprised the next morning to discover the boat at a standstill, entirely surrounded by ice. Except for the uncertainty and discomfort of the cramped quarters, they were glad to have these extra hours together.

Their cabin was near that of a red-haired woman, the wife of a river pilot, who bustled about, talking pleasantly to everyone. "My husband's giving me this trip as a treat," she announced each time. "What are you traveling for? How far you going?"

When she plied Jeff with questions he sat silent, ill at ease. Across the overheated room Varina watched nervously, hoping he would unbend a little. But Jeff became more aloof. Finally the pilot's wife, turning a dull red, shouted: "Well, my name's

McGruggy and I ain't ashamed of it, and I'm going to Cincinnati, and I don't see but what I'm good enough for that man to tell me where he's going." With a sniff she went back to her daughter. "Sis, Davis ain't an aristocratic name, nohow!"

Varina groaned—this was a fine start for a political career. After a proper interval she took a seat beside the McGruggys. At first they were constrained, then the three women were speaking easily. Mrs. McGruggy described her husband's dangerous calling; Varina told of Brierfield and her troubles with new shrubs. That evening, passing with Jeff, Varina stopped before the McGruggys and, when she pressed his arm, Jeff forced a smile. After that, Jeff managed to behave more naturally, although he never became one of Mrs. McGruggy's favorites.

On the third day of the delay a small vessel fought its way alongside of them, and most of the passengers were transferred. As they prepared to climb down the ladder the pilot's wife ran to tell them good-by. She thrust a package into Varina's hand. "That's apricot seed from my best tree. Plant it in Mis'sippi and think of me."

All night the small boat worked its way slowly through the cakes of drifting ice. In the morning they were put ashore a few yards from a narrow ice-covered road which went up steeply from the river. In a biting wind they transferred their baggage to a horse-drawn sled with oak runners, which had been provided by the steamboat company. Jeff and Varina sat on top of their trunks, praying that the sled would not slide off the side of the hill. Varina clung to Jeff's coat, not daring to look at the sharp drop.

They were a quarter way up the big slope when she heard a shout, and then everything slid out from under them. Varina knew a moment of terror and after that only blackness. When she came to, Jeff was rubbing snow on her face. "Thank God you're safe," he muttered. They had fallen twenty feet, and both were scratched and bleeding. When they were able to rise they found that they had suffered no serious damage, and together they helped an elderly man who had broken a rib in a fall against a tree. Eventually ropes were thrown down to them and they were pulled up to the comparative security of the narrow road. And now all transport was gone and together they limped on to the nearest inn. But even at the inn the bed was as cold as ice and Varina spent a wretched night during which she dreamed of death. "I've never been so miserable in my life," she told herself. And for once she failed to notice that Jeff, too, was chilled and badly shaken by the events of the past few hours.

The following morning they started out again by wagon in a wind that howled about them. That afternoon when Jeff stepped down from the wagon he collapsed on the ground. Terrified, she cried to the others and they carried him inside. It didn't take the local doctor long to learn the cause of his trouble. "Ma'am, it's his feet. They're frozen."

For days they stayed in a small roadside inn—more primitive, more uncomfortable than any house she had ever known, while the doctor worked over her husband. Finally he could walk again, though only gingerly. "But we've got to be on our way," he insisted. "I can make it." And against her better judgment, she agreed.

There remained the creaking stagecoach ride over the Alleghenies and beyond. Nothing that could ever happen to them would compare with the horror of this trip, she told herself. One moment they were thrown against the sides, then the roof, then the floor. In deep snow the wheels slipped repeatedly close to precipices deeper than the one into which they had already fallen. Several times there was a cry ahead: "Get out! Help!" The men leaped through the doors to chock the wheels, while the driver whipped the horses, turning them into an embankment to keep the coach from sliding over a ledge. Each time she told herself: "God help us! This is the last of it." Somehow, they survived.

In these gray hours Jeff showed her another side of his nature. He laughed; he took her hand and told stories. "If you think this is bad, you should've been with James and me in the West, that year of the bad freeze." He joked; he sang little Indian songs, including one Black Hawk had taught him on that trip back to civilization. He was still singing to her after three long weeks. The night they spied a cluster of lights far off in the distance she raised her throbbing head. "What's that?"

"Washington City," he told her. She dropped back and went quietly to sleep on his shoulder. As she did her hands tightened about her purse. In it she held the packet of seeds, gift of the pilot's lady. Her last thoughts as she closed her eyes were of the garden at Brierfield and the spot at which she would plant them beside the door.

Chapter 6

On Jeff's arm Varina started down the curved staircase of the National Hotel toward a lobby filled with the best people of Washington City. She lifted her eyes with the expression that Jeff jokingly called "Natchez arrogance." Leaving Brierfield, she had emptied her costume savings box and had bought a new wardrobe. Now she felt at ease in her close-fitting blue serge with its zigzag lines of lighter buttons and the blue hat with the cockade of black feathers. She had just surveyed herself upstairs, and she knew that her eyes were unusually bright, her white skin a little flushed. And Jeff, she assured herself, was at his best, his head held high above the soft stock at his throat, his new broadcloth suit setting off his tall figure.

"Do we look country?" she asked him, her head to the side.

"Well, we are country, aren't we?" He smiled.

"Hush." She dug her fingers deeper into the crook of his arm. "Let's keep our secret!"

At that moment she saw the first sharp glance from one of the women, and her hand went to the edge of her bonnet, while her eyes passed quickly over the folds of her skirt. It must be that hat which was a little extravagant. It was too bad, and also too late. She'd have to carry this through—and then as soon as she returned to her hotel room she'd rip off the feathers. She had been fond of it, but she understood what women meant when they exchanged stares as they were doing now.

But nearly every man in the place was observing her, and she was pleased at that. For a second she felt scorn for the women. What did she care about them, anyway? They were probably like the gossips along the wall at her mother's parties. Her nostrils dilated in anger. Then she checked herself, for she had almost forgotten something she must always remember. A politician's wife had to please the women too!

Someone across the lobby called Jeff's name. Moving toward them, his hawklike face plainly visible over the heads of the crowd, was Mr. Calhoun. Varina guessed that the woman who held tightly to his arm was Mrs. Calhoun, still handsome although no longer young. As Mr. Calhoun made the introductions Varina looked hard at them. The woman interested her as much as the man, for it was she who had snubbed the beautiful Peggy O'Neill and done so much to wreck Andrew Jackson's Cabinet when Calhoun was in the government.

Mr. Calhoun took them firmly under his wing. Almost at once he was talking government affairs. "A lot is at stake for the South, this session!" His yellowish eyes gleamed, and he poked a thin forefinger at Jeff. "We'll have to stand together, all of us." On he went, appealing directly to Jeff, unconscious of the crowd that pushed about him, his zealot's face alight with his own thoughts. Somewhere Varina had heard that a good deal of Calhoun's authority lay in his power to win younger men to his side. Jeff was deeply impressed. As they parted he took Calhoun's hand in a firm grip and assured him, "You can depend on me, sir."

After they had said good-by Varina observed that the attention the great man paid to them had made a stir. The eyes that looked at them were less cold, more speculative. As she stepped into the carriage Varina's chin rose. They weren't so country after all!

Her mood deflated slightly when she took her place behind the rail in the chamber of the House. There certainly were a lot of members; Jeff would be only one of many. She was depressed by the atmosphere of the House and the gloomy pillars of dark stone behind long semicircular rows of seats. Almost everyone, she noticed, was chewing tobacco, and she spied shiny spittoons conveniently placed near each chair. The hall was chill and drafty, and many members kept overcoats on, muffled up to their ears.

When the clerk read Jeff's name she heard a trickle of applause, nothing like the ovation she had anticipated. When she found herself the only person still clapping, she stopped abruptly.

On their way out she asked: "When will you start making speeches?"

She could not understand Jeff's amusement. "Winnie, I suppose all your reading in the journals didn't teach you that a new representative has to watch himself. We barely open our mouths."

"What will you be doing?"

"You'll see, my dear, beginning tonight."

Their first evening in Washington, first of many similar ones, was spent in their room, at the desk. Before them lay a pile of reports, leaflets, newspapers. He read to her; then, while he rested his eyes, she spelled him. Most of the documents had to do with Mexico and Texas and the Army. "That's the big issue of the moment," he explained. "I want to find out everything I can about it."

For week after week they followed the monotonous routine of breakfast at seven, then several hours of work in their room and after that Congress, and then supper and more study. Now and then two o'clock had struck before they were ready to retire. Varina's voice grew hoarse from too much reading, but in his concentration Jeff hardly noticed it.

At last, as they prepared one evening for bed, Varina stood at the window, a frown on her face. Was it going to be like this forever? In her hand she held the inkwell; automatically her fingers tightened about it. Before she realized it Jeff was behind her, his arms encircling her waist. "Don't throw it, dear! It won't always be so hard. I forget you're so young."

"That's not it at all, Banny!" She whirled around, her petticoats swinging against him. "I want to be more than—a clerk. I can help you in other ways, meet people, talk to them." She stopped to catch her breath.

"Well, you'll have a chance to do that, beginning tomorrow night." His eyes had a quizzical expression. "I forgot to tell you about the party." They were to go to a reception at one of the congressional boardinghouses on the avenue. She shook her head in amazement. Jeff never remembered important things like parties. . . .

In a room lined with greens she moved amid the gay confusion from one group to the next while a band played in the background.

There were many bare shoulders, strange glazed dishes, conversations that she could not always follow, and names and names: Mr. Calhoun, two Supreme Court justices, the Russian Minister and his American girl-bride, a Polish lady with a mustache. She tried from the beginning to make these people like her, to fit herself into their pattern. But it was so easy to make little slips.

She found that people looked astonished when she said "cudd'n," which was Mississippi style for "cousin." She told a senator, "I went to the speaking," meaning the meeting at which Jeff spoke, and the senator's scarcely hidden amusement made her realize that she must never use that expression again. She was learning fast that one never needs to make the same mistake twice. She laughed a little too heartily at a sarcastic reference to Senator Benton of Missouri. Jeff nudged her and whispered in her ear that the senator's daughter, Jessie, was standing just in front of them.

When the evening was half over she looked up as a judge came to her, mopping his face. "I had to escape that lady over there." He inclined his head in the direction to point her out. "She's that worst of God's creatures, a controverting female." Varina nodded sympathetically, inwardly amused that some of these Northern women didn't yet know something she had learned as a girl in Mississippi: No matter how hard it was to keep still, always appear to be smiling and listening whenever you were in the room.

She was still comforting the judge when a late arrival appeared in the doorway. Varina noticed that this newcomer was a small man in a vast black overcoat. A servant helped remove it, and he looked smaller still, like a diminutive pea removed from a bloated pod. He was middle-aged, she guessed, and grotesque—a hairless, shriveled face, lackluster eyes, the body of a child with a slightly humped back. "Alexander Stephens, the Georgia representative," a woman said behind her. "Did you know what somebody called him? A fugitive from the graveyard." The man next to her simpered: "They say he looks like a corpse dug up after two weeks!"

Varina's heart went out to him. Poor Mr. Stephens; he must have heard at least a few of the things that were being said about him on all sides. His air of melancholy deepened; he paused irresolutely at the threshold. At that Varina turned to the judge beside her. "I want to meet him. Will you please introduce us?"

She soon found out that Alexander Stephens, besides being queer-looking, was extremely hard to talk to. She stuck to her guns, however, and made conversation desperately for several minutes. Then Jeff joined her, for he had gathered something of her feeling, and his ready sympathy was aroused. Mr. Stephens, she understood, was a Whig, and she knew that he and Jeff were political enemies, but Jeff stayed beside her, apparently interested in everything Stephens was saying, as polite as she could wish. Eventually others came forward to join them, and Jeff and Varina were able to slip away. Much later in the evening Varina was again talking to the observant Mrs. Calhoun while Jeff waltzed with a congressman's young wife. Varina's eyes kept following Jeff, although she was trying very hard to answer Mrs. Calhoun's questions about Natchez. The older woman gave Varina's hand a little squeeze. "Don't worry about him, my dear. He's only doing his duty. By the way, how long have you two been married?"

"About a year."

Mrs. Calhoun gave her a comprehending look. "I wouldn't have thought even that long. You two are more in love than any couple in Washington."

"And we'll stay that way, Mrs. Calhoun," said Varina quietly.

The months went by in a rush. Jeff worked harder than ever, going regularly now to see Mr. Calhoun, though he did not always agree with him. Yet she knew that the South Carolinian had become Jeff's guide in most matters.

They moved to a congressional boardinghouse. That meant congenial people as neighbors but a slight reduction in privacy. Often they were invited to evening gatherings. She persuaded Jeff to attend when the other women told her that the affair was important. He made a varying impression. When he was in a good mood and unworried he became a courteous and attractive guest. All too frequently, however, Jeff appeared in a high-strung, agitated state, sitting stiffly alone, wrapped in his own musings. Once or twice during a lull in such parties she slipped up to him and said, "Jeff, can't you let go a little?"

He shook his head. "I'm sorry, Winnie. I think other things are essential."

After some hesitation she began to go to parties without him in the company of legislators and their wives. "Are you sure it's all right?" she asked.

"Go and be my representative," he advised her with a smile.

That was all right for the time being, she thought, but later when Jeff adjusted himself to Washington and his new position she would see that he went out again. Meanwhile she listened hard and returned to him with news of new developments among the rival Whigs, rumors of new appointments, tidbits of gossip, and stories that might or might not be important to him. She did not try to conceal from Jeff or from herself that she liked such parties; she always had, and she suspected she always would.

She was beginning to forget Brierfield and the life on the plantation and to discover the excitement and fascination of Washington City. True, it looked as ugly in spots as foreign visitors proclaimed it, with its half-finished public buildings, its muddy streets and its pigsties, its odorous drains outside the best hotels. But Varina was stirred by a sense of decisions in the making, by the knowledge that she was witnessing great changes, by the thought that the words of the President which she overheard at a party would affect the lives of people all over the country. She was part of things, part of the sound and fury that were the capital of the United States.

It was not long before she realized she possessed a type of good looks that made an impression even here. She met several women whose features appeared more classical, girls with a regal look, others with especially piquant mouths and eyes. Yet she had what most of them lacked: vivacity and a dark arresting beauty. One evening at a ball she stood beside a blonde who was considered one of the loveliest women in Washington City. It was not long before Varina discovered that she herself was drawing more male attention than the celebrated one. She did not understand the completeness of her victory until the girl, noticing the same thing, made an excuse to seek another part of the room.

It was in those first months at the capital that the state of Virginia dominated a large segment of Washington society. Some of the great Virginia families had been sending representatives to Congress generation after generation. They were recognized, deferred to, admired wherever they went. But Mississippi was not Virginia. One dowager spoke of Mississippi as "the frontier," and she merely smiled when Varina tried to clarify the matter. "But my mother always described such places as the West!" The *grande dame* waved her hand as if to indicate foreign parts. Varina managed a smile at that and said very quietly that her mother had been a Kempe of Virginia.

"Well!" the lady said with more warmth. "Isn't that awfully nice? I should have guessed it, of course. You don't talk quite—quite like those other Westerners." Varina felt more annoyed than ever and escaped as quickly as she could.

Some of her other encounters were disturbing too. A gentleman from Massachusetts startled her when he observed with a deprecatory wave of his hand: "Of course, Mrs. Davis, you know that only a few of you Southerners own slaves?"

"Why—why," she stammered, "nearly all the people I know do!"

"That merely shows"—he was enjoying it, and momentarily she wanted to slap his face—"that you don't know many Southern people."

That night, returning to their room, she taxed Jeff with the question: "He's wrong, isn't he?"

To her astonishment Jeff shook his head. "Well, no, dear. The percentage is, I suppose, small. Only a handful of men are really big slave owners. A few more have a limited number of slaves as we have. Even then, most Southerners have never had them."

"I wish I'd known that," she said. "I'm afraid I wasn't too polite." She would have to think further about this. She went on: "Also, he said something to the effect that we're the last civilized nation that allows slavery."

At that Jeff's face hardened. "Abolitionist propaganda. Yes, England and France gave it up, but only because it was no longer profitable. And a lot of our Abolitionists are descended from people who owned slaves in this country until they couldn't make money with them any more. Now they say it's a sin." He looked at her very seriously. "Well, it's our sin, Winnie, not theirs! Let's forget the Abolitionists." It was a long time, however, before she could put the Massachusetts man out of her mind. He had been so reasonable until he started to talk about slavery.

Now, at last, Jeff was to make his first formal address. Varina sat between two women acquaintances, her hands cold inside her muff. She and Jeff had worked until early that morning over his carefully prepared notes. (After his introduction of Calhoun there would be no more prepared speeches.) Her eyes followed her husband's movements and saw how white his face had become. A quiver ran through her as he started to speak.

"Texas . . . American rights." She was watching the audience; she paid less heed to his words than to their effect. He was speaking eloquently, forcefully, yet without malice, toward those who disagreed with him. All around her men and women were nodding to one another. Jeff's painstaking research into all the facts, his absorption in the subject were beginning to tell. Few men in Washington City had gone so deeply into the subject; few could show such easy familiarity with it. He finished to an explosion of applause, and a dozen well-wishers screened him from her. The hands in her muff had lost their chill.

As she and Jeff got up from dinner that night a servant announced: "Bunch o' people downstairs, want to see Mr. Davis." Before they reached the reception room quite a crowd had arrived to offer congratulations, and through the rest of the evening people kept dropping in. For Varina it was an exciting time. And it was not until the end of the evening that a woman standing near her upset her by saying casually: "Mr. Davis's speech certainly showed that he has had a lot of military experience. I suppose he expects to be in the war?"

Varina could not answer. Was actual fighting so close, and would Jeff be called to the colors?

The same week she had her answer to the first question. On her way to pay a call she met Alexander Stephens, a stern expression on his withered face.

"What's the matter?" she asked in alarm.

"They've spilled blood out in the Southwest," he said bitterly. "It's on now, after all the fine talk."

She learned that Zachary Taylor, in command on the frontier, was moving forward with his men. Mr. Stephens had more to tell, but she turned away, her alarm showing in her eyes.

That afternoon, from her seat in the gallery of the House, Varina looked on as Jeff got up to speak, the tension showing in his face. Through the day there had been strong criticism of Zachary Taylor and his makeshift army. But Jeff referred to his former father-in-law as a great soldier, a man of "desperate daring and military skill of the highest order." He told of the need for trained military men. "Could a blacksmith or a tailor have gotten the same results?" he demanded.

There was a sudden interruption from the other side of the chamber. A heavy individual strode forward, rage in every gesture. Another representative had jumped to his feet. Someone behind Varina whispered, "That's Andrew Johnson from Tennessee. What's he mad about?"

Mr. Johnson glared at Jeff Davis and yelled across the room: "I'm glad to have the world know I was a tailor. I prefer that to an illegitimate, swaggering, bastard, scrub aristocracy!"

Varina was suddenly numb with fear, for she knew that Jeff was not one to take such words. If he struck back at Andrew Johnson there would certainly be a challenge. She held her breath and waited, and then Jeff began to speak again, firmly, quietly: "I wish the House to understand that I am sorry. I meant no reflection on any member; I would never knowingly do a thing like that. I named several trades at random. . . ." Relieved, Varina settled back, thinking that incident was closed. But after the session was over, as she and Jeff waited in the hall, Andrew Johnson swept by, his eyes still furious, his heavy features eloquent of his warm resentment. For a moment she felt sorry for a man who could be hurt so deeply by an accidental word and then could not accept a sincere apology. Then she thought of Jeff and realized that in Andrew Johnson he'd made a permanent enemy.

But that evening the Johnson affair was forgotten in plans for the approaching war. A travel-stained messenger arrived from Mississippi with the news that Jeff had been chosen colonel of the First Mississippi Regiment. The two men sat opposite her, running over the military details, hardly conscious she was there. "Embark from New Orleans. . . . Another hundred volunteers . . ."

Hands clenched, she tried to fight the terror within her. Jeff's eyes had a fevered look, a tension she had never seen before. Now, at last, she realized how much the Army meant to him, more than his plantation, more than his public career which had begun so well.

The next day she had a brief reprieve from anxiety when Jeff was called to the White House and returned with the news that President Polk had asked him to stay in the capital a while longer to vote on the tariff bill. His face brightened. "I did a little trading with him. In return I'm going to serve under Zachary Taylor—and I'm going to get the new percussion rifles for my men instead of the old flintlock muskets." She rejoiced; anything, anything to keep Jeff with her, no matter for how short a time.

Jeff was busier now than she had ever seen him, and also happier. His work in Congress seemed easier now that he was planning a resumption of his military career. Varina knew he was seeing a lot of Winfield Scott, old "Fuss and Feathers," General in Chief of the Army. Washington was filled with stories about the silver-haired martinet, his vanity, his opera-star temperament. One evening Jeff came home depressed and in a bad temper. "I've had a long argument with Scott," he groaned. "It was over the new weapons."

She could tell from his manner that this was no light matter, and she wasn't surprised when the fight went on for weeks. Old "Fuss and Feathers" thought little of the new rifles, but Jeff insisted that they be used. "I won," he told her finally. But she wondered how high the personal cost might be to her husband. People said that old Scott never forgot a slight, and she knew that now Jeff had made another enemy, another important one.

The weeks went by rapidly, and suddenly the session had ended. The brief respite was over. Varina would be returning to Brierfield, and Jeff would soon be donning a uniform and joining Zachary Taylor. Not until now had she understood how much she liked Washington City and the friends they had made. Sadly they made a round of final calls; then on a rainy morning they started back to Mississippi over the same route by which they had come.

This time it was summer. A perfume hung in the air, and the mountainsides were stained with the red of laurel. As they rode along they encountered clouds of dust and soon caught up with a battery on its way to Mexico. Jeff jumped down from their coach, and while the driver waited he talked intently with the men on one of the caissons. When he climbed back beside her she watched him in silence. The coach bumped ahead, and Jeff took out a pocket edition of military tactics and gave his full attention to the closely written pages. More than all the news reports, more than all the speeches she had heard, this moment brought the war home to her.

She stood again before Brierfield, its latticed gallery white against its setting of green. After her months in the great world it seemed so small, so unpretentious—and so much hers. Her throat ached; she was afraid to speak. There was James Pemberton, like a sober ruler among the blacks who clustered around him; the squat Annabelle, a grin on her broad face, and Harry at her side. Varina looked anxiously toward her plants, to the rows of spring roses that Harry had trained in long, curving lines. They had flourished during her absence. Harry was pointing with pride to something beside the door—a new bush that had started to flower.

She suddenly realized what it was. "Mrs. McGruggy's apricot seeds!" she cried to Jeff. "I'm going to call it the 'Pilot's Wife.'" From that day on it was known by no other name.

Joe Davis and Eliza came over from the big plantation. Varina talked quietly with her sister-in-law about Washington manners and Mr. Calhoun, senators' wives and Virginia styles. Joe Davis paced up and down, a cigar between his lips, his pride in Jeff's accomplishments showing in his very walk. Jeff had hardly a moment for his own remarks. Joe took over, tossing out dogmatic statements.

"This war, it's nothing." He tugged at his beard. "A skirmish or two and it'll all be over, all over!"

Jeff said nothing, but Varina, throwing caution aside, asserted firmly: "Joe, nobody in Washington thinks so."

Eliza cast an apprehensive glance at her husband. To her surprise, Joe contented himself with waving away Varina's words. "You'll see, girl. Jeff'll be back here before you can turn around."

Was the big man merely talking flamboyantly, as he always did? Watching him more closely, Varina saw that, despite his delight at his brother's advance, Joe was as upset as any of them over Jeff's going. She felt closer to Joe than she had in a long time. She would try to bridge the gap that had been growing between them. . . .

Her last hours with Jeff had arrived. As she watched the clock Varina tried to be brisk and matter-of-fact, talking of plantation affairs and the way she would try to supervise operations, with James Pemberton's help. She spoke, too, of her easygoing older brother Joseph, who had just volunteered in Natchez and was on his way to join Jeff. "You'll look after him when you can?" she asked. "He's headstrong—and Mother writes that he's so tall he'll be an easy target!"

Jeff laughed with her, and then suddenly both were silent. She kept thinking, "He'll be gone at least a year, at least a year, at least a year." Now she thought of something else: If he didn't come back, there'd never be a child. Suddenly she found herself sobbing and whispering her fears.

"Banny, Banny . . . I've failed you. You're going, and I couldn't—couldn't give you a baby."

His face was gentle as he bent over her. "Please, Winnie. We've got a long time ahead. I'll be back."

"No, you won't!" Her voice rose to a high pitch. "They'll kill you out there!" She had lost all control. He leaned back in his chair and drew her to him. He appealed, he reasoned, and then he asked: "Would you really want me to stay behind?" With his free hand he turned her face until her dark eyes were looking directly into his. She could only shake her head.

"Another thing." His eyes were very steady. "Don't believe the rumors you'll hear. Don't pay attention to gossip over losses and deaths and all that. They're always wrong. And nothing's going to happen to me!" Despite herself, she believed him now.

He was still holding her in his arms when James Pemberton knocked to say his horse was ready. Jeff kissed her for the last time and then walked quickly out of the room. Through the window she saw him ride off against the sunlight. She stared blankly ahead of her. A breeze lifted one of the strands of Spanish moss that hung from a branch beside the house. Then there was stillness again.

Chapter 7

THE DOWN-SWEEPING OCTOBER WIND WHICH HAD SENT THE YEL-lowed leaves scraping against the oversized doors at Brierfield brought Annabelle into the parlor with an armful of fresh wood. Eliza Davis, who had arrived a few minutes earlier, drew her coat tighter around her narrow shoulders and said: "Annabelle, is she taking it any more easily?"

"No'm." Annabelle groaned. "Worse. For a while, at firs', she use' to try to keep busy, sortin' linens and sich. Now she jus' sits, thinkin', an' den runnin' for to git de news from de papers. Den she go for long rides, all alone, like now." Shaking her head, Anna-belle waddled off.

For nearly an hour Varina had been walking in agitation at the edge of one of the marshy spots a mile from the house. Her well-trained horse moved along behind her, nibbling occasionally at tufts of grass. Varina had tried to quiet herself by watching the ripples among the dying lilies until she could stand it no longer.

At first it had not been so hard when months ago Jeff had joined forces with "Old Rough-and-Ready" Zachary Taylor. A warm friendship had developed between him and Taylor. The old warrior had shouted his praise of what Jeff had done to turn raw troops into trained men. Jeff had worked his men steadily, until they had be-come a magnificent aggregation. . . . Varina was naturally happy about that. What a fine man the general must be, to admit he had been wrong in disliking Jeff as a son-in-law, and to make amends this way. Someday she hoped to meet him and to tell him how she felt.

But now for days the papers had been full of stories of the great battle near Monterrey, where Jeff was stationed. More than two weeks had gone by without any word from him. What had happened?

Varina mounted and rode slowly back to the house. At the gallery she gave the reins to a colored boy, jumped down, and walked dejectedly up the steps. At any other time the sight of Eliza Davis would have pleased her, but now she gazed sadly at her sister-in-law. Eliza was shocked at the change since her last visit. Varina's cheeks were hollow, her lips as white as her pale face. Eliza moved toward her, and in the next moment Varina was in the older woman's arms.

"Child, child," Eliza appealed to her. "What are you letting this do to you?" Annabelle brought a glass of warm milk, and together the two women coaxed her to swallow it. They watched her in an uncertain silence; she had nearly finished when, through the window, she beheld a familiar figure. It was Harry with the twice-weekly mail. She put the glass aside, spilling it in her haste, and ran to the doorway before either of them could reach it.

"Jus' one." Harry looked disappointed, but Varina, with a cry, had snatched it from him. It came from her brother in Mexico; in her anxiety she almost ripped it apart. From the first page she learned that the battle was over, the Americans had won, and Jeff had become a hero! She cried out the news to Eliza and Annabelle and raced ahead to the next pages.

Every effort to take the strongly defended Mexican position had failed, until Jeff's men were ordered to attack it. Running forward through murderous gunfire, Jeff had led the Mississippians in a charge up a steep embankment. Just as the onlookers became certain the charge had failed, Jeff's figure emerged from the dust and smoke. The fort had capitulated a few minutes later.

Varina sat down, her eyes shining. Then she picked up the letter again and read the rest of her brother's news. He wrote that the organized fighting had slackened off. More men were now dying of guerrilla attacks and disease than in action itself. The words leaped up at her: "Five men found dead with throats cut; dysentery has taken another dozen; they are shooting at us from ruined buildings . . ."

She stood up, trembling again. "They'll kill him, I know it! They'll kill him!" She was close to hysteria, and suddenly Eliza

Davis acted with decision. "Varina, you can't stay out here by yourself, so far from the rest of us. Come over to The Hurricane, for a while, anyway. Can't you see——" Eliza realized that she need argue no more, for Varina lacked the energy to resist. She waited limply while Annabelle hurriedly packed her clothes and then let Eliza lead her to the door and to the waiting carriage.

The next few weeks were wonderfully peaceful ones. Eliza provided her with a wide room at the back of the rambling three-storied house, usually occupied by one of Eliza's nieces, and Varina went at once to bed, to stay there indefinitely. Joe issued firm orders that there must be silence so Varina could sleep.

One afternoon Varina turned her head and saw that the smiling Annabelle stood beside her. "Sure glad to be with yer." She grinned.

Eliza said from the doorway, "I thought this would help you; Annabelle knows everything you need."

That evening Annabelle carried a pallet to the room so that she could be with Varina night and day. By this time the newspapers were arriving with long accounts of Jeff's deeds, eyewitness stories, and statements made by important men all over the South. Varina accumulated the accounts in a box beside the bed. "They're my best tonic," she told Joe Davis.

She was regaining weight, and the fixed expression of recent weeks was gone from her eyes. Soon she joined the other women of the household—sisters, nieces, cousins—in the music room and the library.

"It's like old times, like the Christmas party you attended," Eliza told her. That Christmas party seemed so long ago. Suppose she had not accepted the invitation but had insisted on staying in Natchez for the town parties she had wanted to attend? Today she might be, instead of Mrs. Jefferson Davis, the wife of any one of a dozen young planters. How lucky she was, the way things had turned out!

She looked down at the newspaper in her lap, and by habit her eye ran down the casualty list and halted. *Amant, Jules, Captain, died in action.* She hadn't heard from him since their accidental meeting on her last visit. She had left him with a curt good-by because he had been unimpressed with Jeff's record. And now he had fought under her husband and given up his life. . . . There, but for an accident or two, was the man she might have married.

Gradually Varina grew aware of a slight friction in the household at The Hurricane. With most of the big family she managed, now as before, to get on without difficulty. The generous Florida Mc-Caleb of Diamond Point took a supervisory interest in her welfare. The quick-tempered, volatile Mary of the dark curls rushed in and out, seeing that Varina had needles and scissors when she sewed, headache vinegar when she felt weak, and warding off petty annoyances. Mary, who had watched her so closely at first, was now a loyal friend.

One or two of the others seemed less sympathetic. Perhaps she had slighted them a little, unconsciously, on that first visit when she had trouble remembering who was which cousin and who was whose mother-in-law. These women looked on her, she suspected, as a kind of interloper who had taken away the Prince Charming of the family. She repeatedly set herself out to please them, talking of things that interested them, but they still seemed cold and aloof.

The girl who gave up her room to Varina was not entirely happy about it. She made several airy references to the subject and after a while implied that Varina was pampering herself. One afternoon in the sewing room, when Eliza was absent, Varina dropped her work in anger. "What do you mean, my 'easy life'?"

"Nothing, Varina. Don't be edgy. You're acting like a star boarder."

"I'm not a star boarder!" Varina's dark eyebrows went up. "My husband has his own plantation. If anybody wants it, I can repay——"

"Oh no! Your husband hasn't any plantation. Jeff's as dependent on Joe Davis as anybody in this house!"

Unsteadily Varina got up and went straight to her brother-in-law's office.

"Does Jeff own Brierfield?"

The big man showed his surprise. "For God's sake, who's been upsetting you?"

He thrust out a chair for her, but she chose to remain on her feet, her eyes fixed on him. "Then it's true."

"Not quite." He spoke slowly and looked toward the window. "Officially, I suppose, the land's mine, but I did turn it over to him. I've never bothered about making any deed. But you need never worry——"

"Then after all the work we've put into it"—her voice was very low—"it could be taken overnight from Jeff and me and our children?"

A spark of anger flashed instantly in Joe Davis's small blue eyes. "You've had no children!"

She faced him, silent, fingers clenched to keep them still. Until then she had never realized that Joe Davis had any feeling on the subject of children. She had heard in Natchez of families that grew bitter when a widow, without children, took property that had been theirs before the marriage. Now, if anything happened to Jeff . . .

Still, there was more to it than that. She had barely sensed it until now, but Joe Davis wanted to keep everyone around him dependent on his favors. She thought of others in the family: to some he made gifts; others he helped in getting a start. Yet he wanted them all obligated to him, within easy reach, and always under his direction. That was the reason why she had seen those half-hidden gleams of resentment in Joe Davis's eyes, those sudden looks of annoyance, for she had never bowed before him as he wished.

The anger had gone from his eyes, but some of the resentment remained. "Varina, this will straighten itself out. Don't take it to heart."

She, too, was calmer now, but there was a wary look about her wide dark eyes. "Just one more thing. Do you intend someday soon to give Jeff the title to his plantation?"

He sat there, silent, stolid, his eyes on some distant object behind her. The minutes dragged by. "Very well," she said at last. "I have had my answer. I'll leave The Hurricane at once."

An hour later her belongings were packed, and she was going down the steps to the driveway, the puzzled Annabelle pounding along behind her. Eliza Davis, much upset, was at her side.

"I'm sorry this happened," Varina told her. "And you know, don't you, how much I appreciate what you've done?" Eliza nodded, her tired eyes on the ground, and Varina went on: "But I couldn't stay now. Come see me when you can, won't you?" As they rode away Eliza remained at the gate, waving.

Late that afternoon Varina was walking by herself in the garden at Brierfield. Their beloved house—and it wasn't theirs after all. They could lose it in an hour, and after they had given so much of themselves to it. . . . Harry Mounger approached with a letter from Jeff. He had learned of her illness, and he was on his way home on a furlough! It would take nearly six weeks to get to Brierfield and back, and he would have about fifteen days at home.

Varina hurried to the house and up the stairs to her room. She summoned Annabelle. "Bring the lamps and my creams." Before the dressing-table mirror, in the strongest of lights, she took rapid stock of herself—the blue shadows beneath her heavy-lidded eyes, the sagging of her chin, the lifeless quality of her hair. She went to work with the creams and called out directions over her shoulder.

"Bring me those light dresses out of the trunk. And let's see those new shoes. And, oh, for tonight I want a good thick soup and plenty of meat and extra milk." Her tone was buoyant. She lifted her head from the dressing table. "I forgot to tell you, Annabelle, Mr. Davis is coming home!"

Annabelle grunted. "You didn' hafta tell me dat, Miss Rina! I knew it de minute you raise your face from dat letter."

As Varina continued to massage her neck and throat she heard the sound of an arrival downstairs. One of Eliza's servants came in with a note. Eliza had written a simple message of encouragement. She had tried to talk with Joe, but so far without success. Varina must have seen how Joe acted when he thought people were trying to change his mind. But Eliza had not given up, and Varina must not worry. Eliza would bring up the subject when next she could and would let her know. . . . Varina slipped the note into her bodice. She had a stanch friend in that frail woman at The Hurricane.

The next day she began to watch the calendar: Now Jeff must have started. Next week he would be passing Baton Rouge, then St. Francisville. Daily she took rides; daily she added to her diet and inspected herself in the mirror. Toward the end she saw that, though still underweight, she looked a great deal better. As much as anything else, the word of Jeff's coming had done that for her.

With Annabelle's help she took in several inches at the waists of her best gowns. And at last, when the day arrived, she had everything ready hours ahead of time; and she stood there against the lighted square of Jeff's outsized doorway, straining her eyes for his approach.

By the time he reined in she was clinging to his saddle.

"Banny, Banny. It's been so long." After that she could say nothing more.

"Yes, darling," he echoed, "it's been so terribly long." And then he had jumped to the ground and was holding her in his arms. Harry, leading Jeff's horse away, stole a glance back. When he reached the stable they were still standing there, just looking at each other.

In the morning she woke early and watched him as he slept beside her, taking in hungrily every detail of his appearance. He had changed and she saw that his skin was bronzed, his body heavier and harder-fleshed. The hollows in his cheeks had begun to fill out, and the lines of worry had disappeared. Last night she had noticed that his eyes were clear and bright. He stirred in his sleep, and she slipped out of bed. Lifting the tray from Annabelle's hands, she took over the serving of his breakfast. Annabelle grinned. "Lots of people give half dey life not to carry food!" Varina left her with a laugh.

At first, as he ate the eggs and liver and sausages, she questioned him in detail about the battles and his part in them, but he preferred other subjects. "Your brother's fine; he's made a good soldier. And did I tell you about John Quitman?" The ever-fiery Natchezian was Jeff's immediate superior; for years, everybody said, Quitman had itched for a war, some war, any war. Now that he had it, he was having the time of his life. His officers laughed behind his back at Quitman's red-hot temper, his dramatic orders, the way he perpetually brandished a sword. "Still, he's a good man in a fight, and a brave one," Jeff told her.

He had more to say, however, about Zachary Taylor. "The boys go anywhere he says, do anything he orders. I've never known anybody so much loved by the men under him." As she listened Varina saw that Jeff, too, had developed a deeper admiration for old Zachary Taylor.

"But the general's not so happy now," Jeff added. "He thinks he's being put on the shelf. General Scott's going down there with a new army, and we'll be shoved to the side." Varina concealed her guilty delight at this news. Let someone else take the glory. She wanted her husband alive.

She carefully avoided any mention of Brierfield or her difficulty with Joe; it would hardly be fair to burden her husband with this additional worry. But then, over his second cup of coffee, Jeff himself brought up the subject. "Joe sent word. I'm"—he stammered—"I'm sorry this came up. Once or twice since we were married I wanted to talk it over with you, but I always put it off. Joe's done so much for me. . . . I've expected all along that he'd deed the land to me sometime. But he's set in everything, and stubborn, as you know." He paused and looked over the cup at her. "Let me work it out, will you, Winnie?"

Her stored-up anger slipped away, and she leaned over to kiss him. "Of course, Banny, of course." It was enough that she had him back.

His time slipped away like snow under the Mississippi sun. Varina hardly left the plantation; she felt a pang of jealousy whenever he rode off, if only for an hour. Several times he went over to see his brother, and toward the end he went to The Hurricane for a business conference. When he returned he stopped at the door, and she knew that something important had happened.

Puzzled, she followed him to the desk, where he took out a paper. "Joe thought it'd be a good thing for me to make a will— just in case. I've asked James Pemberton to come in because he's mentioned in it. After he leaves there's something I want to tell you."

Just then Pemberton knocked on the door.

"Oh, James," said Jeff, motioning to him, "bring your chair here. I've left a blank opposite your name in my will. I suppose you'll want your freedom if I die before you do?"

James Pemberton looked from Jeff to Varina, then out of the window. He said finally in a firm voice: "If you passed away I'd stay on and take care of Mrs. Davis, the way I've done." Varina's face softened. So James had come to like her more than she had thought. His reticence had not meant he was unfriendly, after all.

"Thank you, James," she told him.

He continued, his eyes still steady: "But if anything happened to Mrs. Davis I'd want to be free."

"That's how it will be," Jeff told him. Gratefully Varina's eyes followed the colored man as he left the room. Then, as the door closed, she faced Jeff again. "Well, Banny, what was it you were going to tell me?"

In reply he read the will to her. Brierfield was declared to be Jeff's. In case of his death Varina would share it with Jeff's three sisters and the children of a fourth who had died. . . . He halted and turned toward her.

So Joe Davis had found a way to strike at her. True, the ownership seemed to be cleared up. But she would be denied a wife's normal share. Joe was the rich man, the ruler of the family, and yet Jeff had to provide for the sisters. Under other circumstances she might have forced herself to understand, but now her cold face showed her sense of shock and her hurt.

Jeff took her hand. "I'm not sure it's right, Winnie. I haven't signed it yet."

Varina shook her head. "I'm not blaming you, Jeff. It doesn't matter." She rose. "Now it's about time for you to pack. Go on, up with you." She forced a smile and watched him go to his room.

That afternoon she had a letter from her mother which disturbed her almost as much as the will, but she didn't mention it to Jeff. He had enough on his mind.

Late that evening, with the rest of the Davises, she told Jeff good-by at the steamboat landing. She stayed on the levee top, hand lifted against the sky, until the vessel had become a tiny spot in the brown immensity of the Mississippi. When she started back Joe Davis was waiting. His voice was matter-of-fact. "You'll be coming to The Hurricane with us?"

She shook her head.

"Where'll you be going?"

"Home. To Natchez." With a nod she turned away.

Joe Davis remained there for a time. Then with an angry motion he slammed his hat on his head and walked over to his carriage.

As the old house loomed ahead at the end of the deeply worn Natchez road Varina's hand closed again about the disturbing letter in her purse. After considerable thought Margaret Howell felt it best to tell Varina that her father was on the verge of failure—a bad year coming on top of a pile of unpaid debts. Also, there was another matter. After all these years Margaret Howell was going to have another baby. Varina wondered why she herself couldn't have been favored instead, she who was so much younger and had no children. Then, ashamed, she put the thought aside. It occurred to her that it was extremely dangerous for her mother to have a baby so late in life. She had heard of cases . . . Anyway, her family needed her and she had come home.

Margaret was already several months advanced. Competent as ever and no less hurried, she kissed Varina fervently and shrugged off her first anxious questions. "Child, I had a baby before you, and more of them afterward. Don't bother your head about me." Then, however, as they settled down on the sofa, she admitted that the Howell finances had her worried more than she wished the other members of the family to see. "Varina, I just don't know."

William Howell hurried in with a slightly sheepish look on his bland pink face. He joked as he hugged Varina. "Do we have to have another baby to see our girl again?" He asked about Jeff. "That's all you hear on the streets. Jeff and the Mississippi Rifles."

She told him proudly that Jeff had proved his point about the value of the new rifles, and done it so well that his troops had taken that name. This in spite of the fact that old "Fuss and Feathers" Scott still resented what Jeff had done and told everyone that he considered Jeff Davis, Mexican record or no Mexican record, a military upstart. William Howell asked more questions about Jeff's military feats, as excited over the war as any Natchez schoolboy. He'd never change, Varina assured herself as she patted his hand.

When she and Margaret were alone again and were discussing family affairs Varina explained the situation with Joe Davis. This was a blow to Margaret Howell because she had been counting on him as a last resort in the present financial crisis.

"I'm afraid we can't ask him for anything," said Varina glumly. "If only Father could make a success of planting, but maybe planting isn't the best thing for him. Why doesn't he—why don't we hunt up something else for him?"

Her mother looked away. In Natchez, if a man wasn't a cotton grower or a lawyer or a doctor, most people didn't consider him a gentleman.

"Well," Varina resumed, "I've met some people in Washington who might help. He'd take a place in government service, wouldn't he?" It was a slim chance, but hope began to show again in Margaret's tense face.

That night Varina sent out a dozen letters. Then she and her mother settled down, each to her own months of waiting. For both it would be hard. By the time the replies arrived from Varina's Washington friends Margaret's confinement was close. The mail brought only refusals; Mr. Howell, alas, was too old or too inexperienced. Margaret could no longer conceal her fears about the family's future. Varina worked hard to keep her mother in good spirits. "Please . . . You know you don't have to worry. If nothing else comes up Jeff would never let anything happen!"

Overnight Margaret's condition made Varina forget everything else. It would be a difficult birth. For days the older woman lay in torment, Varina and two Negro girls constantly at her side. Several times the pulse fell dangerously low and, while William Howell herded the children together downstairs, Varina sank to her knees beside the bed.

"Oh God," she whispered, "this mustn't happen. We need her badly, so badly!"

Then just before dawn Margaret gave birth to a boy and came safely through her ordeal. There was no argument over a name for the baby, for William Howell had one all picked out. "It's going to be Jeff Davis Howell, for our hero."

Without warning trouble boiled in the neighborhood of Zachary Taylor's army. At Buena Vista twenty thousand Mexicans were moving fast against a scant fifty-five hundred Americans! Varina, her face ashen, went to her father. "Take me to town to the newspaper office! I've got to find out what I can."

It was a nightmare ride. William tried to talk to her, and Varina nodded but heard nothing of what he said. When an oak branch scraped across the window she gave a cry of fright, then drew back against the cushion. They rolled along the Esplanade until they reached the corner at which she had talked that day to young Jules Amant. They halted to let another carriage cross in front of them, and in the momentary silence they heard one man call to another: "They say Colonel Davis is dead. Killed in the fighting!"

She caught the door in her white hand. "Don't mind me," she muttered to her father. "Go to the editor. Find out!"

With an apprehensive glance he stepped out of the carriage and raced off. Ten minutes later he was back, panting. "Child, it's just a rumor. . . ."

"But the editor heard it too? It's gone that far?"

"Well, there's no reason to believe it." She had sunk against the back of the seat. Her lips moved, but he could hear only fragments of sentences: ". . . should have made him stay. . . . My fault . . . God punishing . . ." The ride back, for both of them, was endless. Was it some ill omen that she had received the word on the same spot at which she had seen young Amant for the last time? And Jules Amant was dead now, buried in a narrow sand grave under the violent Mexican sun. . . . Stumbling, she let her mother lead her to her room.

The christening of little Jeff Davis Howell had been set for that afternoon. An hour after she returned from town Varina walked downstairs, her lips blue-gray, her face fixed. "No." She shook her head. "We won't postpone it. I'm ready."

The younger Howells watched her apprehensively. Her face twisted in suffering, she rode with them to Trinity Church and took her place beside the font, where the baby's long robe trailed over William Howell's arm. She heard the words: "Jefferson Davis Howell." Where was the other Jeff now? Was he already in the ground?

For days she waited in agony. "No news yet, child. . . . The editor hasn't heard anything more. . . . No, nothing." Then a letter from her brother arrived. William Howell pushed open the door and handed it, unopened, to her. Before she unsealed it she shut her eyes for a second and said a prayer. Please, let it be good news, please. . . . After that, with hands that shook no longer, she tore open the paper.

Jeff had been injured, but now he was recovering, and more of a hero than ever! She swallowed, gave her father a quick look of relief, and skipped on. Jeff had led his regiment in an unusual formation, an inverted V, that had saved the day for the Americans. Motionless and silent, he and his men had held firmly until the Mexicans came close along a ravine. Then Jeff gave the signal and the guns crackled. Down went men and horses, writhing in death. She winced at the descriptions of pain and slaughter and read on.

At the climax a musket ball ripped into Jeff's left leg, forcing the spur and part of the shoe deep into the ankle. He had refused to leave but fought on while his wounded leg swelled in its boot. That night the doctor thought it might be necessary to amputate, but a friend had stayed at Jeff's side, pouring water constantly over the injury. The report had spread that Jeff was dead. "Old Rough-and-Ready" Taylor had nearly cried when he heard it. Some were saying that when the general found Jeff alive he told him: "My daughter was a better judge of men than I was." Varina glowed at the words, then jumped to the last passage. Jeff was on his way home!

God had been good to her.

Near the top of the hill at the Natchez port Varina waited for the steamboat that would bring Jeff home. Below, beside the cannons and the militia lined up, thousands were waving flags, screaming and cheering. At her side her mother whispered: "Did you hear that down in New Orleans the Creoles went crazy, saluting Jeff in French, throwing flowers from the balconies, toasting him. . . . And who do you think made the oration, praising him to the skies? Mr. Seargent Prentiss!"

Varina thought of that day when Jeff had first met Mr. Prentiss, the great lawyer, in debate. Then Prentiss had been at his peak, Jeff almost unknown. Now their positions were reversed. Pity touched her; for Mr. Prentiss there was no more future. He had drunk most of that away.

Somebody cried: "There she is! Round the bend!" The cannon boomed again and again. A line of white-clad girls held yard-long ropes of roses, and whistles jangled in Varina's ears. Her cleft chin lifted. And this was Natchez, the town that once sniffed when she prepared to marry Jeff Davis, the country farmer!

The crowd ran forward. The vessel slipped in, churning the water to a froth. A line of soldiers waved to the civilians. Men shoved aside barriers to race to the deck, and for a moment Varina could make out nothing. Then the crowd parted and out came

Jefferson Davis. At her first sight of him her hand went to her mouth. He was white and haggard and he was hobbling on crutches. Then at once she wiped her eyes and raised her hand.

From the distance he saw her and smiled. He started forward, till one of the men shouted something, and then they lifted him on their shoulders. They surged upward, Jeff high above them, bringing him to her.

Part Two

MID–PASSAGE

Chapter 8

THE DAYS WERE WARM AND LONG AND SLUMBEROUS. THEY SAT together on the gallery of Brierfield, in the shadow of the lattice where the lavender clusters of wisteria hung close to their heads. While Jeff rested, with his crutches beside him, Varina went over his correspondence. The mail piled up by the basketful. All the world, it appeared, wanted to tell Colonel Davis how much it thought of him. These were golden hours, when no one had any words except those of praise.

She ran expertly through editorials, tributes from state legislatures, notes from men who had served with Jeff. "Hm. Two more invitations to make talks, another to visit a reunion in Jackson." Jeff began to speak, but she halted him with: "I'll know how to handle *them*. You're going to stay here, sir, and get your health back, no matter who invites you and where!" With a smile he inclined his head. "Yes, Doctor."

She made a face at him and went back to the mail. Her scissors ripped open another letter, and then they clattered to the floor. "Banny, Banny! You got it for him." It was an official communication; a new Navy agent had been named for New Orleans—William Howell. Going to her husband, Varina kissed him on the cheek, then, more eagerly, on the lips. The two families would be separated more than ever, but it would be a godsend for the Howells. Things had worked out as well for Margaret as for her. . . .

The last message in her lap was marked with heavy lettering, "PERSONAL." She handed it to him. "Open it right away, Banny. What is it?" She tipped her head to the side.

Jeff's eyes gleamed as he read. Under a new congressional act,

President Polk wished to make him a brigadier general in the volunteer Army. "General Davis!" she tried the words. "Don't they sound wonderful? What will your uniform be?"

Jeff raised his hand. "Hold on, Winnie. No matter what Congress did, I don't think the President has any right to make an appointment of that kind." He frowned slightly. "It's a violation of states' rights."

Her mouth fell open. "You won't take it?"

"No. I wish you'd write him my regrets." He gave the letter back to her.

If only Jeff could be a little less fixed in his views, she thought. But there was no sense in arguing. Nothing that she or anyone else could say would make him change. For a moment she saw herself beside her general: Jeff in a resplendent uniform, her own fine costume trimmed with feathers. A general's lady could certainly find an excuse to wear feathers, she told herself. Ah well, a colonel's wife was still something. . . .

James Pemberton drove up in an open carriage for Jeff's daily inspection of the plantation. As she helped him in she looked at him more closely. He still seemed drawn, his chest sunken, the lines almost carved into his face. A few strands of gray had appeared in his thick hair, and the high cheekbones and long chin jutted out more conspicuously than ever. As for his bandaged leg, any quick movement that jarred it made him break out in sweat. When he was settled comfortably she climbed in beside him. She, too, was weary; after her year of continuous strain she welcomed nothing so much as the prospect of the long quiet months ahead. Again they were together, with the world far away, much as it had been during those early months of their marriage. They were separated hardly an hour of the day or night, and she wanted nothing more. . . . She took the reins and clucked to the horse.

"Crop's doing mighty well," Jeff said to her. "You and James hardly need me here!"

He pointed with his cane. "I think I'll put up an extra barn in the back. The lumber's ready; I don't see why we can't start Monday."

A few minutes later he asked her to pull up. "That fence is wobbling badly. We'd better replace it." She nodded, pleased at his renewed interest in Brierfield.

They passed Annabelle standing beside the road, looking unmistakably pregnant. Jeff called to her: "Let me congratulate you, and Harry too."

"Yessir, we sure happy, too." Annabelle stared down at her scuffed shoes. "Me and Harry been wantin' to ask, can we name it after you-all?"

Varina blinked. "After both of us?"

Annabelle slapped her side. "You know—a girl for Miss Rina or a boy for Mist' Jeff."

Varina looked quickly at Jeff and answered for them both. "We'd like it, Annabelle. We'd be glad."

As they drove on Varina knew from Jeff's expression what he was thinking about. Would they ever have a child of their own? She wondered too. She had spoken with the doctor, and he had been reassuring. "I know of no reason why you shouldn't have one." Yet that was a scant comfort. Why didn't they, then?

She said nothing, but Jeff, sensing what was wrong, leaned over and took her hand. They drove back in silence, the day somehow less bright. When they got near the house they saw that Joe Davis was standing on the gallery, barely able to restrain his excitement. Ignoring Varina, he called out to Jeff: "Senator Speight's died, and I've just gotten a tip—the governor wants to appoint you to the place!"

Varina's heart almost stopped. It would be a fine thing, but the doctor had been firm. Jeff, lowering himself slowly from the carriage, hobbled to a chair by the lattice. He passed his hand over his high forehead and pushed back his hair. "I don't know, Joe. I don't know." He continued to stare at his feet, then with a tired gesture he lifted his hands. "It's more than I'd hoped for. Still, the way matters are . . ."

Varina saw warning signs: Jeff's heightened color, a nervous movement at the corner of his mouth. He thanked Joe for coming by and, taking his crutches, started indoors.

His disappointment showing in his bearded face, Joe Davis walked down the steps. Varina followed her brother-in-law with her eyes until he had reached his horse. Then she strode after him and called: "Wait a minute!"

They faced each other coldly. "I think you know how much I

want to stay here," she said, "but that doesn't matter. I'm just worried about Jeff—do you think he ought to take it?"

"I certainly do!" He snapped the reply back at her.

"The chance mightn't come again?" Her voice reflected her reluctance, the division in her mind. He nodded, scowling.

"Well . . ." She faltered. "We'll see."

Back in the house, she sought Annabelle. "Will you see that the carriage is ready right away?" A few minutes later, gloved, her hat on, she was giving directions to her driver. "Take me down the road to the doctor's."

She was gone for a long time. Returning, she stood momentarily beside the door, buttoning and unbuttoning her gloves. Then she rushed up the stairs to Jeff. From the sofa Jeff lifted his head, as if he expected some important news.

"Banny," she said quickly, afraid to stop, "I've talked over everything with the doctor. He finally agreed to what I suggested. If we wait two or three months, and then you promise to work only so many hours a day and stop when you're tired——"

Jeff sat up. His eyes twinkling, he put his arm around her. "I promise. Yes, Madame—Madame Senator."

The words had a good ring, but Varina's gaze passed over the scene outside the window—the fields of their Brierfield, the green hill of the levee in the distance. There would be no extra barn now, and no new fences. Again they were taking the long road to Washington.

As Jeff made his way forward in the Senate chamber, leaning on his crutches, many eyes turned in his direction. His war fame had been widespread; not many on the floor were unaware of him or his story. From her place behind the rail Varina saw several men come up to greet him, friends of other years in Washington, and newcomers who wanted to be presented to him. Certainly her husband was a dramatic figure today, tall, lean, his long, unbearded face more intent than ever, with the marks of his illness unmistakable, yet an increased strength in his manner.

The air was tense with the excitement that accompanies the opening of a congressional session—the regathering of opposing forces, the greetings of friends and enemies, the appraisals of new men. As she glanced about the room Varina compared it with the noisy, overfilled House; here was dignity and restraint, the luster of great names. She made out the massive outlines of Daniel Webster.

A hand touched her, and she jumped up with a quick exclamation. It was the austere Mr. Calhoun himself, his yellowish eyes lighting up for a moment. "Things have changed since our last meeting, haven't they?" she asked. He allowed himself a smile and gave a fond look in Jeff's direction. Then almost instantly he was solemn again. "Yes, things have changed, child, in more ways than you think. The North has made up its mind to outlaw all slavery in the territory we won in the war. Unless the South acts, it will be outnumbered, destroyed."

His words shocked her. Mr. Calhoun was a powerful man, with influence all over the South. If he thought that way, there would be trouble aplenty. She looked up. "Is it really as bad——"

They were interrupted by a startling figure in a brilliant yellow coat, flamboyant red tie, and waistcoat of a spotted catamount skin. Calhoun made a motion toward him. "Mr. Sam Houston of Texas."

Mr. Houston bowed dramatically over her hand and shouted: "Lady, I salute you." To her astonishment he added: "And I give you my heart!"

From his pocket he pulled a small object, heart-shaped, and explained that he had whittled it himself while attending Congress. "Years ago, Mrs. Davis," he added in his booming voice, "I met your husband in the West and told him: 'The future United States senator salutes the future President.'" With that ringing pronouncement Mr. Houston suddenly lost interest and ambled away.

At the end of that crowded day, as she tried to sleep, the words came back to her: "Jefferson Davis, President of the United States." She rose on her elbow. "Jeff, did Mr. Sam Houston really say that?"

Her husband grunted: "Oh, something of the kind, I suppose. He says a lot of remarkable things!"

She fell back on her pillow. That didn't sound so remarkable. Mr. Houston must be a wise man. . . .

The next morning she learned that at least one other individual would not share her enthusiasm if Jeff really became President. As they passed through the boardinghouse hallway a man stood coolly aside. He was small, totally bald, with a sharp and intelligent face. "Henry Foote," Jeff told her with a frown. He was Mississippi's other senator. Jeff had had one or two differences with him, but Varina had not realized that they had broken so definitely. Stories came to her of Mr. Foote's eccentric temper, his chameleon politics, the gamy stories he told on the platform.

"If I'm introduced to him," she asked Jeff, "shouldn't I speak to him?"

"No." His tone was frigid. "A blackguard is a blackguard."

"Very well, Banny," she soothed him.

A few days later she learned how difficult it was going to be to live in the same boardinghouse with Mr. Foote. Passing the reception room, she was aware of a sudden hush and realized that Foote had been talking volubly against Jeff. Then a message arrived from Vicksburg which reported that Foote was working hard to discredit Jeff Davis in Mississippi. She decided not to show him the note. She was doing what she could to prevent any contact between the two men.

Despite her efforts to make him rest, Jeff was overtaxing himself and he looked badly tired. He had grown more tense than ever, and irritable. The holidays were approaching, and she looked forward to a respite, however brief. She refused several invitations for evening entertainments although she enjoyed the new deference she received, the way men and women sought her out at the soirees.

On Christmas morning Jeff hobbled downstairs ahead of her; the other senators and their wives were gathering, and she heard a happy hum of voices, the clink of glasses, the slamming of doors. She had bought a new green velvet dress, high-throated, long-sleeved, and though she liked the effect against her pale skin and full red lips, she wanted to readjust the skirt. As she hurried to fix it she heard the noise of a fall downstairs, followed by some loud exclamations.

Rushing into the hall, she saw Jeff being helped up the stairs, his face drawn, his hair falling over his eyes. One of the senators whispered to her: "Foote made a slurring remark, and he slapped him."

Varina went to Jeff's side. "Banny, are you hurt? In your condition——"

He shook his head, fury still in his eyes. "I should have smacked his dirty mouth!"

She helped him to their room, trying to quiet him.

The house was in an uproar even after Foote stamped out. Although Varina and Jeff joined the rest for the Christmas dinner, it was a strained day for them all. That evening she faced him. "Banny, we'd better find another place to stay." He objected, but she argued with spirit, and the next day she found another residence and made the arrangements to move.

They were hardly settled in their new place when Jeff came home one day with a look of quiet satisfaction on his face. "They've made me a member of the Military Affairs Committee, and the President's asked me to the White House to talk about the war."

Varina did not attempt to hide her pleasure. So important a committee, and the President's request . . .

The war hung on, but more important than the war itself became the disposition of the territory won from Mexico. Would slaveholding be allowed in the conquered land? She heard the men about her: "It's the South that's winning this war but the damned psalm-singing New Englanders who are going to rob us of it!" Jeff was spending more and more time with Mr. Calhoun, and the South Carolinian's fiery sectionalism was having its effect on him.

Thus far, she reflected, Jeff had made a reputation as something of a moderate, a strong Southerner, yet not one of the hotheads. She had seen him wince at the violent utterances of the extremists, such men as Mr. Rhett of South Carolina, a fuming zealot who talked constantly against the Yankees, and Mr. Yancey of Alabama, who shouted and hurled threats and shook his fists. Once or twice Jeff had said: "Such men may do as much harm as the worst South-haters. If too many people in the South believe them, and if too many Northerners believe the Abolitionists, we'll have real trouble."

But now when he walked in slowly one evening, his face dark with resentment, he said to her: "They're going too far, these Yankees. I can't stay quiet any longer."

That evening he began to prepare a speech, Varina hunting records, accumulating mounds of data. Jeff stayed at his desk for two weeks, until he was finally satisfied with his notes. The morning he was to speak Varina went nervously to the Senate, praying that Jeff would keep his temper.

As Jeff rose his face looked gaunt and feverish. He spoke less deliberately than usual. It was a talk that brought men running. Varina saw older senators turn in their chairs to listen. Slaves, Jeff cried, were possessions just as surely as wagons and cattle. An individual state might decide to exclude them, but a territory, which was merely a piece of land belonging to all Americans, didn't have the right to make such a decision. Southerners must be allowed to take their slaves and their other belongings to any new territory. Otherwise the South was doomed—and it would never submit to that fate!

His light eyes taking fire, he raced on: "We who represent the Southern states are not here to be insulted because of the institutions we have inherited!" Then, almost carried away, he cried: "Slavery's origin is divine decree. It is the curse upon the graceless sons of Noah. . . ."

Varina's fingers were cold. She thought of James Pemberton and Jeff's respect for him as a man. She remembered the Jeff who apologized when he had spoken harshly to the servants. Did he mean everything he was saying? She had a feeling like that which had gripped her on their first perilous trip to Washington City as the wagon slipped over the edge of the icy road. Now they were all on dangerous ground. A little distance away Mr. Calhoun was nodding to himself, very pleased. The hotheads were staring at Jeff, delight in their eyes. He had moved definitely into their camp.

She was glad that year when the congressional sessions ended. Tempers might cool, she thought, during the weeks before Congress reconvened. They left the capital as speedily as possible and headed for Mississippi.

Brierfield needed paint, but otherwise the place was as lovely as she remembered it. On the gallery stood the graying James Pemberton. She looked for two other figures and found only one —Annabelle, and a different Annabelle, hands folded, disconsolate. While Jeff and James Pemberton went inside she led Annabelle aside.

"What is it?" Her voice was sympathetic, for Annabelle seemed on the verge of tears.

"De baby come." Annabelle's hands were twisting in her apron. "He come dead, and de doctor, he say I cain' have no more."

Varina took the girl's hand. "Oh, I'm sorry." Annabelle was crying now, her head rolling from side to side.

"And Harry?"

Annabelle looked up quickly, a terrible new emotion in her wide face. "He take it bad, worse even den me. After what had happen' to 'im befo', you know, and all dat . . . Tha's why he—he lef'!"

Varina stared. It was the first runaway since she had been at Brierfield. "When?"

Annabelle groaned. "Other day. An I'm scared. Mister Davis, he won' send no dogs dat'll tear 'im up, or anythin' like dat?"

"I—I don't think so. Here's Mr. Davis now." He had just heard the news from James Pemberton, and his face had saddened. "I'm sorry about the baby, Annabelle, and this other thing. If we'd been here, Winnie, Harry wouldn't have left."

Varina went to his side. "I may be wrong, dear, but I have an idea Harry isn't far away. Couldn't we just—well, send word around that we're home, and see what happens?"

"Well, why not?" Jeff slowly nodded. "It might work."

It was a disturbing home-coming. Both Annabelle and Harry were closer to them than most house servants to planters' families. Varina's last thoughts when they retired that night were of the stricken Annabelle. As for Harry, she supposed she should feel bitterness. Harry was valuable property. But, no matter what Jeff said in Congress, she couldn't think of her servants in that way. She was certain that Jeff didn't either.

The next day she took shears and basket and went to her garden. Whatever his mood in the recent past, Harry had kept the garden in excellent condition. The roses, white and yellow and red, climbed over everything: up around the casements of Jeff's oddly built windows, along the trellis, high toward the roof of Brierfield. The Pilot's Wife was in rare bloom, thrusting her blossoms against the side of the house.

Jeff, in old clothes, came out to join her. He had been able to discard his cane, and much of his color had returned. She had succeeded, after all, in getting him through the hard winter after he was wounded. He took a place beside her, working over the flowers, cutting, pruning. They had little to say. He, too, was glad to forget some of the worries that had been crowding about them. Washington was far behind, and so were the problems of the new territories, Calhoun, and states' rights. When they talked it was of the garden. Wasps droned and the white bolls of cotton covered the nearby fields. From the quarters rose the notes of a song that they did not recognize, a minor thing, slow and sad. It was Annabelle.

After a while Varina jumped to her feet. "I know what I've been missing without realizing it—a canter down the road." Jeff started to the stable with her, but before he had reached it he was hailed from the house—a visitor had arrived from Vicksburg.

"That's all right, Banny," she sighed. "I'll go alone."

She rode along, her loosened hair flying behind her, her lips parted in the excitement of the moment. The lines of trees hurried quickly by, with a little rush of sound and a swaying of leaves in the wind. She closed her eyes for a moment to enjoy the caress of the breeze against her cheek and forehead. In that instant her horse quivered and shied. Varina, almost losing her seat, clung to the reins and called out softly: "There, boy, there—steady now." Then she saw what had frightened her horse. A man was standing motionless against a tree a few yards back. It was Harry Mounger. Dismounting, she went to him. At a glance she saw he was ill, his clothes muddied and torn, mouth slack, eyes badly bloodshot. Apparently he had had a bad time of it, hiding in the woods. Even now Harry showed a certain dignity: he did not cringe or drop his head.

"Harry, you're ready to come back with me, aren't you?"

He nodded, his eyes on hers. "I—I was lookin' for you or Mister Jeff, hopin'——" He could say no more. His black eyes were half closed.

"Come," she told him. "You can ride with me."

Harry frowned. "Maybe people wouldn' like dat. Lemme walk behin'."

"Well——" She hesitated. "No, you'd never make it, the way you are. Here, I'll wait by the tree. You ride home."

He shook his head. "Maybe dey t'ink I hurten you and took de horse."

That hadn't occurred to her; she had little patience with the silly tales some women whispered and their unreasoning fear of Negroes. "Look," she told him, "you go straight to Mr. Davis and say to him what's happened. It will be all right."

Again Harry refused, until she took his arm and directed him to the horse. "Up with you!" For the first time he almost broke down. With a little sob he lifted himself up and rode off. She waited there, the silence thickening about her, the sun beginning to disappear behind the distant trees. Perhaps she had done a foolish thing for a runaway Negro who might escape again. Angrily she shoved the notion aside. All her life she had known Negroes with whom she would risk her life. She mustn't think such white-trash talk. As she argued with herself hoofbeats sounded in her ears. She ran to the middle of the road. Around a bend Jeff was galloping toward her.

When he dropped to the road he took both her hands in his. "You did a good thing, Winnie, the right thing. Annabelle has put him to bed now. He nearly collapsed before he got to me. We gave him water, and he managed to get your message to us before he fainted. It'll be all right now." He kissed her.

As she rode home behind him on the horse he told her something else he had just heard that afternoon. "You know people have been spreading rumors about Zachary Taylor, that he'd run, maybe, for the presidency. He's said he didn't want it, and I believed it. But he's mighty angry at the way some of them in Washington City have treated him. Now it looks pretty definite. There's news from upriver that he's going to be a candidate."

She felt the indecision in his voice. "Wouldn't you be for him, Banny?"

"I'd like to. But the Whigs are going to run him, and I'll have to make speeches for my own party."

Yet the next day when the first of many letters arrived, and during the weeks that followed, she saw her husband pulled in two directions. He had become very fond of Zachary Taylor, and the blunt old fellow had been generous in spite of his earlier antagonism. The campaign soon became one of personalities, for neither party dared take a real stand on the issue of slavery in the territories.

"They're both afraid it'll lose votes," Jeff told Varina with a bitter frown. "Politicians, politicians! Look at this." He showed her a crumpled paper. "A lying attack on Taylor—the dirtiest kind."

She picked it up and straightened it out. "Hm. They're reaching pretty low. Stirring up a Catholic scare." A little later she added: "A fool, a traitor—what else could they call him? None of this is true, is it?"

"Certainly not!"

"Then why don't you come out and say so, regardless of party?"

He continued to frown at the paper. "Why shouldn't I?" he asked in a low voice, and his pen began to race across the paper. He wrote to the general and asked him where he stood on the slavery issue. Getting a prompt answer that indicated Taylor was wholeheartedly for slavery, he wrote to friends who had been claiming that Taylor, though a slaveholder, was an "Abolitionist." In several instances he stopped malicious rumors and helped to correct the public impression of the old general, and he knew that Taylor was grateful.

Late in the fall Varina and Jeff waited up together for the election news. Harry, dispatched to the road to bring the first reliable returns, galloped up the drive with the news that Taylor had won, the Democrats had gone down to defeat! Jeff sighed, but Varina knew it was not an altogether unhappy sigh.

Several months after the election Congress reconvened, Taylor was inaugurated, and Varina was back in Washington City again to find a mound of calling cards waiting for her, as well as numerous invitations and letters of greetings. As one close to the new President, her husband had taken on new importance. He came back from his first day in the Senate with pleasant news for her: "They've made me chairman of the Senate committee to arrange for the inauguration." His eyes shone; it was a flattering appointment for a man so new to the Senate. "Also, we have an invitation from General Taylor. He wants us to come to the White House day after tomorrow."

In a heavy snow their driver stopped before the pillared portico of the White House. Varina had been here several times in the past, but she could not suppress a shiver of excitement. She remembered Sam Houston's words now as she was to remember them on other occasions later. Would she one day walk down that curved stairway with Jeff?

A door opened. "The President." Zachary Taylor made the rounds of the room. When she extended her hand she told herself he had the ugliest face she had ever seen—heavy, gnarled, eagle-nosed. A second look, and she thought it one of the kindest. The man was squat and awkward, but she decided quickly that he had a certain simple charm. In some ways he reminded her of her father —perhaps in the way he turned his head when he spoke, or in his easy smile.

They talked of the general's daughter, who had preceded Varina as Mrs. Jefferson Davis. "She must have been a lovely girl," Varina told him. She described their visit to the grave in Feliciana Parish, where she put flowers before the marble slab.

"It was kind of you, very kind," the old man murmured. He had been touched; reaching into his pocket for an enormous handkerchief, he blew his nose.

As he continued to speak his fingers tightened and untightened in a peculiar nervous gesture. For once, she felt, she had met a completely honest man and a badly puzzled one. Even at this early stage it was evident that Zachary Taylor was not cut out for politics or governmental office. Entirely inexperienced in public affairs, he issued contradictory statements. He grew confused over his powers and the way to exercise them. The current quip in Washington City was that Taylor thought he, as President, had only one vote in his own Cabinet!

At the door as she bowed good-by to him she was overcome with sympathy. It was a hard role, this presidency. But she'd want it, of course, for Jeff. What woman wouldn't wish it for her husband? Jeff had the ability: of that she had no doubt. If only things worked out right, if only chance were on their side . . . Her jaw grew firmer, and her eyes looked steadily ahead. If there was anything on God's earth that she could do to get the presidency for Jeff, she'd do it!

About this time, Jeff stayed late at a banquet of legislators, Army officers, and other Washingtonians. She waited up. The dinner lasted for hours, with many wines and liquors and much speechmaking. At last he returned. As he undressed, Varina turned eagerly to the list of guests. "Mr. Stephens of Georgia, of course. Senator Douglas of Illinois . . . Here's a new one," she called. "Lincoln—Abraham Lincoln—who is he?"

Jeff scratched his chin. "Some Westerner, I think. Don't remember him. I don't believe I saw him."

Chapter 9

THE MORNING WAS A DULL GRAY; RAIN BEAT AGAINST THE WINDOWS hour after hour. Inside the Senate chamber the mood was no less dismal. Varina leaned forward, her hands clasped against her knees. During these past nine months the division between North and South had grown ever wider, and now there was violence in the air.

Yesterday Jeff had risen to his feet, his face red with anger, to deny loudly a suggestion that he was a "disunionist." He had shouted: "When that word is used against me, I'll answer to it—with a monosyllable to describe the man who says it!" Then, a little later, he had cried out a defiance such as she had never heard him utter: "Men of the South will know how to sustain the institutions that they inherited"—he paused—"even by civil war."

At another time, in another part of the room, a free-soiler had made a bitter remark, and suddenly two or three men had sprung at him. The room was turned into a pandemonium, with men shouting and cursing. The sergeant at arms ran forward to break up the disturbance, supported by half a dozen officers. Punches were exchanged, heads beaten against desks, and only after a hard struggle were the fighters separated.

Today tempers were just as high. An old woman friend tapped her shoulder and said: "Have you heard? At least three of them out there have guns. Notice how their pockets bulge. That one's got a bowie knife, and he says he'll use it against the first Yankee that insults him. I hope he does!" Varina noticed that one of the individuals whom the woman had pointed out was little Mr. Foote, Jeff's archenemy.

At this point Thomas Hart Benton, the massive senator from Missouri, rose to speak, and Foote hurled an insulting remark in his direction. Benton swung about, and then slowly his bull-like form bore down on the Mississippian. Varina half rose in her chair. Foote, retreating toward the clerk's desk, suddenly reached in his pocket and whipped out a gun. A great stillness descended upon the Senate chamber. Benton shouted in defiance: "Assassin!" and moved closer, thrusting back his coat to make a better target.

Varina found herself screaming: "Stop them, for heaven's sake! Stop them!" That broke the spell, and a senator near Foote leaned forward and grabbed his gun. Benton's friends quickly surrounded him and pushed him away. By this time Jeff had reached Varina's side. "This way, Winnie. I've got to get you out of here."

Outside in the damp air the rain had stopped, but Varina thought for a moment that she was going to be sick. Jeff put her into a carriage and patted her hand. "I'll get home when I can, but I'd better stay here."

"Jeff," she said, "how far can this thing go? What's the South going to do?"

He looked away. "It's going to demand its rights, for one thing! They're refusing to give back escaped slaves, even conniving to help them escape. They want to outlaw slavery in the District of Columbia; they're trying to bring in the new territories—California, New Mexico—with a ban on slavery. It's all illegal, contrary to the Constitution, a fraud against us. Unless we call a stop to it, we're lost. With the new territories, they'll control Congress and then they'll wipe out slavery by one means or the other!"

"Isn't there hope that the President will do something?"

Jeff scowled. "There's a lot he could do. But he won't do it!"

She should have realized that this was a sore point with Jeff. Between the President and Southerners like her husband, a breach had begun to open. Zachary Taylor had broken with many of his Southern backers, and now he was refusing to admit that a territory could not outlaw slavery. And Jeff had been so certain that the general, as a slaveholder, would be on their side!

"Winnie, I don't want to tear this country in half!" Jeff went on. "I fought for it, don't forget, and so did my father and my brothers, too, in the War of 1812. If anybody's trying to wreck it, it's that hell-born crew of Abolitionists. . . ."

As he spoke Varina stared down the glistening avenue. She had met some professional Yankees who were as fanatical as the hot-blooded Southerners, Mr. Rhett and Mr. Yancey. Yet other Northern people, who appeared to be quiet, logical individuals, suddenly turned out to be Abolitionists too. She had slowly become aware that the feeling against slavery was spreading all over the North, in places high and low. Ever more frequently she had heard talk of government payment for emancipation, and she asked Jeff about that now.

His face was grim. "We'll have emancipation finally, when nature says it's time for it, and also when those of us who have slaves agree to it! Don't you realize it would wreck the South to wipe out slavery overnight?"

"But"—she thought of Grandmother Kempe and others who agreed with her—"even some Southerners think we've suffered because of it. Our wealth is tied up in people. You yourself say we don't have enough industrial strength."

"That's our worry. Not the North's!"

By now she knew she had gone far enough and she shifted the subject. "Banny, will the South really try to leave the Union?"

His lips compressed. "Not if we make our enemies realize the danger in carrying out their intentions. We've got to draw a firm line and make them see it clearly—thus far and no farther. Or . . ."

"Or what?"

"We'll have no choice." And now he spoke the words she had dreaded to hear. "No choice but secession and the formation of a new nation. Mr. Calhoun's more worried than he's ever been. We want the Union, but the Union as our forefathers knew it, not the kind they're trying to make it."

His face still flushed, he left her, and she started home, within her heart a greater fear than ever. So much had happened these past few months. Mr. Calhoun had issued his "Address to the Southern People," demanding a convention to consider "a mode of resistance." Southern legislatures were meeting, one after another. Her own Mississippi had gone farther than most of them by calling for a general Southern congress. To Varina's surprise the irascible John Quitman had been elected governor of the state. South Carolina, the birthplace of the hotheads, had even summoned up her militia and armed it. She had heard the daily arguments of Jeff's friends: "The North is reaching out to strangle us." From the opposition had come another cry: "The South wants the territories, and also Cuba and all of Mexico, to overwhelm the North and force slavery everywhere!" She could find no comfort in such thoughts.

Ahead of her carriage she spied a lonely figure on horseback. It was Zachary Taylor, dressed in a baggy suit several sizes large for him. As she drew abreast of him he recognized her, lifted his tall black hat, and smiled.

"I'm out for an airing, child," he called to her. "It's pleasant to get away from—that."

He made a vague gesture toward the White House and shook his head gloomily. "I'm not very popular these days, as you know. I don't see much of you and Jeff any more."

It had been weeks since she or her husband had gone to the Executive Mansion. Jeff had been unwilling to accept the last invitation to a reception.

She said rather lamely, "Jeff has so many duties in the Senate."

"Yes." Zachary Taylor's smile was wan. "This is a busy place, and a strange one too."

The poor general had shown how lost a purely military man could be in a high governmental post. He had made foolish appointments, and embarrassing ones, and he had floundered sadly. Listening to Jeff's friends, she had deplored with them the things the President had done. But, as she told herself now, at least he had acted honestly. And here he was at last hopelessly trapped, caught between those two great grindstones, the North and the South.

Fumbling with his hat, the President stared at her sadly. "Do you think I'm as bad as they say? All I want is to keep the Union together. . . ." And then before she could reply another idea occurred to him: "Come back with me to the house, won't you? I know Mrs. Taylor would like to see you."

It was impossible to resist this frank appeal, and before she knew it Varina was sitting with the motherly Mrs. Taylor in one of the elegant parlors of the White House. "My dear," said the President's wife, "you're as lovely as ever, but you've been such a stranger!"

Varina talked idly of household problems, the cost of clothes, and such matters, for she knew that Mrs. Taylor had little inclination for public affairs. She asked about Jeff's health, and Varina remembered suddenly that Jeff had once been her son-in-law. There was no direct mention of politics, but occasionally there were pauses in the conversation and vague references that made Varina realize how well Mrs. Taylor understood the odds against which her husband was fighting.

"I wasn't anxious for him to take this," she said at last. "I think we'd have been a lot happier back home."

In her voice there was no trace of bitterness, but a deep sadness. Varina looked down at her hands and felt ashamed that she was part of this Washington City, with its schemings and plottings, intrigue and hatred. Was this the thing she had urged upon her husband, the life for which they had left Brierfield? As she watched the tired face of this elderly woman Varina's depression mounted.

On the way downstairs a little later she heard the sound of angry voices. "Good day, Mr. Seward. . . . Very well, Mr. Seward." She caught a blur of movement, a swinging of coattails, as the front door slammed. She was instantly alert, because although she had never met Mr. Seward of New York, the great spokesman of the North, she knew well that he was exerting more and more influence over the President. In fact, many of Jeff's friends blamed on Seward all their troubles with Zachary Taylor. If Mr. Seward was in a bad mood, something was afoot.

Unexpectedly the President himself appeared from an anteroom, his face still red with anger. Almost immediately he got hold of himself. His words were kindly. "Well, Varina, it was good of you to come. Why don't you ask that husband of yours to drop over— say tomorrow night? I'd like to talk over a few things." Her eyebrows went up in astonishment. There must be some connection between this clash with Seward and the President's wish to see Jeff. Hastily she agreed to ask Jeff and hurried out.

As her carriage rolled away she took a backward glance at the White House. Her mood had changed again and she had forgotten her gloom of a few minutes ago. Washington City was an exciting place to live in, and these were exciting days. Things were happening all around her, and she was in the heart of them!

Jeff had preceded her to their quarters. She told him all that had transpired at the White House and then waited eagerly for his comments. He sat still, drumming his fingers. Finally she could wait no longer. "You're going, of course!"

"I'm not sure. It's hardly a formal invitation." The tone was austere.

"Jeff, you're not going to insist on ceremony? It may be your best opportunity to talk to him, plead your side of the controversy!"

"He knows my side." Jeff's light eyes had the quality of ice.

She wanted to shake him; he was behaving like the man his enemies described. But she calmed herself and set to work, as on many earlier occasions, to persuade him. She tried several appeals, one argument, then another; and finally she won.

"Very well, I'll go over there tomorrow." He rose with a shrug and straightened the stock at his throat. "We'll see how it turns out."

She walked out of the room wearily, a thin line of perspiration on her upper lip. She'd done it, but with what an effort! In the hall she glanced at the mail rack and saw that there was another thick letter for Jeff from Joe Davis, another of the older brother's interminable messages of advice and direction. Whenever Jeff heard from Joe Davis his temper rose, for Joe was always egging him on. She thought of Jeff's ominous remark of that morning— if the North went too far, he wanted the South to secede. . . . If she could only destroy this letter, she thought; but obediently she took it out of the rack and brought it to Jeff.

As she expected, he read it avidly and then went back to the first page. "Listen to this," he said with enthusiasm. "Here's what Joe says: 'Any slight concession to Yankee arrogance, any retreat on a single point, means we're wrecked forever.' Don't you think he's right, Winnie?"

She faced him calmly. "Jeff, you're up here in the middle of it all. Don't you think you're better qualified to judge than your brother?"

By the expression in his eyes she could tell that her words had hurt and annoyed him. For a moment she was tempted to tell him that she was sorry. Then she rejected the impulse. She'd be damned if she would. Why couldn't Jeff make his own decisions?

The next evening, as he shaved in preparation for his call on Zachary Taylor, Jeff said with surprise: "Aren't you coming along?"

She had thought about it several times that day. The President had been vague and she might easily have assumed that she was invited too. But she shook her head. Tonight she felt that she should stay well in the background, if only to give Jeff an opportunity for a long uninterrupted talk with the President alone. She went to him, touching his bare brown arm. "Promise me something. You'll be—reasonable?"

"We'll have to see."

She realized he would concede nothing more.

This was one evening when she could not even doze as she waited. Two hours passed, then another. She was biting her lips when finally she recognized his step down the hall. She met him at the door, and his long face and dull eyes gave her the answer. "I tried," he told her. "I didn't get to talk to him alone for very long. We did a little fencing, but we never got down to cases. Anyway, a friend whispered to me on the way to the White House that Seward was with him for hours this afternoon. I knew it was no use."

There was nothing more to say. Slowly she helped him off with his coat, wondering if it would have made any difference if she had gone. Perhaps she could have managed, with Mrs. Taylor's help, to keep the two men together for a longer time. Well, there was no use now in tormenting herself; it was too late. For once she made little attempt to lift Jeff's spirits, for she felt as unhappy as he did.

It was late January of 1850, and the tension between the sections had grown worse. Hardly a day passed without a vicious argument over slavery, but still nothing happened. Varina restlessly paced her room, then, unable to stand the silence any longer, threw on her shawl and went downstairs. In the sitting room three women were picking up their purses and gloves and were starting for the door. There was an air of agitation about them.

"What is it?" she asked.

"Didn't Mr. Davis tell you before he left?" one of them exclaimed. "Lots of fireworks, about to pop. All kinds of rumors, but nobody's sure. We're going over to the Capitol to find out."

"Wait, just a minute. I want to go with you!" She was away only a few minutes. Struggling with the belt of her brown coat, she raced down the hallway. Only when she reached the carriage did she push her dark velvet bonnet down over her parted hair.

As she seated herself behind the rail Jeff flashed her a glance of surprise. She saw that he was writing furiously, making notes, and it was evident that something important was about to happen. Varina looked around the room, noting the new faces and the old ones. In the few years that she had been in Washington City the Senate had undergone a drastic change. Vanished was the serenity, the mature dignity of the Senate as she had known it. Most of these men looked angry, and also impatient.

One chair was empty, conspicuously so. John Calhoun was at home, seriously ill, and Jeff had told her gloomily: "I don't know if he'll ever return to the Senate." But whatever his condition, the South Carolinian was still rallying his supporters, dispatching letter after letter, calling in men for advice and exhortation. Jeff had spent most of the day with him yesterday, and as usual he had returned with determination in his eyes.

Now there was a stir. Voices rose and Varina saw that Henry Clay was getting to his feet, his slim distinguished presence dominating the enormous room. Since her arrival she had heard many stories about the man, his drinking and gambling excesses, the women he loved. Jeff, she knew, disliked him wholeheartedly. Today, as Mr. Clay rose in his place, he was solemn, more solemn than she had ever seen him. His pinched nostrils dilated, his usually white cheeks were slightly flushed, and his hands shook.

He was here to offer a set of compromises, concessions for both sides. He waved his hand; he pleaded: "Let us hesitate at the edge of the precipice before the fearful leap is taken." As a hush fell over the Senate he outlined his plan: California would enter as a state with slavery forbidden, but New Mexico would come in as a territory, with no provision for or against slavery. In the District of Columbia the slave trade would end, but slavery itself would continue there. Congress would adopt a firmer law against fugitive slaves, and the North would pledge itself to accept and enforce it.

Before Varina could decide whether she favored Mr. Clay's compromise plan or not Jeff had jumped to his feet, shouting his resentment. Clay was a traitor to the South, giving the Abolitionists a support that no Northern man could have given them! The South got nothing out of Clay's compromise; the North took it all. But the South had a right to full equality in the territories; it would take nothing less.

He stopped, and hand clapping swept the room. Varina's pride was roused and she looked around, delighted at the response. This was Jeff Davis, her husband, whom they were applauding so joyously. But then she noticed that the enthusiasm was confined largely to the Southerners, and some of them were strangely quiet.

Despite herself she wondered if perhaps Clay was right and Jeff too stubborn, too inflexible. Was Clay's compromise, after all, the one thing that could save the country? Compromise . . . The very word, she felt, was abhorrent to Jeff. She stole a look at her husband. The line of his chin, the jaw, was that of a man who would sacrifice everything before he gave in. She had a sinking feeling. This would be a long battle in which one side or the other would lose a great deal. Which side would it be?

Days of increased agitation and uncertainty followed. Coming home late one evening, Jeff told her, "We've been arguing for hours with Calhoun. He's doing very poorly"—Jeff's voice almost broke —"but he insists on getting out of bed tomorrow to talk against Clay's scheme."

"Then I want to be there," Varina cried.

"I thought you would." Jeff's tone was more cheerful.

The chamber was crowded as she had never seen it. Every corner was filled with visitors perched on upturned boxes, in alcoves, on the edges of desks. Women clustered together here and there or pushed into places their husbands found for them. The mood was anxious expectation, a mood which Varina was to remember years later.

When Mr. Calhoun entered, wrapped to the chin in a heavy shawl, he was supported by a friend on either side, guiding, almost carrying him. The famous face was a death's-head, the lips trembling, the yellowish eyes bright with fever. Varina half rose as he went by in front of her, and he reached out his hot hand. "My child, I'm too weak to stop." Moving on to his seat, he sat down heavily, looking old and sick and spent. A friend got up; he would read Mr. Calhoun's talk.

The old man remained there, his fierce eyes moving all about the room. As the other voice droned on Calhoun shifted his glance from one senator to another, hunting them out as if to fathom their response. Varina shuddered, for it seemed as if a dead man were listening to his own words and studying their effect. . . .

It was a challenge that he offered, a scorching defiance. Clay's compromise was worse than nothing. The old theme of a confederated government was being forgotten in favor of a centralized union run for Northern benefit. The South wanted the right to take any property into the territories, including slaves, and a final end to the agitation over slavery. There must be a constitutional amendment to restore the former balance. Failing that—and here the aged eyes drilled into his fellow senators—the Union was at an end.

At these last words Varina trembled. Secession again! And then she saw that the whole Senate was rising to its feet as Calhoun was escorted from the room. His audience, his friends and opponents, knew that he would never return.

Not many evenings later Jeff came in to her with a heavy step. "I just saw Calhoun. It can't be long." To the very end, he told her, the South Carolinian had struggled, dictating resolutions, writing letters, handing out arguments against his opponents. "But he had to stop tonight. When I was there he seemed to feel he'd take up the work again tomorrow. I don't think he ever will." He described the bare room where Calhoun was spending the last hours of his life, as austere and grim as the great statesman himself.

The next morning as they went downstairs they came upon a hushed circle in the hallway. A man nodded to them. "It's all over. The word arrived a few minutes ago." Shaken, Jeff started back to the room. "I—I'll need my hat and coat."

One of the women looked at her with a curious expression in her eyes. "You know what Mr. Calhoun said a little while ago, don't you, Mrs. Davis—that he expected Mr. Davis would take his place as the South's leader?"

Yes, Mr. Calhoun had told that to somebody, and she had been thrilled to hear it. But now, at a time like this, who was to say what was the right thing to do, for the South or for the country? She went to her room. An hour later, when the maid knocked, she was still there, staring down at her hands.

The situation altered day by day. The country was frightened, but it also appeared angry. Clay's proposals lost ground, gained, lost ground again. One morning in the Senate, Varina was startled when Henry Foote, the other Mississippi senator with whom Jeff had clashed, came out flatly for the compromise. For Jeff the development was not a happy one. "Foote fancies himself as a weathercock," he sighed. "He must believe the votes are going that way."

Slowly it became evident that one major obstacle stood in the path of the compromise—the opposition of Zachary Taylor. He wanted nothing of Clay's devices; he had little use for the man who might have been President in his place had the Mexican War not intervened.

"Taylor won't ever give in!" Jeff told Varina almost gleefully. She gave him an amused look. A few months back Jeff and his friends never said a kind word about the President. Now they were all working, at least for the time being, on the same side.

On July 4, which was unusually hot that year, Varina and Jeff planned to attend a ceremony to be held at the Washington Monument.

"And I suppose we have to be there," Jeff grumbled as he wiped the moisture from his face.

For an hour they sat with the other invited guests on the half-enclosed platform. Even there they could feel the appalling heat. Through the crown of her thin flowered hat Varina's hair seemed to be burning. The main speaker, Zachary Taylor, drenched in perspiration, was unhappily drinking one glass of iced water after another. He bowed to Varina, as friendly as ever. The poor general looked as if he needed, above all things, sleep and rest.

After the President's speech Varina, drying her face, whispered to Jeff: "I don't think I can stand this much longer." Quietly they made their way out. The last thing they saw was Zachary Taylor being led to a final rite in the open sunlight at the base of the monument.

Late the next day a frightened Negro messenger tapped on their door. "De Pres'dent, he real sick. Dey want you should come." Together Varina and Jeff hurried to the White House. The weeping Mrs. Taylor told them the details. "He was in the open sun for a long time at the end of his talk. Then he came home and drank iced milk and ate cherries." Shortly afterward he had suffered violent pains and his temperature had risen. Four doctors were in attendance.

For days Zachary Taylor tossed on his bed. The ancient frame was sturdy, but gradually it weakened. Once or twice he recognized Jeff and Varina and moved a tired hand to greet them. From the next room Varina heard his muttered words: "God knows I've tried to do my honest duty. . . ."

As she listened Varina's head sank on Jeff's shoulder. The presidency had brought the gnarled old soldier nothing but heartbreak and dismay. Would she ever want to find herself in the position of that unhappy woman in the next room, with the knowledge that the office had helped kill, if it had not actually killed, the man she loved?

That night as they left the pillared porch of the White House a bell began to toll in the distance. Despairingly Varina clung to her husband's arm. But when she saw the crowd watching them she straightened her shoulders, held her chin up, and walked proudly to her carriage. They were not going to see Jeff Davis's wife cry.

Chapter 10

ONCE MORE THE LONG FLIGHTS OF WILD BIRDS SWUNG OVER THE levee; once more Varina watched in quiet joy from the window of Brierfield. She had risen early, for they would be here only a month or two, and she must miss none of the things for which she had longed. Already Jeff had begun to ride around the plantation, and she made out his tall figure as he talked with James Pemberton. James's broad back was stooped and he was showing his age in the slowness of his gait.

But they were all growing a little older. The face she saw in her hand mirror still looked fresh. At twenty-four her wide-spaced brown eyes usually had a sparkle and her rounded cheeks were as smooth as ever. Yet she could make out the beginnings of lines below her eyes and a slight set to the lips that had not been there before.

The door opened, and Annabelle brought coffee. The girl's grin was something for which Varina had been waiting. "Yes'm, everythin's fine," she replied to Varina's question. "An' Harry, too. Oh no, he never show no discontent. He won' never do what he did dat las' time."

As she munched the warm bread Varina listened to Annabelle's gossip: "Mister Joe, he bin over nelly ever' day dis week to see how it go wid de new work—and tell us how to do it." Annabelle gave Varina a fleeting glance. It was as far as she would go, but she had succeeded in telling Varina what she thought her mistress ought to know.

Varina turned and looked out the window at the framework of a house which was being built a few rods away. This was to be their new home. For a long time she had hinted to Jeff that they needed a larger place and had talked about the spaciousness of Governor Quitman's pillared Monmouth in Natchez and the charm of the house her mother and father had taken near Algiers, across the river from New Orleans. Her meaning seemed to elude him; she caught no answering response until one day, with a grin, he handed her a contract. "Winnie, they're ready to start that house you've been thinking about so much."

For a second she had been provoked. Then she kissed him. "Well, if it has to be a surprise, this is the best kind I know!"

Now, taking her last sip of coffee, she hurried out of the house and walked over to see how the building was progressing. It would be a house rather like the one she had known as a child in Natchez —large square frame structure of ten or eleven rooms, slightly raised, with the upper story covered by a sloping roof. There would be three galleries along the front of the house, a middle one dominating the approach, the side ones recessed.

Varina walked about, admiring the big square hallway, the high-ceilinged parlor, the bedrooms with delicately carved moldings near the ceiling line. As she went to a window she stopped. What was this, marble?

"Are you surprised again?" Jeff was chuckling behind her.

"Marble fireplaces!" She wheeled about. "I hadn't thought——"

"Madame, I thought ladies liked that kind of thing."

"Yes, Banny, but the cost!"

"Well, I think the Davises can afford a few. These may be the last we'll ever have."

She nodded, pleased by his thoughtfulness, but already figuring on little economies to make up for this splurge. They went together through the half-completed house. His worried look of recent months had returned, and as he spoke again she understood he had something important on his mind.

"I'm going up to Vicksburg," he began, "to attend a meeting of the states'-rights people."

She seized his arm. "Banny, isn't that fight over? Nobody could say you didn't do your best, but when the President died Clay's compromise was bound to pass!"

"Yes, it passed." His face was brooding. "But the battle's still on. We still have to band together to protect our interests. Things are happening all over the South—mass meetings, rallies. Quitman's called a special session of our legislature, and when that convenes we'll see the fur fly."

Her face clouded in the realization that Jeff was now taking his political guidance from such a wild radical as Governor Quitman. "Banny," she said, "do people really want this fight between the North and the South to go on?"

For an answer he handed her two papers, just arrived. The first was a recent resolution of the legislature warmly backing him in his stand on Southern rights; the second—her eyes opened wider at the words—a notification that the same body of men had just re-elected him to a six-year term in the Senate.

She took his hands. "I'm happy, Jeff, about the election. But this other thing, this bitter political feud—if you go on with it, isn't there danger of real trouble with the North? If we go too far they'll send troops."

"In that case the Union will be broken up already, Winnie. Let them try that if they dare!" His gray-blue eyes looked angry, but a moment later he went on in his usual tone of voice: "The way things are, I don't know whether we have to secede or not. We can hold that as a last alternative, to be resorted to if necessary. . . . We'll see what happens at Vicksburg."

Long after Jeff had left her for the long ride to Vicksburg, Varina sat on the gallery, thinking what a perilous course he was leading. One step either way, and who knew what would happen? And men like Quitman, men whom Jeff was now working with—nobody ever called them people of discretion or calm judgment. . . . She was still staring into the distance—and into the future—when Joe Davis rode up to Brierfield and jumped off his horse. It was their first meeting alone in more than a year.

He stopped at the sight of her, his small blue eyes moving uncertainly. She put out her hand. "How are you, Joe? Jeff won't be back today, but come in."

Reluctantly he followed her into the parlor and sat down without saying a word. Varina began to talk nervously about the discomforts of Washington in the summer. When Joe merely grunted, her annoyance increased. Regardless of her past trouble with Joe, she determined not to give into it. Still trying to placate him, she changed the subject and said: "Jeff has certainly gone far. The longer he stays——"

Joe Davis's dark head jerked up. She had accidentally touched a sore point. "Some of us aren't too sure of that!"

"What do you mean?"

"That he ought to keep closer to what we think at home!" He half swallowed his last words and she got the impression that he was blaming her because Jeff was gradually asserting his independence. He gave her no time to reply. With a gesture of impatience he headed for the door. Over his shoulder he called out: "Will you tell my brother I'd like to talk to him about the expenses on the new house? That extra back porch is useless!"

She held her hands tightly before her, reasoning with herself. This was a small thing. Wouldn't it be better to keep peace over it? Then she remembered the way Jeff had stood so long in the shadow of Joe Davis, the way the older man had never given up trying to control all of her husband's activities.

"Just a minute," she called out sharply. "I want that porch, and we're going to have it! Jeff and I will be living here, and I suggest you let us decide what kind of a house we want." She found her chin trembling.

Joe Davis swung around, glaring. Now that the break was in the open she threw caution to the skies. She advanced toward him. "You resent me, even my being here. You want to rule him the way you rule everybody else around here. But you won't. I'll see to that!"

Joe Davis with a great effort controlled himself and stamped out of the house. Never would she forget the look of rage and frustration and hatred on his face. She realized that had she been a man he would have knocked her to the ground. Unsteadily she returned to the parlor, her mind in a furor. Hardly an hour ago she had been groaning that she wanted rest, an end to argument. Now she told herself she must be feeling just as Jeff did about Clay's compromise. No matter what was involved, she'd fight this out.

For most of that day and the next she moved in agitation from room to room, debating with herself while she waited for Jeff. Late in the night, when Jeff came back from Vicksburg, she was sitting up. She had made up her mind; this time she would bend no more to Joe Davis. It was important to her, and to Jeff too. Coolly she told him the whole episode, ending quietly: "It's up to you to decide this."

Jeff started for the door, his face expressionless. "I'm going over to see him now."

She could hardly guess what her husband thought, whether he blamed her or Joe. It was close to midnight, but it never occurred to her to suggest that he wait until morning. For the next hour or two she walked up and down the hallway. Then she tried to read a letter from her mother in New Orleans: Everybody was well. Varina's older brother hoped to find a job in a broker's office; little Maggie was growing tall; the baby, Jeff Davis Howell, was a chubby child. . . . She dropped the note. Hoofbeats sounded from the drive and she knew that Jeff was back.

When he opened the door of the sitting room he said abruptly, without preamble: "My brother won't interfere again."

His eyes staring blankly ahead, he went to his study. She had won! She understood the effort it must have involved, how much he must have gone through. . . . She knew that he wanted to be by himself for a time, and she went to bed ahead of him. When he joined her much later he touched her gently, and she moved toward him with a sigh. There was a new understanding between them.

In Washington City a month later the turmoil had lessened, at least for the time being. The bitter fight over Mr. Clay's compromise had been referred to the individual states and the capital wanted to see how they would react.

For weeks Varina had been hearing vague rumors of secret expeditions in preparation against the Spanish rulers in Cuba. Now the story was out in black headlines on the front page of the newspaper. Varina pointed it out to Jeff and looked at him inquiringly.

He scanned the article and then gave the paper back to her. "Yes, Winnie, I've known about this for a long time," he told her. "You know that I've always thought Cuba ought to be ours. Geographically it's a close neighbor of the South, with somewhat the same climate and some of the same crops. And it ought to be brought into the Union as a slave state. But"—and now he looked puzzled, upset, and she realized he had thought a long time about the problem—"I'm not sure that an invasion with guns is the right way at this time."

She closed her eyes. So Cuba was all part of this same endless conflict between North and South. She didn't like the sound of this conspiratorial thing aimed against another nation. Jeff, sitting opposite her in the long sitting room of their boardinghouse, looked guiltily behind him. "They're all anxious that it be kept quiet. A lot of Yankees would die rather than see Cuba come in as a slave state. . . ."

That night as she returned to the sitting room she was surprised to make out, in the far corner with Jeff, several men with obviously Latin features. Their conversation was low-pitched and nervous. Though she tried to read, her eyes were drawn several times to the anxious movements of a small man whose white hair gleamed in the gaslight. The rest deferred to him, and he appeared to be pleading, appealing. At the beginning Jeff seemed much impressed. She knew nothing of what they were saying, but she felt a twinge of apprehension. She managed to catch Jeff's eye. He read the meaning in her motion and smiled briefly to let her know that he was not committing himself.

Then Jeff rose. "I'm sorry, I couldn't. My duties are here." The callers said something else, to which Jeff answered: "I'd suggest Colonel Lee. Oh yes, I have the fullest confidence in him."

Politely, their regret showing in their manner, the strangers left. "That was General Lopez and the Cuban revolutionaries," Jeff told her. "They asked me"—he looked suddenly proud—"to lead their expedition." His eyes warmed and his voice quickened. "They offered to deposit a hundred thousand dollars in my name before I left and then another hundred thousand after we won!"

Abruptly she went numb. "Banny, you'd be a foreigner invading Spanish soil. If they captured you . . ."

Jeff was laughing at her. "Winnie, I turned them down flat. You don't have to convince me!"

She felt reassured. Now she could admit to herself that it had been a fine compliment to Jeff and his military reputation. Of all the men in America, they had sought out her husband. . . .

A few days later, coming into the boardinghouse, she heard a polite cough. There stood a stranger, robust, well poised, with a look of strength in his attractive face. He touched his hand to his dark mustache. "Colonel Robert Lee, at your service."

She thought him the handsomest man she had ever seen; there was a friendliness in his manner that was unfeigned. In her years in Washington she had learned to tell the difference between adopted manners and natural breeding.

Colonel Lee was there to see Jeff, and as they waited for him he mentioned something about Virginia. "Oh yes," she told him, "my mother's people came from there."

"So do mine." He spoke quietly, modestly.

"That's nice. Who were they——"

Jeff entered. She noticed by the way they greeted each other, in the looks they exchanged, that they were already good friends. She rang for coffee, which had been brewed, as usual, by her instructions, in the potent Mississippi-Louisiana style. After his first sip Colonel Lee looked startled, but after the second he smiled at her. "It's a little overpowering at the beginning, but it grows on you!" With most visitors she would have taken it for a cheap compliment. This man wasn't given to such things.

With an air of slight embarrassment Robert Lee thanked Jeff for recommending him to the Cubans. "I had to decline too. But I wanted to let you know how I felt. I'm going to stay in the Army. . . ." At that his manner changed and he suddenly seemed depressed and sad. Varina was still puzzling over it when she saw that he had risen and was about to depart. He thanked her gravely for the Mississippi coffee, and they both escorted him to the door. As Lee walked briskly away she and Jeff remained there, their eyes on the well-set shoulders disappearing down the street.

"Jeff"—she turned about—"what made him change just now?"

Jeff frowned. "Lee isn't really happy in his assignments. I know what he did in Mexico and I'd back him for practically any place in the Army. But he's been discouraged. He's been wondering, I know, if he has the makings of a good soldier."

"He seems such a—gentleman."

"Yes. Some people think he's too much of one, and he certainly isn't pushing. He doesn't try to use his influence the way some do. I don't think he'll ever get the recognition he deserves."

She thought over Jeff's words. "His influence—would Lee have any?"

"Surely, my dear, you've heard of the Lees of Virginia?"

"Oh! He's one of *those?*" Comprehension was growing in her eyes.

"His father was Light-Horse Harry Lee of the Revolution."

Again she said, "Oh." Then her nose wrinkled. She'd started to ask their guest who the Lees were! She felt as she had that day when, as a mere representative's wife, she first faced Washington City in that awful blue-feathered hat!

Jeff Davis and Robert Lee had turned their backs on the Cuban revolutionaries, but plans for conquest continued. Down in Mississippi, Governor Quitman was giving money and advice to the Cubans and Americans backing the expedition to the Caribbean. Rumors spread that he planned to head up the attacking party himself and lead the insurgent forces, provided he could induce a large number of Mexican War veterans to join him. Quitman was showing a lack of finesse, a flair for indiscretion remarkable even for him. At the same time he was tossing out ill-timed statements that embarrassed even his supporters. Shaking his head, Jeff handed Varina one of the latest Quitman exuberances.

Varina's hands made tight fists at her sides. "Banny, if you keep this up, you'll be ruined by the man. Don't you see, his wildness is committing both you and the party, driving you into a corner. Who knows what's going to happen next down there?"

Finally the day came when a Federal grand jury indicted Quitman for violating the neutrality laws. Worse news followed: Quitman announced with a flourish that he would not give himself up. It was a matter of states' rights and he was governor of a sovereign state, while the United States was a "foreign power." The story ran through Washington that Quitman was going to barricade himself in his office and call on the local populace to help him shoot it out with the Federals! But at that point Quitman suddenly quieted down, resigned as governor, and for a while kept his mouth closed. Varina sensed that although the immediate danger had ended Quitman had hurt Jeff's position enormously. All over the country men and women were alarmed by what had almost happened.

Ominous notes came to her from Natchez, center of the conservative planters: "Can't you make your husband realize we need an end to this battling?" "Our cause has everything to lose by continued disturbances. . . ." Jeff pushed them aside after a brief perusal. She should have understood that her husband was hardly the man to be persuaded by letters from people who didn't agree with him! He pulled out a sheaf of letters and editorials demanding that he fight "Northern insult and aggression." This is what the voters really wanted him to do, he told her.

One morning Varina went to Jeff with hands that trembled so badly she could barely hold the paper. The American expedition had reached Cuba—and it had been wiped out. Spanish soldiers hunted down the fleeing men with guns and bayonets and then dragged them through the streets. The natives spat at them and cursed them as pirates. Her eyes stopped at the names of three or four young men she had known as children in Natchez. The report said they had been shot by firing squads.

Even worse was the end of Lopez, the man who had finally taken command of the movement. In a sun-bright courtyard, while crowds outside screamed their approval, he had been strapped down and strangled by the iron collar.

"He took the place they offered you," Varina told Jeff, and slowly he nodded. She saw again the swarthy face, the head of white hair that glowed beneath the light as he argued with Jeff.

"There, but for the grace of God . . ." she sighed. It was a murmur of protest, a lament, and a whisper of thanks. At least Jeff was alive and their future stretched before them.

Yet to Varina that future had a disquieting look. Quitman asked that the party renominate him for governor and vindicate him. The leaders invited Jeff home for the campaign.

In her new white-columned Brierfield, Varina watched the mounting progress of the fight. Actually, she found, two campaigns were on at once—one for governor, the other for a constitutional convention Quitman had called to plan further resistance to Clay's compromise. To Varina's dismay, Henry Foote, Jeff's old enemy who had changed sides, raced back to Mississippi, summoned "Union meetings" in many places, and tossed challenges at Quitman and Jeff himself. Foote was running for governor in opposition to Quitman and his states'-righters.

"How's it going?" she asked Jeff.

"Badly," he groaned. "They've talked Quitman into debates with Foote, and there he's at his worst. He's a miserable speaker, and Foote's sniping at him, setting traps and watching Quitman fall into them."

Jeff left on a campaign trip, and Varina turned gratefully to the final furnishing of the new house. She and Annabelle struggled over the new damask curtains from Royal Street in New Orleans. They trudged up and down stairs, bringing books and pictures from the attic, filling library shelves. From New Orleans, Varina's mother sent some of her heavier pieces of rosewood—a long sofa, chairs, and bed. "I've no use for them, child," she wrote.

When she read the letter Varina's heart turned over. Her mother had been prouder of that great sofa than of anything she owned in Natchez. It had been brought from Virginia by her mother; it had floated down-river on a raft, and Grandma Kempe had told how it was once partly submerged when the boat tipped over at Natchez-under-the-Hill. It must have been an effort for Margaret to give it up.

Varina was glad she had a mother like that and a sister-in-law like Eliza Davis, who dispatched an occasional message, gifts of jelly, seeds from the big gardens at The Hurricane. She was doing what she could with Joe, thus far without success. "But I'm not sure," Varina assured herself, "that this mightn't be for the best." Jeff was standing on his own feet now, making his own decisions. The wrong ones, she sometimes feared, but definitely his own.

When Jeff came back from his campaign trip James Pemberton rode with her to the boat landing. She stood at the levee, her plaid umbrella shading her face. As the vessel slid toward them she looked for Jeff in vain. Finally the boat backed in, the gangplank was lowered, and she caught sight of him, surrounded by a group of passengers. She would hardly have known him.

His face was shrunken and yellowish, and one eye was hideously swollen. Two men supported him as he staggered forward. Varina and James Pemberton exchanged glances of alarm. In the Negro's bright eyes she read all his love and admiration for her husband. Together they helped him into the carriage. Before she had touched his hand she realized that he had a raging fever and was in even worse shape than he'd been after his first campaign tour several years ago.

As she got Jeff to bed he held a trembling hand over his eyes to keep out the blinding light. Dispatching Annabelle for water and cloths, she closed the shutters. When she looked closer at the eye she cried out, for it looked as if it were almost ready to burst. Repeatedly, as she applied cold compresses to it, he moaned: "Oh, oh . . . It still feels as if a hot iron rod is being pushed against the eyeball!"

She had the good sense to send a colored boy for the doctor, and he must have understood her great need, for he fetched him very quickly. The doctor worked for a long time at the bedside, then came out to speak to her. "Acute inflammation—danger that the cornea will ulcerate. He'll have to be in the dark for weeks, anyway. Even at that, there's a chance he may lose the eye."

She had been expecting just such a verdict and she had steeled herself to face it. "Thank you, Doctor," she said very quickly, "but we're going to save that eye."

He watched her with admiration as she summoned her staff. "James, you go right away with the doctor to get those new medicines. Annabelle, we're going to reorganize things, beginning now. You and Harry, get the couch in the hall and put it at the foot of the bed. I'm going to be here from this moment on!"

For two weeks she stayed with her husband day and night, leaving the room only when Annabelle approached with a discreet knock and a message of importance. "Keep everything away from us, unless nobody else can handle it!" Her voice had grown imperious, almost threatening, and Annabelle, understanding, obeyed.

After that fortnight Jeff was able to rise. But now Varina made sure he slept through the day in the dim room, while she sat nearby, ready to apply new cloths and medication at the proper time. Only after dusk did she let him get up and walk about the house in the dark. Then she remained near him, sometimes guiding him, again sitting near him and talking.

At dawn, when the sky began to brighten, Jeff rested on the big rosewood sofa which had belonged to the Howells, while she read to him. The campaign still roared on, and so she selected the most vital documents and, though she could scarcely make out objects in the room, she managed to read the words to him and take down his replies. It was in this same spot that, a little later, the doctor brought her the word for which she had longed: "The eye's been saved, Mrs. Davis." Then he added: "But he still needs time to recover."

Another two weeks passed, and still Jeff could not face a direct light. Late one afternoon a message arrived that delegates were now selected for the constitutional convention to pass on Clay's compromise. The states'-rights side had lost badly, and Varina realized immediately that Jeff had been wrong, for he had misjudged the temper of the people. They wanted peace, after all. . . .

Less than six weeks before the election for governor, Quitman withdrew from the race and the party was without a candidate to send against Henry Foote. A letter from Vicksburg concluded with the ominous words: "You, Mr. Davis, are the only member of our side who could win at this time. It is necessary, therefore, that we ask . . ." When she read that letter to Jeff her voice was unsteady and the palms of her hands were wet with perspiration. Jeff made no comment on the letter but sat thinking. All at once she could stand it no longer. "Banny, you've just been re-elected to the Senate for six years. To give that up for two years in a position of less importance—and you're not even sure that you can win, the way things are going in the state . . . And besides, you aren't well enough to campaign!"

He said slowly, "I'm going to do it."

"But how? You can't even leave the house. It will be over by the time you're better!" Her voice broke.

Now, standing up, he took the bandage from his face. His bad eye blinked desperately, slowly adjusting itself to the light. "Winnie, they need me. I don't have a choice. Don't you see?"

Her shoulders slumped. She didn't see it at all, but she had to say she did. She left him so that she could enjoy a quiet cry by herself. Then she washed and dried her face and returned to Jeff again in complete control of her emotions.

"I'm ready, dear," she told him. He dictated a letter, resigning his seat in the Senate, then worked out plans for a gradual return to active life. Varina adjusted the shutters each day a little wider to allow additional sunlight, and by the end of the week he was outdoors, wearing dark glasses.

As he packed for his three-week canvass Varina filled a trunk of her own. He shook his head, but she was resolute. "This is one time I'm going to be with you." She had not anticipated how brutal an ordeal it would be. Often she sat back in their carriage, her handkerchief against her lips as she saw him, eyes squinted, face quivering with pain, while he talked to the crowd. Why didn't the committee make him stop? The doctor had warned: "Only three quarters of an hour at the most." But, caught by enthusiasm for his subject, Jeff went on and on.

In the weeks of his illness he had gone through a remarkable change, for now he was the old Jeff again, calm, deliberate, almost judicial. If the people of the South wanted to compromise, they would have it, though he thought they might live to regret it. Meanwhile the Southern states must still draw together to protect their rights. . . .

After his speeches were over Varina worked with water and medicines at grimy hotels, at the homes of strangers, to prepare him for the next stop. Twice the eye grew so badly infected that doctors had to be summoned, and she prayed outside the room: "God, let the eye be saved again. . . ." Only once, in spite of all this physical trouble, did he miss an engagement.

When the campaign ended he went to a hotel in Jackson, to sink exhausted on his bed while she sat beside him in the dark. That night a letter reached them from Brierfield. Reading it, Varina felt as if she had suffered a physical blow. James Pemberton had died. . . . He had weakened a little during the past year or so, but the shock came as a hard one. When she told Jeff he broke down completely. One of the campaign workers who looked in on them a little later was shocked to see the expression on their faces. "I'm sorry—is something wrong?"

"Yes," Varina answered softly. "A death—in the family."

When the man had gone Jeff talked about James Pemberton, repeating stories of his earlier days, of the times James had shielded him from illness and financial loss, of his worth and dignity as an individual.

Varina thought of her own relations with the good man. He had not quite liked her at first, and in his eyes there had been doubt and mistrust. Then in a hundred ways, quietly, with instinctive tact, James Pemberton had made the way easier for her. Under different circumstances, under freedom, what would have been the life of this remarkable man?

Jeff, holding his hand before his eye, wrote a long letter to

James's wife, offering her help and consolation. Turning back to Varina, he sighed: "I'll have to have a white overseer now, the first time I've ever used one. But I'll never find a match for James Pemberton."

The election returns came in slowly. Jeff and Henry Foote were running neck and neck. In one district after another only a few votes separated them. If Jeff could make a gain here, or in the next county . . . For hours the result hung by a thread. "You've moved ahead!" she cried, a fury of hope in her face. "Another one in your favor." But then a new batch of returns, and he had dropped a little, then a little more. An hour later he was ahead once more. And so it went. . . . He and Varina stayed together in the hotel room, whispering, wondering. A friend brought them the final results. His look told Varina the story.

"There was a difference of only 999 votes," he whispered. "But it's Foote, 29,358"—he looked down at his paper—"and Davis, 28,359." Jeff had cut down his rival's previous lead from 7,000 to 1,000. Yet he had failed.

Varina shut the door. Her arms went around her husband, and she tried to find words with which to temper this blow.

Chapter 11

THEY SAT OPPOSITE EACH OTHER IN THE DEEP ROSEWOOD CHAIRS Margaret Howell had sent up from New Orleans. All about them in the library of the new Brierfield were the books they had accumulated these past six years, histories she had chosen because they would interest him, bindings he had ordered from New York. These last few weeks since their return had not been easy. At her side lay a novel by Sir Walter Scott that she had tried to read to him. He had only stared into the distance, and she had finally given up.

Jeff moved restlessly. "To think of losing to a creature like Foote. The lowest of low demagogues! But"—and the bewilderment returned to his light eyes—"all the letters I got, and the way they'd voted me for senator just a little before that . . ." His voice faltering, he spoke bitterly of the recent months when he had been hailed as Calhoun's successor, spokesman of the South. One day he had been a man to whom his people gave practically every honor; the next, a cast-off politician. He had anticipated a close vote, but he had never really prepared himself for the prospect of defeat.

"Well, this trouble's not over yet." He spoke in short, despairing sentences. "We'll see something yet. The South got nothing out of it, nothing." He shrugged, but the hurt was still there.

As she had done many times during these past few days, she pressed his hand. "Banny, you did what you felt was right, didn't you?" She was thinking of something else. Jeff had never lost his stiffness with the average man and woman. She had watched him closely during the campaign. True, he had been ill and handicapped; and yet if only he tried to smile and joke a little more . . . Even when entirely well, he seldom seemed to unbend. Foote had scored tellingly when he had suggested that Jeff was uppity.

She tried to indicate this problem as tactfully as she could. But Jeff's eyes blazed. "I couldn't be a demagogue, Varina. And I wouldn't if I could!" When he called her Varina, and in that tone, she knew he was annoyed. In the silence that followed, her eye fell on the shaggy outlines of the apricot tree, The Pilot's Wife. She had finally persuaded Jeff to make his peace with Mrs. McGruggy; certainly that wasn't being a demagogue. . . .

"I'm glad you're out of it, Banny," she cried suddenly. "Yes, I admit I miss something—the parties, our friends, things happening in Washington. But that's over and behind us, with the fighting, the troubles, and the hates. This is our home and the life we were intended for, before they pulled you away from it."

Jeff nodded. Was he thinking, as she was, of their first happy days on the river, when they were content with the slow passage of the seasons, the bird-swept isolation of their delta acres?

There was an interruption from the doorway in the person of Mr. Williams, the overseer hired in James Pemberton's place, a youngish, slow-moving man with freckles, red hair that was beginning to disappear, and pale green eyes. Ambling in, he launched into a complaint: "Those niggers, they don't show me respect, Mr. Davis."

Jeff looked up, a question on his face.

"I mean"—Mr. Williams frowned and gave a pull at his galluses —"they don't bow down or say 'Yessir' or anything. You seen that for yourself yesterday when you was with me. Dammit—begging your pardon, ma'am—they act like they was white folks!"

Wearily Varina picked up the novel again. She had caught the man last week raising his hand against James Pemberton's two boys, and she had given him a firm lecture of her own. She felt an extra duty toward the Pemberton children, and she wasn't going to have this red-neck abusing them.

Jeff scratched his chin. "I noticed them especially yesterday, Williams. They were respectful to both of us."

The man's green eyes showed a spark of anger. "Well, if that's the way you think. But a nigger's gotta drop his head when he sees *me!"* The words were sullen, almost whining. "I still cain't see how I'm to make 'em work if I'm not to whip 'em once in a while."

"No." Jeff had iron in his voice. "That's not the way it's been here, and we're not going to start it now."

As Williams left, Jeff said absently: "I'm afraid we won't have Mr. Williams long."

Varina's eyes passed over the page; Scott, with his knights and his talk of nobility, was very remote today. Her brows knitted. This feeling of some Southerners toward Negroes—she had thought little about it before. Poor-white-trash talk, that was all. But of late she had been hearing more and more about the curious structure of the South. There were far more Southerners without slaves than with them, and many of these people hated the blacks in the same way this bully Williams hated them. If emancipation ever arrived, what was going to happen between the blacks and the Williamses? It wasn't a happy prospect, and she put it aside. Shaking out her skirts, she went to Jeff. "It's time for our ride, isn't it?"

Without alacrity her husband agreed. Soon they were on their way down a tunnel of cool green, fragrant with the sweet olive and the smoky scent of moist leaves that rustled beneath them. It had been a long time since she rode the Mississippi woods in deep winter, and she beheld a forgotten beauty—the glory of close-pressed evergreens, moss that hung like frayed folds of gray lace. Occasionally a rabbit streaked across their path and disappeared; the only other sounds were the thud of their horses' hoofs and Varina's laugh when now and then she maneuvered her horse into the lead.

Her hat fell back; she gave a tug at the pins that held her coiffure, and her thick black locks were flying behind her, tangling in the wind. As she dodged a tree branch she had a glimpse of Jeff. He was looking far ahead, his mouth slightly parted, head raised as the breeze sang past his cheeks; and there was the beginning of a smile on his lips, the first she had seen in weeks. This was what they had first enjoyed together. Let the world keep to itself; let them be here in their own private world!

Approaching a clearing, they halted by unspoken agreement and dismounted. It was the slaves' cemetery, a white-fenced ridge marked by a double line of weathered tombstones. Beyond the big tree lay James Pemberton's resting place. As they reached it they heard a movement. James's two young boys stood there, big-eyed at the interruption.

"We jes' want' come 'ere a lil while," John, the elder, apologized.

"That's all right, son. We're sorry we're intruding." Jeff's tone was warm and sympathetic.

A few green tendrils had climbed the boarding that bore James's name, and Jeff stooped to pull them away. Then, without hesitation, he sank to his knees and dropped his head in prayer. The boys, unused to such demonstrations, looked on, abashed. Varina drew them aside. "You're keeping up with your reading, the way your father wanted?"

"Yes'm." They talked simultaneously. "An' we savin', too." John spoke, his mouth widening. "I got fo' dollars and seven'y cents. Paul, he got t'ree-twenny."

"T'ree-thirdy!" Paul cried in rebuke. And John picked up the subject: "We wanna buy ourself free, ma'am."

"Well, what's all this about finance?" Jeff had risen and joined them. The boys hesitated, and Varina talked for them: "They hope they can save enough for their freedom, dear."

Unexpectedly Jeff's face changed. "You're not happy here?" His words had a cutting edge that made Varina flinch. Paul's head dropped and his toe sank into the earth; but John, though his eyes seemed to bulge out in his anxiety, spoke up: "Yessir, we happy, still, ever'body want free, don' dey?"

Thinking it over later, Varina wondered if she could have put it any better herself. "After all, dear," she said, "this is pretty much what you taught our first plantation Negroes. They have stores, they sell fruits." Then she remembered that none of their blacks so far had won his freedom. In such matters Jeff's opinions hung in delicate balance, and they sometimes changed. She realized that this was not the moment to discuss slavery and its ethics. Well, she'd try to work it out later.

Day by day she saw Jeff improve. The tension in his eyes was lessened; no longer did she find him pacing the floor, hands clasped tightly behind him. His body was filling out, the hollows of his face growing less pronounced. She, too, looked better than she had in a long time; her old serenity had returned. From moving about so much in the sun, her skin was taking on a slight tan. Most of her Washington friends, and also the Natchez ones, would have disapproved of it as extremely unfashionable, not to say improper. Annabelle, too, protested. "No lady I ever knowed had skin lookin' dat way. Mulatta, I say!" Varina smiled to herself. She preferred it that way. Let the milk-and-water women stick to their own style.

In the management of the plantation Jeff was changing confusion to order. As he predicted, Mr. Williams went, to be followed by Mr. Bostick, an ever-smiling individual with an obsequious air. "I've never had no trouble yet with blacks," said Mr. Bostick. Whatever Jeff told him, he agreed with, but although the plantation ran smoothly Varina had her doubts.

Yet she welcomed the respite from worry, the calm of the early spring, her hours in the hospital at the back, with the old women and the children in the nursery. She and Jeff went together to the steamboat landing for special packages; they had the McCalebs and other neighbors in for suppers of choice beef and well-cured ham. Best of all she valued their hours in the room that had become their favorite, the library. Here they enjoyed long evenings, reading the journals together, talking over new books and old ones.

When she told women callers of these quiet evenings some did not conceal their surprise. "Don't you have chores to do?" they asked.

"Whatever they are, I do them early, so I'll be there with Jeff."

One matron was baffled. "Do you *like* talking politics?"

"It isn't exactly politics." Varina smiled. "It's everything. You see, Jeff and I are interested in the same things. We've always been." A moment later she asked the woman: "What do you people around here think of the compromise?"

"Compromise?" The lady tittered. "Who was compromised?"

When Varina returned home with the story Jeff threw back his head and laughed. "I'm not so sure she wasn't right!" he cried.

Varina was delighted because it was the first time he had been able to joke about the matter. His face still relaxed, he handed her three new letters from friends who wanted him to know they still had faith in him. More than anything else, this was the sort of affirmation Jeff needed. She noticed that he prized one in particular and looked down at the signature. "Albert Sidney Johnston," she read. "He was with you in the Western service, wasn't he?"

"Yes." Jeff's tone was affectionate. "He's in Texas now, still in the Army—one of the finest soldiers I ever knew, and one of the finest men. I suppose he won't ever leave the service." Then his eyes dulled, and he looked through and past her. Was he thinking now, as he did from time to time, of his own Army days and regretting that he had ever left the military?

To fall in with his mood she opened one of the boxes she had brought from the attic. "These are certainly antiques," she mused as the papers crumbled to her touch. "Look—here are the records of your military campaign in the West." Her finger ran idly down the lists. "Yes, here's Johnston. And here's that man Lincoln, Abraham Lincoln. He's that Westerner who was in Congress a while back, isn't he?"

Jeff considered. "I suppose so. It's funny, but I don't have the faintest recollection of the man."

"Couldn't have impressed you much."

"I guess not." Jeff's words faded; he was thinking of something more important. He gave her a quick glance and cleared his voice. "Winnie, the Democrats are trying to come back in Mississippi." He spoke as if he were trying to convince himself. "They'll accept Clay's compromise; they're asking all members to join again on that basis. They want me to make a talk. No"—he read her meaning— "I won't run for anything, ever. But I owe something to them, if I can help."

She said nothing, but she began to realize that for all their apparent seclusion they would never be really free of the Democratic party, Southern politics, or national problems.

A week later she was waiting upstairs on the sofa for Jeff's return, her dark hair lowered over her shoulders, a bright shawl about her. There was a stillness in the air, a light movement of birds in the trees outside the window, and then sleepy silence. At the back of the house one of the women worked at the butter churn, and in the parlor Annabelle sang two verses of a Negro spiritual and then her voice trailed off. Varina, her eyes on the clouds above the live oaks, heard nothing, saw nothing. Her mind was filled with the new thing that had happened to her.

Jeff's steps sounded in the hall below, and Varina came to with a start. She heard Annabelle telling him she was upstairs, and then he was in the room, a perplexed look on his face. He dropped to his knees beside the sofa and put his arms around her, his hunger for her in his touch. Her black hair, with the blue lights that shone in the sun, enveloped him with its faint musky scent. Then he drew back. "Winnie, you're so—— Is something wrong?"

"No. That is, I hope not——" She stopped, and the words came all together. "You see, I'm going to have a baby."

His eyes widened, and there was a new expression in them, an expression of joy, of pride, of love—she couldn't analyze it. He pulled her to him again, and they talked quietly of their great happiness.

"Yes," he murmured. "The plantation's the best place for him. I'll get a pony and a cart and . . ." That it might not be a boy had not occurred to him.

Varina had never seen Jeff in such a state; his joy was that of a twenty-year-old boy. How urgently, all along, had he wanted this child! He must have suffered more than she had during these barren years. Lately she had given up hope; she suspected that he had too.

Downstairs Annabelle waited, a smile on her lips, keeping the supper warm until it began to dry up in the pans. Harry sat on the doorstep. After another hour passed Annabelle scraped the food into cold plates and set it aside. "Sure ain' gonna be down now," she told her husband, slapping her side. "She think I don' understan'. I guess it de day she know herself. Lord love a duck, tha's one time no 'oman can hol' a secret!"

It was not until breakfast the next day that Varina remembered. "What about your trip?"

Jeff looked pleased. "I think the party is getting back on its feet. They're doing better. Governor Foote"—his eyes darkened as he used the hated name—"Foote's making a lot of mistakes, and we'll be profiting by them." He had first said "they," then "we." Her heart sank a little, but Jeff whistled as he rode to the fields.

Her world of Brierfield had become suddenly more beautiful, the earth more fragrant and tranquil. The white blossoms of the delta spring were showing against the sky. Along the wet spots she stopped at the sights of the lotus with their lemon-hued chalices and green leaves almost a foot wide. With a heightened spirit, a new sense of her duties, she went about her visits to the sick in the Negro quarters.

Jeff became apprehensive. "You better not go back there. You might catch something."

She laughed. "Don't worry so soon, you goose. It won't be for months." After a while, however, she rode less and gradually cut down on her activities. At times she grew faintly disturbed. Did she know enough? Would she understand the things to be done when the hour arrived?

In her letters to Margaret Howell she told of her fears. Her mother replied promptly: "If you have room for me I can come up and be with you. You've asked me before, but this time I have a good excuse to leave the family."

Jeff not only gave his approval to the visit but added: "Maybe she'll want to bring some of the children with her?"

At the steamboat landing Varina embraced her mother with delight, and they clung together in tearful excitement. The white in Margaret's hair had increased, her figure was heavier, and new lines crisscrossed beneath her quick-moving eyes. Yet she remained the crisp, capable woman who had safely shepherded her husband and her family through many crises, a good woman to have on hand in emergency.

"Where's that husband of yours?" She craned her neck. "Oh, hello, Jeff. Handsomer than ever, I see. Are you sure we're not inconveniencing you? Has it been raining?" Before she had the answers to those questions she had started on others. "Oh, I brought your brothers' and sisters' baby dresses. My, aren't the children with me?" She wheeled about to find a trio of younger Howells standing diffidently together behind her.

Varina threw out her arms: "Children! Kiss me, all of you." She encircled them, the five-year-old Jefferson, the plump little boy who was Jeff's namesake; Maggie, blond and freckled and good-humored in her green silk dress and flowered hat; and Becket, the reserved older boy, his hair parted precisely in the center, observing them with a look that bordered on solemnity.

"You're pale and peaked, all of you," she told them. "Wait till you get some country sun."

Her mother took her arm. "And you, Miss Varina, no more sun for you—not until after the baby comes."

Varina nodded meekly. Once again she would relax while her decisions were made for her, do nothing but rest and wait. Within an hour Margaret had fitted herself into the life at Brierfield. Varina felt a quickening pride as her mother praised her household arrangements, admired the kitchen, and paused to exclaim at the marble fireplaces. Annabelle was suspicious at first, but by the time Margaret asked her opinions about several points and then followed her advice, Annabelle had been won over. "Yes, Miss Marg'ret, glad to do dat. What else you wan'?"

"Now, missy," Varina's mother said to her, "here's something you'd better get accustomed to. You'll have to drink it from now on." It was thickened cream. Varina had never liked it, but she understood that this fact would hardly matter now.

The children made themselves at home immediately and, watching them, Varina concocted a few plans of her own concerning the size of the family she would raise. Maggie was in a fine mood, chuckling over everything, asking Jeff interminable questions: "Where's the stable? You have any ducks?" Little Jeff would be no problem, for he was apparently delighted with everything he saw. It was Becket who disturbed her. He appeared oddly constrained. She discovered he had not been altogether happy in New Orleans. "It's so different," he told her with some intensity, "and so smelly." The Creole boys laughed all the time at things that weren't funny and talked their peculiar talk.

The morning after the arrival of the Howells' tribe Jeff came through the doorway of the dining room, carrying Maggie on his shoulders. The smaller Jeff crawled down the stairs, shouting: "I'm a wagon rolling down the road!" By the time Varina reached the table Margaret was waiting for her with the neatly dressed, freshly combed Becket, who held out her chair. After breakfast, as they lingered over the last cup of coffee, she managed to draw the boy out.

"I'm going to be a lawyer," he said. "And make a lot of money and buy the family a house—a big one like we use' to have in Natchez."

Varina lowered her eyes; she was glad her mother had already gone into the parlor. "Why, it'll be a long time before you have to worry about that, Becket."

"Oh no," the boy told her gravely. "Mama always says every bit counts. Brother William, you know, has gotten a place with the brokers, and Brother Joe may get one next year. If Papa's pension comes through things will be that much better." So, despite the

Navy post Jeff had obtained for her father, they were not doing as well as Margaret wanted her to think.

She got up. "Let's look around the place, Becket." She took him past the stables, the blacksmith shop, the bushes in which the mockingbirds had their nests. "Don't you remember the mockers in Natchez?" she asked. He nodded, all too seriously. Then she spied one of James Pemberton's sons. "John, you take Becket. Show him everything!" The Negro youth, flattered at the assignment, laughed and led away the half-willing Becket.

Hours later the front door burst open and a begrimed, tousled figure ran toward her. "Look! An alligator, a baby!" Becket's shirt was torn, his face scratched, but he was happy. Varina pulled back from the squirming thing in his hand, then reached over and pushed the hair from his face. John Pemberton, hanging back in the doorway, grinned at her and she smiled back. This was what Becket needed.

At supper she saw Becket, somewhat subdued again, studying Jeff with eyes in which there was awe—for he had heard a great deal of Jeff and his deeds—and also a shade of jealousy over Jeff's attention to the younger ones. As the meal ended Varina pressed Jeff's sleeve. "Banny, I want you to do something for me."

An hour later Becket started as his tall relative threw an arm over his shoulder and said: "We've been annoyed lately, Becket, by a bull alligator that's eating our pigs and calves. Harry and I are going to hunt him this evening. Think you want to come along?"

Without bothering to reply Becket dashed upstairs to change his clothes. He rode off in triumph, to the annoyance of Maggie and little Jeff. For days afterward Becket told all the details of the capture, the snapping of the great jaws, the grunts and slashings, the slapping of the leathery tail—"and then Brother Jeff took aim, and *boom*, it was over!"

Mid-June arrived, and Varina's confinement was close. Jeff stayed near her, his apprehension deepening with each passing week. He talked frequently in a low voice with Margaret Howell. Varina asked herself: Was he remembering that other crisis, when his first wife had died slowly before his eyes?

On one of these occasions she looked up at Jeff with a laugh.

"Don't be so sad, Banny. I have no intention of dying!" When his face showed pain she took his hand. "Don't mind me, Jeff. I guess I'm more nervous than I want to let on."

The doctor rode over every day or so. Varina had a strong constitution, he assured them, "and a strong mind, too." He grinned when she told him: "I'll be no trouble. I want this over so it won't interfere with the crop. We have a good one this year!" Toward the end, however, she lay in bed, exhausted, her body heavy, praying that it would stop.

Early one afternoon Margaret, sitting in the next room, heard her cry out in pain. Varina was rolling back and forth, groaning, the sweat beading her face. Expertly her mother dispatched her helpers. "Annabelle, to the kitchen, but first find Mr. Jeff and ask him to go for the doctor, fast. And you, girl, don't gawk; take those children to a back room—and keep them there!"

Then, as Varina's moans increased, Margaret Howell did something she had been planning to do for weeks. She asked Harry if he would ride over to The Hurricane and see if Eliza Davis would come. She knew the unchanged antagonisms between the branches of the family, but now she was sure that Eliza would want to be at Brierfield.

She was right, for Eliza came immediately, tears of sympathy in her tired eyes. Whether she left without a word to Joe Davis, or whether there was a clash, Varina never knew; but Eliza had arrived. As the two women kissed, Margaret sensed something of gratitude in those tears. "It's been a long time," Eliza whispered, and then she went to Varina and kissed her tenderly.

The three women—Margaret, Eliza, and Annabelle—waited at the bedside, watching, commenting in whispers. To Varina, as she beheld them in pauses between the spasms of pain, they looked like the three Fates. Once she tried to tell them, but before she could explain she was lost again in agony.

By the time the doctor and Jeff raced up the stairs Margaret Howell and her assistants had done their work. She walked forward with a bundle in her arms. "A boy, and a big one."

Jeff's eyes went to Varina, tired and white-faced. She managed to lift her head. "I'm all right. Everything's all right." The delight that spread over his face made her want to smile, but her head dropped back on the pillow and she slept.

She was happy in the days that followed as Jeff hovered about her and the baby, holding him by the hour, touching the light hair that formed a swirl on top of his head, and the buttony nose that might in time look like Varina's. Yet there was something about the baby—the cheekbones, the brow—that made Varina think most of all of the stern face of Jeff's father, almost scowling from the wall at The Hurricane. She hoped the child would be a little less set in his look. One day after she was up again she came back to the room and heard Jeff singing to the baby in a strange minor key:

> "Cora wankee shangmonee
> Sheereerra notty hiee, notty hiee . . ."

"What's that?" she demanded.

"An Indian song that's supposed to calm children. I learned it in the West." He smiled and resumed the chant. For a moment she was annoyed because the incident reminded her that she would always be separated from Jeff by the many experiences he had had before she knew him. Every now and then some little thing like this showed her the gap between them. But that was scarcely Jeff's fault, she told herself sternly. She came back to the present to hear him say: "What shall we name him, Winnie?"

She had been thinking about this for a long time and she was ready with her answer. "We'll call him Sam, after your father," she told him. Holding the baby between them, he thanked her, first with his eyes, then with his lips.

As soon as Varina was able to move about easily a traditional ceremony was arranged. Jeff set up a chair on the gallery, and every Negro on the plantation came to see her, each with a gift and a few words. Old women carried squawking hens; men carried sacks of yams, and their pockets bulged with other produce. All of them bent to admire the baby, to touch the pink hands and cheeks and to feel the toes.

One crone, nearly eighty-five, cried out as she stepped forward: "Law, baby Sam. You never gon' work. We do it all fo' you!"

Laughter greeted this prediction, but Varina shook her head. "Little Sam's going to work, and hard. I wouldn't want it any other way."

A few hours later Jeff tiptoed into her room to see if she were asleep. Finding her awake, he placed a document quietly in her lap. It was a new will, replacing the earlier one that Joe Davis had directed. In case of Jeff's death, it divided the property among Varina, Sam, and any other children they had. As she read the old hurt slipped away. That earlier document had been a continuing evidence of her brother-in-law's power and hostility. And now that it had been destroyed she could hardly speak. She kissed Jeff silently, and he pressed her head against his shoulder.

They were still together when Margaret Howell walked into Varina's room. She spoke crisply, a little too crisply to be entirely convincing. "Time for me to be getting back home. I've been on your hands too long already." She brushed away their protests. "We'll be on our way by the end of the week."

That Saturday when the carriage came for them Margaret and Varina embraced with a heightened emotion. How many more months must pass before they met again? Maggie went to Varina with a sob, and she caressed the freckled face with its blond pigtails. Young Jeff begged to be held. Becket stood at the gallery edge, hands in his pockets, close to tears, until Varina put her arms around him. "Don't cry," she told them. "We'll all be together again. You'll see, you'll see. . . ."

Not long after the departure of Margaret and her brood Jeff came home one evening obviously excited.

"Winnie," he cried, "some of our party men in the East, all war veterans, are getting together to talk about the next election." Then, seeing her face, he said more deliberately: "Anyway, I have some business in Washington and I can make my visit serve both purposes."

Varina sat still, her hands in her lap. She was about to protest, but then she stopped herself. She mustn't try to restrict Jeff, for certainly his interests should extend beyond the limits of their plantation.

When he came back he seemed disturbed.

"The situation's confused," he remarked, frowning. "There are three or four candidates for President, none strong enough and none good enough. That fellow Stephen Douglas——"

His tone was contemptuous, and she already knew what he thought of the ambitious young Westerner.

"Still, most of us agreed on a likely man for Vice-President, Franklin Pierce of New Hampshire. I hope we'll be lucky enough to get him."

She had heard Jeff talk before about his old friend Pierce, a New Englander but no Abolitionist. She had a vague impression of one or two misfortunes in Mr. Pierce's life—a liking for the bottle, now conquered; a sickly wife who feared Washington. Oh well, that was all far in the future and far away, and she had the baby Sam to occupy her attention.

Yet when the Democratic convention met and surprisingly enough nominated Franklin Pierce for President, she realized that the election might be important to them. The hitherto unknown New Englander had been introduced as a dark horse and a stampede had followed. Jeff was both surprised and jubilant. "I'd thought of him from the beginning, but only as a running mate for some other candidate."

Pleased as he was on the good fortune of his old friend Pierce, Jeff was not happy about the party's platform. It called for acceptance of Clay's compromise as a means of establishing peace between the North and the South. "I suppose we'll have to accept it," he sighed.

Jeff's interest in the election increased when the Whigs nominated Winfield Scott, the crusty old warrior who was one of Jeff's particular enemies. "Fuss and Feathers" Scott, the admirer of his own comely legs, was referred to in the Davis household as "that old windbag."

As the campaign started Jeff became more and more incensed with the things the opposition was saying about his friend Pierce: a drooling full-time drunkard, a coward in wartime, his military record "two somersaults and a faint." He wrote an angry letter to Pierce's managers. The reply was prompt: Would Mr. Davis take the platform? He would be delighted to. And before the week was up Jeff was off on another barnstorming tour, Varina secretly amused by his protestations of annoyance over this new turn of events. She was sure that he was enjoying the campaign as much as she was enjoying her first baby.

When Pierce and the Democrats won that fall she was as delighted as Jeff, but she sensed without really knowing why that the pleasant days at Brierfield were probably at an end. Still it wasn't until early February that two letters from Washington arrived in the same mail. As she opened the first a clipping fell out: "President Pierce is giving serious consideration for the post of Secretary of War to former Senator Jefferson Davis." She turned inquiringly to Jeff, and he handed her a note from Franklin Pierce himself. Pierce wrote that he hadn't yet made up his mind on the composition of the new Cabinet, but he wished Jeff to come to Washington to talk with him as a friend.

Jeff glanced up at her and then shoved the letters into his pocket. "Don't worry, Winnie," he said in answer to her unspoken question. "I don't think I'd take it."

Yet there was a tinge of uncertainty, an edge of regret in his voice. She thought of the tensions, the hatreds of Washington City, and yet . . .

All at once she was saying: "Jeff, you know how I feel. But—a place in the Cabinet—I don't have any right to ask you to say no. Whatever you decide up there, that's what I'll want."

It had been hard to say those words, but for a long time now she had known that she was married to a statesman and not a farmer. As her husband kissed her she understood that he would accept the post if it was offered to him. Her eyes, staring beyond him, saw the early spring bloom through the window, the filmy pink branch of a fruit tree. In Washington City there were no flowers in February.

Chapter 12

As the railroad cars lurched and the grimy outskirts of Washington City moved slowly into view, Varina clutched the hard seat in front of her. For the past few hours she had been caught by a feeling of rising excitement. At Brierfield during the weeks just past she had gone mechanically through her duties, dreading the change ahead of her. But now, with her trip near its end, she found herself warmly anticipating the future.

She remembered again her afternoon walks down the crowded streets, diplomatic receptions, balls at which she met justices and senators. Her old love of action, of participation, had returned; and back, too, were her ambitions for her husband. Now and then during the past two years she had suffered a twinge of nostalgia when she thought of the capital city at her favorite moments of afternoon and evening. She had firmly rejected those musings in Brierfield and had turned to her plantation chores. Today she knew for the first time how strong within her was this attraction for another kind of life.

Little Sam was resting quietly in her arms. She fondled his soft pink cheek, his round nose that seemed more and more like hers, and then, remembering that she had other responsibilities, she handed him to the nurse. She turned her attention to her brother and sister, Maggie in her braided coat that somehow hung wrong, and the serious-faced Becket, dark and spruce as usual.

On her way to Washington she had gone through New Orleans and had been greeted so warmly by the children that it suddenly occurred to her that she might take Maggie and Becket to Washington City.

"Mother," she had appealed, "could we take the two oldest with us, for a season anyway? They'd meet everybody up there; it would be an experience for them." She had not added another argument that was on the tip of her tongue: Surely it would lift some of Margaret Howell's many burdens.

For a long time her mother had sat silent, watching the boy and girl in the yard. Then she replied in a voice that was gentle and also a little sad: "It would be best, wouldn't it? And I'd see them when you were home on trips."

The decision had cost her a great deal, Varina knew, and made up her mind then that Margaret Howell must never regret the arrangement.

The train stopped and Maggie and Becket were darting forward. "Brother Jeff! Jeff!" He strode toward them, vibrant, smiling. As he held Varina her hand touched the smooth face with its sunken cheeks, the firm lips, the light wave of the hair at the forehead. "Banny, Banny. Only a month, but it felt like years."

"We'll make up for it," he assured her, then swept up baby Sam. "He's grown a lot; every time my back turns he's bigger."

Maggie was clinging to his hand and Becket was beaming, his eyes on Jeff's every movement. As he led the way out Varina began a running fire of questions: "Have you arranged about the schools? It's a nice house, isn't it? And how are the Pierces——"

"You'll know about the Pierces soon enough—tonight," he interrupted. "The President's giving a dinner, and he expects you and me."

She hid her frown of momentary annoyance. It was like a man to accept an invitation like that. She would be expected to leave for dinner before she had time to do more than dust the cinders out of her hair. But the prospect was a thrilling one. Would she ever grow so blasé that a party at the White House would not stir her?

Soon Jeff was taking her through the partly furnished house he had rented. It had twenty-three rooms, and even though many of them were small, she thought the house too big and too expensive for them. Jeff persuaded her that, everything considered, it amounted to a bargain.

"We have our position to maintain," he told her.

She nodded. "Well, I'll have to send home for more things again."

As she walked about the sprawling house she added: "I'll have to redecorate here and there and replace those pink curtains and the wallpaper in the hall. But you've done far better than I hoped, Banny." She squeezed his hand. "How is the administration going?"

"Magnificently, Winnie," he replied with real enthusiasm. "There's harmony, peace, in Washington for a change. It's all different and you'll hardly believe it. Of course the Abolitionists are still stirring things up and still refusing to return runaways. That editor in New York, Greeley, he's never stopped sneering at the South. . . ." Then with an effort he returned to his subject. Harmony was the keynote, Pierce was giving representation to all factions, and nearly everybody was pleased.

"It sounds almost like a miracle," Varina ventured.

"But it's working," he told her. "Big things are going to happen this time, things I've always hoped for."

"What things?"

"For instance, a railroad to the Pacific. It's been talked about before, and nothing ever happened. Now I've persuaded Franklin Pierce to back it, and he's given his word. My department's going to make the surveys. In fact, we've already started. We'll be opening up the Far West, cutting through deserts, finding sites for new towns." His enthusiasm was contagious. "That land out West is a great reservoir of natural wealth. There's thousands on thousands of miles of it waiting to be developed!"

She had never expected this. "What about states' rights, Banny?"

He had thought it all out. "It's a matter of military necessity, don't you see—a national undertaking?"

She nodded, though she was still not sure. What a change had come over Jeff! Was he like those other men who spoke of states' right when that fitted their plans, and of "national necessity" when it didn't? She felt a little confused. "Also, Winnie," he was saying, "there's a chance that we may get Cuba—without revolution—by purchase or peaceful dealing with Spain."

This indeed was not the Jeff who had once talked of taking Cuba by some method and had spoken of a defiant South and a break with the North. Now he saw the future of the South within the Union, an expanding Union. The South would benefit, but so would everyone else. She felt a quiver of excitement. These would be great years!

Dressing for dinner that evening, she chose a heavily embroidered silk with a more than normally tight waist. Of late she had taken more and more to white, for it emphasized her almost Latin coloring. She added a single string of pearls and, for her hair, a single white rose from the garden.

Returning to the mirror, she applied a little rouge to her pale cheeks, then washed it off. She did not require such coloring. Her thick straight hair, blue-black as ever, had a superb sheen. She had lost the slight tan of her recent plantation days, and her wide-spaced eyes were deep and luminous in the direct light. Her figure remained firm, excellently rounded, and her breasts had grown fuller. She was a little heavier, but she did not have to be told that it became her. Jeff's arms enveloped her as she sat before the mirror. "Don't waste your time. You'll be the loveliest woman there, whatever you do or don't do to yourself."

She turned and made a rapid survey of Jeff's costume. "Hm . . . Those trousers are a trifle snug. But I like the blue coat. Your stock——" She cocked her head to the side. "No, you'd better get a black one." When he protested she was resolute. "Banny, you'll be on trial tonight too."

On their way out she glanced at the card tray. Within an hour it had filled and overflowed. "It's nice to know we're remembered." She smiled. But long ago she had gained sufficient experience to understand that there was something more than that to it. A Cabinet member and his wife were figures of considerable importance.

At the White House she noticed that the portico, the windows, the walls had been elaborately repainted and retouched. Inside she stared at the freshly frescoed walls and heavy draperies, remembering how different it looked on her last visit, the day poor Zachary Taylor had died.

A door opened and a voice called out, "Mr. President." Two or three couples ahead of the Davises stood to one side, and Franklin Pierce came toward Varina, holding out his hand. His words could be heard clearly across the room. "Mrs. Davis. Even the descriptions hadn't led me to expect such a beauty."

It was a compliment that only a man of considerable self-possession could deliver. She saw at once that Mr. Pierce was above all a poised and socially experienced individual. The handsome face, lean and symmetrical, had considerable charm. In his smile she read understanding and a desire to please.

As he talked with her quickly and easily, forgetting the others about them, she became aware of the nervous gestures, the weariness in the circled eyes. Some hinted that the President was weak, too easily led by others, often changeable. She already knew that Mr. Pierce was not a man of great depth and yet she liked him enormously from the start.

"Is Mrs. Pierce down yet?" she asked.

The President's face saddened. "Poor Jane. She isn't up to affairs like this." He leaned toward Varina. "You and your husband stay after the others go. I'd like you to see her."

After the President moved on to other guests she was introduced to the various Cabinet members and their wives. She discovered very quickly that most of the Secretaries were bachelors or widowers. Not only was there a shortage of wives, but those who came seemed naïve and unsure of themselves. It became evident that Varina at twenty-seven could consider herself the Washington veteran.

A group formed around her, and soon she was dominating the conversation in her part of the room.

"That was the day I met Alexander Stephens . . ." She was defending Mr. Stephens against the malicious jokes about his appearance.

"Do you know Mr. Stephen Douglas, the Westerner?" said one of the women.

Her first impulse was to express her real opinion of the man, which was far from favorable, but she checked herself and changed the subject.

As she talked her eyes sought Jeff. He stood against a window, two men and four or five of the younger women clustered about him. One of the prettier girls seemed to be following his every word. Despite all she could do, a flush of jealousy rose to Varina's face. Would she ever be able to control her feelings when she watched him with other women?

A chime sounded, announcing dinner, and the guests filed ceremoniously into the long dining room. As the elaborate meal was served President Pierce tried hard to put them all at their ease. The absence of his wife was something of a handicap, and Varina noticed that, while the new White House appointments had elegance, they produced a chilling effect. The conversation languished until Varina began to draw out the people at her end of the table. Before long she had worked up the discussion to a point where she could afford to drop out of it. She caught a grateful look from Franklin Pierce. He was relaxing at last.

Jeff had managed to whisper: "I was right. You're the best-looking woman here." And the President's attentions to the Davises had not gone unobserved. Without question Jeff would be one of the dominant men of this administration. Her husband turned, and they smiled at each other. This was a moment of true triumph.

When the party was over and the President had said good night to the other guests, he returned to Varina and Jeff.

"Come with me, please," he said, offering his arm to Varina.

At the top of the stairway he led them to a door which he knocked on softly and then opened. A small woman in a pale taffeta dress stared up at them from the depths of a chaise longue with an expression almost of fright. Without a word Jane Pierce extended an uncertain hand and listened while her husband said: "The evening went well, dear. We're all hoping you'll be joining us soon."

As he continued his nervous monologue the uncomfortable woman answered in a few broken words: "Oh yes . . . That— would be nice, I think." Her weak eyes, red-rimmed, moved timidly from Jeff to Varina and back to her husband. Her white hands, the nails bitten, tugged at the waist of her dress. Varina's heart softened. This woman had suffered a terrible loss, a series of them. Her last remaining child had recently been killed in a train accident. She had had many illnesses, and she feared the cruelty of public life. Even when she was young she could never have been a pretty woman, or an assured one.

Not until her husband mentioned Varina's baby did Jane Pierce respond, and then her interest was immediately apparent. The sad face turned in appeal to Varina. "What's the little one's name? Is he pretty, and well?" The voice wavered. "Will you bring him to me? You promise?" She was pathetically fearful that Varina would forget.

"We'll be here whenever you say." Varina smiled reassuringly.

"Then tomorrow," the sick woman replied quickly.

Outside Franklin Pierce thanked Varina in a husky voice. "It's the first time in weeks that Jane has shown a concern over anything outside the family." He, too, seemed apprehensive that Varina might not return. "You'll remember?"

"I'll remember." She nodded.

On the way home she thought about this couple who had suddenly found themselves the most famous people in America, and also about Jeff and herself. It had been a curious fate that brought the Pierces to Washington—one day living in comparative obscurity, the next in the center of the limelight. Yet no more curious, was it, than the luck which had touched Jeff? Years earlier, accidentally, he had met Franklin Pierce in Washington, and then again in the Mexican War. But for this chance acquaintance she and Jeff would still be in Mississippi.

The next morning Varina, passing the drawing-room door, spied a familiar face, that of Robert Lee of Virginia. She stopped on the threshold, and he greeted her with a grave bow. Whenever she met him the manners of other men appeared suddenly crude. "Let me get you some coffee," she suggested, "in our Mississippi style. Remember it?" His eyes twinkled as he said: "Well do I remember. For weeks afterward, whatever coffee I tried tasted like muddy water!"

As he stirred the fragrant brew Colonel Lee told her of his new post. Less than a year before he had become ninth superintendent of the United States Military Academy. A little later he was replying to her question: "Yes, I like my work. I'm learning a lot." It was an example of his usual modesty that had nothing of affectation in it. "And now, with Mr. Davis as the new Secretary, it will be much easier for us. He understands what we need. You know, Mr. Davis and I were at West Point together," he reminded her.

Jeff arrived as she was pouring Colonel Lee a second cup of coffee. He was incensed over a political scandal he had just discovered. "One thing I can assure you, Lee," he said sternly. "There'll be no more political interference at West Point." Colonel Lee asked him if there were any new plans under discussion, and Jeff's eyes lighted. "The Army's dropped far below strength, to a new low point. It's poorly supported, badly equipped. While the country grows, the Army shrinks. Only eleven thousand men are in service, and a lot of them ought to be retired! But unfortunately we don't have a retired list, and the dead wood never drops out."

Jeff was warming to his subject. "I'm going to build it back and modernize it. We want new tactics, more installations, better pay. I'm going to ask Congress for two new regiments of riflemen, another of dragoons." He pointed a long finger at Colonel Lee. "In the next war things will be very different, and the United States has to be ready for it." Robert Lee was obviously impressed.

"There's one thing more I'm going to give the Army," Jeff concluded somewhat truculently. "I'm going to bring on camels."

Varina started. Robert Lee, well mannered as he was, did not hide his astonishment.

"Yes, camels." Jeff shrugged. "They're the only way to handle our transportation over the Western deserts—the only animals that can cover long distances without suffering, without drinking up precious water. I'm going to try to import them and show their value!"

Before Varina passed a vision of the American frontier, populated by herds of camels moving slowly across the sands. . . . Lee rose. "Anyway, it's time I must go." As the trim, well-set figure left them Jeff nodded his head in approval. "Lee doesn't know it, but when we get those extra regiments he'll find himself one of the top officers. He's never received what he deserves. But he will now."

The three children occupied more and more of their thoughts. Maggie flourished in the new atmosphere. Bright ribbons in her blond hair, her blue eyes bright, she was finding Washington City all that her sister Varina had promised. Her older brother Becket remained something of a problem. His school work turned out to be rather more difficult than they had anticipated, and he had trouble in keeping up with it. But she and Jeff gave him a hand, and he was improving.

Most of Varina's day centered about the baby. To the wonder of some of her women callers, she seldom allowed the nurse to give

Sam his bath. "It's my right," she insisted. Almost always she succeeded in cutting receptions or her visits, to get home in time for the event.

Soon after his arrival in the capital Sam had started to walk; now he was getting around without help. Plump and good-natured, he looked more and more like Jeff. He pattered behind them from room to room; sometimes when Jeff had an official guest he eluded the nurse and ran in, to stand beside his father, mumbling half words that Jeff translated to the caller. He learned the hour when Jeff was due at home and would go to the hall and wait patiently for him, to jump in his arms as the door opened.

Whenever he picked up the child Varina saw her husband change, become a younger, gentler man. If only those who called Jeff cold and humorless could be with him at such moments! Jeff seemed to be giving Sam all the affection he had stored up during their childless years. The depth of his love for the boy gave her an occasional pang of fright. Suppose something took Sam from them; could she or Jeff bear it? Then she would smile as, from the next room, she heard Jeff's voice singing that strange Indian song:

> "Cora wankee shangmonee,
> Sheereera notty hiee . . ."

There was someone else to share their love for Sam—Mrs. Pierce. For hours every week the two women sat together in the Davis home or at the White House, watching the boy. Varina was beginning to understand the tortured woman who was a mystery to Washington City. Alone with Varina, Jane lost much of her habitual tension. One day, unexpectedly, she described her early life as the daughter of the president of Bowdoin College.

"You see, I had a very strict religious upbringing," she half whispered. "The pleasures of social life and such things were not for us. And I—I was always shy."

Her strait-laced family, Varina gathered, had not altogether approved of the easygoing Franklin Pierce, with his breezy manner. "Oh, I've not regretted my marriage," she cried, alarmed lest Varina misunderstand. "Franklin is always kind and understanding." But during much of the time her husband had been in Congress she had stayed in New Hampshire. Varina remembered that this was the period of Franklin Pierce's heavy drinking. Now

Franklin barely touched liquor. Enemies who observed him in the White House were disappointed.

"If my health were better," Jane was sighing, "I might make myself do things. As it is, I feel so weak . . ." Her voice trailed away. "You know I have my despondent days, when I do nothing but cry and pray." Her hand touched the Bible at her side, and Varina saw that constant use had almost worn it out.

"At times," Jane Pierce confided with a nervous glance over her shoulder, "I think God took my last boy so that Franklin would have no disturbance in his new duties. We sacrificed him to this new life." Varina shuddered at the words.

Almost always, in parting, the President's wife told her: "You're good for me, Varina. Don't ever stop coming." Varina promised herself she never would.

The tempo of Varina's life had gradually been accelerated. She had managed to fill the big house with pieces contributed by Margaret Howell from the furniture she was not using in New Orleans, and from Brierfield itself. She sent down for her finest possession, the great rosewood sofa her mother had given her, and placed it in the most prominent spot downstairs. She reflected often on the vicissitudes of that favorite sofa—Virginia to Mississippi, then Natchez to New Orleans, then back to Brierfield, and now Washington. Where next?

More than ever she found it easy to hold her own in the drawing-room discussions. Many women sat silent with fixed smiles on their faces while the men talked of political theory, the happenings in Poland, or touched on the classics. Varina could make contributions of her own and enjoy it when the men seemed surprised.

"Why, madame, you're very clever," a Cabinet member told her. "I wouldn't have expected it. You're so—so——" He stammered, and Varina colored pleasantly; in payment for the compliment she introduced him to the comeliest new arrival.

She was winning, too, a reputation as a sophisticate. But in spite of all this flattery she usually managed to bear in mind one of her first Washington lessons. No matter what they said to the contrary, men did not like a woman who knew too much. She tried to conceal her knowledge to some extent and thereby maintained a certain intellectual margin in favor of the man. It was, after all, a fictitious margin, but it was a device which increased Varina's popularity and indirectly Jeff's.

All too frequently Jeff was away from the capital on business. A Washingtonian of long residence told her: "No Secretary of War ever worked as hard as Mr. Davis." He found an ever-increasing volume of detail to occupy him. He was making a few enemies, Varina heard, by the way he insisted on passing on all phases of the department's work. There were whispers that Mr. Davis was jealous of his authority, that he hampered his subordinates. She went to him with the stories. "Jeff, even if there's nothing to them, wouldn't it be wiser——"

She got no farther. Jeff flared: "Whenever somebody thinks he can do my job better than I can, let him apply for it."

In any case, everybody agreed that Jeff was making a remarkable Secretary of War, one of the best in American history. A dowager repeated a joke to Varina: "Under Mr. Davis it's impossible for the government to be cheated out of a brass button." Then the lady added: "Still, I think he could attend my parties sometimes!"

Varina made a face; if only he would come to more of his wife's. He left for his office in the early morning; he had lunch brought there, and he stayed long after regular hours. No matter how late he returned for dinner, she saw to it that there was warm food on the fire. He was losing weight again. When she protested he shook his head. "I can rest later. There's too much to be done now."

She watched him stand up against political pressure. One evening, after he appointed a chief clerk, a Democratic delegation called. From the next room she heard the exchange. "Mr. Davis, they say you named a Whig to the place."

"Certainly not." There was anger in Jeff's voice.

"We *thought* you weren't aware of it," the reply came unctuously. "Mr. Goodloe is a Whig." The voice went on, explaining, urging. Then Jeff interrupted:

"Gentlemen, it's you who are deceived, not I. I appointed a *clerk*, neither a Democrat nor a Whig, but the man best qualified for the place. And I'm going to follow that rule in every case." The delegation left in a huff.

But later that week Jeff's "strict-construction" theories made her pause. He said to her very seriously: "I don't think we ought to send orders for flowers to the congressional greenhouse. Oh, I know a lot of officials do it. I'd rather not." The same day, when a War Department messenger called, Varina asked him to drop one of her parcels on the way back. Learning of it, Jeff reprimanded her. "Pat's services are for the department. Get another servant if yours aren't enough." He added, "Winnie," with a smile, and that took away some of the sting. Still she wished Jeff weren't always so uncompromising.

The Fourth of July arrived, and with it the occasion for a review of troops at Fortress Monroe in Virginia. Together with the President and several Cabinet members, Jeff and Varina made a leisurely excursion to the Virginia coast. With Maggie and Becket and the energetic Sam, Varina walked around the fortifications, with their thick walls impregnable against attack from land or sea. For Jeff, Fortress Monroe held a particular interest, for it was here that Black Hawk had finally died.

This was a great day for Jeff. On a big black horse he rode back and forth commanding the maneuvers. Varina was thrilled by the exclamations over his magnificent horsemanship, his air of easy control. The review ended after dark with a display of fireworks. Children shouted, the cannons pounded, and the ground trembled. After the rockets and flares had burst in all their glory two set pieces were touched off. The first of these carried the name of Franklin Pierce in brilliant lights. The second—and Varina caught her breath—read *Jefferson Davis*.

The President leaned over to her. "What do you think of that?" There was a boyish excitement on his handsome face. She had heard that he wanted to run again and that Jeff might be a possible running mate.

Her voice shook. "I don't have to tell you how I feel." On the way home she recalled Sam Houston's flamboyant prediction. President Jefferson Davis. Would it ever come true?

Jeff's duties as Secretary of War were not always as amicable as the occasion at Fortress Monroe. Trouble soon developed over Winfield Scott, commanding general of the Army. Old "Fuss and Feathers" was now serving under a Secretary of War whom he hated. Jeff was now giving direct orders to a general whom he referred to privately as "that pompous old antique." Their greetings were stiff, their communication very sparse. But the temperamental rooster had been accustomed to run the Army his own way, under a succession of mild Cabinet members. With a strong-minded Secretary of War in charge of the Army, Varina realized sparks would fly. General Scott touched off the fuse by refusing to secure Jeff's approval for travel expenditures.

"We'll make this a test case," Jeff cried savagely. "We'll see who's in charge here." Varina groaned; if Scott had tried deliberately, he could not have picked an approach better calculated to infuriate Jeff. Each held firm, issuing ultimatums, challenges of authority.

"How much does it come to?" Varina asked Jeff.

"Five hundred and seventy-seven dollars!" Jeff spoke as if it were five million.

Over that amount the Secretary of War was at swords' points with the general in charge of the Army. Here, Varina knew, was the making of a white-hot dispute that could injure them all. She had made up her mind. It was up to her to halt this feud and thus help Jeff in spite of himself.

Over breakfast she said innocently: "You know, I've never entertained General Scott." Jeff shook his head, but she persisted. "If I don't do it soon, there'll be gossip." Eventually, as she had expected, she won his consent.

Days before the dinner she began to make plans. She consulted her oldest Washington authority in making the seating arrangements. She arranged for an extra servant upstairs to keep the children invisible and silent. With the cuisine she took profound pains. The general, a terror among hostesses, was known to sneer when a dish did not please him, and wave it away as unfit for human beings.

At last the day of the dinner party arrived and she stood ready in the drawing room in close-fitting blue velvet, white-trimmed, the most formal of her costumes. The excitement of the event made her dark eyes glitter. Jeff, having taken his time dressing upstairs, gave her an enigmatic look. All the other guests arrived, and they waited together nervously. What had happened to the general? A half-hour passed, then another half-hour.

There was a great banging on the door and the general strode in, pushing the servant to one side. At her first glimpse of the military terror Varina's impulse was to laugh. She had never seen so much man, so big all over, and so enamored of itself. The general stood nearly six feet and a half tall in high-heeled boots, and he was proportionately wide. From the florid face, dominated by a big reddish nose and a mop of gray-white hair, his eyes peered with extravagant pride. His uniform was a fury of color, red and blue and gold braid, great plumes atop the cocked hat, and gold epaulets of an astonishing luxuriance.

Varina bowed. "Fuss and Feathers" made a majestic response. "Ma-dame!" She led him around the circle of the guests. Some of them he merely recognized coldly (such as Jeff, his host). Others he favored with a slight nod. Varina hastily gave the signal for supper. One of the servants brought the soup, and Varina leaned toward the general. "Your favorite kind."

General Scott glared, as if challenged. The company waited while the ancient relic lifted his spoon for a delicate sampling. Then, with a look of disgust, he dropped the utensil.

"Anything wrong?" Varina inquired.

"It is not good." The answer was almost bellowed. "It's useless for anyone except my cook to try to make that soup."

Varina's smile grew only more amiable. Despite herself she raised her voice a trifle. "That's odd, General. I went to your house today and had your cook prepare this." The general applied himself to the soup; she would have no more trouble with the curmudgeon.

It was a Sunday morning, January of 1854, and Varina and Jeff were watching the children as they played together on the floor. An unexpected holiday present had arrived the previous day. In the mailbox they found a letter from Joe Davis, his first communication in years. As if there had been no interruption in the family solidarity, Joe had written his brother a long, rambling note.

Jeff, his arm about her on the sofa, talked of the year ahead.

"Will it be easier than the last?" she asked dreamily.

"Maybe." He smiled. "In spite of what they say, things are rocking along."

She looked away; there had been a slight strain in relations between the two sections of the country, largely over the fugitive slave matter. And, as she had feared, Franklin Pierce had shown himself a blunderer, an indecisive man without marked strength of purpose. A saying had started: The winner in any contest was the man who reached the President last. She had resented it, but she now admitted to herself that it had an element of truth. Yet she found the President always charming, and certainly he had been good to Jeff.

"Please God," she whispered in prayer, "send us a good year, one free of worry."

She opened her eyes to find a servant standing before her. "Sen'tor Douglas for Mr. Davis." She felt her lips tighten. The more she saw of the blustering Westerner, the "Little Giant" of Illinois, the less she liked him, and she knew that Jeff had never revised his unfavorable opinion of the man.

"Do you have to see him?" she asked Jeff.

He nodded. "I won't be long."

Her husband was gone longer than he planned. Looking out of the window, she saw him leaving with Douglas. He didn't return for several hours, and when he finally joined her in the parlor he was noticeably excited.

"We've been to the White House!" he exclaimed. "Douglas has a new bill to organize the Nebraska Territory. The President wasn't sure at first; now the administration will back it all the way. The bill prohibits the people of a territory from acting on slavery either way until they decide to apply for admission as a state."

Varina's eyebrows went up. "Nebraska! Why, that's above the old Missouri line, where there's not supposed to be slavery!"

"Oh, I forgot to say," Jeff added impatiently, "the new bill will repeal the old Missouri line."

She still wasn't satisfied. "Banny, it all sounds too easy. Douglas is a hunter of votes—for himself; you've said that a lot of times. What does the South get from this, really?"

Jeff said quietly: "The right to bring slaves into a territory, like any other property—the thing I've contended for all along. The right to compete with the North to keep them there!"

Compete. She grasped at the word. "What a prospect that opens up. Didn't we all agree there was to be an end to competing, to fighting between one section and the other?"

But Jeff has started up the stairs, intent on carrying out the new scheme. Her feeling of premonition was growing.

Chapter 13

As varina stepped from her carriage near Jeff's office a group of men were arguing on the street corner, shaking fists, cursing. "The goddamned South! This whole Nebraska bill's a trick, a dirty outrage, to force the slaves down our throats!"

She hurried past them, her chin deep in her collar. The incident, though it shocked her, did not come as a surprise. She was on her way to show Jeff a paper just delivered at the house—a united protest from a caucus of Northern senators. Thousands of copies were being circulated about town, proclaiming that the new territorial scheme was a black repudiation of a solemn pledge of American honor, a gross violation of the old Missouri line. . . .

With this paper she carried something yet more ominous, a denunciation by several thousand ministers. The South, they said, was growing brazen again, reaching out to take the Union in its grip; the new bill was a crime before God. And Greeley, the New York editor who was growing more and more powerful, was exhorting his readers like a prophet of old to beware of the South and its intentions.

As she crossed the sidewalk Varina almost collided with an old friend. The woman clutched her arm. "Have you been hearing what the Yankees are saying? Why, the whole thing's a matter of principle. They've been waiting for a thing like this—a chance to strike at us."

"Yes?" Varina replied coolly. "Then why give them the chance?" The woman stared in astonishment, and Varina continued on her way. A few minutes later she sat in Jeff's office while he read the papers she had brought him.

"It's bad," she told him, her voice breaking. "The whole dispute's been revived, after everybody agreed it was compromised!"

He shook his head wearily. "I expected something of the sort, though not as violent. Still, I don't think they'll get far with this —this screaming propaganda."

She tried to argue. "Call it what you want, Jeff, it's started people all over again——"

"Winnie," he interrupted, "this issue has to be settled. The question of the new territory can't hang in the air forever. Anyway, it's too late for the administration to change its stand. We're committed to it." His eyes took on a new intensity. "And don't forget —our party's in control, and we're going to carry this out the right way, our way!"

Her mouth dropped. Here was no longer the man who had talked to her of harmony, of great projects that were above sectional prejudice. The unrelenting Jeff, the man who followed Calhoun and his zealot's programs, had returned. And this bill had been concocted that Sunday morning at her house. Had she been able to see Jeff before the decision was made, had she argued with him in advance, might it have been different? But it was useless to think about that.

She rose to go, her skirts murmuring about her.

During the harried months that followed, little Sam suddenly became very sick. He had been ill for several days, but there was no indication that his condition was serious.

Jeff bent over the bed, his hand stroking the burning head with its thick light hair. "Mama! Hot!" The child was kicking at the covers.

As Varina strove to quiet the baby Jeff whispered: "The doctor just left. The fever's gone way up and there's some intestinal inflammation." He was more disturbed than he meant to show.

For days Varina stayed in the child's room, sleeping on the sofa near him, rising when he called. He improved a little, but soon the fever returned. For an hour or two he would be in a lively mood, reaching for his toys, catching at Varina's hand. Then he fell back, and the playthings dropped to the floor. "Mama! Hot! Hot!" The moan echoed through the rooms.

"If only we were somewhere else," she muttered to Jeff. "Anyplace but this stifling city, with the stench from the water." It was late June, and she was remembering that other broiling day when Zachary Taylor died. But they could hardly move Sam now, and she knew it. Her eyes went back to the child, to the almost transparent skin, to the bones that showed skeleton-like against the sheets. Nothing must happen to Sam! It couldn't. They'd planned so much for him!

One afternoon while Jeff was leaning over the crib little Sam opened his eyes and recognized his father.

"Sing my song. My song," he pleaded. Jeff hesitated, and then he began to sing very softly the Indian lullaby: "Cora wankee shangmonee . . ."

After a while the rhythm of Sam's breathing told them he was asleep. Without premeditation they both dropped to their knees and prayed.

They were still in prayer when the President entered with Mrs. Pierce. The two women went together to the next room, and there Jane, who had suffered so badly in the loss of her own three children, tried to comfort Varina. "Please, please, don't worry so," she begged in much the same tone Varina had used in trying to console her during those first days in the White House. As Jane talked Varina suddenly became aware that the house was completely silent. Jeff came to the door of the room, his knuckles white against the frame. "Winnie——" he began. "Sam's gone." As she sobbed she recalled that scene on the gallery at Brierfield and the old Negro who had said: "Baby Sam, you never gon' work!" The words had come true; her baby would not know the cares of this existence.

In the political world the fury over slavery and the Nebraska bill was spreading and there was trouble with Spain over Cuba. Nothing went as Jeff had hoped, but Varina paid little heed. She turned her back on Washington City. When callers came she greeted them with dulled eyes. Had God struck at her as a punishment for pride or self-will?

Her sister Maggie, in her new, longer dresses, hovered nervously about her, bringing toilet water and headache powders. "Let me bathe your forehead, Varina; rest here awhile." Maggie was gaining in dignity and understanding. Already she reminded Varina of their mother, continually bustling about, helping everybody in the household. Now twelve, she was developing a habit of talking quickly, like Margaret Howell herself.

Sometimes Varina's pain seemed unbearable. At the sound of Jeff's returning steps she remembered how Sam used to run to meet him at the door. When evening came she thought again of the times she had given little Sam his bath and put him to bed. Yet she had one consolation—her second child was growing within her.

Through all of a chill January and February she stayed restlessly in her room, awaiting this second baby. Nothing must happen to this one, nothing! When she slipped one evening on a rug, an agony of fear ran through her. Please, God, spare her any injury.

When her time came, Jeff, disregarding urgent messages from the war office, stayed in the house, walking up and down outside Varina's door, nervously clasping and unclasping his hands. Inside she lay moaning softly. The doctor, listening, heard her say: "Mustn't fail Jeff, mustn't." Pain tore through her body and she lapsed into coma. When she woke Jeff was beside her. "A girl," he whispered.

"Good," she sighed. "Can we call her Margaret, for my mother? I've always wanted——" She could say no more.

"Of course," Jeff assured her. "Of course."

For hours Jeff sat beside the new baby, his lean face calm again, the shadows lighter beneath his eyes. Margaret was a plump baby, with wiry hair that would almost certainly be as dark as her mother's, placid brown eyes, and a disposition that struck Varina as oddly serious.

"She's as earnest as you are," she told Jeff as the child slept in her bassinet.

"And she has a will like yours." Jeff grinned.

Jeff held the baby in his arms with a look of love that had something of desperation in it. If anything happened to this one, Varina thought, Jeff could not stand it, nor could she.

Once she was sitting in her room as Jeff started the plaintive Indian lullaby that he had sung so often to the dead Sam. After the first few words an abrupt silence fell; the memory must have been tormenting.

After that he never attempted it again.

The coming of little Margaret, who was soon nicknamed Polly, marked another change for Varina. She soon began to resume the life she had led before Sam died. "I've got to spruce up this house," she told Jane Pierce, "get rid of the atmosphere of gloom. And I want to see people again!" She superintended an intensive house cleaning, added new carpets and draperies. She and Jeff entertained once more.

Although President Pierce forced through the new bill, it only increased the administration's troubles over territorial legislation. Varina tried not to listen to the shouts of dissension and thought instead of the progress Jeff was making in the War Department. He told her excitedly that they had approved the new equipment, with the improved rifles; that thousands of men were being added to the Army, and top rankings were going to Robert Lee and to Albert Sidney Johnston, his long-time friend in the West. Moreover, the first retirement system was introduced.

"It will cause a lot of grief," he admitted to Varina. "But the Army's going to be the best we've ever had."

Jeff was also making progress in his demand for camels, though few people in Washington City could talk about them with a straight face.

"Why not try them—make an experiment?" he pleaded.

He got the funds, and a mission was dispatched to the Far East to find the best animals, learn all it could about them, and transport them to the Western plains.

"If you have anything to do with it"—Varina smiled—"the West will look like Arabia."

"And why not?" Jeff asked. With him it was no joking matter.

Varina was not too sanguine about the camels, but she was deeply interested in Jeff's plan for a Pacific railroad. After his office closed in the afternoon young engineers were beginning to come to the house with reports of Western exploration, thousands of pages of documents, tales of strange birds that swept like death over the deserts, peculiar rocks that men had never seen, springs that steamed high in the air.

As she listened Varina's eyes sparkled. "Jeff, this is information of a sort that most people have never dreamed of—a whole new Western world!" He nodded. "And the more they find out about this, the better for your plan?" This time he looked at her and grinned.

After that she planned her dinners carefully. On the same nights that the explorers called she brought in senators and representatives. To these she added a sprinkling of scientists, members of the Smithsonian Institution, geologists, geographers. Occasionally Jeff returned from the Capitol elated.

"It looks as if Congress is going to do something at last about the railroad." He would beam. But the surveys went on and nothing definite came of them. The increasing agitation over the territories was overshadowing everything else.

One evening at a party which Jeff could not attend, Varina met a handsomely dressed woman about her own age, with a rippling voice and gay manner. "Mrs. Joseph Johnston, the colonel's wife," a friend told her. Varina had heard a great deal about this energetic lady who led her own capital set. Lydia Johnston's greeting was hearty, and there was an unhidden curiosity in her eyes.

"Mrs. Davis! So many people have mentioned you; I'd hoped we'd be introduced. You're a Western belle, aren't you?"

There was an awkward pause. Despite herself, Varina was taken back; it was some time since she had heard the word "Western" applied to herself. Then she remembered that Lydia Johnston was from Virginia, which still tended to regard the Mississippi River as rather a frontier. Mrs. Johnston, realizing the mistake she had made, immediately made up for it. "We Virginians are sometimes rather provincial, you know." And she started to tell an amusing story about her husband.

Varina liked the forthright Lydia from then on. Publicly or privately, they laughed at much the same things and they enjoyed each other's company. No one would have called Lydia Johnston a beauty, but she had tact and style and wit.

It was not until several weeks later that Varina met Joseph E. Johnston. At first glance she recognized him as a complex person, one who would not reveal himself with ease. He was a short, solidly built man who wore a mustache and a goatee, and he was beginning to get bald. He introduced himself and smiled. "Lydia has spoken of you. I trust my wife's judgment—and follow it."

A little later that evening one of the men at the party made a facetious remark about "Army attitude," and Varina saw Joe

Johnston flush and grow furious. For the rest of the evening he was grim and tight-lipped, unwilling or unable to regain his sense of humor. Varina was amazed at the touchiness of the man. She saw him often from then on, and most of the time he seemed overly stern, almost dour. She learned that Joe Johnston had a reputation for such behavior.

"People like him," she told Jeff, "but he certainly seems to carry a chip on his shoulder."

Jeff, who had known Joe Johnston from West Point days, had the same opinion. "He's a man who thinks more about the Army and his career than any I've ever met. If Joe has anything to do with it, he'll go a far distance." From her husband's manner she gathered that he had no great affection for the man. Yet they got along well enough in public, and she found herself becoming more and more friendly with Lydia.

Some months later a delegation of rabid Southern sympathizers had called on him.

"Do you know what they wanted?" Jeff cried, still bristling from that meeting. "They were discreet, but they made it clear enough. They asked me to favor certain Southern states in fortifications, supplies, and assignments"—his face darkened with anger—"as a 'protection for the future.' I told them my job was to serve the whole country; I took an oath to that effect. And as long as I hold this office I'll serve the country without favoring any one section against another."

Varina was so proud of him she could hardly speak. This was the Jeff she would always love and admire, the man who could not compromise with dishonor. She tried to tell him how she felt, but he abruptly changed the subject.

"We're sending a mission to observe the Crimean War," he told her. "I envy the boys who are going. Someday our Army will be making good use of the things they'll learn. They'll be studying weapons we've never seen, and new techniques." He frowned. "We're having a little trouble, though, in getting final passes and permissions from the two governments."

She thought for a moment and then offered a solution: "How about a dinner for the ambassadors and the mission too? We've smoothed out other things at our dinner table, haven't we?"

The invitations went out almost at once. Though Jeff scowled, she included General Winfield Scott. Whether through her efforts or for other reasons, an uneasy peace continued between the two men. She hoped that the difficult old warrior would refuse, but he came, practically ignoring Jeff, while paying elaborate compliments to her.

Included in the dinner party was Captain George McClellan, a stocky, swarthy young man who had caught Jeff's attention in his explorations in the West. Varina had met him once or twice before.

"I think we'll be hearing a lot in the future from this McClellan," Jeff said. "He's one of the most promising of the young officers on the Crimean mission."

Varina found that McClellan had a manner which approached timidity. When others addressed him he colored, and he had little small talk on any subject. She went to work to make him feel at ease. She introduced him to the ambassadors, placed him next to the most poised of the women guests. Even with Winfield Scott on hand, the dinner started off very well. Then, during a lull in the conversation, Varina heard young McClellan talking quietly to the girl beside him about traprock in the West. The expansive Scott, at the word "trap," pointed his fork. "No, sir! I say no. Buffalo are never caught in a trap!"

McClellan sat transfixed, his dark face very pale. General Scott was hardly an officer whom subordinates, especially captains, corrected in public. Others tried to explain, but the general ignored them and shouted at McClellan: "Captain, I tell you I've never heard of buffalo taken in traps!"

When the meal ended an hour later the general was still discoursing on the subject; thereafter, whenever she thought of shy young McClellan, she remembered him as he sat there hunched over his plate, misery in his eyes. There was, she decided, more than mere pomposity and eccentricity in Scott's behavior; at least a little malice was involved. Someday, she hoped, the junior officer would be able to pay back the older one for that evening's torture.

It was shortly after that dinner party that Jeff's truce with General Scott came to an abrupt end when the old soldier claimed a large back payment for his Mexican War activities. Jeff blocked the payment, and it was substantially reduced to Scott's intense annoyance. Congress raised Scott's rank and he promptly asked for back salary amounting to twenty-six thousand dollars.

Two days later Jeff came home early, his face twisted in anger. "The President's given in to Scott. I can't stay in the government and keep my respect!"

"What do you mean?"

"I mean I'm resigning, today."

She sank into the chair opposite him. "Please, Banny, think of all your plans—the railroad, the new Army. And the family——"

With quiet desperation she argued for hours, and at last she succeeded. Jeff reached over and slowly signed the order in Scott's favor. Then, his mouth tightening, he added the statement that he still considered it wrong! How like Jeff, she thought, smiling weakly.

Varina heard rumors of trouble in the administration, but late that month she was surprised when the President himself paid her a visit. His handsome face was worn, his shoulders slumped.

"I need a refuge," he told her hoarsely. "Just a little quiet for a while. They're hounding me to death over there."

As soon as she could she placed a tray before him with warm food and milk. He ate and drank gratefully, speaking meanwhile in broken phrases, as if to himself. "I never thought—thought it would be like this. . . . That job will kill any man." Then he grew silent. His chin dropped on his chest and he dozed.

She remembered the rumors his enemies were always circulating: The President was drinking heavily; he had appeared in a befogged condition at a public meeting. They weren't true, she was certain. The man looked dog-tired and close to exhaustion. She tiptoed toward the door. Before she reached it Franklin Pierce woke from his light sleep and with a murmured apology made his departure. What a change had come over the gentle statesman of that reception at the White House.

When Jeff returned he explained why the President was in such a state. "It's that same trouble about the territories. We put over our bill, of course, but at what a price. . . ." The new territory had been divided in half, into Kansas and Nebraska. A furor had broken out over the lower region, Kansas. A race had started between North and South to see which would populate it. In New

England emigrants' aid societies were being formed, with the help of the ministers and such men as Editor Horace Greeley. From the South, slaveholders, egged on by their papers, were rushing toward the goal.

"They're killing one another every day," Jeff groaned. "Rioting, grabbing land, ambushing people, slaughtering women and children." Slowly, the pain showing in his face, he broke the news she had expected: "It looks as if the President can't be re-elected. The bill's aroused too many hatreds. . . ."

And so the man who had tried to please everybody had ended by pleasing very few of them. Senator Stephen Douglas might have been guilty of tricking Jeff and Franklin Pierce with his Nebraska scheme, but it was more probable that none of them had quite understood the resentments which would be stirred up by that bill.

"There are some times, Winnie, when I wish I had never taken a job in the administration. No matter what you do, it turns out wrong."

He took an envelope out of his pocket, opened it, and handed her a letter. "They want me to run for the Senate again. The legislature's to pick a new man soon." His voice was low, doubtful. "It's been a long time since I faced an election in Mississippi."

He gave her a searching look. "How do you feel about it?"

She thought of Brierfield, the white fields under the sun, the low flights of birds. She remembered that defeated politicians usually retired to their homes. Her chin lifted. "How do I feel? Take the chance, of course!"

Before the month was up she wondered if she had been right. A letter arrived from Joe Davis saying that it was going to be a tight race. For one thing, his post in Washington had kept Jeff away from the Mississippians too long. He was out of touch with them and they with him. For another thing, the legislature was split and a handful of ballots might settle it.

On the day of the contest they stayed awake until after midnight and then decided it was too late to get the returns that night. They went to bed, though neither could get to sleep. Suddenly Varina sat up in bed. Someone was banging on the outer door below. She ran down to receive a telegram and tear it open. ". . . a tie; no one would change, until chairman cast deciding vote—for Mr. Davis." It was hardly the victory for which they had hoped, but Jeff would be going back to the Senate, and his voice would be heard again.

There remained the national election, and they waited together tensely for the result.

"The Democrats have won!" She cried the news up the stairway to Jeff, but his face clouded when he compared the figures. A new, third party had come forward—the Republicans—and their vote was amazingly large.

Jeff made a grimace. "A conglomeration of discontents, reformers, Abolitionists, free-soilers, and Horace Greeley followers—haters of the South, all of them!" With a shiver Varina drew her shawl tighter. The days of uncertainty were upon them again.

Whenever she felt glum, Varina remembered: A new baby was forming inside her. The barren years had ended. . . . Then one day she grew upset when a letter arrived in Annabelle's scrawl.

Harry Mounger was dead. Three weeks before, as he was sawing in the swamp at Brierfield, a tree had fallen, crushing his chest. He died soon after Annabelle reached him. So Harry, the black man who had labored so hard for them, was gone—Harry, who had seen his first wife and children taken from him, and then his other child die at birth. Varina lived again that day along the road when she had found the runaway waiting against the tree. . . . She read on: Annabelle found that things were not the same without Harry; it had been a long time since she saw "my fambly," the Davises, and she hoped she could serve them in Washington.

Jeff sent for her immediately, and when she came clumping in the back door the years seemed to drop away from Varina. At the first sight of her old helper's miserable face, tense and worn after the long journey, Varina caught her in her arms. Both were crying, and it was some time before they could speak.

"You're a little peaked," Varina told her.

Annabelle, shaken as she was, could still joke. "An' you lookin' pret' bad you'se'f!"

She was looking with amusement at Varina's ungainly figure, for the new baby would arrive within a few weeks.

Annabelle waddled into the kitchen. Soon she was back, coffee-pot in hand, sniffing. "Dey say dis coffee. I see how much you needs me up here!"

Varina smiled; yes, Annabelle's presence would make things easier for them all.

The child was overdue. Varina was listless and dispirited. She could hardly get up in the morning, and Annabelle, expert in such matters, was clicking her tongue. The doctor arrived and Varina, straining her ears, made out some of the words: "Complications . . . difficult birth." When Jeff came back, the line of his jaw showing through his skin, she knew that another crisis lay ahead for her.

The thermometer dropped. Snow was drifting steadily, day after day, against the house and on the street. As Varina tossed in her bed the day grew darker and a high wind shook the house from cellar to roof. The children watched from the windows in fascination. It was a blizzard, one of the worst in Washington's history.

Varina, left alone for a moment, began to whimper softly and then to scream. By the time Jeff and Annabelle reached her she was almost out of bed and the blankets had fallen to the floor. With firm hands Jeff forced her down and threw the covers over her again. Then she was crying hysterically: "I'm smothering! The snow's all over me, all over. . . ."

Her eyes stared glassily at nothing. When Annabelle caught her hands she found them icy.

Alarmed, Jeff cried out to the other servants, and the butler and two maids came running. Annabelle quickly gave them orders: "Warm water, towels, an' de quickes' you can git 'em!"

She spoke sharply, too, to Jeff. "Ef you know where 'at doctor is, we need 'im fas'!"

For an hour the colored woman hovered over the writhing figure on the bed. The Negro girls ran up and down stairs, carrying supplies. Annabelle, moving in the shifting candlelight, threw a grotesque shadow on the white wall. Above Varina's deep groans and Annabelle's agitated mutterings came the howl of the air.

"Lawd God"—Annabelle was weeping—"what kin I do now? Ev'thin' I know, and not enough . . ."

Finally the doctor arrived, dropped his snow-caked coat in the hall, and rushed upstairs to Varina's room. He sent Jeff out, gave whispered instructions to Annabelle, and for another hour the two remained at the bedside. Then, during a momentary lull in the whining of the wind, the baby came. It was a boy, small but healthy.

"Praise de Lawd," cried Annabelle.

In a few minutes, however, they were giving all of their attention to Varina. The doctor stayed by her, muttering swift directions. Once when Varina lay very still the Negro woman began to weep.

"It's all ovah, all ovah . . ."

"Quiet!" the doctor hissed at her. "We've got work to do."

Only toward dawn did he let up, and as he left the room he told Jeff: "She's been pretty low, but she has the will to carry through, I think. I'll be back."

That day silence dropped over the town. The wind and snowfall stopped, but Washington City lay under the thickest covering it had known in decades. All street traffic halted and roadways were blocked for miles. Like every one else, the Davises were isolated.

No word arrived from the doctor, who lived across town. The baby appeared well, but Varina's fever had increased. "What we gonna do?" Annabelle turned toward Jeff, while the servants stared apprehensively from the doorway. There was nothing they could do, for Washington was snowbound. Jeff paced nervously up and down the room.

"Banny, Banny . . ." Her words were almost undistinguishable. "I feel so—so poorly. . . ."

The padded stillness had grown yet more pronounced; they seemed to be inside a great white vacuum.

Suddenly Varina sat up in bed. "Listen!" she cried. "Listen, they're coming."

Jeff tried to quiet her, but she shook her head.

"No, Jeff, it's no nightmare. I can hear a sleigh."

To satisfy her he went to the window. There, sure enough, was a heavy drag sled drawn by a pair of magnificent horses coming slowly toward them through the drifts.

A few minutes later one of Varina's women friends stamped in brandishing a box of drugs from the doctor. "He managed to send these to me and told me to try to get here with them." She waved a hand toward the driver, who had followed her diffidently into the house. He was bundled up to the ears, but his ugly face appeared vaguely familiar to Jeff.

"If it hadn't been for him," the woman exclaimed, "I'd never have gotten here. When he heard about your trouble he volunteered and saw that we got through." She stopped in surprise. "Oh, you haven't met? Mr. Davis, Mr. Seward."

It was William Seward, the fervent Northerner, who had worked against Jeff and his party for these many years. Of all the people in Washington, he had come to Varina's aid.

When she was told about Seward's visit several days later, Varina was recovering rapidly.

"And to think"—she smiled at Jeff—"I've always thought of Seward as a devil. I guess I've been wrong about him. Right now he seems to me much more like a saint."

Chapter 14

THERE IT WAITED, WHITE AND SHADED, HER BRIERFIELD. THE ROOF
was showing signs of wear, and several of the overhanging trees had
fallen in storms that broke over the delta land. But it was her
house, and even the natural fragrance of the place seemed familiar.
She walked through the garden, less bountiful than in the days
when Harry Mounger watched over it. Yet the rosebushes were in
bloom along the brick walks, and the Pilot's Wife, now a heavy
apricot tree, grew sturdier with the seasons.

She came back to the gallery to join Jeff and review the file of
servants which had been assembled to greet them. "John . . . Jack
. . . Charles . . . Big Marie . . . Myra Number Two." She was
puzzled by the new faces she did not recognize and the absence of
some of her favorites. Her eyes met Jeff's. "We've been away longer
than I realized."

Afterward she and Annabelle settled little Polly and the new
baby, who had been christened Jeff, and then she went through
the rooms of her house. Hastily aired, it still smelled of damp
neglect. There were gaps where pieces of furniture such as the rosewood sofa had been removed and sent to Washington City. The
rooms, after those in the capital, looked small, the furnishings
plainer than she remembered. She passed the library, where she
and Jeff had spent their long evenings together. She picked up a
book, still lying on the table, which she could almost recite by
heart, so often had she read it to Jeff. Yes, she was home again.

She heard the wheels of a heavy carriage approaching up the
drive, and before she could reach the gallery Joe Davis walked in
the door, his head high, a grin showing above the graying beard.

Behind him moved a procession: Eliza Davis, tremulous in her pleasure at the moment; Florida McCaleb, a warm smile on her face; cousins, nephews, and other relations. It was Varina's first meeting with Joe Davis in years. She had hoped to pass off the occasion as easily as possible, but Joe made a ceremony of it. He took Jeff's arm and Varina's as well.

"The family's together again, at last," he announced, as if to an audience. "Everything's going to be the same, isn't it, Varina?"

She smiled uncomfortably. Actually, between her and Joe things wouldn't be quite the same; neither of them expected that. Then she remembered that she had handled malicious dowagers in Washington, spinsters who took no pains to conceal their jealousy, professional opponents of her husband. If she had to draw on every reserve of tact, she would see to it that this night went by without incident.

When Joe had marched off with Jeff she took Eliza into a corner. Shyly her sister-in-law told her: "Washington's done a lot for you, Varina." Her tired eyes showed her admiration, her happiness that Varina and Jeff had made a success of these recent years.

It was true, Varina realized. Her own world had shifted several times, but along this edge of the Mississippi things went as always, in an atmosphere of somnolence.

That night as Varina combed her black hair she studied the look of strain beneath her eyes, the depressions in her cheeks, the new lines at her throat. She still showed signs of her recent illness. Some of the damage she could repair by using her mother's old recipes of cream and custard, but she needed a long rest too. She would have to have all her strength, she suspected, for the days ahead after their return to Washington.

The next day Jeff started off on a canvass of the state. She and Annabelle, with one of the other girls, were busy working on the curtains when there came a knock on the door. A handsome young Negro entered, and for a moment she failed to recognize him. Then she smiled. "Of course. You're John Pemberton, aren't you?" He nodded seriously. It had been a long time since she thought of John, but now she recalled the morning at his father's grave, when he had mentioned his hope of buying his freedom someday.

"Are you still saving your money, John?"

He showed his pleasure at her question. "Oh, yes'm, tha's what

I'm here for to see you about." His embarrassment grew; he tugged nervously at his belt.

To help him Varina added: "How much do you have?"

"T'ree hun'ed dollars and twelve cents. An' I'm gittin' more. I raises stuff and sells it all the time!"

Varina ignored the disapproving frown on Annabelle's face and looked at the boy with new respect. "That's fine, John. To think, at your age . . . You keep it up, and eventually we'll ask Mr. Davis, I promise you."

John's eyes fell. "Well, I'll wait some longer." He must have hoped for more definite word, but Varina wondered if she could have said more. That would be up to Jeff. What would it cost— twelve hundred dollars, fifteen hundred or more? In any case, the boy had made a good start.

When John Pemberton left, Annabelle sniffed. "He sure ain' like old James, dat 'un. Buyin' himse'f free!"

Varina returned to her sewing. He was different, yes. After a while, however, she said: "Everything's changing, Annabelle. The boy's been trained, and he's making a beginning for himself."

Annabelle's lower lip jutted out farther than ever. "Dat ain' my kine, dat 'un. Humph!"

Varina was in the sewing room when Jeff returned to Brierfield toward the end of the month. He bounded up the stairs, threw his arms about her, and upset her sewing things all over the floor. "Winnie, these people are furious at the North, angrier than I've ever seen them! Down here they're ready for anything. Once, I suppose, I got ahead of them, back in the time of Clay's compromise." His face wrinkled. "Now I'm afraid I've lagged behind. When you have time I want you to help me with a few letters."

He dictated one message after another, and Varina's face grew a little troubled. As he paced the floor, his nostrils dilating, his mind working rapidly, there was still no outright defiance in what he said. And yet, subtly, a new tone had intruded itself—or was it the old one that he had adopted in that feverish period that had ended with his defeat? She thought once more of Mr. Calhoun and his influence. Was he beginning to speak again through Jeff? . . . Through the open window she made out a line of field workers bending low over the cotton plants. Slavery, slavery—would it and its questions haunt them all their lives?

He stopped. "Well, we'll see what develops." At least, then, his mind was not made up. She dropped the pen and looked down at the note she had just finished. On the desk near it was one in Jeff's handwriting, but the two letters looked as if they had been written by the same person.

Some time back, copying message after message from his original, she had found herself writing just as he did, the same unornamented letters, the identical short circles. She could not say just how or when she had started, but by this time her script was very close to his. One or two people, getting a letter from her, had told her how nice it was that Mr. Davis took time to write personal notes. She smiled. It would be a help to Jeff; she needed no other motive. . . .

As the weeks went by there were answers to the letters, hurried conferences at Brierfield, and Jeff seemed more and more impatient to get back into action. At last the time came for the Senate to reconvene and they took the long and tiresome journey north. Washington City looked unchanged to Varina. Though out of the Cabinet, Jeff continued a figure in Washington, a force in the administration. Now he was laboring with a fury beyond human endurance. Varina wondered if he was trying to make up for the years he had lost away from Congress, or whether he was merely searching for facts to settle his own doubts. He seemed driven, harried, as if the South's whole cause depended on him. A coffeepot at his side, he bent over books on agriculture, treatises on slavery, volumes about Northern industry. Keeping Polly and the baby Jeff as quiet as she could, Varina took up part of his burden whenever she managed to find the time.

Jeff had caught a severe cold on the way up to the capital. He didn't seem to shake it off, and she soon noticed that he was pressing his hand against his forehead.

"Is anything wrong?" she asked.

He shook his head. At two o'clock in the morning, when she went to the children, he was still at work. He rose the next morning, nerve-racked, his eyes bloodshot. She watched him that day and the next as he grew more agitated and more irritable. She dosed him with every remedy she had in the house. He improved a little, but he refused to take the hours of rest that he needed above everything else.

"Well," she told Annabelle, "at least I can keep pouring medicine into him and hold off a real sickness." But she wasn't sure how long she could do it.

The next morning, soon after he left for the Senate, she called the maid. "I'm going to Capitol Hill for a while." There she found a seat behind the rail in the Senate gallery. She had barely settled herself before she was witnessing the kind of incident she had feared.

Jeff was arguing with his colleague, Senator Judah Benjamin of Louisiana, an able lawyer-planter who had been a casual friend of his for some time. As Jeff spoke he gradually assumed an air of haughtiness, of disdain. His words became ever sharper, and a taut silence came over the chamber.

Benjamin, normally one of the most easygoing members of the Senate, reddened and said bitterly: "It's very easy for the senator to give a sneering reply to a respectful question."

Jeff faced about and remarked coldly: "I consider that an attempt to misrepresent a plain remark."

"That's enough, sir!" Benjamin cried.

Whispers went around the room. Jeff glared at Benjamin and sat down.

Varina waited until the session was over and Jeff had joined her in the gallery. He was greatly disturbed. He looked about for Mr. Benjamin, but the Louisianian had gone.

"I made a mistake," he told Varina. "I'm sorry already."

They had hardly reached home before a stranger rang the bell to hand Jeff a formal challenge from Mr. Benjamin. The next day, as the session opened, Jeff stood up.

"I was in error yesterday," he said in a firm voice. "I acted thoughtlessly, unfairly, and I want to apologize to the senator from Louisiana."

Mr. Benjamin responded gracefully, and Varina saw the two men shake hands; she was as proud of her husband as she had been at any time in her life. At the end of the day she sought out Mr. Benjamin. "Won't you come to dinner with us?" she asked him, hoping to show how grateful she was for the generous way in which he had settled the difference. Mr. Benjamin accepted with alacrity.

A trifle constrained at the start, the dinner gained in enjoyment as it progressed. She liked the charm of the heavily jowled Benjamin, his pleasant voice, the quiet understanding in his dark eyes. He was one of many Jews for whom she felt admiration. She tried to remember what she had heard about him. Born poor, he had made his way to Creole Louisiana, forced his way up by merit and also, perhaps, by adaptability and a winning personality. There'd been some gossip behind the fans about an unfortunate marriage. He had a gay, well-born wife who preferred to live alone in France. . . .

Tonight the three of them talked of everything but that one subject, and now and then, beneath Mr. Benjamin's banter, she thought she sensed an undertone of sadness.

"Life," he assured her with a lift of his hand, "it's never what one hopes. Doesn't the wise man do what he can and accept the rest?" Mr. Benjamin, she guessed, was accepting the rest. The heavy lids dropped; behind them lay a culture, a seasoned wisdom that were new to her.

Early the next week she and Jeff were guests of Mr. Benjamin. The food was succulent, prepared with imagination, served with Old World grace. She marveled at the man's deft and brilliant conversation; as she sat there she felt gauche. Jeff, though he looked very tired, was stimulated. Mr. Benjamin, she thought, brought out the best qualities in his guests.

At one point in the evening the Louisianian turned to her, the attention in his liquid eyes a compliment in itself. "But I want to hear what you have to say about that." And she discovered that he possessed the art of listening as well as the art of talking.

It was Senator Benjamin who, just before they left that night, first alarmed her over Jeff's eye condition.

"Don't tell him I suggested it," he murmured. "But please get him to a doctor. I know what that trouble is like. For a long time I had to give up everything to rest my sight. Believe me . . ."

She left in a haze of uncertainty. Yet she led up to the matter as they were going to bed. Jeff waved it away. "I've survived worse than this cold and inflammation."

The next morning she found him much worse, the face badly inflamed, both eyes swollen, the left one filmed over. He opened his mouth, and no words came. Motioning for a pad of paper, he scribbled a message: "Please—call somebody." Running downstairs, she dispatched Annabelle for a doctor. Racing back, she brought water, liquids, cloths, anything to reduce the inflammation. The doctor was a long time coming, and for hours she stayed at Jeff's side, working desperately.

She was there early that evening when three doctors, the other two hastily summoned by their family practitioner, held a consultation. They lifted him into a chair beside the window and looked carefully at his eye. He winced in agony as they examined him, but she held tightly to his hand.

One of the doctors finally said: The cornea has ulcerated. . . . Also, he has facial neuralgia with complications." He paused. "I don't see why the eye hasn't burst already."

At this Jeff reached for the pad to write: "My wife saved it!" As she stood beside him, the gaze of the doctors upon her, she realized that this was only the beginning of another long siege.

For two months at least Jeff would have to live in a darkened room. Whether he would ever fully regain the sight of the left eye, the doctors could not tell. As during those earlier years at Brierfield, he now slept during the day and walked the dim parlors by night. For days she left his side only when the children needed her. Maggie and Becket, her sister and brother, went promptly to school in the morning under Annabelle's direction. Varina looked in occasionally on little Polly and the baby Jeff in the nursery. Sometimes she took the baby in to see his father, for the doctors recommended these visits if they weren't too long. Jeff, eyes covered, reached out hungrily and held him at his side, whispering, caressing him.

"Don't take him," he would appeal to her. "A little longer." And the baby, clutching at Jeff's thin finger, was content to stay.

The doorbell never seemed to stop ringing. Apparently all Washington wanted to learn about Jeff's condition. But there were some notable exceptions, such as General Scott and Senator Andrew Johnson. Until now she had not quite realized the general respect her husband had won. Many of his opponents were calling. That anxious, twisted little man, Alexander Stephens of Georgia, who had differed strongly from Jeff on many a measure, came regularly. Northern dignitaries, known to her mainly through their attacks on slavery, arrived in delegations. Joe Johnston and his witty wife Lydia, Mr. Benjamin, Robert Lee . . . Gratefully she read the cards.

Yet the most regular of them turned out to be Mr. Seward of New York, the gaunt-faced Abolitionist. One of their Texas friends, spying Mr. Seward in the hall, couldn't believe his eyes. The New Yorker had first appeared in their lives in Varina's hour of danger. He reappeared now that Jeff was sick. In the earlier period Jeff had found much to talk over with the ungainly philosopher-agitator. Now Mr. Seward sat daily for a long time at Jeff's bedside.

She listened, in the room or through the half-opened doorway, as Seward summarized the day's events carefully, often with pungent humor: "Your side outtalked ours; you would've enjoyed it, but I didn't." Or, "We put you in the shade today." And Varina heard the two men laughing together. Might there not be hope for peace in a country where two men, so firmly opposed on the main issues, could meet so happily?

Family opinion of Mr. Seward was divided. Becket, the gangling youth who had little in the way of conversational skill, disliked the man intensely. On the other hand, Maggie found him wonderful. "He knows so much," she told them, "and about so many things!" Varina reflected that he had a remarkable way of fitting himself to the mood and the interests of almost anyone he met. It was a fascinating thing to watch, and yet Varina never quite understood Mr. Seward, though she did like him. In some things he appeared too direct, in others cynical, almost devious. He smiled disarmingly one day and then said something that shocked her: "With me the ends justify the means. I decide my goal; everything must serve it." When he told her that, his eyes took fire in a way that reminded her of Jeff's. Yet how different they really were!

Through it all William Seward was as sympathetic with human pain as anyone she had ever known. As he descended the stairs one day he faced Varina. "He mustn't lose the eye! He's such a splendid figure of a man. . . ." Many times in the days that followed, as Mr. Seward stormed at the "slavocracy," Varina thought of that remark.

Slowly Jeff improved, and now he could work in a half-darkened room. She had to tell him then that the sight would never wholly return to the bad eye. He would be able to make out dim shapes with it, but that was all the doctors promised.

He took it more easily than she had anticipated. After a moment a thin smile crossed his face. "Well, I'll have your two good ones to make up for it." It was the conventional answer, but it reassured her. The damage, she told herself, was barely noticeable. Many people, meeting Jeff, never guessed.

The doctors wanted him to remain away from all duties, but one night word arrived that a friend's position in Congress was endangered.

"I'm going to speak for him!" Jeff cried. "I've got to, if it kills me."

She protested, then realized if Jeff were to get through the day ahead he would need every assistance she could give him. She bundled him into heavy clothes and shawls and went with him, carrying beef tea and wine. Looking like a wraith, he spoke steadily for an hour and a half. When he was finished he nearly fainted. On the way home it occurred to her that, above everything else, Jeff was loyal to his friends. Was he perhaps too loyal?

Unable now to take his place regularly in the Senate, Jeff was forced to stay at home while his plan for a transcontinental railroad lapsed into failure. He had provided the senators with ten thick volumes of reports, colored maps, elaborate descriptions. "This is America's hope," he whispered to Varina. She didn't need to be reminded that he had set his heart on this scheme.

The senators glanced at the data he had assembled and continued to wrangle over "bleeding Kansas" and the territorial question. After another long wait they voted to allow the President to call for figures on possible costs. That was all, and for years to come there would be no Western railroad. As to Jeff's hopes for acquiring Cuba, they had collapsed in the general failure of President Pierce's efforts.

"Still," she reasoned with him, "you've accomplished a complete reorganization of the Army. Everybody admits it's the best we've ever had. And look at the camel program. It's working beautifully; they're breeding all over the place in the West."

He gave a dry smile. "Winnie, you can find comfort in anything."

With the session's end the doctors recommended a summer in a cooler climate. They decided on a boat trip to New England. The moment the boat left the pier Jeff seemed to get better, and soon he dispensed entirely with his dark glasses. They were on the water for the Fourth of July, and the captain asked Jeff to favor the company with a few words. As the passengers lined up, Varina could not hide her concern. How would this audience take a Southerner?

Jeff spoke quietly, telling the passengers that politicians, South and North, were causing trouble to the Union, but they were "like the mosquitoes around the ox; they annoy, but they cannot wound and never kill." There was no reason for hostility between the two sections. The South provided raw goods, the North factories to handle them. He told of his love of the Union, his father's services in the Revolution, but he insisted on slavery's rights and states' rights under the Constitution. He caught the imagination of his audience as he had done so often before, and men and women stood up to applaud him.

Afterward, in Massachusetts, he talked to greater crowds, Democratic audiences in Boston and elsewhere, whose response overjoyed Varina. It would be a long time before she forgot the enthusiasm of one Massachusetts man, a stout committee member with a cast in one eye, who took Jeff's hand and shook it repeatedly.

"Who was that, Banny?" she asked him later.

"Um . . ." He looked at the card. "Ben Butler."

"I'll remember him." She smiled. "Do you know what he said when the ladies were around you?" (As usual Varina hadn't missed that detail.) "He told us you ought to be the next Democratic candidate for President!" Jeff shrugged, but Varina's eyes were serious. She still dreamed of her Jeff in the White House.

Meanwhile there came leisurely weeks in New England—distant hazy hills, bays with small boats that were white against the cool blue, old-fashioned gardens bordered by fruit trees. One evening they rode with friends to a high sky-bordered plateau. While the children picked blooms among the green mosses, dark descended and the stars appeared one by one over the mountain peaks. Used to the insect clamor of Mississippi summers, they settled against a boulder to enjoy the silences.

Reluctantly they went back to Washington, into the vortex of new bitterness and new hatred. "These Republicans are gaining all over the North," Joe Johnston told Jeff on their first day back. The self-possessed Lydia Johnston was no less disturbed. "Kansas seems to be going over definitely to the North," she said. Jeff told her with real bitterness that their mercurial friend Seward had gone farther than any of the other Northerners. He had made a raging speech about a "higher law," a law beyond the Constitution.

Moreover, Joe Davis wrote that Jeff's New England talks had not set well in Mississippi, and a dozen letters confirmed the opinion. "What is Mr. Davis doing," a Natchez man wrote, "selling out to the Yankees?" A keen-witted editor had labeled the story of Jeff's steamboat address, "Davis at Sea." To offset this reaction, Jeff decided to take a quick trip back to Mississippi.

Worried over the effect that an aroused South would have on Jeff, Varina now waited impatiently in Washington. A clipping, mailed from Vicksburg, told her what had happened. Jeff had told a turbulent meeting that the Abolitionists were gaining, taking over the new territories. Soon, he said, they might have the power to end slavery in the states themselves. In that case the South faced a revolution in Washington City. A separation from the Union would be their last remedy, "a great—but not the greatest—calamity." Worse would be the loss of honor, the loss of a chance to survive. "Sooner than see Mississippi's star degraded, I would tear it from its place, to be set even on the ridge of battle!" Her breath caught; he must certainly have been carried way. . . .

At the railroad station, on his return, he poured out his feelings. "They're pretty upset down there, Winnie. They know what they want—a firm hand with the North. We've got to stand up and fight back!" She had never seen him so stirred, so inflexible.

He went fiercely into the Senate the next day, his hand clenched over a set of resolutions. As he read them out she felt the atmosphere crackling about her. He proposed flatly that Congress had no power to limit slaveholding in a territory. For better or for worse, he was demanding a showdown on a strong slavery platform. Above all others, she realized, he was aiming at the hated Stephen Douglas, the Westerner who was trying to appeal to both Northern and Southern elements.

Behind Varina a man from Maine whispered jubilantly: "It's happening! The Democrats are split wide apart. After this they'll never get back together again!"

When she heard Jeff's footsteps in the hall that night she got up. "Jeff," she said seriously, "are you sure this time that you're doing what's wisest for us?"

He gave her a sharp look. "I'm sure. It's what we've got to do." His words rolled forth, passionate, convincing. So many men, all over America, were arguing that night, just as passionately, just as convincingly. She could think of no more arguments, no more replies. Sadly she went to the desk. "Do you want me to take any letters?"

At once he was beside her, dictating furiously. Southern governors, other congressmen, other Southerners, Mr. Rhett, Mr. Yancey. He was working again with that pair of radical Southerners who had always wanted secession, who had never stopped agitating for it. Even now, she was aware, he did not go as far as Mr. Rhett. He shook his head. "The man's violent tongue . . ." Yet Varina remembered John Quitman. Jeff had never accepted all of that irascible man's opinions, and yet it had been Quitman, as much as anyone else, who led them into that disaster of 1850. That was nearly ten years ago.

Nervously Varina waited for the Democratic convention. As she had feared, it broke into two Democratic meetings and two candidates.

Now came the Republican convention.

"There isn't much doubt who'll get their nomination," Jeff told her soberly. "Seward, of course."

She took it for granted their friend, the Abolitionist, would be nominated, and she lost interest in the convention returns. She was all the more startled when Lydia Johnston burst into her parlor one afternoon, calling out excitedly: "Seward didn't get it all, but that man Linclon. Abe Lincoln!"

Of late she had been hearing more of that name. Yes, it was the same man who had been on Western duty with Jeff, the one who had spoken on the same program with Jeff back in Zachary Taylor's day.

"What's he like?" she inquired.

"You mean you don't know?" Lydia Johnston was calming down slowly. "He's a baboon, a foul-mouthed backwoodsman, that's all. To think of a thing like that in our White House!"

Could he be all of that? Varina asked herself. Some said that

Lincoln was not half as radical as some Republicans, that he had never come out flatly for forced emancipation. . . . Time would tell.

In the middle of all the turmoil over Abraham Lincoln's nomination Varina's fourth confinement occurred. This time there were no complications. The baby, when it came, was another boy, dark-haired, lively, and squirming. Holding him in his arms, Jeff walked to her bedside. He started to speak and then hesitated.

"What is it, Banny?" she asked.

There was an expression of embarrassment on his face when he finally said: "Would you mind—if we named him after Brother Joe?"

"Of course I wouldn't mind." She squeezed his arm. "It's a good name. And Joe and I—there's peace between us."

Gratefully her husband took her fingers to his lips. That night they sent the word back to Mississippi.

The unrest in Washington began to find its way into her bedroom. She heard echoes of "Yankee insults." Even Mr. Benjamin, with his calm philosophy, admitted that he was alarmed at the violence on both sides. Jeff seemed morose. "An Abolitionist in the White House! Some people think it ought to be a signal—just that—to secede." Yet now she suddenly saw that Jeff had become more cautious. If others, like him, were growing more careful as a final test approached, wouldn't that save them? It was a good sign, she reassured herself.

Yet when she was able to go out again she was astounded. The issue of North and South intruded into everything. Once upon a time they could be sure, when they attended a party, that good manners would prevent the introduction of awkward subjects. Now, in the middle of a reception, at the end of a dinner, there were often angry words and sometimes blows. Sadly Varina observed enmity widen between families that had once been intimate.

Oddly enough, Jeff and others about him continued to grow more conservative as the situation grew more heated. "There may not be a war," Jeff told her, "or even secession. If we stay firm and cool and let them see we're in earnest in demanding our rights . . ."

Already it was evident that there would be many problems if the Southern states decided to secede. Those nearest the Mason and

Dixon line were not of the same mind as the cotton states. Differences were developing among all Southern factions.

The election was over. A panting messenger brought them the news. Varina tore open the envelope and read the three words on the paper inside: "LINCOLN HAS WON." Jeff's face, caught in a shaft of light from a window, went suddenly haggard. It showed all of his fifty-two years.

In Jackson the governor of Mississippi called the state's senators and representatives to a long caucus. Jeff returned to her graver than ever. "I had to argue against all the others. They want secession right away. I told them we should wait and see and try to get every concession from the other side!" And yet, she sighed to herself, some were whispering that Jeff was involved in a plot to end the Union.

But each day brought more ominous word. South Carolina's representatives withdrew from Congress. Her troops were mobilized to face the Federal soldiers. For weeks efforts at compromise went on between committees of both sides; meetings and more meetings were held before Lincoln took office. . . . Mr. Lincoln watched from a distance. Finally Varina heard a compromise proposal was taken to him which he firmly rejected. The North could make no more concessions; it had come down to a point of principle.

Finally Jeff came home one evening, his face so worn that she thought at first he was sick. "There's no remedy now," he told her, his voice flat. "It will be secession."

"Then—you mean there'll be war?"

"There shouldn't be. We have a right to leave the Union. Our compact has been violated; the North denies us our rights. We'll be trying to preserve those rights outside the Union." He started to leave, then turned back. "I've offered to serve in Mississippi's militia, and the governor's accepted me." He smiled at her, and there was a look of candor in his eyes. "I'm better suited to military service than to the politician's ways."

. His last words were almost a question, and she found herself nodding in agreement. Yes, yes. They'd be free, at last, of this eternal jockeying and bargaining. Jeff had never been really fitted for the life of a politician. Now she could be frank with herself. . . . Then her thoughts shifted to military service and she remembered again those hideous days of the Mexican War.

Behind the rail in the Senate, Varina took her place for the last time. She could see Jeff's tall lean figure pushing through the crowd to his old seat. Her eyes searched his weary movements, the tightening of his lips. He had been unable to sleep for nights. She looked about her, taking in the details, the columns, windows, dark walls. Would she ever be here again? A sudden tenderness took possession of her. Until now she had hardly realized the hold that the place had upon her.

Jeff stood up, and there was silence in the room. Her eyes passed over his sunken cheeks, the narrowed mouth, his hand as he raised, then lowered it. He was speaking with obvious emotion and sometimes his voice faltered. His state had seceded; the time had arrived for him to tell them good-by. "To maintain our rights, we must leave. My state is convinced that her constitutional rights will not be honored. . . . Her safety requires that she provide elsewhere for their maintenance. . . ." His voice grew hoarse, but he went on: It was only what the American revolutionists did when they withdrew from a government that threatened destruction of their rights. . . . He saw men with whom he had long served; in some cases there had been differences between them. If he had injured any, he offered his apology. "It only remains for me to bid you a final adieu."

His head dropped; he was close to tears. About him others were crying. Varina made out one or two men who had witnessed the first struggling years of the young nation. Were they now watching it die? With lagging steps Jeff walked off the floor. She rose, and together they went through the corridors to the street.

A few minutes later as they were passing the White House she craned her neck for a last glimpse of the high portico, so serene while the country it symbolized came close to wreckage. Then her eye caught an American flag flying in the wind.

The sight of it jarred her. All of her life she had watched it with pride. During the Mexican War, when she passed through the streets of Natchez, she had paused before the flagstaffs; her husband was far off to the West in those days, fighting under that banner. Her father had almost given up his life for it in the War of 1812. She had stood before it on that July day when Zachary Taylor died; she had stared at it with President Pierce—and how many other times?

Now they were turning their back on the flag. They might yet, though God forbid it, be fighting against it. She must remind herself that it would be the banner of another country, perhaps even an enemy country. That would be hard. And now she remembered; she was leaving in this capital another part of herself, the body of her dead child, Sam. If she ever came back here again . . . She found herself sobbing against her husband's shoulder.

Several weeks later they were working together in the garden at Brierfield. Jeff was bent over an old rosebush, pruning knife in hand. There was a buzz of insects over the blossoms; two or three birds flew down from the trees that led toward the distant river. Around the small hill of green the Mississippi flowed on toward New Orleans, slow and yellow-brown and unchanging.

It was peaceful under the February sun, in the serenity of this rich earth. If, somehow, they could stay here during these years ahead; if things could be managed so they would not be wanted elsewhere . . . It was a wild, foolish hope, and Varina realized it.

Inside on the sofa Jeff's new uniform lay ready. He was to command Mississippi's troops, and already he was restless to join them.

In the distance a horseman rode toward them. She glanced at Jeff. "Another of those messages from Vicksburg, I suppose." He nodded and got up from the ground, a cutting in his hand. The rider pulled up near them. He was a youngster, and much excited, Varina noticed.

Standing beside her, Jeff stiffened as he read the paper. She caught his hand. "Is something wrong, Banny?" There was a long silence; the drone of the wasps sounded louder in her ears. Then he told her: "They've elected me Provisional President."

He spoke as if he had received a sentence of death.

Part Three

"QUEEN VARINA"

Chapter 15

As her vessel neared the high-piled landing at Montgomery, Alabama, Varina got to her feet, patted down her wide blue collar, and reached for the drooping ornament in her hat. "Does everything look right?" she asked Maggie. Her voluble sister assured her it did. "Stop worrying, Varina. You're fine. The children are in good hands over there. Stop worrying."

Varina nodded absently. Somehow she felt like the naïve girl who had first left the river country at her husband's side those long years ago. A new adventure was beginning and she was a little afraid of it. For the past month, ever since Jeff left her for the Confederate capital in the Alabama city, she had been unable to shake off her vague depression. When he disappeared in a mist down the road from Brierfield she had wanted to call him back. Were they doing the right thing? Would it be a colossal failure?

In New Orleans, where she had stopped on her way, a Creole company had marched gallantly to the Howells' house to serenade her. The captain handed her a bouquet of spring violets, and her mind had dwelt on the color—purple, the shade of pomp and ceremonial, and also death. We who are about to die salute you. . . .

Her brother Becket had stayed behind. His schooling was finished and he was already talking of joining the Confederate service. Her father spoke endlessly, and blithely as usual, of the Confederacy and of the way Jeff would handle everything; while her mother smiled and, also as usual, kept things going. Margaret Howell, upright and resolute, was the last figure she saw on the pier as the steamboat left.

All along their route soldiers drew up to honor her, but her mood had hardly changed. Today jubilant men behind her were shouting their feelings, thumping backs and exchanging opinions. It was all the same opinion: "Not the slightest danger of a war." . . . "One skirmish and the Yankees will turn tail." As she heard it she remembered Jeff's final words to her: "If this does come to fighting, it will be the bloodiest war the world has ever seen."

Two men approached the bow where she stood and took off their tall hats. The first told her gravely: "I don't mind that Mr. Davis was a little slow at first. Now he's here with us, he'll bring the Yankees to boot." The second smiled and said: "We got to worrying a little, though, that he'd stayed up there too long with the Yankees!"

Again she reminded herself: In the North they were calling Jeff an arch-conspirator, a man who schemed it all, coldly, deliberately. Here many thought he had not been fervent enough. In her coat pocket her hand touched Jeff's last letter to her. In it he told her of the inauguration; Mr. Yancey and Mr. Rhett had been with him on the platform. The two hotheads had come to see the fruition of the thing for which they had worked through the years! But although these two men had exchanged messages with Jeff, she sensed that they had never quite approved of his selection as President.

There was more to his letter. Things seemed to be going well, yet he admitted an undercurrent of something like foreboding: "Upon my weary heart were showered smiles, plaudits, and flowers; but then I saw troubles and thorns innumerable. We are without machinery, without means, and threatened by a powerful opposition. . . ."

The boat pulled in to the landing, and there stood Jeff, bareheaded, in a spruce business suit of the new Confederate gray, squinting as he searched for her. Her sister Maggie and little Polly and the boy Jeff crowded close to the rail. Annabelle, beaming at her side, held up the youngest baby, Joe. Her husband saw them at last, sprang forward, and took her in his arms.

"Winnie, I've needed you so much," he whispered.

His hair had grayed a little more; his long face revealed the strain under which he had been living, and there were heavy lines at the corners of his eyes and beside the tight lips. But at his first sight of her she had seen a change come over him. She knew beyond any doubt that her husband loved her as much as he ever had. What woman could ask for anything more?

The crowd gave way and they went forward toward their carriage. Men lined up in brisk salute. In back of them a band started up a gay march and a cannon boomed.

"It's all for you," Jeff said as he handed her into the carriage. "Look, they're waving to you." She leaned out; women were smiling, children lifting their hands, men removing their hats. A small girl tossed a bouquet, and Jeff, bending forward, caught it by the ribbon and handed it to Varina while the crowd applauded.

Her spirits rose. This was her new country, this their capital. A new day in the making, her husband the leader of it all! Her eyes took on a brightness that was feverish, and her full lips parted. Her hand covered Jeff's, and he caressed it in both of his. When they stopped at a corner an officer addressed Jeff as "Mr. President." It was the first time Varina had heard the new title used, and she was instantly thrilled by it.

Opposite her Maggie's wide blue eyes had misted, and Annabelle, with the baby in her arms, showed her elation too. Varina looked happily about her; Montgomery was a pretty, rural town, turned overnight into a crowded military-civil center. She was going to like it here. Then, like an echo, a line or two returned to her from Jeff's letter, and her face sobered. She'd have things to do, for Jeff and for the new nation.

Their vehicle drew up before a large wooden building.

"The Exchange Hotel, our quarters for the time," Jeff told her as he helped her out.

Another crowd appeared from nowhere and she heard whispers: "Mrs. Davis . . ." "Over there with the blue hat." And then, for the first time, those magic words: "The First Lady."

A group of women came down the steps to meet her. Several of them were old friends from Washington.

"Varina, didn't you know I was here?" said Lydia Johnston. "I'm here with Joe on a visit."

Varina's heart warmed at the sight of those who had been close to her in former years. She called out greetings. "Yes, Jeff says there'll be a reception this evening. . . . I'll be lookin' for you tonight. . . . Yes, let's ride out to the camp—tomorrow."

The hotel servants finally cleared a path for them, and they made their way up the stairs. Varina could still hear people saying, "The First Lady . . ." Every eye had been on her these past few minutes; never had she experienced quite that sensation. Jeff's hand tightened on her arm. "I needn't ask how you feel, Winnie." He appeared amused.

"Does it show that much?" She laughed. Then she thought of those other two women, bearers of the title, who had been her friends, Jane Pierce and Zachary Taylor's wife, and her mood changed.

When they reached the door of their suite her hands had gone cold. "Too much excitement?" Jeff asked her solicitously.

She nodded. "I'll be all right once I rest a bit." Later, as she loosened her black hair and began to brush it, she noticed that it still glistened like a young girl's. She was nearly thirty-five now, and a little heavier than she had been a year or two ago. There were the beginnings of blue shadows under her eyes, but she knew that she remained a beautiful woman.

Annabelle broke in, grumbling: "A cer'mony, they says, right away. We git in jis' in time. You better finish combin' you'se'f and git into dis!" She held up a stiff white dress that she had persuaded a hotel employee to press. As she grew older Annabelle was becoming more and more domineering, and Varina found herself enjoying it. How many people, she wondered, liked her as well as Annabelle, or knew so much about her?

That afternoon she and Jeff waited on a platform, eyes raised toward a flagpole. A young girl stood in front of them with a folded cloth in her hand. "John Tyler's granddaughter," the all-knowing Mrs. Johnston whispered. This descendant of a former President of the United States, from Virginia, had been chosen for a purpose as the leading figure in the rite. "Virginia is the mother of Presidents," Jeff explained. "We're showing that we follow the principles of our old government, not that new one in Washington."

The girl tugged at a cord. It held for a moment and then it ran free. Slowly a new flag rose against the sky—a flag with red and white stripes, and in the corner, on a field of blue, a circle of seven white stars. It fluttered, and as a firm breeze lifted it, Varina caught her breath. It was the flag of their new country.

After the ceremony was over she had to hurry back to the Exchange Hotel to prepare for that evening's reception. She had only a few minutes in which to check the ingredients of the punch, to sample a cake, and order the supply of coffee doubled, before Annabelle summoned her to her room. Without being asked, her maid had chosen a dress for the occasion—a cream-colored taffeta with a regal skirt. Yellow flowers for her hair, and she was ready. But her eye halted at her décolletage.

"What do you think?" she asked Annabelle.

Her maid sniffed. "Nothin' wrong. I notice' in Wash'ton City —dem what has, shows. Dem what don', covers!"

In the national capital the dress would not have aroused undue attention. Already, however, Varina had learned that the Confederacy represented many elements, some rural and Puritan, that might not understand. She found a lace handkerchief, deftly pinned it inside the front of her dress, and called to Jeff. Annabelle looked disappointed.

Downstairs she moved easily through the crowd, waving to old friends, extending her hand to strangers. Jeff brought forward, one by one, the men who would assist him. She saw first the smiling face of Judah Benjamin. He was to be the Attorney General, and she congratulated him warmly. Some of the other Cabinet members were men she had heard little about.

"Still another non-entity for the Cabinet," someone whispered behind her.

By this time she knew what she had begun to suspect a week ago. Jeff's choices were not universally popular. Each state had been given a representative, but many were protesting that he had picked mediocrities and "lukewarms" rather than warm partisans of the Rhett and Yancey type.

Jeff himself had been something of a compromise choice for President. He was a man on whom all could agree and, moreover, he had an excellent military record. The thought of a soldier-president, in case of hostilities, had met with much favor.

The people in front of Varina moved away, and she made out a man whose appearance was causing a stir among newcomers— the yellowed, shrunken Alexander Stephens of Georgia, Vice-President of the Confederacy. When she had first heard of this choice she had cried out: "Oh no! You must be mistaken." Mr. Stephens had fought harder than anyone else to keep his state from joining the Confederacy. To the very end he had voted against secession. But now he was the Vice-President.

As she saw him again, she felt the same rush of pity that had come over her that first evening in Washington. What a pathetic wisp of a man, a first-class brain in a secondhand body. His eyes shifted uneasily, for he must have realized that everyone in the room was either staring at him or making rude remarks about him. As on that other occasion, Varina hurried to him. "Mr. Stephens, I'm happy to see you again!"

Again, too, Alexander Stephens showed his gratitude. He stayed at her side, smiling, bowing awkwardly. She tried to draw him out, and he answered briefly: "Yes, we're old friends now. . . . Yes, a lot of people tonight." But he contributed nothing to their conversation or to those of others about them. Looking closer, she detected an expression of wariness in his eyes. The Vice-President was taking care to commit himself about nothing. Beyond that, his mummy-like features indicated only a profound melancholy.

Only once did he allow himself more than a banal agreement with her. She had just said something to indicate that she thought the Confederate government was getting a good start.

In a voice that seemed all at once to grow louder—as if at last he did not care who heard—the Vice-President of the Confederacy replied: "That's a statement, madame, that many of us wouldn't agree with!"

His eyes swept the room, and in them she read distaste, clear and undisguised. So that was how the man felt.

At Jeff's side she managed to convey what she had seen. Jeff's face lost its smile. "He's been like that since his arrival," he said. "It's as if he wanted us to think the whole thing's a mistake. But he accepted the place and I'd certainly think——"

The rest of his remarks were drowned out by a woman who hurried up to her and said: "Varina, we've been talking about that Lincoln up in Washington. He's turning the White House into a barn!"

Another woman chimed in: "Scenes such as you'd never imagine. Lincoln barefoot, telling barnyard stories—even answering the front door himself."

Varina's first impulse was to laugh and tell them that on occasion she had answered her own front door; if people were so careful of their dignity they couldn't be very sure of it. But before she could reply, another woman had cried: "And that wife of his! If she stays up there, Kentucky born or not, she can't be a true Southern woman. Have you heard the crazy things she's doing?"

Again Varina wanted to protest, and then it occurred to her that perhaps they were telling similar stories in the North about Jeff and her.

The talk turned to Army officers and their wives. Quite innocently Varina spoke of "my friend, Mrs. Emory.'"

A Charleston matron peered at her curiously and said: "You mean the wife of that Yankee general?"

"Why, yes." Varina sipped at her punch. "He's an awfully good soldier. I wish we had him on our side."

She felt a tremor of resentment around her, and then the circle broke up. Her sister Maggie, who had been watching, gave her a sympathetic glance. Despite the scattered freckles that remained here and there on the oval face, Maggie looked quite grown up.

"I'll try to do better," Varina whispered. "But everybody in the North isn't a villain"—she paused—"nor everybody in the South a saint."

The next morning Jeff rose at dawn and hurried to his office without even stopping for breakfast. At noon, after she sought him out, she found him in a tiny, inconspicuous set of rooms with a hand-lettered sign tacked to the door: THE PRESIDENT. A heavy throng was waiting for him, and the space was so packed that she had difficulty forcing her way through. There was only one clerk in attendance, and he was harassed and ill-tempered. Almost everybody in the South seemed to want to see Jeff, and almost everybody, she said to herself, seemed to be doing it. Gratefully, mopping his brow, Jeff pushed some papers off a chair and made room for her to sit down.

She asked him about the crowd outside and he said with a touch of pride: "I see anybody who asks for me. I want to be fair."

"The drain on your time," she protested, "when you need that time to make decisions on more important matters."

He shook his head. "I couldn't trust these interviews to a clerk. How can I tell, until I talk to these people, what's important and what isn't?" She sighed; as she had feared, Jeff was taking on himself, all too conscientiously, too many burdens of administration.

Though he had done magnificently in the War Department, she had heard the same criticism of him then. He did not delegate responsibility. He wore himself out in the routine of the office.

She hadn't believed it then, but she did now.

"Anyway," she said, putting on her coat, "I hope you'll be back early tonight. I'm having some people in for dinner. One"—she mentioned an important name—"needs a little persuading from what I heard last evening, and I think you can win him over."

Jeff's eyes lighted, and then he looked through the half-open door at the line waiting to see him.

"I'll try, Winnie."

His tone was not enthusiastic.

As she expected, he arrived too late. She asked no questions as she helped him off with his coat and vest and drew him to the sofa beside her. For a few minutes he rested, his head in her lap. Then nervously he sat up. "If we're to have a war, Winnie, neither side is prepared! But the South's even less so than the North. No factories, very few railroads, hardly anybody trained for industry. We don't have a real Navy yard and we will certainly need ships." He grimaced. "Yet in South Carolina they're calling for an attack on Washington City tomorrow!"

She shook her head. It sounded so familiar. Ever since their first years in the capital South Carolina had been the center of almost every disturbance.

"The South isn't really united," Jeff continued, "at least we're not united yet. Even Virginia isn't with us——"

"She will be," Varina interrupted, "if the North tries to use force against us. She's given them fair warning."

"Even so," he conceded, "we aren't sure of Tennessee and Missouri, and also Maryland."

She faced him. "You're doing everything to win them?"

"Yes, Winnie," he said impatiently. "We're sending men to argue, we're using every appeal. And we still have commissioners in Washington City demanding that the South be recognized as a separate country." At that his face reddened. "Some people down here claim that I'm trying to worm my way back into the Union! But what I want is a peaceful settlement, a treaty with the North. I'm afraid others are after just one thing—war."

"Banny, it must never come to that."

"It wouldn't be popular in the North, I can tell you. There's already been a reaction against the Abolitionists, and of course the businessmen don't want it. Most Northerners are ready to let us go our own way. They don't propose to give up their lives or their sons' lives to keep the South in the Union."

He reached into a drawer and pulled out a ball of fluffy white cotton. He looked at it almost with affection, and when he spoke there was a ring of triumph in his voice.

"This may be our salvation, Winnie. The North needs it—and so does Europe, for England's mills depend on it. We're holding every bale we raise. When Europe's present supply is gone, their ships will come over here to get it. Should the North try a blockade, then English ships will break it. That will mean war between England and the North. If those damned Yankee agitators want trouble, let them remember that we still have cotton on our side."

Varina looked with awe at the handful of raw cotton. King Cotton, King of the South. Would it stay King and win for them? Most people agreed with Jeff, but she suddenly began to wonder if they were not putting too much reliance in it.

They had moved the next week into their official residence, a simple white building in the main part of town. Varina was finishing the arrangements for her first afternoon reception. She hummed as she and Maggie superintended the placing of the potted plants. More and more Maggie was proving a blessing to her, reminding her over and over again of Margaret Howell in her anxiety to help and to accept responsibility. Already she had become a belle, and Varina discovered that the younger bachelors were following the girl as they had once followed her older sister in Natchez. Her mind slipped back to that party with Jules Amant. Well, she'd see that there were no kisses behind the house as far as Miss Maggie was concerned! She stopped herself. Could this be middle age creeping up on her?

The first guests began to arrive, among them James Chesnut, formerly a Carolina senator, now a Confederate officer, and his wife, a modish and witty woman of Varina's own age. The two women had met before, and Varina admired and appreciated Mary Chesnut.

"Do you know what just happened?" Mrs. Chesnut bubbled.

"A friend rushed down from Washington, gasping, 'Their troops are the finest body of men I ever saw!' I felt like telling him: 'If you liked them that much, why didn't you stay and make friends with them?'"

Varina smiled; if she knew Mary Chesnut at all, she would warrant that, sooner or later, she would be saying it to his face.

At that moment she caught sight of Vice-President Stephens, whom she had not expected at all. He bowed solemnly, dispiritedly, and she wondered why he attended. She introduced him to Mary Chesnut, who began in her forthright way to question him about his loyalties. "Mr. Stephens," she said, "you're halfhearted about all this. You're looking back—toward Washington City. Look ahead with the rest of us!"

Varina and Maggie exchanged smiles. Mary had the Vice-President on the griddle and he hardly seemed to be enjoying it. . . .

Jeff approached Varina with a pleasant man whose alert eyes were missing very little.

"Winnie, this is Mr. Russell, the British journalist. He's writing a series of articles comparing the North and the South."

Varina steered him toward the punch bowl, out of earshot of Mary Chesnut and the unhappy Vice-President. That was one conversation she didn't want reported and discussed in England. Mr. Russell brought her a glass of punch, and while she sipped it she began very artfully to paint for him a glowing picture of the Confederacy.

Mr. Russell, obviously impressed by what she had said, finally made his excuses. Feeling pleased that she had maneuvered an important interview successfully, Varina made her way to the pantry to see how Annabelle was making out with the refreshments. On the way back she stopped just long enough outside the parlor door to hear a voice say in a sharp feminine treble: "The Queen! Queen Varina!" Her eyes blazed. So that's what they were saying. Well, let them. If they thought that would stop her, they were going to be disappointed. Her chin rose in what Jeff called her Natchez manner, and she sailed back into the room.

It was April 10, 1861, a calm and sunny spring day in Montgomery, Alabama. Varina and Maggie had driven out into the country to escape for a few hours from the tensions of the Confederate administration. As they rode home Varina began to talk about the crisis which was developing at Charleston. A marooned Federal force at Fort Sumter must be relieved, or it would starve to death on the sandy island. The Confederates controlled the harbor, and they were insisting on the surrender of the fort.

"Aren't our commissioners still in Washington, arguing with the Yankees about it?" Maggie's face wrinkled in its intensity.

"Yes." Varina frowned. "Mr. Seward's the Secretary of State now." She no longer referred to him as "our friend, Mr. Seward." "He's been telling us everything will be adjusted. He says one thing and Lincoln another. Jeff's worried, very worried."

She stopped speaking as the carriage pulled up at their door. Jeff was waiting for them, looking white and shaken.

"They've shown their hand in Washington," he said slowly when they were inside. "Lincoln's sending supplies to Sumter—the vessels are already on their way. I've summoned the Cabinet to meet within the hour. And now in the time that's left I—I'm going upstairs to think as clearly as I can."

Going to the window, she stared blindly down at the half-empty street. Her husband's footsteps sounded above her, steadily back and forth, back and forth. The Confederacy must act now, and quickly—one way or the other. And Jeff must make the decision. Oh God, she prayed, give him wisdom. . . .

The footsteps overhead had stopped, and suddenly she realized that Jeff was standing in the doorway, his face cold and determined.

"We've got to take the fort before they get there."

She reached out her hand to protest, then drew it back. He had made up his mind and, right or wrong, she would be with him.

Two days later—on April 12—Mary Chesnut was telling her excitedly that Charleston was like a town on holiday, the battery crowded with people holding umbrellas and chairs and spyglasses, watching Fort Sumter. It seemed hardly like a picnic to Varina.

Through the open window she heard people shouting, one phrase repeated over and over again. As the crowd came nearer she made out the words: "The first shot's been fired! The first shot's been fired!"

Varina's hands clasped in her lap. The hotheads had gotten what they wanted at last.

Jeff came dashing by for her a few minutes later.

"They want us at the hotel," he cried. Now he, too, seemed quietly elated. The hour of indecision was past.

"We acted, for better or for worse," he told her. "We acted at last."

As they reached their carriage a shouting mob formed around them. Men pushed forward, beaming, to shake their hands; women came up and asked questions.

"Hurray for the President!"

"Damn the Yankees! God damn 'em!"

Then, as on that first day in Montgomery, she was thrilled by the spirit of the South. On the streets before them, from everywhere, came lines of people. A file of soldiers stopped short and swung about to salute them. Out of one window, then another, women leaned, smiling, waving the Stars and Bars.

Varina squeezed Jeff's arm against hers. With unshed tears she watched this spontaneous demonstration of enthusiasm for the Southern cause.

"Mr. President! Mr. President!"

Jeff stood up, and the cheers redoubled. An old woman ran out to kiss his hand.

In the torrent of exultation girls tossed flowers, papers, handkerchiefs. Men were shouting: "I'm volunteering tonight!" "Where can I register?" "God damn 'em to hell, we've got 'em running now!" Carried forward on the crest of this tide of loyalty and emotion, she hardly realized that the South had plunged into war.

That week and the next she stood beside her husband at the telegraph machine while one important message after another came over the wire. The South was aflame. Headed by Virginia, the border states were coming in. The Old Dominion, having thrown in her power and her great prestige, promptly invited the Confederacy to transfer its capital to her soil. Jeff hesitated, then agreed to move to Richmond. The Confederacy's center would shift from the New South to the Old.

Jeff called out the names of the other border states that were joining up: "North Carolina . . . Tennessee . . . Arkansas!" But the telegraphed reports from other sections told her that in some cases it was too late. Kentucky, Maryland, and much of Missouri were lost. Sentiment was divided in these states, and neighbors faced one another in hatred, families broke apart. The worst loss, Varina knew, was Maryland. It meant that the vital territory, controlling the approach to Washington City, stayed in the Union.

And meanwhile from a dozen sources Varina followed developments in the North—developments that were not pleasant to contemplate. From Maine to Kansas swept a wave of revulsion, of wild resentment. The South had fired on the American flag, and that act had united the North as nothing else could have done. . . .

Varina shuddered as she read the reports: Lincoln called for five hundred thousand men, one of the greatest armies the world had yet seen. Loans for hundreds of millions were being subscribed. A blockade of Southern ports was declared. A vast war machine clanked into action—and now there would be heavy bloodshed.

Jeff tried to comfort her, but she was beyond comfort.

"It isn't as bad as they're trying to make it sound," he told her. "In a few weeks we'll be in Richmond, and you'll see how it looks then. We're getting in so many men we don't know how to handle them. We've revised all our estimates upward, and then upward again!"

Yet he was less exultant than his words would indicate. After a while he grew quiet, and she dropped her head against his shoulder. They sat there in the silence while the crowds swept by on the street. Somewhere a long way off a band was playing "Dixie."

Chapter 16

IT WAS RICHMOND IN THE LATE AFTERNOON OF A BRIGHT HOT DAY in July, and Varina was riding back from a trip through the outskirts with a party of women friends. She liked the look of the city with its red brick buildings whose white galleries were ornamented with iron balconies. She liked the vine-draped private gardens. It had an atmosphere of quiet, of leisure—or at least it had when she first came. Now it was filling with newcomers, with signs of turmoil and crowded living.

During the two months since her arrival there had been scattered skirmishes of troops at distant points, but no important battle. Gradually, however, the tempo of preparations had been speeded up, for the Union forces were forming their lines outside Washington City. Opposing them stood Confederates under Joe Johnston and the picturesque Beauregard, hero of Fort Sumter.

Lydia Johnston, her old friend from Washington City, was with Varina's party today. They talked casually of the changes that had occurred in the Confederate capital. A few Louisiana Zouaves went by in flashing reds and yellows, their wide pantaloons a sight for the children along the line of march. Ahead of them moved several high-stepping Texas volunteers, ready to finish the war singlehanded. The outskirts of Richmond were alive with banners, with the echoes of rolling artillery, of horses that strained to dray supply wagons to camp.

They were laughing over the "gentlemen's units" that had arrived with supplies of champagne and dancing pumps and black servants, one to a man.

"And did you hear about the lieutenant from Savannah who

challenged his superior officer to a duel because he gave him too sharp a command?" The question came from Mrs. Bartow, the wife of a high-ranking officer.

Varina smiled. "Jeff says that they had some of that sort of thing in the Mexican War. . . ."

"But when the men got their first smell of gunpowder," Lydia Johnston added, "all that changed!" At the word "gunpowder" a silence fell. There were too many husbands at the front to make the word anything but a disturbing one.

By this time they had reached the main streets. Lydia pointed to a crowd of men gathering in front of the telegraph office.

"Look," she cried, "something must have happened."

Varina remembered suddenly that Jeff had left that morning for Manassas Junction, and she had had no message from him all day. In Mrs. Bartow's face she read signs of growing alarm. A man detached himself from the crowd and came up beside their carriage.

"Haven't you heard, ma'am?" he asked, removing a battered hat. "Word came in a little while back. There's been fighting, big fighting, all day at Manassas. Some claims President Davis's pitched right into it!"

Varina's face drained of color. Lydia Johnston sank slowly back against the seat. At the sight of Mrs. Bartow's eyes Varina remembered that her husband, too, was out there. In silence they drove over to the Spotswood, their hotel and the center of Confederate activities. There they were greeted by other women with terror in their hearts, who had husbands, brothers, sons in the front lines. Their voices rose in a babel of terrified questions.

Varina lifted her hand. "Please. I have even less information than you. But the minute I know something, you will. Come upstairs whenever you want." She walked briskly up the stairs, outwardly calm but inwardly as worried as any of the women in the lobby. She found Maggie waiting for her, cold and frightened, her hands trembling.

Varina embraced her, then turned to the children. "Are you all right, Polly and Jeff? That's fine, Joe. You're always the quietest of them. Go back to sleep." Behind her hovered Annabelle, serene, competent; only her eyes, which never once left Varina's, made it clear that she understood the gravity of the hour.

A silence fell, the silence of women who wait. Mrs. Bartow and

Lydia Johnston, eyes lowered, came up to join her. Together they listened to every footstep in the hallway. Each time they asked: Could it be news? Then as the sound disappeared in the distance they looked away. Varina paced up and down, her hands clasped. Why didn't they hear? The battle must be over by now.

There was a quiet knock at the door, and Varina ran to open it. Mr. Benjamin stood there, his face for once unsmiling, an unlighted cigar clamped in his mouth.

He told them quickly what he had learned. "The fighting's very heavy. Neither side's won yet."

That might be good news or bad; and it might mean, she reasoned, many dead on both sides! Mr. Benjamin, his bearded face softening, had a special word for Varina. "The President's on the scene, but he isn't in the fighting. He got there too late."

"Oh thank God," she exclaimed. She suspected that Mr. Benjamin had come on purpose to give her that information, but in his instinctively tactful way he had conveyed it casually. How kind the man was, she thought as Mr. Benjamin excused himself and hurried out.

And now her other fears returned. Was the South losing? Perhaps the Union men were already marching on the capital itself! Mrs. Bartow, who had been sitting intently beside Maggie, got up and said quietly: "I'll be in my room if any word comes." Maggie lowered the light and, despite herself, Varina dozed off. Hours went by.

Long after midnight she woke with a start. Someone was tapping at the door. A messenger handed in two telegrams for her, and she ran with them to the light. They were both from Jeff and the first one contained the three words: "A GREAT VICTORY." The second was longer, and as she read it she caught at her throat. "Dead and dying cover the fields. . . . Sherman's battery taken. . . . Lynchburg regiment cut to pieces. . . . General Bartow, rallying his men, died gallantly. . . ." Gallantly! It would be a small help to the woman down the hall.

Word spread through the hotel. There were repeated knocks on the door, and the room filled with women, among them Mary Chesnut. One woman sobbed hysterically in relief; another, whose man was in the battery reported cut to pieces, wandered blindly out. Others reread the words: "Dead and dying cover the field."

Were their husbands, their sons among those corpses? Lydia Johnston, alone in the corner, murmured a prayer, for apparently Joe Johnston had been spared.

Mary Chesnut came up to Varina, put a hand on her arm, and looked very seriously into her face.

"We think you're the one to tell Mrs. Bartow," she said in a flat voice.

Varina went down the hall, stopped for a minute outside Mrs. Bartow's door, then knocked and went in.

"My dear——" she began, and could go no farther.

Mrs. Bartow looked from Varina's face to the telegram in her hand.

"Bad news for me?" she whispered, her eyes round with fright.

Varina nodded, unable to speak.

"He's dead," Mrs. Bartow said, and began to sob, quietly at first and then wildly.

Varina gathered her in her arms and tried to still the frantic cries, the convulsive tremors. Outside in the hall Varina could hear Mary Chesnut saying to another woman: "God help us if this is what we prayed for!"

The next morning the telegraph wires were down, put out of order by a driving rainstorm. For nearly twenty-four hours there came no further word from Manassas Junction. All day the city waited, and in each face was the question: What has happened to my man? Looking from her window at the sodden, empty streets, Varina asked Maggie: "Who'd think this was a victorious capital?" What was the price of their victory?

The following morning the sun came back, and the telegrams stacked up in the offices. The worst of the news had now arrived, and here and there through the town crape appeared on the doors. For others it became a day of joy. Men ran down the streets, shaking hands, shouting, smiling. At the hotel entrance Varina heard the wild rumors: "We're chasing the Yanks all the way to Washington City. . . ." "They say it's over—the whole damned war!"

For a moment she almost believed them, and then she remembered Jeff's stern warning before he went off to the Mexican War: After a battle, put no faith in street gossip. Wait, wait and see. . . .

Late that afternoon a tremendous noise brought her to the front of the hotel. There, through a screeching throng, Jeff was pushing his way. He looked badly tired, his sunburned face more hollow than usual. His clothes were rumpled, his hat awry, but in his eyes shone the light of victory. She put out her arms, and he clasped her quickly. "Winnie . . . Winnie." She drew away, embarrassed to have the crowd see her in his arms, but he caught her to him again. She felt the trembling of his body, the tight control under which he held his nerves.

For a few minutes the crowd allowed them to be alone in their own room. She made him comfortable in an easy chair and asked him how far their troops had gone.

"No, we didn't try to march on to Washington. You know most of it now, Winnie. I want to forget it for a while." The intensity faded from his face, and he sat reflecting. Then he spoke again very slowly. "You know, Winnie, when I reached the field and saw the United States flag in the distance, I had a strange feeling." His light eyes dimmed.

"For a minute my mind went back to my Mexican War days, and I thought it was my flag and I was fighting under it again. . . ." She could think of nothing to say. In the silence she heard the distant hum of the crowd and then steps pounding down the hall toward their room. "Mr. President! They're calling for you!"

She went with Jeff to the steps of the hotel, and there he spoke to the crowd. At first he could not be heard above the tumult. The shouts, long, endless, drowned him out, and he remained there in the glare of the lights, arms raised happily, mouth a little open, enjoying this tribute. A man shoved his way forward and cried: "Mr. President! My wife just had her baby an hour ago. And we're going to name him after you—Jeff Davis!"

Jeff himself had been named for another American leader—Thomas Jefferson—and now people were being called after him.

His voice rang out: "We've thrown back the invader." His words were lost again. "We've taught him a bloody lesson. . . ." At those words she heard, from somewhere back in the crowd, a noise which started low and rose to a shrill of triumph. Other voices took it up, and the crowd screamed its pleasure. "The rebel yell!" Mr. Benjamin whispered at her elbow. She felt a tingling up and down her spine and she knew she would never hear that sound again without thrilling to it. And now Jeff was praising the two new hero generals, Beauregard and Joe Johnston; one had taken the left wing of the Army, the other the right, and together they had achieved their glory. He spoke of Tom Jackson, who at one crucial point had saved the day and won the name of Stonewall.

Over the shouts she heard the thin echo of music in the distance. She looked around; down another street, unnoticed by the crowd, a cortege was passing. Her friend General Bartow was on his way home.

Three days after the victory at Manassas Junction she was driving by the railroad station when her attention was caught by a group of soldiers, weary, disheveled, many of them wearing bandages.

Her sister Maggie stared at her, distress in her pale face. Varina halted the carriage. A man, running by, cried out to her: "They're the wounded. Plenty of 'em, lady! So many they hada dump 'em into anything they could find to get 'em here."

Varina stepped down. "Maggie," she called behind her protectingly. "Please stay here. I'll only be gone a few minutes."

As she started toward the wounded men she almost tripped over a man's body lying in the grass. Near him a youth—he was little more than a boy—was clutching the bloody bandages across his stomach, lips bared, white teeth clenched in agony. A third man was moaning on a stretcher, the stump of one leg covered by dirty wet sacking. And she saw a man who had died on the way, stretched stark and stiff under the sun, the flies thick about his mouth.

Already other women had appeared on the scene. A determined matron was saying to a young lieutenant: "I have room in my place for five beds. Help me get them there." A girl in a drab patched dress was whispering timidly: "There's a barn near our farm, just on the outskirts." Everybody knew the hospitals of Richmond could not care for half of these men.

Varina saw one or two women bending down over the men, cutting away at dirty uniforms and applying fresh bandages. She ripped away her white petticoat and went quickly to work, calling to Maggie: "Come over here. You take that one. . . . Of course, your skirts!"

As the first blood streaked her green silk dress Varina stared in dismay. Then, biting her lips, she went ahead. A moment later, when she looked closely at an infected wound, bluish and filled with pus, she thought she was going to be sick. The soldier himself gazed up solicitously, and she swallowed twice and began to bandage.

The time for champagne and dancing slippers had come to an end.

Before another month was over Jeff had rushed in with some tremendous news. "It looks as if the British are coming over to our side! Manassas did it!" He lifted a finger to caution her. "It's not official, but we've heard from Europe that England may recognize us. And then"—his voice grew hoarse—"and then we'll be certain of winning."

She was aware that one British journal after another was openly favoring the South. The nobility and the upper class were strongly inclined toward the Confederacy, but she had been hearing during the past weeks that the working people of England favored the North because they hated slavery. After all, Britain had long ago abolished it.

"How about the working people over there?" she asked.

His face showed his scorn. "Once they lose their jobs because there's no cotton, they'll find they don't object so much to slavery!"

Yet she couldn't feel as certain as Jeff did. If a large part of the British public disliked slavery, things might not go so easily for the South. Again she wondered about the King Cotton theory on which Jeff was banking so heavily. But now her husband had turned to another subject, and as he spoke she sensed the alarm behind his words.

"It's this matter of optimism, Winnie. The South thinks the war's over. Why, some of our soldiers are starting to leave the Army. They're slipping off, saying we don't need them! One day we've had to turn them away because we didn't have enough guns. Now they quit because they claim we've won already. . . ."

Maggie came in, bringing an armful of Northern newspapers, and Varina raced through them—skimming accounts of vast recruiting, purchases of thousands of tons of new supplies. Jeff stared gloomily through the window. "Manassas has had an opposite effect up there. It's solidified them, taught them they face a hard fight. And"—his knuckle beat against the folded journals—"and they're getting ready for it, as we aren't!"

He got up and walked nervously to the door. "Joe Johnston will be in the next room with me in a few minutes for a conference. Maybe you'd like to see him?"

"Well . . ." She had no particular desire for such a meeting. As much as she liked Lydia, her dour little general of a husband was not a favorite of Varina's.

Jeff cleared his throat. "Joe's a trifle dissatisfied these days. And you can usually get on with him."

"Then of course I'll see him."

Jeff gave her a grateful look and waited while she preceded him into the parlor. They were both amused a few minutes later at the staccato rapping which announced the arrival of the general. Before he came in Jeff had time to say to Varina: "Joe Johnston makes even a door knock sound official."

But Joe Johnston was not in flippant mood. He appeared petulant. Solemnly he took her hand, then dropped it with a hint of rejection. He seemed to be waiting for her to leave, and when she did not go he transferred his full attention to Jeff, asking at once about General Beauregard. "What will his part be? Is he to control that . . ."

Long before this Varina had understood that the two generals did not get along. A friend had told her: "With so much glory to be divided, you'd think there'd be enough for all. But military men are monopolists, aren't they?"

Jeff was speaking with firmness. "I've told you several times, Joe, and so has the War Department—you outrank Benjamin."

At first Johnston appeared relieved, but Varina gathered that Jeff's tone had nettled him. He made several false starts, apparently having difficulty in broaching his next question. Finally it came out: "And when will you fix the relative rankings of the generals?"

"That hasn't been decided." Jeff looked coldly into the distance, and Johnston again looked hurt. Even though Varina felt annoyed at the man, she asked herself whether Jeff should not be making more of an effort to placate him. She tried to signal her husband, but he either did not see, or he was ignoring her deliberately. She tried changing the subject, but Joe Johnston answered her only in monosyllables. At last he rose to go.

"By the way, Joe," Jeff said casually, "I'm expecting Robert E. Lee. Would you care to wait?"

Clearly General Johnston didn't, and he left with a curt bow.

This time she did not require a suggestion from Jeff. She really wanted to see Lee.

"The poor fellow!" She shook her head. "Things haven't gone so well with him, have they?" When secession broke he had been in Washington City and had been given to understand he could have the field command of the Northern armies. As Varina had known, Lee was no advocate of slavery. In fact, he had freed those slaves which he owned. Nor had he previously favored a separate confederacy. But when Virginia left the Union and joined the Confederacy he felt that his allegiance belonged with his home state. He had turned down the Union offer and joined the South.

For a time he had been in charge of Virginia's state troops, but later these had been transferred to the Confederacy, and Jeff had called Lee in as his adviser.

"You know, Winnie," Jeff said with a frown, "there's a little matter of rank between him and Johnston. . . ." Johnston and rank again! Would they spend the whole war trying to humor an ambitious general?

Lee came in soon and they both rose to greet their old friend. As Varina's glance passed over his calm face with its dark mustache and strong eyes she remembered their intermittent meetings through the years and the way Lee's fortunes had gone up and down. Jeff agreed with the military men in Washington City who considered Lee a remarkable soldier, and yet Lee had still to win a fraction of the attention others had gained.

Jeff, with a sidelong glance at Varina, opened a sheaf of papers. If that was a hint to leave she wasn't taking it.

"I have a new assignment for you, Lee," he said. "It's going to be a hard one. But if anybody can do it, you can."

There was a pause.

"I'm giving you western Virginia," Jeff concluded.

Western Virginia, thought Varina, that mountainous and difficult region where many of the people were strongly pro-Union, having little in common with the plantation South . . . West Virginia, where dissensions had already broken out among the Confederate forces.

Lee's finger touched the edge of his mustache. Then he squared his shoulders.

"I'm ready whenever you say."

Varina's brown eyes filled with admiration. How different the two generals were! After he had gone Jeff looked at her quizzically. "And did you notice"—Jeff's eyebrows rose—"Lee asked no questions about rank or anything like that? That's certainly unusual."

"Unusual?" Varina's eyes twinkled. "With a general, I'd say unprecedented!" They laughed, and then they grew solemn again. There was so much ahead, so much to be done.

A few months earlier, over her protest, he had begun to wear a tuft of whiskers beneath his chin. It made him seem older. He was fifty-three now, she was thirty-five. The gossips had been wrong when they said there was too great a difference in their ages, for theirs had been a good marriage. Through everything there remained the solid core of their happiness.

Walking past a mirror, she thought to herself, I'm showing the years too. She noticed a number of white strands in her thick black hair. She didn't look too hard, for she was afraid there would be more. For several weeks now she had known that she was to have another child. Ordinarily she would have been overjoyed by the discovery, but now in the midst of war, with all the duties of the President's wife suddenly thrust upon her, she had moments of feeling unequal to the task that lay ahead. It occurred to her bitterly that the women who had called her "Queen Varina" had no conception of what was going on in her heart and in her mind.

They were moving at last to their Richmond home, the Confederacy's White House. Young Jeff was poking baby Joe whenever he thought no one was looking. Little Polly was trying to impress the others with her accomplishments. Only Joe, always the best behaved of the trio, sat quietly in the carriage, minding his own business.

"From now on," sighed Varina, "I'm going to have a little disciplining to do."

She could hardly blame the children, she supposed. They had been spoiled during these past few months—pointed at by strangers, patted by colonels, their names called out as they walked along the street. It would be good to have a house of their own again with fewer interruptions and a little privacy. At first her sister Maggie had been excited by the hotel life, but now even Maggie had grown tired of it.

As she stood before their new home a feeling of delight came over her. It was the former Brockenbrough house, a three-storied brick building, gray-stuccoed, facing a terraced garden on the edge of a high hill. An establishment of rich simplicity, it had a small portico at the front, with marble stairs to the street. A line of heavy pillars faced the plantings at the rear. There, Varina decided, was where the family would spend most of its time. The garden, dotted with fruit trees, gave off a cool fragrance that made her think of Brierfield. Going around to the back of the house, she walked through the brick kitchen, carriage house, servants' building, and stables.

"We'll like it here," she told Maggie.

Inside the house she found a high-ceilinged elegance with elaborate cornice work, white-paneled folding doors, and wide windows. She stopped before the marble mantels that reminded her of those others at home back in Mississippi. Jeff had once said: "We may never have other mantels, so let's enjoy these." Well, they had others now.

She arranged a new routine for the family, insuring greater quiet for Jeff and freer movement for the children. She made over rooms, changing their purposes, turning a wide chamber into a nursery.

When her first callers came she was surprised to find that they disapproved of these alterations. She overheard one old beau murmur: "This place was perfect when Mary Brockenbrough used to have it. I remember how she used to walk about these rooms, singing to herself."

"You know"—she smiled at Jeff when she told him the story later—"I almost feel that Mary's still here with us."

"Our patron saint." He grinned.

That night, when she decided to move a highboy from the dining room into the hall, Jeff laughingly protested. "Do you think Mary would approve?" he asked.

When she misplaced a comb the next day she insisted that Mary had pushed it off the bureau. Thereafter it was one of their private jokes.

Varina found that Richmond was a tight little traditional world of its own, making no efforts to follow the fashions of New York or Paris. Richmond was Richmond, and that seemed enough. There was no attempt at the fashionable small talk of, say, Washington City. The Richmonders belonged, and they knew it. Already Varina was aware that some Virginians regarded her Mississippi as the frontier.

She said to Jeff: "Richmond resents the coming of so many strangers. It's never had such a lot of 'foreigners,' people from everywhere, and some of them loud and pushing. They're crowding the town, changing its ways. I can feel a kind of 'English hospitality' here, polite but wary."

Jeff, intent on other matters, shrugged.

For a time her social life proceeded smoothly; if she made any mistakes, she did not know of them. She joined a women's sewing group, and then one evening her sense of humor got her into trouble. They had been working on underwear for the soldiers, and one forthright old lady who had been trying without success to follow a pattern finally dropped the cloth in her hands and cried: "My! Every one of the men's drawers are cut wrong—all right legs!"

This remark was greeted by a shocked silence. Despite herself, Varina laughed. Several elderly women turned and looked at her coldly; one got up and left. Afterward Varina chided herself; would she ever learn? She was not surprised when she heard the echoes of this incident passed on by the gossips. "Mrs. Davis . . . She's too flighty. And not serious about the war—not serious at all."

Several weeks after they were installed in the Brockenbrough house Varina was seated at her desk, shaking her head over another of those letters from people who mistook her handwriting for Jeff's. Opposite her, through the doorway, her glance settled on her favorite piece of furniture—the great rosewood sofa which had been with her in so many places. Now installed in the place of honor in the parlor, it would show the doubters that, even on the lower Mississippi, she and Jeff knew civilization!

She was still at work when Jeff came into the room, walking slowly, his face drawn.

"You remember I fixed the order of our generals with Joe Johnston fourth?"

Varina nodded.

"Joe has just sent me a burning letter, nearly ten pages long." He tossed the letter out to her, and her eyes tightened as she read it. Johnston insisted that he belonged at the very top, ahead of Lee or anybody else. He claimed that the order of generals was a blow aimed only at him, that Jeff was trying to tarnish his fair name as a soldier and a man.

"Why, he's even brought in his father's sword!" Varina snapped. "I don't understand what the sword has to do with it."

Jeff argued the justification for his choices—technical rankings, prior services in the American Army—but she did not try to follow the delicate points. She watched anxiously, however, when he sat down to write his reply.

Her throat tightened as she read: ". . . arguments and statements utterly one-sided . . . insinuations as unfounded as they are unbecoming."

"Don't you think you ought to be a little more tactful with him?" she asked.

"No," Jeff snapped, ending the discussion.

At once she felt repercussions. As she had realized, Joe Johnston had many connections, many high-placed friends; whispers against Jeff's action were heard in the Confederate Congress and elsewhere. Lydia Johnston had been expected at a White House party, but she sent brief regrets. The following afternoon, riding to the drill grounds, Varina smiled as Lydia rode by. Her old friend looked in another direction.

She was sorry; for several years she had liked Lydia as well as any woman she knew. Their association was over. She understood at once that there was no hope for a reconciliation. Lydia wouldn't be that disloyal to her husband, nor, for that matter, would she.

Returning home that afternoon, Varina found another friend eagerly waiting to pass on the news that Lydia was talking angrily against Jeff.

"She says Mr. Davis is incompetent and has a grudge against her husband. And you—she called you a 'Western woman'!"

Varina chuckled. Lydia had first called her a "Western belle."

The next day that term of approbation was changed. One of Lydia's intimates, she learned, had converted it to "coarse Western woman."

Maggie Howell, hearing about it, flamed with anger. "We can't let this go on," she cried. "It's a shame! Why, everybody knows——"

"No, child," Varina stopped her. "There's nothing we can do. It's like the old story of a piece of gossip changing each time until you can't recognize the first version."

Although she tried to put the best face on it, the thorns were growing thick among the roses, for her as well as for Jeff. How had Mr. Benjamin put it months ago in Washington City? Life never worked out just as one hoped. The wise man "does what he can and accepts the rest." To be a wise woman; was that beyond her?

Jeff came home one afternoon, his face cold with fury.

"They're wrangling in Congress over why our forces didn't push on at Manassas and carry the war to Washington City."

Joe Johnston's friends were saying that he wanted to do it. A House member, a volunteer aide to Beauregard, was charging that the Creole, too, had been anxious to shove ahead.

Jeff's fist clenched. "It's not true, it didn't happen that way. We talked about going on, but the Army was disorganized, the weather was bad. We waited overnight; the next day rain turned the ground into gruel, and the three of us agreed we should not proceed."

He slammed down the desk cover and started to write out his replies. This time she could not blame him.

But that night as she lay beside him she slowly realized what those replies might stir up. The two Confederate generals had idolators everywhere, while to the Southern people Jeff was still a remote figure in Richmond.

"Jeff," she asked suddenly, "have you sent those letters yet?"

"A long time ago. Why?"

"Nothing. Nothing, Banny." It didn't matter now.

As she was putting little Joe to bed one night Jeff came to the nursery to help. From his nervous and distraught manner Varina sensed that there was bad news from the troops.

"Yes," Jeff replied, his words muffled as he held the child against him. "Yes, I'm bringing Lee back from western Virginia. Things are almost over in that campaign. Maybe it was an impossible assignment."

Her lips drew together. "And now they're calling him 'Granny Lee' and "Evacuating Lee.' It's so unfair."

Lee's reputation had suffered badly during recent months. She thought of Lee's old doubts, his uncertainty as to whether he would ever be a good soldier. How would he hold up under this blow?

She had her answer at once. Lee returned to Richmond, and his friends immediately suggested that, for his own good, he should explain the problems he faced, among them the fact that his subordinates had quarreled constantly among themselves. Lee decided that he would make no apologies, that he would let matters stand as they were.

When she heard about it Varina almost snapped her fan in half. "That's not what I'd do!" she exclaimed.

"You aren't Robert Lee, my dear," Jeff replied.

With a slight smile he told her the new development: He had given Lee another command, along the South Carolina coast. Already people were saying that he should have dismissed him, that the South would pay for another mistake.

This time the fan in Varina's hand did break.

Late summer gave way to a smoky fall. Another confinement approached for Varina. Sitting on the big gallery at dusk, watching the lights blink on in the valley below, she found Richmond a place of shadowy beauty. Let troubles hover outside; for the moment she had respite in her garden.

Jeff came around the corner of the house and she could tell by his air of suppressed excitement that there was important news.

"What is it, Banny?" she demanded from the chaise longue.

Eyes flashing, he told her that their new commissioners to Europe, Mr. Mason and Mr. Slidell, had been slipped off on a British mail packet, but a United States ship had fired across the bow of that packet and taken the two men prisoner. The South was electrified. England threatened war, and already a British fleet was on its way to Canada!

Varina was as excited as her husband. What a windfall. As they sat together in the soft twilight it seemed to her as if all of her forebodings had been wrong. Victory lay just ahead.

Chapter 17

FOR HOURS, EVER SINCE DAWN, A TWISTING WIND HAD BEATEN THE rain against the walls; a curtain of gray had fallen over Richmond. Varina, her face pressed against the windowpane, stared down the sodden passageway before the Executive Mansion. It was the morning of February 22, 1862, Washington's Birthday, the date selected for Jeff's inauguration. In the recent election he and Alexander Stephens had been chosen to succeed themselves for six-year terms. The brief provisional period of the government had ended, but what should have been an occasion of celebration had turned into a day of anxiety.

Through the opened door Varina saw that Jeff was praying on his knees. She made out a few words: "I ask Thee, Lord, for Thy support. . . ."

How badly did they need support! In the late fall war between England and the North over the Mason-Slidell affair had not materialized. The past few weeks had brought one piece of shattering news after another, and more disasters were in the making. Fort Donelson, the key to Tennessee, had fallen—a man named Grant having defeated Jeff's close friend, Albert Sidney Johnston.

The rain poured more steadily than ever against the windowpanes. The door creaked, and Jeff stood beside her. Before leaving they went to the cradle of the new baby, Billy, who was named after Varina's father. They watched the round face flushed in sleep. Her earlier fear had begun to return; what would be the future of this boy of theirs, or of any of them? Jeff reached out to touch the sleeping child, then withdrew his hand.

"We better not wake him." His voice was muted, mechanical. As he turned to her he added: "Are you ready?"

The carriage waited in the downpour. She and Jeff silently took their places for the ride to Capitol Square. The vehicle moved slowly, the drip of the water endless in their ears. Jeff sat absorbed. Looking out, Varina found eight Negroes in heavy black marching solemnly under umbrellas ahead of them. She rapped and shouted to the driver: "What does this mean?"

The answer was prompt: "Tha's how we always does for funerals and sich-like." With an exclamation she dismissed them from her mind. She might laugh about this later, but for the present this incident depressed her still further.

After long preliminaries at the Capitol they were placed with others on a temporary platform near the monumental equestrian statue of George Washington. The crowd before them shivered under raincoats and umbrellas, and a thin mist hung outside the overfilled platform. The Vice-President, his yellowish hands gripped before him, looked ahead like a carved oriental figure. Jeff walked forward, his face tense with emotion, and his voice rolled out over the wet crowd: "We have reached a black hour. . . . But we will fight on. . . ."

As he stood, painfully lean, his high square forehead wrinkled, shaggy brows overhanging his smoldering eyes, he seemed suddenly like a victim going willingly to a sacrificial pyre. If she stayed, she would break down. Whispering an excuse, she went home and sat for hours beside the baby in the cradle.

The next day she caught sight of a man she had not seen for a long time. Luckily she was not forced to speak to him, for it was their old enemy, Henry Foote. When she asked Jeff if he knew the man was in Richmond he said, "Of course. Hadn't you heard? Foote went to Tennessee, and now they've elected him to our Congress!" Her heart contracted; she thought she knew how potent an opponent that little man could be.

She found out that Mr. Foote was even more dangerous than she supposed. Daily he was marshaling opposition to Jeff and his words were carried back to her. "He's the man that's brought everything down on us," he was telling Richmond. "Him and that Benjamin!"

Sometime before, Jeff had brought in their old friend Judah Benjamin as Secretary of War to take the place of the first incumbent who had resigned. But the choice had been unfavorably received and many people in the capital referred to poor Benjamin as "that arrogant foreigner," or "that Jew that Davis favors."

Angered by these remarks and by Foote's fresh outburst, Varina discussed the matter with Jeff.

"They're against Mr. Benjamin *because* he's a Jew! Isn't that so, Banny?"

Sorrowfully he shrugged.

"He's one of our best men—efficient and quick and dependable in everything. He runs his office—any office he's in—better than anybody else we have." After a moment he added: "He's not to blame for these new losses. We couldn't send supplies or men because we didn't have them to send."

"Why don't you tell the people that?"

"I can't." Jeff had a stricken look. "Even the North doesn't guess how badly off we are at some points. Benjamin came to me this morning and offered to resign immediately—anything I want." Jeff's fist clenched. "I won't let him do it," he cried. "I can't surrender to an attack like that!"

An experienced Washingtonian had once told Varina that a wise official is ready to sacrifice anything for the main goal. Certainly Mr. Seward would have sacrificed Mr. Benjamin under similar circumstances. But Jeff couldn't, and suddenly she was glad of it.

"Isn't there another place for him in the Cabinet," she asked, "a place where he'd fit just as well? Couldn't you give him a new office?" For more than an hour she talked earnestly, then left Jeff to his decision.

The next day the announcement was released that Mr. Benjamin had resigned as Secretary of War to become Secretary of State.

Shortly after this shake-up in the Cabinet Varina was interviewed by a perfect stranger, a persuasive youth who indicated that he wanted a commission. Frankly curious, she tried to find why he had come to her.

"Have we met, or did someone send you?"

The man stared and said calmly: "No, ma'am. Just thought you could swing the thing."

Was this stupidity or arrogance? She jumped up, her skirts rustling. "I've nothing to do with such matters."

His face flamed, and he started for the door, but at the threshold he shot back over his shoulder, "Well, lady, everybody says you got a lot to do with running this whole shebang!"

Her fingers ached to slap him. By main effort she kept her hands at her sides. So that was what Richmond was saying about her! "Queen Varina," and now this . . .

When Mary Chesnut called a little later Varina questioned her carefully. Her gay South Carolina friend sought to evade the point, then told her the truth. "Oh, they peddle all sorts of wild stories, that you and Mr. Benjamin handle things all alone, that you even tell the President what to say to the generals——"

At the sight of Varina's face Mrs. Chesnut stopped.

One evening a few days after the inauguration she drew up behind Jeff's chair, her eyes on an ominous set of figures spread out on the desk before him. The Federals had nearly a million men under arms, the South less than three hundred thousand.

"And our one-year enlistments are ending." Jeff frowned. "We can't depend on volunteers any more. We've lost these last two battles because we just didn't have the man power."

"Then"—she spoke deliberately—"draft the men you need!"

"I've thought of that, of course. But think of the hullabaloo, the animosity that would stir up!"

Her voice grew firmer. "If we don't, we'll lose the war?"

"As usual, Winnie," he groaned, "you put it very forcibly."

He sat silent for a long time, and then his pen moved across the paper, drawing up a plan to summon to the colors all men between eighteen and thirty-five years of age.

Jeff had not underestimated the disturbance the draft bill would cause. Congressmen called it unconstitutional, an insult and an outrage. The fiery Mr. Foote made capital of it in a speech which was reported to Varina later.

Beating his fists against the table, he had cried: "Conscription would make that man Davis a dictator, that's what! We were born free; are we to hold out our wrists for this man's chains? Davis! The worst tyrant man ever saw, and the stupidest, the lowest . . ."

In Georgia, Governor Brown issued a broadside attack: "This draft would make slaves of our white Southern people."

As a final blow she learned that Vice-President Stephens was also against it, not openly so far; but in the back rooms he was saying that he thought it must be defeated, or the whole Southern government would be destroyed.

"Why," she cried to Jeff, "Stephens prefers the letter of the law —the law as *he* sees it—to winning the war! And Governor Brown is just as bad. He's worrying over whether it violates the rights of the states!" She caught herself suddenly, remembering how often in Washington City she had heard that complaint from Jeff himself! Now the shoe was on the other foot.

The debate over the conscription bill dragged on and on, and as the South debated, the North moved. From the generals who came and went in the White House, Varina heard reports of a great Federal offensive which was churning its way toward Richmond. Coupled with those reports was the name McClellan, the newly appointed commander of the Federal forces on the Virginia front.

She said to Jeff: "Why, that must be the shy officer you sent to the Crimean War—the one who had so much trouble that evening with General Scott."

"Yes." He nodded.

And now McClellan had become the most important of the Northern generals and was rising above the cantankerous old Scott. That aged hanger-on, she heard, was soon to go. So McClellan had his revenge on the man who had once tormented him.

Varina thought of something else. "Jeff, didn't you say that the men on that mission would someday be using what they learned in an American war?"

Grimly Jeff inclined his head again. The Army for which he had laid the groundwork, the modernized American Army, was moving upon them.

Overnight the Federals were advancing through crumbling defenses. And now she saw Congress act. Jeff got his draft law, and a few days later he called on Robert E. Lee as his special adviser. In spite of the gravity of the situation, Varina took fresh hope. The South was going to fight back. . . .

Good news came earlier than she expected. On March 8, at Norfolk, the Confederate Navy, patching something together out of steel and wood, had scored a dramatic naval victory with a thing that looked like a brown beetle—the first ironclad.

At the White House men were milling about, trembling with excitement.

"Wiped out everything in sight!" they shouted. "We can go anywhere we want now—Washington, that's the next step!"

Varina called for wine, and there were toasts and cheers. A naval officer came in, proudly carrying an American flag, trophy of the day's victory. He clicked his heels and with a conscious flourish presented it to Varina.

"Our men wanted you to have it, ma'am."

The shouts loud in her ears, Varina held the banner. Happiness surged through her. They were winning again, the bad times were over! Only then did she remember that these Stars and Stripes had once been her flag.

Less than a month later, while they were finishing their morning coffee, a courier dashed in with the news that a great battle was under way in Tennessee under Jeff's old comrade, Albert Sidney Johnston—and the Federal commander, Grant, was losing! She took Jeff's arm. "Maybe this is what we've been hoping for, the one big success." Through a joyous day men and women hastened to the White House for new reports, and now there were no sneers at Sidney Johnston, only words of fervent praise. Jeff and Varina retired very late.

At six the next morning they were wakened by another courier. As he read the message in the chill hall Jeff went gray. Sidney Johnston had been killed in the battle; his troops had lost momentum—and now the Confederates were in retreat from Shiloh! Varina felt for the chair behind her. A thin shaft of sunlight outlined the edge of one of the brick columns of the gallery. Beyond the paneled glass, near a handful of blossoms on a branch, a bird began to sing. Another day had started. Another day like the ones before it?

From the lower South three weeks later came another blow. New Orleans, where her family lived, had fallen! Ben Butler of Massachusetts—the Northern Democrat who had once wanted Jeff for President—had become the tyrant of the Creole city. Annabelle watched Varina with frightened eyes as she moaned to herself: "What's happened to them? What's happened?"

For two weeks she stayed close to her room in wretched suspense, fearing that the Howell family had been captured. Then a letter came with the familiar handwriting. Margaret Howell wrote that her family was safely reunited in Montgomery. They had been separated when New Orleans fell, but now they were with friends in the Alabama town. She sighed for her mother, who was now uprooted once more.

But Margaret ended her letter with firm instructions for her daughter: Varina was not to worry about them and they didn't want to come to Richmond. They preferred to stay quietly in Alabama, out of the limelight. From her words Varina knew that it would have been hopeless to try to change Margaret's mind.

The next week Jeff eased one of Varina's worries. "A government place is opening at Montgomery—for an older man. A government alcohol plant, not a big office, but——"

"He'll be happy to take it," Varina hurried to reply.

A few days later Varina was glad that Margaret Howell had decided not to come to Richmond. Through her window she made out a frightening sight—slowly moving wagons piled with furniture, and sad files of men and women. General Joe Johnston, in charge of the forces opposing McClellan's army, was withdrawing point by point, and the people were fleeing to Richmond.

And still Johnston dropped back. Jeff was frantic.

"I don't know what to do about the man. He's a fine organizer; he can maneuver magnificently. But he won't attack."

Jeff's pale eyes had a flame of intensity.

"Everything has to be ready, he tells us, everything to the last detail; and of course it never works out that way, and he pulls back again. He complains that he's outnumbered. Aren't we always outnumbered?"

Yes, Varina reflected, and some generals won victories despite those odds! In Joe Johnston's case, could it be a fundamental unsureness of himself? He had overpowering ambition, no question of that; but with it went an unwillingness to take a risk.

As weeks passed and the whole region became alarmed she began to notice a change in Jeff. In these hours of trial he was speaking more and more often of religion. Though he had attended the Episcopal church in Washington with her, he had never joined it.

Now he suddenly said to her one evening: "Winnie, I've thought a long time about this. I want to join the church."

"I've expected it, Banny. And I'm glad."

That Sunday, in a private ceremony, Jeff was baptized by the minister of St. Paul's. As he stood in the yellow light Varina thought she saw gradual peace settle over his well-chiseled face. Only a few were present, and the low voice of the minister made the ritual personal and close. For the rest of the day Varina and Jeff remained with the children in their garden back of the White House. Toward dusk a bell tolled, and Varina remembered what a neighbor had said, that the Federals were so close "they can sometimes hear our chimes." A shiver ran through her, and she looked away so that Jeff would not see her fear.

The next morning he said to her quietly, but with an intensity that did not escape her: "The enemy's gunboats are almost on the city."

"I want to be with you, here!"

"I thought you would." His face was gentle. "But I'll have one less anxiety if you go away with the children."

She knew she had to agree.

Early the following day she and the children, with Annabelle and the nurse, waved good-by to Jeff as the railroad cars pulled slowly away. She had left her house, the place where she had made her home, where all of her hopes lay.

The placid town of Raleigh, North Carolina, was her destination. They had several friends there, but at Jeff's suggestion she went to a hotel. She found signs of panic, men and women selling their furniture, packing goods to be removed at the first warning. During the greater part of the time she stayed quietly in her room. Most of the people did not recognize her, and for this she felt grateful. Her mind and her heart were in another place.

Joe Johnston continued to retreat. Jeff wrote her a disturbing letter. He had unexpectedly visited one of the suburbs and found Johnston's men already encamped! Without consulting or informing the government, Johnston had decided to bring his men into

Richmond. But at this point Jeff called a meeting of the Cabinet. It was decided that Richmond must be defended, the withdrawals had to stop.

But Jeff concluded his letter with this statement: "I packed some valuable books and the sword I wore for some years, together with the pistols I used at Monterey and Buena Vista. These articles will have a value to the boys in aftertime, and to you now."

Was disaster so close?

When she put the children to bed that evening she kissed them with sudden tenderness. Annabelle looked on, pity in her big eyes. Joe went off to sleep at once, curling against the wall, his arm over his head. Jeff, even more restive than usual, had to be coaxed. Polly was beginning to take in a great deal. She looked at Varina curiously and finally asked: "What's the trouble, Mother?"

But Varina, unable to speak, could only shake her head.

For a long time Varina sat quietly next to Annabelle. The Negro woman, getting old in the service of Jeff and Varina, creaked back and forth in her rocking chair, her dress billowing about her, her arms folded over her gingham waist. From below, an occasional footstep echoed along the street, and the flickering lights left a reflection on the ceiling.

Finally Annabelle said: "When we know?"

"Soon, I think." Varina stopped. On an impulse she asked: "Annabelle, how do you feel about this war?"

Annabelle's lips puckered, then relaxed. "Well . . . Well, nothin' in partic'lar. Ain' my concern, I s'pose."

"I mean, about slavery and all that?"

Annabelle rose. "I ain' studyin' dat, Miss Rina. De young, dey seem to worry at it. Me, maybe I'm too ole. Happy like I am, I guess. Happy 'nough."

Varina pressed the black woman's arm. She knew now, if she had ever doubted it, that Annabelle would stay with her through almost anything.

As she sat there it occurred to Varina that there were many Negroes like Annabelle in the South, house servants, whose contacts with their white owners had been close and continuous. Yet what of the rest, the vast mass of field workers, and what of the young generation? If matters became worse for the Confederacy, how strong would be the call of freedom?

The news from Richmond during the following week continued to be alarming. She heard that a great battle was under way, that Joe Johnston had been wounded and taken from the field, finally that Lee had assumed command of the Southern troops defending Richmond. Her reactions to these events were mixed, for while she was glad that Lee was finally getting his chance, she was worried that Johnston's organizational ability would be missed.

She returned one afternoon from a fruitless visit to the telegraph office and found that Billy had contracted a fever.

"How long has this been going on?" she asked the colored nurse.

"Jus' a lil while. I thought it'd go down——"

"Get the doctor right away!"

By the time the physician arrived Billy had grown much worse. He was struggling for air, his fists beating against the covers. The doctor shook his head.

"I have to tell you, Mrs. Davis. I'm afraid—it's pneumonia."

That day, and for the rest of the week, she stayed constantly at the baby's side. She felt agonized as the throat filled and the breath rasped in the small throat. There was nothing she could do, nothing except force the medicines into Billy's mouth and pray.

At a time like this she wanted Jeff with her, but that was out of the question. Everything for them, for the whole of the Confederacy, depended on what happened in Richmond. On the seventh day of Billy's sickness Varina collapsed from overwork and strain and was put to bed herself by the redoubtable Annabelle.

Then slowly the baby improved. Varina was able to leave her bed and attend more closely to him. The fever was beginning to drop; the pain of Billy's breathing lessened. She knelt at the bedside and offered up her thanks to God.

Now she could turn again to the news from Richmond. She learned that Lee was doing peculiar things, splitting the Army, shifting men in a way that older military minds questioned. But Lee's strategy succeeded. Again she held a message from Jeff in her trembling hands, a message which said: "GREAT VICTORY." Again the crowds cheered and banners waved, but this time a new name was shouted in the streets and toasted in the parlors, the name of Robert E. Lee, the defender of Richmond, the new hero of the South.

More months had passed, and again she was home with Jeff in Richmond. Lee had pressed on toward Washington, but he had lacked the forces to carry all the way through, and he had finally withdrawn. The flush of Lee's first victory had begun to pale, yet they were safe now, safe for some time.

On a warm September afternoon she was passing the front door of the White House when the soldier on guard, drawing up stiffly, handed her a bulletin. Abraham Lincoln had announced that on the coming January 1, 1863, all slaves were to be freed in states that had left the Union. Apparently the news had already spread through the town, for outside in the streets people were shouting in anger and derision.

"Huh! Let *Abe* try to free 'em!"

"Why don't he free the niggers up there too?"

As she caught the full significance of the bulletin, she was remembering her grandmother's word: "This slavery, it's got to go, sooner or later." Now, if the North won, it was gone forever.

Her mind returned, too, to those first days at Brierfield when she shook James Pemberton's hand and talked with Jeff about slavery. Yes, he had told her, emancipation would come sometime in the future. Sometime . . . And then those years of heated debate, provocation, reaction, and insult . . . Was slavery going to end, anyway?

One thing she understood without asking Jeff or Mr. Benjamin or anyone else. The Emancipation Proclamation would help the North. Mr. Lincoln had coupled his side forever with the cause of freedom. In England, in Europe, his words would have vast weight. The South could argue, call it unconstitutional, illegal. It wouldn't matter.

An hour later, to steady herself, she picked up the paper. She must do something, anything to keep from thinking about the war. But her eyes, by this time trained to hunt through the news, stopped at the death columns. They halted at a familiar name. *McGruggy, Jack,* and *McGruggy, Rob.* At first she could not remember where she had heard it. Then it came to her—Mrs. McGruggy, the pilot's wife.

She couldn't be sure, but these men might well be the sons of the Mrs. McGruggy she had known. They had died fighting for the South, for slavery. Then it occurred to her that the McGruggy's weren't slave owners. Hadn't a politician in Washington City once told her that most of the people of the South had no slaves? Still, the McGruggys, most of them, were fighting as fiercely as the plantation owners. But they were fighting for their homes, their families, their very lives—not for the things the orators argued about in their debates.

Chapter 18

VARINA WENT TO THE WINDOW OF THEIR ROOM TO THROW BACK THE curtain and admit more of the warming October sun. The leaves were flying, and from a distance the lowlands of Richmond stretched serenely toward the far-off horizon. The trees against her garden wall and those that spotted the expanse before her were a glory of red and brown and yellow. But her mind was on the small dark roofs of the houses below her. Did the people in them alternate, as she did, between hope and apprehension?

The odds were so overwhelming against a Confederate success. How could they survive? Yet they did. Yet they managed to hold on, making what they had suffice, patching together, scraping up the rest. And how much of it was due to the man who lay near her?

Jeff was stretched out on the couch, his face contorted by suffering.

"Are you well enough for me to read again?" she asked.

He nodded and closed his eyes. During the past month his health had broken under the heavy work and worry. Before that, from time to time he had had to take to bed, with a recurrence of his old neuralgia and attacks of nerve strain. But now he had been in his room for weeks. Relentlessly he ran the government from the sickroom. Varina kept callers away and saw to it that only the most vital matters were brought to him. At last he had an adequate secretary, Burton Harrison, a scholarly youth with an instinct for organization. With his help and Varina's, Jeff forced himself to attend to the problems which could not wait.

As she looked at him now, lying on the couch, she saw how much he showed the struggle, how old and tired he looked.

A gray uniform appeared at the door, and Varina leaped to her feet. It was Robert Lee, now the great soldier of the South.

Lee paused. "Perhaps I could come back——"

Her exclamation of welcome reassured him. Jeff, craning his neck, managed to sit up, and a wan smile played over his lips.

"Come right in," said Varina, "and let me take your coat."

As she took it and placed it over a chair her hands passed over the rough places. How worn it felt, and how much patched!

Lee caught her expression. There was a flicker of amusement in his eyes. "I'm afraid I'm feeling, just now, as broken as my coat—and without any patches."

His boots, well splashed, were dripping on Varina's white carpet. For once, meticulous housekeeper though she was, she ignored it. She searched the face of this man who was their hope and assurance in these days of confusion. In Lee's face, too, she found that the strain had left its mark. There were deeper furrows, new creases along the strong nose and lips. His hair was rapidly whitening.

They talked of the new "starvation parties," entertainments without refreshments; the rumors of spies who slipped in and out of Richmond. Then the conversation shifted to the speculators who grew fat while the town suffered, and the blockade runners who brought in profitable luxuries rather than badly needed food. She tried to shift the conversation from these dreary topics and inject a lighter note.

"Here we three are"—she smiled—"just as we were in the old days in Washington."

"Almost," said Jeff. Though he was trying to be light, his tone had become sepulchral. In the silence that followed, the only sound was the settling of coal in the grate. Lee's eyes dropped to the day's newspaper, which had castigated Jeff and the whole administration.

"Our trouble," he drawled, "is that our best generals are working for the papers."

It was rare to hear such a remark from Lee. So he, too, was feeling the unending criticism.

"My men are hungry," Lee was telling Jeff, his voice low. "Sometimes, you know, we get less to eat than even the people in Richmond."

Desertions had grown more and more alarmingly. Some of those who remained were fighting with broken shoes, their feet bloody as they marched.

"Sometimes"—Lee's look was grave—"they race each other to reach a Union body and to rip off the shoes." His voice died.

Varina stared into the fire.

But Jeff surprised her by saying hopefully, "No matter how bad things seem down here, they look as bad or worse in the North."

A wave of uncertainty had set in at Washington City, a mood close to despondency. There was resentment over Lincoln's leadership.

"They claim he's interfering with the Army," Jeff added, and there was ironic satisfaction in his voice. His own enemies said the same thing of him.

As Lee got up to go General Joe Johnston was announced. She recalled that morning of the previous year when both the order of their rank and the order of their visits had been reversed. She wondered what would have been their fate had Johnston remained in command at Richmond.

When he came in there was an expression of resentment on Johnston's face. His eyes were cold and even his mustache appeared to bristle with annoyance. Yet could he blame Jeff because he had been wounded and Lee, taking his place, had scored a magnificent victory? From his couch Jeff, with some difficulty, reached up and shook his hand. Varina remembered to be cordial.

"Joe, I'm so glad you're better," she said. "You're looking awfully well."

"I am well, thank you."

That should have warned her, but she was more than anxious to restore good relations with Joe Johnston.

"And Lydia?" she added. "I haven't seen her in months."

"Indeed?" There was frost on the word. Reluctantly the general added: "Lydia is, I trust, well."

He faced Jeff with an abrupt gesture. "I'm here, sir, to discuss my new assignment. I believe it's to be in the West?"

She had been dismissed. A touch of color on her cheeks, Varina bowed and went to the door. There she heard Joe Johnston raising questions, as usual, about his command.

"Is my authority to be unlimited?" he was asking.

Downstairs Maggie had just returned from one of the hospitals, and Varina, meeting her on the stairway, spluttered: "If Joe Johnston thought less about his privileges and more about winning battles . . ."

She was still frowning an hour later when Mary Chesnut called to take her to a reception. Mary was full of new developments. "Have you heard Alexander Stephens's latest?" She laughed. "He thinks we ought to drop the draft and disband the Army whenever it's cold weather. According to his plan, the men would go home in December and come back in the spring."

Varina's look was wry. "We fight a war, and he theorizes!"

"You know," her friend fumed, "no matter what the administration wants to do, he says it's against states' rights!"

The break between Stephens and Jeff had grown considerably wider. He no longer came to the White House and he barely spoke to the man he was supposed to follow in the office of Chief Executive. They had never been close friends, but now Stephens was a fully functioning oppositionist.

Varina went to the reception with Mary, but she was too worried to enjoy herself. She left early and came home to find Jeff still awake, shaken and angry. There had been another serious development. Governor Brown of Georgia had issued circulars to the troops, telling them that the draft violated the state law.

"Thousands of them are taking him at his word," Jeff cried, "and they're running away from camp."

In North Carolina, Governor Vance was asking state judges to issue writs releasing drafted soldiers.

"And in South Carolina"—his voice dropped—"they're talking about seceding from the Confederacy."

Varina, watching her husband, thought of some fine high-strung animal trapped in a maze.

Jeff said to her one day, "Winnie, we're on the move again. Can you arrange to be here at the White House most of the time? There'll be many visits from generals, state officials, and the like."

After a little thought she decided she could no longer return social calls, for her White House duties were too heavy and too important.

She had anticipated some complaint, but not the high-pitched protests.

"As bad as Mrs. Lincoln!" some said.

"That puts me even with you, Banny." She laughed when she told him. "A lot of them in Congress say they'd prefer Lincoln to you!"

Troubles began from another direction, rising out of the Emancipation Proclamation. Annabelle ran in to say: "Dat Phemie, she gone!" Phemie had been one of their new black staff.

The next day a colored manservant slipped out and did not return. There were rumors that Yankee spies were making the acquaintance of her servants and offering them two thousand dollars each if they would run away. Varina doubted that Northern agents were involved. Many of her friends were losing their slaves just as frequently. They didn't need any special encouragement when freedom was a matter of a few miles.

During one of her receptions she had a bad scare. She had been busily pouring tea when all at once one of her guests cried: "I smell smoke!" Sure enough, there were wisps of it trailing through the hall, and as Varina dashed up the stairs, her heart beating wildly, she prayed that her children were safe. She found them sleeping quietly in their beds with their room quite free from smoke. In fact, she soon discovered that the fire was confined to a small room in the cellar and that it was now out.

Little damage had been done, but Annabelle said after the guests left: "Dey says at de back dey saw a man hangin' aroun' a while ago."

So the fire had been set! Varina shook with fear. Her children might have been burned to death. To think that someone would hate them so much!

She went to Jeff, sank into his embrace, and sobbed against his shoulder. He took her to their room, and she went to sleep with his arm about her. Twice during the night she woke in a spasm of terror. Repeatedly during the weeks that followed a nightmare haunted her, a wild dream in which she and the babies were suffocating while Jeff tried vainly to reach them.

The odds against them in Richmond were increasing. Whites as well as blacks were leaving them, and the Footes and the Stephenses were gaining recruits. Varina worked even harder to help Jeff socially. With the help of his secretary, the methodic Burton Harrison, she arranged additional teas, luncheons, and sent invitations to every disaffected individual who appeared willing to accept—and some, it turned out, who were not.

"If there's the slightest chance that we can bring them into our camp, I'm willing to try," she assured Jeff. Though he did not seem optimistic over the prospect, his look conveyed his gratitude to her. She was succeeding pretty well, she thought, until one day Maggie brought her a newspaper clipping. It accused her of seeking to create a "royal court," of throwing away the people's money on fripperies.

Raging, she reached into her desk and tossed another clipping to her sister. "They ran that a little while ago when I cut down on our parties because the war news was so bad!" At that time the papers called her and Jeff misers, accusing them of hoarding the government's pay.

"Hoarding!" Varina fretted. "For months I've dug into our reserve money to keep the house going. We've had dry biscuits four days a week so that I could afford two chickens for a party at twenty-eight dollars each!"

The gossip about her now began to acquire new twists. People said that her father was "lowborn" and that as a girl Varina had "done housework." Sooner or later, regardless of the Howells' background in New Jersey and the Kempes' in Virginia, she had expected someone to make capital of the fact that William Howell had not been a successful planter, but she had underestimated the maliciousness of the attacks.

While the gossips of Richmond were vilifying his and his daughter's names, William Howell passed away in Montgomery. Margaret sent Varina the details in her clear, nervous hand. On the day he died he had been talking about Varina and Jeff, how well they were doing, how he had realized from the start the man that Jeff would be. William had liked his government work, though it had not kept him as busy as he expected. He seemed to know every second person in town, and people said that no old settler had ever had a bigger funeral. . . .

Varina's tears blotted out the words. To the end William Howell had maintained his happy air, his quiet charm, and his impracticality. She remembered his teasing, his mildly reprimanding manner when she had done something wrong—and the guileless smile that took away what sting his words carried.

Hardly anything had worked out the way he planned. William Howell would be forgotten when others of his day were remembered. But William had injured no one intentionally, and she could think of few men of whom this might be said. Wherever he had lived, there would be people who recalled his good deeds.

When she told Jeff the news he put his arms around her and then said at once: "We'll send for your mother to be here with us."

"Thank you, Banny. I'd hoped you'd say that."

Margaret delayed for weeks, saying that she didn't want to intrude, she didn't like the turmoil and formality of Richmond. Then at last she agreed to come, "for a while only."

Margaret's arrival in Richmond was one of the few happy moments Varina had known in a long time. After the two women embraced, Margaret kissed Maggie and then turned to Billy.

"This is the one"—and her eyes showed the pain and joy of the memory—"the one you named for him?" Then, blowing her nose in a businesslike manner, Margaret threw back her head, prepared to face Richmond and anything it held for her.

That night Varina and her mother talked together for hours. "Yes, the boys are all right, as far as I know," Margaret told her. "Scattered, scattered . . ." Her eyes dropped. The oldest one, Joseph, who had fought in the Mexican War under Jeff, was on remote Army service. Becket continued in the Navy, and his letters were infrequent. . . . Tonight the last one would be with them, for young Jefferson Davis Howell was to follow his mother to Richmond.

When Jeff Howell appeared several hours later he kissed his mother and looked at Varina diffidently. "Don't you know me, boy?" Varina demanded, and caught him against her. "Don't you remember your days at Brierfield when you rode the pony?"

"I sure do," he said in a strange falsetto. He blushed; his voice was changing. "I still like horses, but I don't want to get in the cavalry any more. I prefer the Navy."

Varina saw her mother flinch.

"You're too young!" she snapped.

Young Jeff Howell argued long and persuasively. Margaret was unyielding, yet Varina suspected that in the end she would lose. There was something in the boy's face.

The next day Jeff grinned. "Jeffy isn't one to let grass grow under his feet. He waited his turn at my office today, then applied for a cadetship in our naval program!"

"I won't give up my last one!" Margaret protested. But she seemed to realize that he, too, would soon be gone.

Later that month Jeff Howell packed a grip and started off. As the wagon rocked away from the stuccoed gray house on the hilltop Varina and her mother stood with Maggie in the fanlighted doorway.

Margaret Howell sighed. "We're grinding our seed corn, that's what we're doing." It was true, Varina knew, but they needed man power badly, so badly. The last time she saw Lee's army there appeared to be no young men in it—only haggard old men and children like Jeff Howell.

As she left the door she encountered her own son Jeff with a big grin on his face, pointing with pride to the uniform he was wearing. He had been begging for a soldier suit, and Jeff had finally ordered a replica of a Confederate gray uniform. This was the first time he had ever worn it.

"Papa say he get me a pony," the boy cried, "and I ride just like big soldier!"

The smile on little Jeff's face faded as he looked first at his mother, then at his grandmother. They both had such strange expressions on their faces, he thought. . . .

One quiet afternoon soon after Margaret Howell's arrival Annabelle waddled up to Varina in her most ingratiating manner.

"Miss Rina, what you say," she began, then paused and added finally, "ef I ask to git married?"

Varina's eyes opened wide. In her preoccupation with other matters this was something that had escaped her.

"Who is it? Robert, the coachman?"

"Oh no!" Annabelle said scornfully. "He too ole. It's dat butler Pete, de one Mr. Davis brung in a while back." She looked almost ashamed. "You know I'm a widder 'bout seven year. A woman's nature, it crave comp'ny."

Varina took Annabelle's hand. "That's all right, Annabelle. I'm glad, and I'm sure Mr. Davis will agree with me when I tell him."

Varina herself had not been greatly impressed with Pete, who appeared willing but not overbright. He must be much younger than Annabelle. Still . . .

The marriage followed promptly, and it gave every indication that it would work out well. Clearly Annabelle was dominating the situation, and now she went about in a somewhat better humor. Her slight inclination to grumpiness had gone. For that, too, Varina gave thanks, for in these days they needed as calm a household as possible.

They still lost slaves. Varina was only sure of Annabelle and old Robert, the dignified coachman. One evening she approached Jeff on the subject. "Banny, I've been thinking about this for some time. You remember John Pemberton, James's son at Brierfield? Why don't you bring him here? He's hard-working and ambitious."

Jeff nodded, and eventually a new face joined the household. As soon as he got the opportunity to talk to her alone John said to her: "Miss Rina, if you don' min'—I sure glad to be here, sure glad. But I was wonderin'. It was you 'at thought of it?"

"Well, yes. Why?"

"Er—I was thinkin', tha's all."

He was about to go when she called him back. "John, what about your wanting to buy your freedom?"

"I still hanker to. But the mos' I could save was six hun'red dollar. 'At ain't enough."

"I'm afraid not. Still, you're building it up."

He frowned and shook his head in a discouraged fashion. She suddenly remembered his brother at home. "How about him? Is he saving too?"

"Him!" John's scorn was apparent. "He ain' got the want to be— to be a man, a free man!" Then he looked away, as if he had betrayed a secret.

"Well, we'll see."

It was a long time before she forgot that look of anger and hope combined. Freedom . . . It was a potent word.

That night she glanced at the paper on her desk, and the same word stared up at her. The Confederate government had been appealing to the growers to plant less cotton, more foodstuff for soldiers and civilians. Now a former Secretary of State was announcing he'd raise as much cotton as he wanted to. The government was interfering with his freedom, his constitutional rights!

In icy December new crises developed on both Eastern and Western fronts. "I've got to go to the West." Jeff frowned. "Things are moving badly." It would be his first long trip from Richmond, and, though she would miss him sorely, she was glad he was going. Now he might really know what was happening to people in other parts of the South, people who complained that the administration in Richmond never thought of them.

But when he returned after weeks of traveling he was almost in a state of collapse. After she got him to bed she sat beside him and stroked his weary face. "It was bewildering," he told her in a husky voice. "At some places they seemed friendly, but again they were cold, hostile."

Friction had broken out between Joe Johnston and his subordinates. In Tennessee, General Braxton Bragg was quarreling with his own staff.

At the mention of Bragg, Varina winced. That nervous man who looked like a religious zealot . . . How could Jeff maintain confidence in him? Already many people were blaming Jeff for keeping him in command. For once she felt a little sorry for Johnston, having to deal with Bragg.

As winter gave way to spring she heard again the name of Grant, the Federal commander, and the name of a city—Vicksburg, where she and Jeff had often visited. Grant, gaining in fame, had been assigned the task of taking Vicksburg, heart of the Confederate defenses on the lower Mississippi. Jeff brought her the added news that Lincoln was backing Grant to the limit.

"If Vicksburg goes," he told her, "we'll lose most of the West."

For Varina there was another consideration. Just below Vicksburg lay Brierfield, their home.

The Vicksburg campaign dragged on and on as Varina and her mother ransacked the papers for every word about it. Grant was making frantic efforts, exploring back bayous, trying to alter the waters of the Mississippi which protected it. He failed, yet he did not give up. There came a respite.

"They'll be starting again soon," she told her mother. "But for a while we don't have to think about it."

There was enough to worry about anyway. Food prices had gone shockingly high. There were days when she found it hard to get milk for the four children. Biscuits were gray, flour more and more scarce.

"There's a lot of food in the South," Jeff told her. "One of our main problems, though, is to transport it."

She put her hand to her head. A statement like that meant absolutely nothing to women with families to feed.

Once when the cook proudly displayed a piece of fine bacon she almost wept. "It looks as good as gold to me!" At the table she and Jeff and her mother each refused it politely, until, reaching over resolutely, Varina cut it into three equal pieces. Then, catching the ravenous look in Maggie's eyes, she gave her portion to her sister.

She was eating less, watching leftovers more carefully. Though Annabelle protested, she took a basket and did her own marketing. Thus it was that on a bright April morning, as the elms of Richmond were showing their first green, she came upon a throng of women converging on the shops near Capitol Square.

"What is it?" she asked the coachman.

He looked around at her, his eyes scared. "They says it's trouble about food. They gonna get it to keep from starving, they says!"

She watched from a short distance, her heart beating rapidly. There were sounds of a heavy pounding and then the tinkle of glass. Women screamed and several ran away with bread, vegetables, or sides of meat in their hands. The crowd pushed on. More store windows were smashed, and some of the storekeepers were resisting. Women and children were being hurt. A girl went by with a bloody head; in her arms she carried a box. Whatever it was, it wasn't food. Then Varina realized that the crowd was entirely out of hand, stealing jewelry, clothing, hats, anything that came to hand.

"Soldiers!" someone cried.

She wheeled about in her seat. Between a file of marching men she saw a carriage with city officials. They forced their way to the edge of the wild mob.

One of the officials stood up and shouted at the top of his lungs: "Unless you disband, the men will fire!"

Nothing happened. Then on the other side of the crowd a familiar figure jumped up on top of a dray. It was Jefferson Davis.

Her hand clutched her throat. Suppose someone shot him? Suppose the mob turned on him? So many were blaming him for their troubles.

Jeff raised his arms, and this time there was silence. His words carried a power, a conviction she had seldom heard.

"Go to your homes," he pleaded. "What you're doing is lawless. It will only hurt you in the long run. Nobody will send food here if this happens!"

From a distance his cheeks were deeper-sunken than ever; his tired face showed the lines of suffering, mental as well as physical. There were angry murmurs from the crowd, and one woman in a torn sweater shook a fist at him.

Jeff lifted his hands again. "You say you have no money. Here's all I have!" He emptied his pockets into the mob. Then he took out his watch. "We don't want to hurt anyone, but this has got to stop. If you aren't gone in five minutes you'll be fired on." His calmness had sobering effect, but still no one left.

The soldiers took their positions; the captain gave his command: "Load!" For a tense minute there was no movement, and then a little sullenly the mob began to break up.

Varina, almost in tears with her sudden relief, told Robert to drive straight home. She was in her sitting room when Jeff returned, pale as death.

"These people were stirred up by enemy propaganda!" he said bitterly.

Perhaps that's what started it, she thought, but there was another reason behind the riot, a reason more powerful than any propaganda ever invented. She had seen women stuffing bread into their mouths and children gnawing ravenously at raw vegetables. Today she had seen hunger.

The news from the front lines was worse. Joe Johnston had failed in his attempt to outwit Grant, and now several thousand Confederate soldiers were bottled up in Vicksburg and a hideous siege was under way. Grant was ready to starve the people out.

Varina received letters from many friends in Mississippi. The men and women of Vicksburg were hiding under their houses, in cellars, or digging caves to escape the shelling. They were eating acorns, berries, chewing leather, swallowing bread made of spoiled flour, and eating mule and horse meat. Diseases of hunger and filth were plaguing them. . . . These were her people, her land. This was her part of the South.

"Banny," she cried, "those people can't hold out forever. What's going to happen?"

Jeff had no answer. As disturbed as she was, he paced the floor for hours. Varina knew that the major force on which they might call for reinforcements was Lee's army in Virginia. As she listened to her husband's footsteps she realized that a choice must be made —Old South or New, Virginia or Mississippi.

When Jeff came downstairs he was still shaken, undecided. "I've called the Cabinet, Winnie."

As she waited outside the parlor where they were conferring the sound of voices reached her. Lee was speaking in a soft, firm tone. He had a new plan. He asked them to let him use his men for a paralyzing thrust into Pennsylvania that would endanger Washington City. The North would have to pull men from elsewhere to save the capital. The scheme could save both fronts. Listening, Varina sensed that the Cabinet was hesitating. Jeff's South, or Lee's?

Feet scraped, chairs were pushed back, and Jeff emerged, his step unsteady. He told her quietly that Lee had carried the day.

On a hot summer evening Varina walked desperately up and down the wide gallery overlooking the garden. Jeff sat just inside the door, receiving telegram after telegram. "Lee's attacked. . . . His men are making a new assault. The Federals are entrenched on a steep hill." The scene was Gettysburg, and hour by hour the messages multiplied. The Confederates were moving slowly, slowly, under withering fire, dying by the thousands. Nevertheless, they advanced.

"They're on their way to the top," Jeff told her. In the dark she prayed.

"They've carried the top!" His voice broke.

Then Lee had done the impossible, achieved the thing they said he couldn't do! She settled herself comfortably in a porch chair, happy for the first time in many months. Jeff's voice went on and on, but now it was jubilant.

Then came the terrible climax. A courier dashed in, almost

collapsing before them. Jeff caught the man and took the message from his hand. The Confederates had not been able to hold their gains. They had lacked the man power, the reserves, and they had finally withdrawn. Jeff's words fell in a low whisper: "We took the risk and we lost."

The next morning came the news that Vicksburg, too, was gone. It had surrendered on the Fourth of July!

"And now the South's cut in half." Jeff's voice trailed away and Varina drew her husband's head against hers. How long would it be now, how long?

Brierfield, their Brierfield, had fallen to the enemy. Federal soldiers had triumphantly ransacked the Jeff Davis home. They had stripped the stables of animals, and now General Grant had a new mount from Brierfield which he called by the name of its former owner. Furniture had been tossed out of the windows. The library which she and Jeff had collected through the years was now scattered over the countryside. Brierfield, the place she had loved most on earth . . . Would she ever see it again?

Fortunately, before the Union victory Joe Davis had moved his family and most of his slaves to a point of comparative safety. For Eliza it was only a brief stopping place on a far longer journey. Her long years of illness, her strain and suffering, had ended. Eliza, Varina's closest friend through so many years along the river; Eliza, who had done so much to help them both, was finally at peace.

Chapter 19

VARINA HAD RISEN EARLY ON THIS CHILL SPRING MORNING. JEFF was again away in the troubled West, and she was going to do something she had planned for days. She could no longer afford the feed for the pair of horses for her carriage, and she was going to sell them. Jeff would object, but she had to think of her four children and of the new one which was now taking shape within her. It was due in June, and she shuddered when she wondered where she and Jeff would be when that month came.

As she threw on her clothes she frowned over her much-resewed dress. In the eight months since Vicksburg's fall food prices had jumped astoundingly. Confederate dollars were selling at fifty to one, and their value dropped daily. Yesterday she had gone to a store for eggs and found them twenty-five dollars a dozen.

Pulling her veil over her face, she went stealthily to the small dark shop whose address she had been given. Her voice betrayed her agitation. "I have a carriage and pair, good condition——"

"Why do you want to sell?" Seldom had she heard so harsh a tone. They said that this hard-faced speculator had become a rich man on his profits during the first month of the war.

"Do I have to explain that to you?" She was so angry she forgot her nervousness.

At that the man turned obsequious. "Of course, madame." Then recognition lighted his face. "Mrs. Davis, isn't it?"

"I am Mrs. Davis, but if you buy the carriage and pair I don't want it known where they came from."

"I'm discreet." There was a touch of amusement behind the words, and for this she hated him the more. When he named the amount she was about to walk away. Yet, sharp as this individual was, she had been told there were worse ones.

"Very well," she sighed.

The war had brought up vultures like this, and they had multiplied and prospered. Yet, she reminded herself, the war had brought out the best in people too. Wherever she went she saw signs of sacrifice—families who moved without complaint from once-handsome homes in the country to squalid rooms in town; tired women who smiled cheerfully and worked day in, day out, at the pitifully ill-equipped hospitals.

From the speculator's shop Varina hurried to another store to make her purchases before the prices rose again. She handed the money to a girl and said to her: "Send me as many barrels of flour as this will buy." At least they would have bread.

But late that afternoon she heard the familiar sound of wheels and horses' hoofs. Robert, the coachman, who had tried to dissuade her from the sale she had made that morning, came beaming to her with an unsigned note. Her carriage and horses were being returned to Mrs. Davis with the compliments of a gentleman who preferred to be nameless. Her eyes softened. It meant a great deal to know they had such a friend.

Early one evening Varina and Maggie, riding in from a friend's house, came upon two Negro boys who were fighting in the street. One of them, a full-grown youth, was pounding his smaller opponent unmercifully. With little regard for her personal safety, Varina stepped in between them, slapped the big Negro, and drove him off. She saw then that the little one was bleeding badly from the mouth and nose. He was indescribably dirty and dressed in old rags.

"He's coming home with us," she told Maggie.

At the White House, Annabelle looked sternly at the still weeping boy. Robert, too, had a hint of disdain in his eyes. "What you doin' wid trash like dat?" Annabelle demanded. "We ain' never had nigger like dat aroun'."

"That's enough, Annabelle," Varina ordered. "You wash him for me. There, son, don't worry. We'll talk later."

When the wretched little object stood before her, clean at last but still forlorn, Varina's heart went out to him.

"You look half starved. When did you eat last?"

"Yestiddy, ma'am." To her next question he answered promptly. "I'm a orphing, freeborn. Dat boy, he claim he own me, but he don'. He don'!" He sniffled. "Kin I stay, ma'am? I'll be good."

"What's your name?"

"Jim Limber. I'll take any name you wan'!"

"That's good enough, Jim. We'll see." She faced Annabelle. "We'll try him for a while. Annabelle, get him an old suit somewhere and burn what he's wearing."

Annabelle, grumbling to her husband down the hall, led the child away.

The next morning the young Davises, after gazing warily at the newcomer, agreed to let him play with them. By afternoon Jim Limber had been accepted as companion and helper. He and the small Jeff became special friends, the Negro boy following him around for hours.

That evening, however, Annabelle reported: "De lang'age dat Jim Limber use! You better do somethin'."

Varina summoned Jim for a talk; it ended with a promise. "Yes'm. No mo' bad word. Hope God kill me!"

At once Jim discovered a fellow spirit in the back, John Pemberton, the youth from Mississippi. John took the boy under his care, and whenever Jim was not with the Davises he sat beside John, watching him polish the kitchen utensils, helping him in the garden.

Annabelle, who had never changed her opinion of John Pemberton, sniffed: "Birds of a fedder, all right!" But Varina was soon aware that, despite herself, Annabelle had developed a liking for Jim Limber.

Jeff returned from the West. It was several hours before he spied the young stranger, and he promptly asked Varina for an explanation. As she told Jim's story Jeff's face showed a customary response to human suffering.

"Come here, boy," he said. He rumpled the close-cropped hair. "They've certainly treated you badly, haven't they?"

Early in April, Annabelle's husband Pete broke into Varina's room, badly frightened.

"Dey say Yankees all aroun' town, huntin' down de fambly to shoot 'em!"

Downstairs she discovered two officers talking in low tones to her husband, and she caught some of their remarks: ". . . Union raiding party, somewhere near here. There's been shooting already on the outskirts."

She needed no one to tell her that most of the Confederate forces were at the front, not near enough to Richmond to be any help in this emergency. The officer added: "We're putting extra men on guard here, and we advise you to stay at home, sir, at least for the present."

At these words Jeff straightened his shoulders. "No. I'll go about my duties as usual."

As he reached the door Varina started to call him back, to argue with him, but she caught herself in time. She mustn't think of his personal safety when the Confederacy itself was in such danger. But after he was gone she found it hard to follow that philosophy. Her mother and Maggie tried to quiet her, but she preferred to be alone. From the tall windows her eyes swept the town below. The garden shone under a bright new carpet of yellow-green foliage, but she saw none of it. Death was somewhere near them.

Twice as she moved back and forth she saw John Pemberton standing nervously near the door. "What is it?" she asked.

"Nothin', ma'am. I jus' thought I'd stay aroun', in case anythin' happen to you."

By dusk Jeff came back, unharmed, subdued excitement in his light eyes. "It's over now. It was a magnificently organized raid, up to a point." Several thousand picked cavalrymen had headed toward Richmond, dividing into two parties. "But our men broke them up and captured a lot of them. On the body of one of the leaders"—Jeff's fingers trembled as he handed her a paper—"they tell me they found this."

She read quickly. It was an order to release all Federal prisoners in the town, set it afire, and kill Jefferson Davis and his Cabinet. Jeff paused, and then he added: "The leader was young Ulric Dahlgren, son of Admiral Dahlgren in Washington City."

"The boy we knew?"

Slowly her husband nodded. She was quivering. She remembered one day in Washington City when the father had brought the boy to her in his black velvet suit with the Vandyke collar. He had been a gentle boy with the eyes of an angel. She had touched his head because he reminded her of her dead boy Sam. And now they said he had led a band to murder her husband. . . .

It was mid-April and the new child was due in two months. Despite her condition, Varina hurried from home through town and into Jeff's office rooms, carrying the warm food that he needed. Burton Harrison gave her an apprehensive glance and made room for the plate on Jeff's desk.

At that moment the door burst open, and the coachman ran in. "Lil Joe hurten bad!"

Jeff jumped up from his desk, and they all ran for the stairs. On the way Robert told what he could: "He playin' on de gal'ry. Climb over de rail, and den fall down on bricks. Ain' come to yet, no'm."

Varina found the child on the sofa where Annabelle had placed him, his mouth open, his eyes rolling. He tried to say something, then his head fell back and he lay very still. When the doctor came a few minutes later there was nothing he could do except ask for a sheet and cover the little body.

Varina buried her head on Jeff's shoulder, and slowly the others filed out to leave them alone with their dead.

Her second son to be taken! As she wept she thought of Jane Pierce, that unhappy woman in another White House. What had Jane said? God had taken their boy so that they could devote themselves more fully to their official life. Was Joe's death a payment that she, Varina, had to make for her new rank? Or, she asked as she had on that other occasion, was she being punished? For what? Surely she had given her babies all the time, all the care they required!

Her mother came to her later and took her hands. "Varina, you've got to think of the child that's coming." Taking charge with her old firmness, Margaret Howell put some powders in a glass of water and made her daughter drink it. She stayed beside her until Varina's head nodded and she dropped off into a deep sleep. . . .

At the funeral in the morning there were countless armloads of flowers. Half the children of Richmond seemed to have come, bearing blossoms or sprigs of green. A procession led toward the quiet cemetery on its elevation above the island-spotted James

River. The reds and yellows of the April foliage made a lacework pattern against the skies; a light breeze lifted the edges of the leaves. Varina, in black, saw nothing but the spades as they cleared away the soil, and then the small coffin as it was lowered into the hole in the earth. Jeff stood straight, head bared against the bright sky.

She thought of that other woman who had come to Richmond and had given balls and parties—telling herself that she favored them mainly because they advanced Jeff's career. Yet there had been more to it than that. She had enjoyed them, as she enjoyed her costumes, her extravagances in hats.

How futile, how ridiculous it all appeared now. She hadn't had a new dress in more than a year. The parties she attended had become a trial to her. In these days, when she looked around her, she saw little but the harsh lines of hunger in the faces of the women on the street. Her eyes went to the children with pasty cheeks, with legs like sticks, dull lassitude in their manner. Jeff talked no more of her "Natchez arrogance." And nobody now called her "Queen Varina."

Jeff had brought Braxton Bragg, the highly unpopular general, to Richmond as an adviser, and the cries of complaint increased with every month. This time, alas, she feared that Jeff was wrong, entirely wrong. So many people thought the man incompetent, and what a record of failures he had! Yet Jeff kept him on. The few times she tried to talk about the matter he flared up. She remembered something from her Washington days. Jeff could be over-loyal, beyond reason. And, beyond that, he had been criticized so much about Bragg that his back was up!

Their cotton policy had failed. Thousands of Southerners listened to the government's appeal and burned their bales before allowing them to be taken by the Federals. But others did not, and when new Confederate territory fell in the lower South, more and more cotton passed to the North. Sometimes, as Varina was well aware, the Union forces planned specific campaigns to get access to the precious stuff. Europe did not have to break the Federal blockade. It got the cotton anyway. Cotton did not remain King.

All around her she heard complaints that Jeff had adopted the wrong military strategy. He should not have tried to protect all of the Confederacy's borders but concentrated men for swift, powerful lunges at the enemy's heart. He should have let this section or that one go and risked everything on one or two supreme efforts. He should have . . .

The weeks passed, and the echoes reached her of new developments. General Grant, in high favor with Lincoln, had been assigned to the Eastern lines. As new Union commander he was preparing the most powerful of all onslaughts against Richmond. He had two hundred thousand men, and the North was predicting a triumph, an end to the war.

She overheard remarks made by Jeff's advisers: "They say Grant wants to knock us off before the fall!" . . . "There's never been an army that big before!"

Badly outnumbered, Robert E. Lee prepared his defenses. Grant, using the same tactics that had won at Vicksburg, poured out man power by the mounting thousands of corpses. Grant, the butcher; Grant, the crazy man . . . But still Lee held him off.

From her window she listened to the shouts: "Lee—they'll never get by 'im. No, sir, never!"

In all the new excitement, all the elation, she thought bitterly that no one ever mentioned Jeff. When the Confederate armies failed it was her husband's fault; when they won he was forgotten. But he had helped plan all of this; he had marshaled the men, the supplies. . . .

Obviously John Pemberton had been thinking about Lee's victories, too, but in a very different way. He said to her one evening: "How's the war gonna end, ma'am? Will I be free?"

She stared at her hands. "I don't know, John. No matter which side wins, many people think that slavery will be over. Still, I'm not sure——"

"Still, if the South come on top——" He paused.

Varina wished she knew what else to tell him, but she could think of nothing.

After he had thanked her and gone she sat thinking: How many colored men and women all over the South were asking themselves the question James Pemberton had put to her?

While Lee was still gallantly holding back the Federal armies Varina reached her confinement. Again the same scene with Margaret Howell and Annabelle hovering near her, again the doctor giving orders, again the hours of blinding pain and the weakness that followed it.

She woke to find the child beside her and Jeff at the door.

"A girl," her mother whispered, and left the room.

"I'm glad," she told Jeff. "You wanted one, too, didn't you? After all the boys."

It was their sixth, though there would be only four with them in these years ahead. From her husband's eyes, as from hers, something of the recent strain had gone. Whatever happened now, they had this new symbol of their union. Whenever she saw the child she would remember this year in Richmond, and remember it more happily.

In silence she and Jeff caressed the tiny thing with its scowling red face and swirl of dark hair. Varina's tired face brightened.

"What'll we call her?"

Jeff took the baby's hand.

"Varina," he said. "We'll have another Winnie."

It was early summer, and Varina was resting on the wide gallery with the baby. As Jeff came out to join her she sensed his sudden excitement.

"What is it?" she demanded.

"It's the elections in the North," he told her. "They'll be voting for a President in November, and already there's a new peace party that's making great headway."

He described the resentment in the East against the war and anything that had to do with it. Grant's ruthless bloodletting had shocked the North. The cries of grief had been drowned out by cries of rage. "And who do you think will be the candidate against Lincoln?" he asked. "George McClellan, now out of the Army! The odds are in our favor, Winnie. They say even Lincoln thinks he's going to lose. If we can only hold our own, prevent any Federal victory between now and the election . . ."

McClellan, she thought to herself, first the shy young officer at their table, then the man who commanded the mighty Federal offense against them; and now, perhaps, the instrument of their salvation . . . Fate had placed him in strange relationship to them.

But Mrs. Chesnut, her ribbons flying behind her, brought

Varina the first dark news from the Western front. "Sherman's moving forward in Georgia, and Joe Johnston's retreating."

"Can't he do anything but retreat?" Varina exclaimed to Jeff later.

"Well"—Jeff wet his lips—"to be fair, the concentration against him is a hard thing to overcome."

"But there's a terrific concentration against Lee and against other generals. Somehow, they manage to win!"

He sighed and left her. Week by week the bad tidings multiplied, with Johnston steadily retreating. Varina, listening in the house, heard a high-ranking officer describe it as a "masterly performance," conserving men and materials.

"Still," she told Maggie, "there has to be a point where it stops. If it doesn't, we might end up with a 'masterly withdrawal' down to Cuba!"

Meanwhile Governor Brown of Georgia was shouting frantically for men, more men from the government. Brown, who had done as much as any man in the South to reduce the Confederate armies, was now appealing for aid. "We have no more to give." Jeff gritted his teeth. "After Brown's own performances, he of all people should know that!"

Joe Johnston was evading Jeff's questions.

"I can't even find what he plans to do." Jeff scowled.

Still the withdrawals went on. All at once they discovered that Johnston was only twenty miles from the strategic center of Atlanta and falling back rapidly toward it! Varina remembered how Jeff had unexpectedly come upon Johnston's men after he had withdrawn them, without notice, almost into Richmond itself.

"I'm going to make one final appeal to him," Jeff told her.

The next day, receiving no response, he summoned the Cabinet, and Johnston was removed from command in Georgia.

"Now, at least, we'll have a battle," Varina assured Maggie.

Johnston's successor attacked—and was defeated. In Atlanta panic spread, and the mighty Federal Army rolled on.

Now in the North the peace movement was dead, forever.

One afternoon Varina came upstairs after nursing the baby and found Jeff in his room, his hands pressed to his face. With an effort he told her what had happened.

"I've had a visitor from the Senate. They want me to leave office or agree to give over the handling of the war. They've talked about a military dictator." The words came with an increasing strain. "Some of them think I ought to step aside for Lee."

"I'd make them hang me first!" Varina bit out her sentences. "I'd never do it, never!" Then she said more slowly: "Lee . . . I don't think . . . What does he say?"

They would know at once. She heard a voice from below: "Tell him it's General Lee."

She went to the next room. For a few minutes she could hear the rumble of words, but she could only guess at their meaning. The general's footsteps went down the hall, and Jeff called her back. He was close to the breaking point. "Lee won't have anything to do with a dictatorship. He's willing to take command of the armies, but only under me."

She smiled a bitter smile. Of necessity Jeff's opposition had gone to the man least inclined to turn against him, least ambitious to become a military dictator.

Christmas of 1864, New Year's Day of 1865. In the big house on the hill Varina felt the tension about her, almost unbearable in these days. Her eyes swept some of the letters the women were sending their men: "Come home, for God's sake. We need you." "I don't know what I'll do for food." Deserters were being shot as examples; still men ran away. Their only bulwark was Lee's army, "Lee's Miserables," often hungry, often in rags, decimated by bullets and sickness. Could they maintain themselves forever against the weight of superior numbers?

Like a whisper, as she rode about the town, she caught the words: "Use the Negroes." At the corner of the house she overheard two men:

"Why, if that happened, we'd have to free 'em!"

"Maybe. Why not?"

"Why not?" The question was shouted. "What's the war been for?"

"Whatever it was for, slavery's practically over now, and we'd better admit it."

"I'll be damned if we will!"

But slavery was over. Uncounted thousands were making their

way toward freedom. One evening Annabelle ran to her room with the news: "That John Pemberton! Gone, gone to de Yankees. I said it'd happen. I told my husbing it couldn' las'——" Her tone was scornful.

"Well . . ." Varina began to speak, then fell silent. She had expected something like that, and somehow she could summon up no great bitterness. What could she say to Annabelle that she would understand?

After Annabelle walked away a slight sound drew her attention to Jim Limber's forlorn little figure in the doorway. Jim, she knew, had almost worshiped John Pemberton.

"Miss Rina," he began, "John—John, he say to tell you somethin' tonight, after—you fin' out." He stared up at her, unable to continue.

"Don't be afraid, Jim," she murmured. "Go on."

"He—well, he say to go to you when nobody aroun' and say he sorry he do it like dat. But he hada do it, he say." The boy was crying now, his sobs deep and convulsive. He put his head against the edge of her chair. "Miss Rina, why he hada do it?"

For the second time Varina knew there was nothing she could say. She reached out and touched the boy's head.

"Don't cry, Jim. Don't cry."

The whisper grew. Everywhere she went she heard the murmur: "Arm the blacks!"

Judah Benjamin, his deep eyes troubled, arrived for a long conference with Jeff, and she knew what the subject would be. Years ago Jeff had stopped talking of eventual emancipation, for he felt that slavery had become a blessing, a positive good. After he had fought for it so long she doubted if he would ever change his mind. But when he came down to join her after his session with Benjamin she realized from the expression on his face that he had made an important decision.

"We've got to use them," he said slowly. "We've got to free them. If we do it, we may get recognition from Europe, and that's our last chance. We've got to do it or lose!"

He had made a choice, finally, between slavery and his hope of winning the war.

A Southern agent was secretly dispatched to Europe to make

the offer of emancipation, but Varina, watching the stratagem closely, shook her head. Congress was still undecided on the emancipation question and was doing nothing. She heard such protests as: "It would make Jeff Davis a worse tyrant than ever—give him more power!" And again she heard the cry: "It's against states' rights!" Would those words haunt them to the grave? Soon it hardly mattered, for a dispatch from England told them that, whereas the plan would have made a great impression a year or two before, now it was too late.

Toward the end of March, on a week end that saw the first buds tentatively opening in their garden, Varina basked in the afternoon sun with the three older children about her, the baby Winnie in her arms. From the distance, when the children's voices died down, she could sometimes hear a soft thud. The artillery fire was closer than ever before. But she resolutely put it out of her mind, for she did not want to think of the present. It was peaceful here, and for this hour it was all she wanted.

The central door to the pillared gallery swung open, and Jeff was coming rapidly down the steps. By the time he reached her she was on her feet. His face had a stricken look, and she guessed what he had to tell her.

"Lee's Army is starting to break. You'll have to go in a day or two."

"No! Let me be with you, help you——"

"Winnie, you can help me, you can help us all by taking the children away to some safe place. There's still hope; things may change or our lines may re-form to the West." Then his voice grew husky. "Anyway, you can join me when it's over—if I live."

She gripped his hands.

"In the name of God, Banny . . ."

Polly looked up from her play, and the little Jim Limber also stared. Lowering her voice, she argued insistently, but Jeff's mind was made up.

As they went together to the house he said to her: "I want you to go to North Carolina with Maggie and your mother and wait for me."

At that Margaret Howell entered. Varina took her mother's hand. "We have bad news, dear——"

"I've expected it for weeks." Margaret's words came quickly. "I'm not going with you; I'd be in your way. I want to be with a few friends I have in Georgia, where things will be quiet." Varina realized that her mother, in her own way, was trying to help them too. Reluctantly she agreed to the separation.

With her sister's help Varina hastily got together her belongings. She had so much to take—her dresses, silver plate, glassware, gifts from friends. Stopping on his way out, Jeff said gently: "Winnie, there'll be no space for all that."

"But my silver! Can't I ask people here to keep it, then?"

The sympathy in his eyes tempered his firmness. "No. If the worst happens and the Federals recognize it later, wouldn't our friends suffer?" With an effort at humor he added: "We'll be marked people, you and I."

She shivered. Then as she saw how few dollars they had she found another reason to get rid of her possessions. Early the next morning when the dealer arrived she sold him, among other things, most of her wardrobe, her embossed volumes, some of her jewelry. Many of the things he bought represented an occasion in Varina's life—a birthday in New Orleans, an anniversary in Washington City. She was selling her memories.

To add to the dealer's meager allotment Jeff handed her all the money he had except a five-dollar gold piece.

"I may need that," he told her with a dry smile.

Little Jeff ran to her, weeping, holding his suit of Confederate gray.

"I got to take it!" he cried.

Varina relented. "All right, I suppose we can manage with it."

Now they had finished, and she could no longer fight off the depression within her. Jeff took her to his study, and before she could protest he had taken out a gun and was showing her how to use it. "If worst comes to worst," he said in a harsh voice, "you can make them kill you. But no matter what happens, when you hear the enemy is close, move South. I'll get word to you somehow."

He stared up, and a look almost of optimism came into his face. "Even if Richmond does fall," he said, "we may regroup ourselves and fight on."

She stood silent. As she had always told herself, Jeff would be the last man in the Confederacy to give up.

As they had planned, Margaret Howell was to leave first. When the carriage came that redoubtable woman kissed each member of the family in turn and headed for the door. But before she reached it Varina ran to her and gathered her in her arms. Maggie embraced her, too, and for a moment Margaret Howell seemed about to collapse. Then she cleared her throat, pulled up her collar, and let Jeff lead her to the carriage. Varina buried her face in her hands. When would she see her mother again?

It was still early morning. Varina said a quick good-by to the staff. Alone, she went through the house for the last time. She fingered a curtain at the upper window from which she had looked over the city. She ran her hand over the edge of the rosewood sofa she had taken with her from place to place. Now it would stay here, and what would happen to it, she could not guess. As she closed the front door, scenes from the past came to her mind— the death of Joe, the birth of Billy and Winnie, the day the fire was set, the hours when the raiders were near. So much of her life, so much that was good, so much bad, had taken place here. . . .

At the station, as the moment of departure arrived, Jeff was grim and dry-eyed.

Little Jeff cried: "Can't I stay with you, Papa?"

Polly tugged at her father's trouser leg. "You come with us!"

Desperately Varina busied herself, settling the children, talking over household details, anything to keep from breaking down. One last brief kiss, and she said good-by to him.

The train started off. She began to wave, then dropped her hand. He was staring at her as if he were seeing her for the last time.

Chapter 20

FOR THREE MISERABLE DAYS THEY RODE SLOWLY IN THE CREAKING car. Like nearly every other train left in the Confederacy, this one was in a state approaching ruin, but somehow it still ran. There were no sleeping arrangements, and during most of one day it rained continuously, the roof leaked, and their crude bedding was soaked through. For nearly twelve hours the train stopped while the engine was being repaired. The baby Winnie developed a cold, and Varina huddled over her. If the child got sick, what could she do? Gradually, however, Winnie began to recover and kick at the covers with her normal liveliness.

Even then she could not rest. What was happening in Richmond? Was Banny safe? In any unsuccessful effort of this kind, she knew that the leaders were held responsible. Would the Yankees do something to Jeff?

Burton Harrison, Jeff's earnest secretary, accompanied them. His somber face alarmed her, for she suspected that he knew worse things than he had revealed to her. She felt as if their world were collapsing around them.

She had taken with her not only Maggie and the four children, but Annabelle and her husband, the children's light mulatto nurse, and then, at the last minute, Jim Limber, Robert the coachman, and James Jones, Jeff's mulatto attendant. There were far too many, she realized, but it had been hard to say no. She wondered now if she could bring all of them through to safety—if there was any safety left, anywhere.

Across the aisle she saw a familiar face, the face of a woman she had known in Richmond. Varina raised her head and smiled at her.

Perhaps the woman did not recognize her, for she averted her glance and looked out the window. A few minutes later another acquaintance approached, started to speak, and then went rapidly by. Varina's face hardened as she realized that they were already beginning to snub her.

A little later, however, a kindly woman came up to her with an extended hand. "Aren't you Mrs. Davis? I just wanted to say I thought Mr. Davis has done as well as any man could. You've been a fine wife too. No matter what happens, I'd like to wish you God-speed." A little embarrassed, the stranger smiled and left.

Varina's heart beat happily. There were some, then, who weren't turning against them. They were not entirely alone. . . . It was her final thought as she sank into the sleep of exhaustion.

At Charlotte, North Carolina, Jeff had rented them a small house, and there they settled down. Mr. Harrison left, and she and Maggie busied themselves, arranging clothing, sorting the children's things, writing letters. The baby Winnie had begun to teethe, and that added to their problems. The first evening found Varina so fatigued that she went to sleep early and did not wake until dawn.

The second day turned out to be torture. Two or three neighbors dropped in to pay their respects, but that was all. In the main the people of Charlotte were leaving them entirely alone, and once more she felt hurt and a little angry.

That afternoon Mr. Weill, the agent for the house, stopped by and brought them a basket of warm food.

As she thanked him her throat contracted.

"It's nothing." He waved his hand. "I thought you might have trouble getting settled."

Mr. Weill sat with them for more than an hour. Varina recalled other Jews who had helped her through the years, and now this man had come forward when she needed comfort most of all. Saying good-by, he stopped before a small photograph of Jeff on the mantel and looked at it with obvious emotion.

"Would you like it?" she asked.

"Oh yes!"

She handed it to him immediately. If Jeff could realize that even now there were people who felt this way . . .

Late in the evening, as they prepared to retire, Maggie called from the window: "Varina! Here's Mr. Weill running up the walk."

At the door their new friend panted: "We just found out at the station. Richmond's lost! Our Army evacuated yesterday. . . ."

His eyes burned as he told what he had learned: Part of the town afire, warehouses sacked, men and women fighting for food, some lapping up whisky in the gutter. Lincoln had arrived there, walked through the streets, and then gone to the Confederate White House. "They say he went from room to room and then sat in Mr. Davis's chair."

Their home taken, and Lincoln in it, and soldiers ransacking the rooms for loot. Panic took possession of her. She spent the night in a chair by the door, wide awake and listening for the sound of tramping feet. When Maggie went to her she motioned her sister away.

Early the next morning a letter arrived by courier, and she ripped it open. Jeff was in Danville, below Richmond. He had his Cabinet with him, and she was not to worry. Lee and his men had retired farther west, and Jeff expected to join Lee's men and the remnants of other Confederate forces. Thank God he was safe! But there'd be more fighting, more danger.

Robert came in with a proclamation which Jeff had issued a day or so earlier. They would fight on, he declared. The Army of Northern Virginia, largest and finest of the Confederacy, no longer had to guard Richmond. Now it would be free to strike at the enemy far from his base. "Let us meet the foe with firm defiance, with unconquered and unconquerable hearts."

How like Jeff were the words. Would he ever admit their defeat? Hurrying to a table, she wrote him with as much encouragement as she could muster. She knew that he was at his best in adversity, that "your strength when stirred up is great, and you can do with a few what others have failed to do with many." She trusted God would permit him to save the South, even now.

They had an unexpected visitor that morning. Varina stared at the tall young man dressed in the uniform of a naval cadet and suddenly realized that it was her brother, Jeff Davis Howell. She wept as she embraced him, for his familiar face was like a bright light at a turn on a dark road. Jeff Howell told her that with other cadets he had been sent to guard the government's Treasury on its way South.

"Look, Varina," he said, his face eager, "why don't you come along? You'll be a lot safer."

Mr. Weill helped to convince her by rushing in with the news that trouble was starting all over town, that people were getting panicky. At that Varina made up her mind. A few hours later, her party around her, she was seated in a ramshackle railroad car. Repeatedly her eyes sought the fine-looking cadet opposite her. How well the boy had turned out; she was proud he bore Jeff's name.

For several days they rode unsteadily on their way. The weather became worse. Under the pelting rain Annabelle, her stanchest of helpers, caught a bad cold and began to breathe heavily. By this time the tension and the irregular food had also made Maggie ill. Varina tried to sleep but could not. So many questions, so many problems—and the wild stories that were spreading; that Jeff was lost, that his party were trying vainly to locate him.

Then abruptly the train stopped for the last time. The track had ended, and they were in the town of Chester, South Carolina. As they stepped down from the coach, uncertain of what to do next, a large woman ran toward them, waving her parasol—their old friend, Mrs. Chesnut. Varina suddenly remembered that this was her home.

"Varina! I wasn't sure——" The two women clung together while the children danced around them. "Come on," Mrs. Chesnut ordered. "We have room for everybody, and I think you could do with a little rest."

At the Chesnuts' the welcome was overwhelming. Word spread through the town, and men and women came in groups, sent over notes and flowers and dishes of food. For the first time in days they enjoyed a warm meal. After a few hours in bed Maggie sat up and drank warm milk. Annabelle, on her own cot, seemed better. On the gallery, little Jim Limber ate so ravenously that she realized only then how hungry the child had been.

As the children slept she wrote a note to Jeff: "Would to God I could know the truth of the horrible rumors I hear of you. One is that you have started for General Lee but have never been heard of. . . . May God have mercy upon and preserve your life for your dear wife. . . ."

When she had finished it Jeff Howell appeared and told her: "Our guard is pushing on, by wagon and anything else we can find. I scratched around and found an ambulance; it ought to hold all of you."

The Chesnuts pressed her to stay, but she remembered Jeff's directions: "When in doubt, push on South." She rose and said firmly: "I think we ought to be going on."

At the departure the Chesnuts waved to them with a semblance of gaiety, and Varina managed to look composed as they rocked off. But the pose fell away in the dark. Heavy rains had fallen, and the road turned into sloughs. As they lurched forward, sinking into water holes, the mud splashed through the cracks in the floor boards into their faces and over their clothes.

Their male Negro attendants had been assigned duties with the other vehicles; the women and children were alone in the ambulance.

Their driver finally pulled up and said abruptly: "Ma'am, we're just too heavy. Somebody's got to walk."

Maggie could barely move, and Annabelle's sickness had returned. The puny mulatto nurse was half terrified, half sullen. Varina thought it over quickly, then lowered herself to the ground. When the driver objected she quieted him. "No. We mustn't fall behind the other carriages. I'll manage." Other people were walking; she could do it too.

For miles she trudged through the night in muck that occasionally reached her knees. Once or twice she nearly fell into the deep ruts, and the mud splattered into her mouth and eyes. Holes broke in her thin soles, and she felt a blister forming. As she limped on she could taste the drying dirt on her lips. She was thirsty, terribly thirsty, but she couldn't halt for that. Oh God, when would this end? An ironic expression came back to her from the past: "Queen Varina!" Her heel twisted, and her ankle throbbed. She was no Queen now.

From inside the ambulance she heard sobbing; it was her sister Maggie, weeping to herself. One of the children asked drowsily for Varina.

"I'm here," she called. "Don't worry."

Finally they stopped for the night at a church along the road. The party filled the building. Men stretched out on pews or threw blankets in the corner and attempted to sleep there. A young bride helped Varina wash the mud off her dress and her broken shoes. Then she pointed to the communion table.

"I left that for you."

With a wan smile Varina refused and found an empty space on the floor. In the crowded church she knelt, facing the altar, and prayed, then tried for several hours to sleep.

With dawn they started once more. Her head gave her agony, her eyes stung. Sometimes she walked, again she rode. She was spending her money rapidly to get food—fifty cents for a glass of milk or a biscuit.

When she felt as if she could go on no farther they reached Abbeville in South Carolina. She was perplexed as to her next step. "I don't know whether Jeff would want us to go much beyond here," she told Maggie. The Burt family, friends of Jeff's, lived in Abbeville, and she sent them a note. They responded promptly, riding to the fork of the road where Varina waited.

"Child, child!" Mrs. Burt embraced her. "The house is ready for you. You won't have to do anything but sleep and"—she looked at them—"all of you certainly need that!"

And now Varina had to say good-by to her brother Jeff; the Treasury wagons were pushing on. The boy, whom she had comforted many times in the past, tried awkwardly to console her.

"We'll meet again soon," he whispered. "Don't worry."

She waved, and then, heart heavy, rejoined the family.

At the Burt house they ate with wolfish appetites. Varina talked on and on in nervous excitement until all at once she stopped in the middle of a sentence and said apologetically: "I think I'm going to collapse." Mrs. Burt helped her upstairs, and Varina stayed in bed for nearly twelve hours. Waking finally, she dressed quickly and hurried down the stairs. Maggie was waiting for her, looking very grown-up and very sad.

"Lee's surrendered to Grant!" she said, and turned away.

Varina heard in a daze that Lee and Jeff never reached each other, that Lee's army was falling apart and so he surrendered.

Late that morning a sweat-streaked messenger dashed up to the house. Varina tore open Jeff's letter and read that he and the government were carrying on despite Lee's action. Jeff was moving farther south to meet Joe Johnston and Beauregard and prepare for continued resistance.

Varina went to the window, more confused than ever. Their most powerful army was gone now. Was there any sense in fighting on? . . . For days she waited. Every time she heard a horseman coming down the road her eyes betrayed her tension. Then a note arrived that first thrilled her, then made her tremble: "I will come to you if I can. Everything is dark. You should prepare for the worst by dividing your luggage."

So she might see him again! But what did he mean: "Everything is dark?" Signaling to the messenger, she wrote an urgent reply: "Where are you? How are you? What am I to do with these helpless little unconscious charges of mine? are questions which I am asking myself always. Write to me of your troubles, freely. Do not attempt to put a good face upon them. . . ."

Whispered information was passed on to her. When Jeff reached Greensboro, North Carolina, the people had been fearful, unfriendly. The Federals were approaching, and those who showed courtesies might suffer. Some of the Cabinet members had to sleep in railroad boxcars. For Jeff there was only a narrow bedroom, unwillingly provided.

Next came the report that Jeff had brought his Cabinet together in that same tiny room in a meeting which included Johnston and Beauregard. He had called for continued resistance, pointing out that they could reassemble the scattered troops, rally the people again. And the generals had said no. . . . When she heard that, Varina smiled bitterly. So Jeff's two old enemies had gained their revenge at last.

"Right now," her informant ended, "Johnston's talking general peace terms with Sherman. They've sent the papers to Washington City for approval. Mr. Davis has moved on south again."

At least Jeff was still alive and headed her way. Oh, if she could only see him again!

The doorknob rattled, and Maggie burst into the room, crying: "Abe Lincoln's been murdered—by a Southern sympathizer! They tried to kill Mr. Seward too."

Varina shuddered. What dreadful brutality, what a horrible crime. Most of them had cursed Lincoln at the beginning, but of late there had been much less vindictiveness. And Mr. Seward . . .

She would not have wished such a thing to happen to him. Her eyes suddenly grew round, for she remembered that if Mr. Lincoln were dead, then the Vice-President, Andrew Johnson of Tennessee, would be President. Jeff had no more implacable enemy anywhere.

That afternoon Burton Harrison arrived, close to the end of his endurance, with the information that he was to help her move on.

"There's a terrible excitement," he told her, "over the killing of Lincoln. Washington City is in an uproar. Andrew Johnson's in charge, you know, and they've turned down Sherman's peace plan. Too friendly to the South, they say."

He handed her a note from Jeff, and she sped through it. She should go on, he told her, to Mobile, or a town in Texas, and then make her way to a foreign country. He hoped to keep a group of soldiers with him and eventually force his way back across the Mississippi. If that failed he could "go to Mexico and have the world from which to choose a location." She read on:

Dear wife, this is not the fate to which I invited you when the future was rose-colored to us both. But I know you will bear it even better than myself, and that of us two, I alone will ever look back reproachfully on my past career. . . . Dear children, I can say nothing to them, but for you and them my heart is full, my prayers constant, and my hopes are the trust I feel in the mercy of God. . . . Farewell, my love; there may be better things in store for us than are now in view. But my love is all that I have to offer, and that has the value of a thing long possessed and sure not to be lost. . . .

She touched her eyes. The day would never come when she would forget these words from her husband. She sat down and wrote her reply:

It is surely not the fate to which you invited me in brighter days. But you must remember that you did not invite me to a great hero's home, but to that of a plain farmer. I have shared all your triumphs, been the only beneficiary of them; now I am but claiming the privilege for the first time of being all to you. God bless you, and keep you. . . . I believe He will restore us to happiness."

With Burton Harrison as their escort they set forth again. Somewhere behind, moving in the same general direction, were Jeff and his dwindling Cabinet, the members leaving one by one. That first night Burton drew her aside and said: "This country is filled with outlaws, some Federals, some Confederates. They're hunting loot, food, horses, anything. We'll have to be careful."

For several days they traveled on, stopping at night, making camp as best they could in the awkward manner of city people. Sitting around the fire one evening, they heard a commotion. Out of the bushes strode several hard-faced men in faded Confederate uniforms. Their intent was obvious, but Burton Harrison and another man in their party took the former soldiers aside, and for several nervous minutes Varina heard them conferring. Her name was mentioned, and then the leader squinted and came forward toward her.

"You Miz Davis? You reco'nize me? Don't you remember the day you dressed my arm in that Richmond horspital?"

He waved his friends away and stayed talking with them for several minutes.

"We need anything we can get, and we sure meant to have a divide with you-all here. But I wouldn't let nothing happen to your folks, ma'am." He backed away. "Wouldn't hurt you. Never did think much of Mr. Davis, but I still say he weren't always to blame, like everybody claimed. . . ."

When her heart stopped thumping she thought of those last words. This soldier didn't go as far as some of Jeff's Southern enemies, but he had no great opinion of him. If he could realize, if everybody could, what Jeff had done with so little, and against such opposition . . . Her husband had been wrong many times. To herself she would admit that he lacked the gift of getting along with others, and he had remained isolated, withdrawn in office. But who in the South could have done a better job?

There were no more letters. The whole South was demoralized, fields abandoned, cattle destroyed, markets empty. In the faces of uniformed stragglers, the men who trudged every road they took, Varina read only defeat and a sick despair. Their wagons rolled into Georgia, to the little town of Washington, where they stayed for a short time. As they pushed on a horseman raced up to them with the news that he had left Jeff only a few miles away.

"Tell him," said Varina, "that I want to see him more than

anything in my life, but he mustn't try to come to us. It would only delay and endanger him."

That night the ground felt very hard as she lay on a thin blanket and stared into the dark.

Two days passed, and still they journeyed slowly southward. At last a rumor reached Burton Harrison that another band of bush-whackers was somewhere on the road ahead. They had heard of Varina's party and were planning to rob it. At dark, after they fixed camp, Varina managed to get the children asleep, then sat tensely waiting. From her tent door she followed the play of moonbeams over the leaves. How peaceful, how like other days . . . A thud of hoofbeats made her jump. She heard voices, and a figure stepped into the moonlight. It was Jeff.

She ran to him, sobbing. "Banny! Thank God!"

After a time he explained: "I changed my route. I heard that you were in danger from bushwhackers and I wanted to be with you for a little while, anyway."

The children, hearing the sound of Jeff's voice, came running to join them. That night, as they lay in each other's arms, Varina asked Jeff few questions. They were together; that was enough.

The next day the two parties continued south. Varina sat beside Jeff, and the children watched him with adoring eyes.

Eventually Varina whispered: "You've got to leave us, Banny. With so many along, you're an easier target."

"A day or two more." He nodded.

He looked rested, his face somewhat more serene, but there was a profound melancholy in his gray eyes. His hair had turned much whiter since their last meeting.

He spoke musingly. "I gave away my last money a few days ago" —he told her sadly—"that five-dollar gold piece. They brought a little boy to me and told me his name was Jefferson Davis, named after me."

Would many Southern children in the future be called Jefferson Davis? She turned her face from his.

At last, close to tears, Jeff said good-by to them, then rode swiftly away. It began to rain, and Varina's little caravan moved slowly ahead. Hours went by and the rain had turned to heavy fog. They suddenly came upon a band of horsemen and recognized them as Jeff and his advance party.

"I knew we should have gone faster, but we were lost for a while," he told her, "and then we heard rumors of bushwhackers again. . . ."

She knew that, above all, he wished to be with her and the children. Again she pleaded with him to think of his own safety, and he agreed to push on ahead in the morning.

More and more apprehensive, she watched as they made camp for the night. Fully dressed, Jeff lay down on a cot next to hers. His horse was tied to a tree some distance from the tent. Before long he was snoring, but Varina lay awake.

Just before dawn she heard the crackling sound of gunfire and sat up. One of the Negroes ran to the tent flap to warn them.

Jeff peered out. "Winnie, they're Federal troops."

"Ride off, for God's sake! Get to your horse!"

He hesitated. "I can't leave you."

"You're the one they want, not me!" She shook his arm. "You've got to go."

Reluctantly Jeff took up a light raincoat and put it on. It was Varina's, almost identical with his, and it would do. As he started out, hatless, his sharp features clear in the growing daylight, she snatched off her shawl and threw it over his head.

"Pretend you're going for water to the spring!" she cried.

She spied Annabelle near the tent and motioned her to come quickly.

"Here's the water bucket, Annabelle," she said firmly. "Take it and follow Mr. Davis to the spring. Pay no attention to anybody you see on the way. Now start!"

She had taken charge, and both Jeff and Annabelle were obeying her. A single soldier on horseback was near the tent. He stared, puzzled, at Jeff and the Negro woman. Then he lifted his musket and cried, "Halt!" Jeff was still some distance from his horse. He muttered something, dropped the shawl, and raced toward the mounted man.

What happened next would always be confused to Varina.

"Stop!" the soldier shouted, and aimed at her approaching husband. Then, without reasoning, Varina ran forward, caught her husband, and threw her arms around him. He dropped his hands. No matter what happened now, she had saved his life. . . .

Other Federal soldiers ran toward them and suddenly discovered the identity of their prize.

The commanding officer shouted in exultation: "Well, old Jeff, we've got you!"

The ride was chill and silent. They came to a Federal camp where at first the Union soldiers were content to hoot and shout. A brass band blared out "Yankee Doodle" in derision. Then in a cloud of dust a horseman clattered toward them with a dispatch. The Federal officer snatched it, frowned, and passed it around to his men. Narrowing her eyes, Varina was able to make out several lines: President Andrew Johnson was offering a $100,000 reward for Jeff Davis's capture—for helping plot the assassination of Lincoln!

Varina's hand sought Jeff's. "So that's going to be the claim!" She tried to laugh in scorn, but she failed. For now she saw a change in the manner of the soldiers on all sides of them—bitter glances, looks of hate.

"They believe it!" she whispered. Then she heard some of them cry:

"Look at 'em! Murderers!"

"Kill the bastards, all of 'em!"

Polly had drawn closer to her father, and now she put her arms around him. He stroked her head, and Varina heard him pray. They rode on, and repeatedly they heard gibes and shouts of anger.

They had no way of knowing where they were being taken. They continued overland to the coast, and then they were transferred to a steamer. By now Jeff's neuralgia twisted his face. His eye gave him trouble, and Varina sat beside his berth, trying to bring him ease.

In another part of the vessel was Alexander Stephens, who had been the Confederacy's Vice-President. As she heard how weak and broken he was, she forgot how much she disliked him. When she stood beside him the man looked up at her with great desolate eyes, the eyes of a child in a gnome's head.

"Can't I do something for you?" she asked.

It had been months since she exchanged a word with Mr. Stephens. The face he raised toward her was pitiable, and she bent down to catch his words.

"I'm cold, very cold," he said.

She went to one of the soldiers, who shrugged at her request. She sought out another, who referred her to a third. The shining eyes of Alexander Stephens followed her; when she returned, a blanket over her arm, they were brimming.

A day or two later Mr. Stephens was walking slowly on deck. He came to her, hand outstretched. She offered him a seat next to hers. Jeff, his face bandaged, came to join her at that moment and, seeing Mr. Stephens, he was about to pass without a word. Varina reached out, grasped her husband's hand, and made him sit down beside them. Then she left the two men. From a distance she saw that they were talking hesitantly, then less diffidently. She felt easier in her mind; at least one breach had been healed.

For days Varina had listened to the remarks of one of the officers, an unpleasant man, who had developed a keen interest in the Negro boy, Jim Limber.

"I'm going to take him away," he announced to all who listened. "I'll see that he gets brought up right and knows what these people"—he jerked a thumb toward Varina—"were trying to make out of him."

The boy slid over to her. "Dey won' do nothin' wid me, Miss Rina?"

Alarmed, she appealed to another Federal officer who seemed more sympathetic. "Won't you see to it that somebody looks after the boy—some good people?" After a little thought he nodded.

But when Varina approached Jim Limber the child became frantic. "I don' wanna. I wanna stay wid you!"

A tug came up beside their boat and the friendly officer pointed to it and then to Jim. She understood and nodded her head. "Wouldn't you like to look at the nice boat, Jim?" the officer asked. At first the boy was suspicious, until his curiosity got the better of him. She watched him descend the ladder.

Almost immediately the tug began to pull away from them. When the child realized what was happening he screamed. Varina, standing at the upper rail, could only call to him: "Don't cry, Jim! They'll take care of you. Don't cry!"

The next morning little Jeff pulled at her skirts while she was standing with Jeff and the children on deck.

"They say they're coming for Papa," he said in a childish treble. "Make them let us go with them! Make them!"

Varina turned white. Jeff stiffened, and a look of defiance came into his light eyes. A file of soldiers moved toward them.

"Try not to weep," he told her in a low voice. "They'd enjoy it."

She mustn't give way, she mustn't. She lifted up the baby Winnie, and Jeff petted her. He leaned down to kiss Polly and Billy and the boy Jeff. Then he held Varina against him, trembling. He whispered: "No matter what they say, remember—I had nothing to do with the assassination. I never did that, or anything unworthy of our fight."

He released her suddenly and went with a firm step toward the line of men who waited. The tug slid away. The day was a gray one, and he would soon be out of sight. She ran to the rail; between the soldiers Jeff was standing, his gaunt face toward them, gray hair swirling in the wind.

Only then did she hear where he was being taken. "Fortress Monroe, way over at the side there!" Fortress Monroe in Virginia, so close to the scene of his years as the Confederacy's President! It was there, as Secretary of War, that he had reviewed the troops of the new American Army he had been building. Before the fort, on a well-remembered day, she had seen the fireworks light up the skies with two names, Pierce and Davis; and she had thought Jeff might someday be President of the United States. . . .

Another memory came to her. It had been to Fortress Monroe that Black Hawk was taken after Jeff had delivered him to the authorities. Black Hawk had died within the gray walls.

One of the Federal soldiers passed her a newspaper clipping. The editor of the paper expected soon to see "the arch-traitor Davis dangling and blackening in wind and rain." He demanded "the most disgraceful end known to our civilization—death on the gallows." For the first time Varina realized fully that Jeff was on his way to die.

Chapter 21

HER EYES STARING BLANKLY AHEAD, VARINA LEANED HEAVILY AGAINST the rail as the ship edged into the Savannah harbor. The past week had been a continuous horror. Soldiers had broken open their trunks to steal money and clothing. They had tried to seize little Jeff's gray Confederate suit as a souvenir. Women detectives had stripped and searched her and her sister. An officer with a file of men had forced her to give up the shawl she had thrown over Jeff before his capture. She had first refused, but he had told her: "If you don't, God damn it, we'll take everything else you have." . . . Later Maggie had become very sick. There had been a rule of "no communication," and it had been impossible to get a doctor.

But beyond everything else was the question: What had they done with Jeff? Her blood ran cold when she heard how Andrew Johnson had issued a statement that the government had facts to convict Jeff beyond any possible doubt. He claimed that they had found accomplices who knew all the details, that weeks before Lincoln's death Davis had said it was going to happen! . . . There must be something she could do, but what, and how?

On the way down the coast they had passed Charleston, and now she said to the officer in charge: "I have very little money left. We have friends in Charleston. Can't I go there?"

The answer came promptly: "Ma'am, all I know is you got to go to Savannah and stay there under our watch."

"Am I a prisoner? For what?"

There was no reply.

A little later her servants were summoned and told they could leave whenever they wished. The mulatto maid, who had never lost her fright, chose to depart at once.

Robert, the coachman, walked up to her and said simply, "Ma'am, I'd like to stay."

"But I don't have the money to pay you, Robert."

"I stay anyhow. Where I got to go?" He smiled, and his eyes were sympathetic.

As Varina thanked him a very sheepish and troubled Annabelle approached. "Miss Rina," she began, "my husbing, he have friends round here. We been talkin', and he say it best for we to try dat."

Annabelle's head sank and Varina patted her shoulder.

"I know, girl. I know," she said soothingly. "Here, I want you to take this."

She dug into her purse for a jeweled pin. She had planned to sell it, but now she could think of no better use for it. Annabelle, crying, shook her head, but Varina pressed it into her hand. As Annabelle turned away Varina felt that another door had closed on the past.

And now Varina gathered her greatly reduced party and they walked down the gangplank. Then all at once she understood what her lot would be for a long time to come. A crowd had collected to gape and point at her. Bayonets glistened; soldiers looked at her with hostile eyes, while men and women of Federal sympathies sneered openly and called out: "So that's the Queen!" . . . "Damned lucky she's alive!"

Somehow they found their way to a hotel, and after another delay they were taken to two narrow rooms, gray and cheerless. When the guard closed the door they deposited their meager belongings on the floor and Maggie produced a bundle of newspapers which she had managed to pick up along the way. Varina opened them up and stared with horror at the garish headlines and the story below. She read that Jeff had been thrown into chains; he had nearly lost his life in a struggle with the guards. Soldiers, with a blacksmith and his assistants, had gone to his cell to shackle him. Jeff jumped up to protest; when the blacksmith advanced upon him Jeff struck out. The man, furious, lifted his vise and hammer; a soldier with a gun stepped in, and four men tried to subdue the prisoner. After a fierce struggle Jeff had been pinned to the floor.

Finally he lay helpless, his legs in irons. The account ended with the taunting sentence: "The former chieftain of the Confederacy, 'chief devil of it all,' fell back, weeping."

"Oh, Banny, Banny," she said, choking, "what are they doing to you?"

In her misery she turned frantically to another paper.

"Davis can never escape," it gloated. "The South could raise men and women to conspire to assassinate that noble man, Lincoln, but she can raise none to rescue Jeff Davis, that pseudo President and de facto deceiver, robber, and murderer."

Still another headline drew her attention: JEFF A COWARD— HIDES IN WOMAN'S SKIRTS! She discovered then that the news had been given out in Washington that Jeff Davis had tried to escape capture in an elaborate woman's disguise. A cartoon showed him mincing in a woman's bonnet, hoop skirts whirling while spurred boots showed beneath. So that was why the officer had demanded her shawl, why others had stolen her costumes!

She said to Maggie with her old determined look: "I'm going to see the Federal commander."

It took her the better part of the afternoon to locate the commander and gain an audience with him. When she faced him at last she said quietly: "Mayn't I write my husband?"

"No'm. Wouldn't be allowed."

"Then my friends?" She persisted.

"Well, maybe through regular channels. We have to pass on everything."

"May I write the officials in Washington?"

"Same way. We got to approve it."

She had a last question: "They'll let *him* write me?"

"No'm. He's under investigation."

The Federal commander seemed to enjoy making his answers.

On her walk back she discovered that two men followed her wherever she went. She bought a box of handkerchiefs (the soldiers had robbed her of these too), and as she left the shop one of the detectives walked up and talked to the clerk who had waited on her. Back in the hotel Maggie reported that she and the children were being trailed, too, everywhere they went.

That afternoon she discovered that the newspapers were continuing their attacks. One had somehow secured letters she had written to Jeff and was printing them under the headline: DAVIS INTIMATE LETTERS. Moreover, agents were scouring the country, interviewing Jeff's friends and enemies, purchasing documents. They were making a rigorous hunt through every War Department document of the period when he was in the Cabinet. Her head lifted; let them look there. They'd find nothing.

The next day the baby Winnie tossed restlessly in her cradle. Varina found she had a rising fever and sent Robert out for help. The doctor said it was whooping cough. The worst days of summer had arrived and their tiny room was like a stove. For a long time they watched the baby slowly decline. Hour after hour Varina sat by her, fanning the hot brow, shuddering over the coughs that racked her little body.

If anything happened to the child, if she lost a third one, how could she bear it? Hadn't she suffered enough? Maggie pleaded: "Varina, you're hurting yourself. You've got to rest, you've got to." But she remained there, day and night, until at the week's end the doctor nodded reassuringly. "She's better, Mrs. Davis. A whole lot better." So she could sleep again, the restless sleep of the overburdened.

Then came one reassuring message. Her mother managed to get a letter to her from Augusta, Georgia. Margaret Howell was in a comfortable house; they must not worry about her. Somehow she had contrived to accumulate a little purse, and she was sending "something you may need." It was a hundred and thirty dollars. And how they needed it!

Varina again tried to get a message through to Jeff and again she was refused with a curt "That wouldn't be allowed." On her return from the office of the commander she found little Jeff at the window in tears. He told her finally that an officer's wife had clutched him by the collar in the hotel lobby and screamed at him: "You're a murderer's boy, that's what you are! He'll soon be killed, but that'll be too merciful. They ought to tie him to a stake and burn him, little by little." The woman had raised her hand to beat him, and he had run away. When the child finished he stared at her and said sadly, "Will they burn Papa that way?"

Varina was wakened the next morning when Billy marched into the room, singing loudly: "We'll hang Jeff Davis on a sour apple tree!" When he saw Varina's expression the little boy stopped, but almost immediately he was whispering a kind of doggerel: "You think you is somebody, and Papa too. But you not and he not. Only me—and I'm a Yankee every time!"

The older child Jeff broke in, shamefaced: "Mama, don't mind him. The soldiers hand him nickels and teach him those things. They gave him something to do it. Billy doesn't know what it means. . . ."

After her sister had taken the children into the next room the old coachman tapped on the door with the newspapers. He paused, then said, "Ma'am, thought I'd tell you. Yestiddy de boy Jeff, he pass one o' dem black soldiers and call 'im 'Uncle.' Well, the soldier lif' his rifle and I think he wanta shoot, till somebody stop 'im."

Varina pressed her hands together. This couldn't keep up. What could she do? What was there for her to do? As she paced the room her glance fell on the papers, and she picked them up. New charges, she read, were being developed against Jeff. They said he had stolen tens of thousands from the Confederate Treasury. . . . Varina almost cried out her denial of the ridiculous accusation. If that were so, would she be half frantic now, trying to scrape together enough money to keep her little family going? The next charge was more serious. She read that Jeff Davis was responsible for the deaths of thousands of Federal prisoners in Southern camps. One of the Confederate prison commanders, Wirz, was to be brought to trial. It was hinted that Wirz would save himself by "telling the whole story about Davis's part in it."

She closed her eyes. Several times she had talked to Jeff about this matter, and he had asked her: "What can we do? We have barely enough food for our own soldiers, for our civilians. The prisoners get what our men get, no more, but no less." And some Southerners had cursed Jeff because he had not been harsh enough to prisoners of war. . . .

Now she understood. They were rigging a case, any kind of case to hang her husband! Already they were trying Mrs. Surratt and those other bedraggled people for Lincoln's death, and who was certain they were responsible?

Later she learned that Jeff was sick. According to the papers, he had grown ill during the past ten days. Some thought his condition rather serious. . . . The shackles had already been removed, but he was being kept under close confinement in a small cell beneath tide level. Three sentries were on constant duty outside his cell, each peering regularly at him through peepholes. He was inspected every fifteen minutes, night and day. A strong light was kept constantly burning over him.

She thought of Jeff's bad eye, his nervous state, his poor health. How could he survive such conditions? And what had she been doing here in Savannah while her husband was being treated so cruelly, while her children were in daily danger? She must take hold of herself. She had two things to do—first get her children to safety, then go to work to save Jeff.

An hour later she stood again before the commanding officer. "Can't I take my children somewhere else—anywhere in Georgia? Can't I go with them to my old mother in Augusta?"

"No." The eyes closed slowly, then reopened. "You have to stay here."

Her temper cracked. "Well, try to keep me from escaping! You can't watch me that closely. I can go to Canada——"

"Ma'am, just you try that, and you'll never be allowed back in this country. No matter what happens to Davis!"

She had no doubt that he was telling the truth. She started away, then braced herself and returned. "Please, I don't think you can object to this. Let me send my three older children away, with my mother and sister, to Canada, or anywhere. I promise you I'll stay."

Never, she decided later, had she pleaded so hard. For days there were conferences over the plan she had suggested, and at last a reluctant consent to it arrived. Varina had been putting aside a small reserve, but this, when added to the money she now got for her jewelry, still lacked seventy dollars of the passage money to Canada. For hours she paced the floor, for she could think of no other source of funds. Then a letter arrived from an anonymous friend in Atlanta. "You must accept this as a mark of Southern regard," he wrote. Enclosed were several hundred dollars.

She cried at the sight of it.

Mrs. Howell came from Augusta to take charge of the children, and as Varina embraced her she realized that her hair was snow white now. But she had lost none of her quick competence. Varina knew that Billy and Polly and Jeff would come to no harm in her hands.

"Don't worry, child," Margaret told Varina. "Don't worry."

At the last moment Varina decided to send Robert with them. He was the object of suspicion and some hate in the Federal-regulated city. He could serve them better, and be safer himself, up in Canada.

Now the boat was sliding away from the wharf, the children standing sadly at the rail. Jeff was clinging, as if frightened, to Mrs. Howell's gown; Polly, always adult in her own way, was trying to wave. The usually phlegmatic Billy had broken down. He was rubbing a fist into his eyes. And her sister Maggie was sobbing quietly. In the middle, her lips firmly together, was Margaret Howell, dominant to the end.

The boat had gone, and Varina turned slowly about. She was freer now to do the things she had set out for herself. . . . As she approached the hotel an older woman walking near her appeared to stumble. As Varina helped her up she whispered: "Mrs. Davis, I'm a friend. Wirz, the prison commander, has told them they can kill him, but he won't lie about your husband!"

She was careful to hide her relief over that news from the plainclothes man who was only a few feet way. When she reached her room she found an envelope on the dresser: PRIVATE. It told her that Burton Harrison, Jeff's secretary, had been offered his freedom if he would testify to certain things. "*But he will not. We wanted to get this word to you.*"

So there was hope after all; people did care, and they were working with her, for her and for Jeff! In the morning her pulse raced as she picked up a paper in which there was marked criticism of the Federal officials. A reaction had begun. Editors, North and South, were starting to raise questions about the military trials. Complaint was being made that Jeff Davis was subjected to needless mistreatment. She immediately began working through various channels, asking questions of her own: "What's happening among the Federal officials here? The commander—is he on permanent assignment? . . . I'd like to know about that too. Can you get word to me?"

She was accumulating information of a sort that had never interested her, but she knew that someday she would have need of it. Meanwhile the people of Savannah began to show their sympathy. Flowers arrived with notes of encouragement. (How many messages were kept from her she never knew.) Women sent garments they had sewed; would she take them for the baby Winnie? She accepted several invitations, but most of them she rejected. Several times she had to explain that she couldn't see anyone who was prominent in the Confederacy. It would bring suspicion on everybody present.

Overnight her informants brought news that the Federal commander was to be transferred. Daily she walked past Federal headquarters. She could see the commander's desk from the street, and when a new face appeared there she walked right in. When her turn came she introduced herself and spoke rapidly, urgently. "My money is almost gone; I can no longer afford to stay here with prices so high. Won't you let me at least go to Augusta, where I can be with friends?" She held her breath; the young man riffled through the papers before him, then pursed his lips. "Provided you follow our regulations, I can't see any reason why you shouldn't——"

She heard none of his other words. She had won the first step. Waiting only to thank him, she sped away. Her heart was pounding, her mind rushing ahead. "My tether's being lengthened, and how I'm going to take advantage of it!"

In Augusta, two days later, she started her labors. All that day, the next, and the next, she huddled at her desk, dispatching letter after letter. She must stir up Jeff's friends, try to get concessions from his enemies. One by one she went over names of lawyers, former officials, men and women she had known in Washington. Would it help to ask this one, or would it hurt? Should she take a chance and find out? Generally she followed the latter course. The only way to learn was to try.

She wrote passionate denials of all the offenses with which Jeff was charged, demanding that the records be checked, asking the addressee to search his own memory, explaining that since Jeff was silenced she was speaking for him. Some ignored her; many wrote notes that were icy, bitter. Yet repeatedly she received reassurances, pledges of assistance. Old friends sent information to contradict charges, data to be used in any way she wished.

She collected all this information and poured out to editors and friendlier officials a flood of facts, anything she could discover to refute the rumors, the claims against her husband.

"You can use this in any way you want," she wrote. "Please see that the truth is known."

Often at the end of the day, when she stopped for supper, her fingers were blistered and aching from so much writing. Often she plunged them into warm water, then when the pain subsided she started again and worked as long as she could.

Late one afternoon she found a thick envelope waiting for her at the post office. It was from Dr. Craven, the physician at Fortress Monroe. At last she had managed to make contact with him!

He told her that Mr. Davis had been ill, worse than most people realized. At one point they did not expect him to survive—but now, although he was better, he was listless, emaciated. His eye gave him increasing pain; his neuralgia had returned. Mr. Davis ate very little; yet he seemed, for the past few weeks, to be holding his own. She might be sure that as her husband's doctor he was doing all he could.

Unaware of people staring at her, Varina lifted the letter to her lips. During the following weeks she learned how true a friend Dr. Craven was. There were interruptions in their correspondence, for he must avoid offending his superiors. Yet he managed to get news to her and to let Jeff know something of what she was doing. He wrote her that Jeff had suffered extreme depression for a time. He had thought the world had turned away from him. But now he understood that something was being done in his behalf and he was grateful. Yet he longed, more than ever, for a glimpse of his wife and children. He asked constantly about the baby.

Dr. Craven had made sure that Jeff's diet was improved; he had helped provide a slightly warmer, drier cell. He offered a few personal items: Jeff had grown calmer, almost humble; he spent much of his time in prayer. Once, as the doctor was about to brush away a few crumbs near his bedside, Jeff asked him to stop. They were for a mouse he was trying to tame. "It's the only living thing I can help," Jeff had said. He was teaching it to approach him, to nestle against his arm. "The only living thing I can help . . ." As she read that line she put the letter down and wept quietly.

One afternoon, however, a letter came from Mr. Charles O'Conor, the celebrated New York attorney. He was ready to accept Jeff's defense without payment. Varina was startled because she remembered that Mr. O'Conor had been a leading Unionist! But the tone of his letter left no doubt of the sincerity of his offer, and she wrote him at once that she and Jeff would be honored to have him on their side.

The lawyer went to work immediately and asked the authorities if he could visit Mr. Davis. No reply. He wrote again, inquiring about his letters, but they appeared to be "missing." Mr. O'Conor, with the aid now of several other attorneys, applied to the Attorney General, to the Secretary of State, to the Chief Justice. None would grant them the slightest satisfaction. The unvarying answer was that the Davis case was in the hands of the military. So O'Conor went to the military. They told him that the Davis trial was "under advisement." He asked if it would be a civil or a military affair. There was no answer to that question, and O'Conor knew how important it was to have that question answered.

Yet the very strangeness of the government's course gave Varina a certain amount of hope. Gradually the conviction spread that the government "didn't know what to do with Davis." Mr. O'Conor advised her that Lincoln had once told someone he hoped Jeff would escape the country if the South were defeated, taking the problem off the government's hands. Added to that was another turn of events which considerably altered the case. The men who had sworn they could prove Jeff's part in a Lincoln plot now admitted they had lied!

But Jeff was not yet out of danger. Whenever she picked up a Northern paper she saw vengeful comments. Curious things were happening in Washington City. Andrew Johnson was breaking with the radicals; Jeff's case had become an issue between them, and his enemies were charging that Johnson was "too easy on Davis"!

And some of the Confederates, she told herself grimly, were turning against Jeff too. They were beginning to write articles, grant interviews that reflected on him as an incompetent who was the cause of their failure.

She'd fight now, harder than ever, for her husband and his reputation. She was struggling for Jeff's future, her children's future, in the life they must resume together.

Fall passed, then winter. One morning she did a thing she thought she could never attempt. By now she understood the value of the help that Northern men were giving. There had been indications that Horace Greeley, the great New York editor, was growing doubtful about the treatment Mr. Davis was receiving. Difficult as it was, she decided to appeal to him. Hesitantly, shrinking from the unhappy task, she started to write. Then her pen raced, and she told him everything she knew, everything she suspected.

A reply came promptly. It was circumspect; Mr. Greeley was surprised at some of her statements, but he would investigate. A few days later he wrote again, stating firmly that Mr. Davis was being unfairly handled, that he was due a trial. . . . Greeley would do what he could.

Varina realized that another powerful Northerner was now on their side.

In the spring a letter arrived from Jeff. The words were carefully guarded, and yet they were his, in his beloved handwriting. She replied at once, telling everything she thought would pass the scrutiny of his guards. Apparently they were now allowed to write each other regularly.

In one of his letters he described how, as he sat one night in his room, he had an optical illusion. "I saw little Polly walk across the floor and kneel down between me and the fire in the attitude of prayer. I moved from excitement, and the sweet vision melted away. I am hungry for the children's little faces. . . ."

In another he said: "If I alone could bear all the suffering of our South and relieve it from future calamity, I trust our Heavenly Father would give me strength to be a willing sacrifice."

But whether he was thinking of the South or his children, to Varina these letters were a blessed light.

More months went by. Then abruptly things grew more difficult for Jeff. The tyrannical young commander of the fortress discovered that Dr. Craven had ordered an overcoat for Jeff to protect him from the weather. He made an issue of a technicality and the doctor was removed. Varina was dismayed. For exercising normal precaution their friend had been dismissed. Would this mean that she could no longer get medical reports on Jeff? She wrote the new doctor and appealed for his help. At last she had word from him and knew that she had made liaison. The new man told her much less than his predecessor, but she had the comfort of knowing he would write if anything serious happened to Jeff.

Meanwhile she was little by little gaining freedom of movement. After several long arguments and much letter writing she even obtained permission to visit Mississippi. She had felt that someone must look into the family finances and find out what had happened to the plantation.

At Vicksburg she once more encountered Joe Davis, her brother-in-law. Joe had broken badly; he was heavy in body, uncertain of movement. His white beard moved up and down as he spoke, and his eyes were filmed and dim.

"Well, Varina," he said, staring off into the distance. "After all this time . . . Who knows what will happen to us next?"

The anger between them was gone. As he took the baby and played with her Varina found herself saying things to comfort him. They sighed together over Eliza, dead now for nearly three years. She told what she knew of Jeff, his condition, the progress of the war she was waging in his defense.

"I want to go to Brierfield to see what's left," she ventured.

But he shook his head. "You wouldn't like it, Varina. The Freedman's Bureau operates the place. You'd only be grieved."

It was a blow. Her Brierfield, where she had spent those sunny years of peaceful isolation by the river . . . And now she learned from Joe that there was nothing to recover from the estate. It was beyond reach. She suppressed a shiver. The years ahead would be harder than even she had guessed. But when she looked around her she saw that they were all poor. This was Vicksburg, scene of the terrible siege, of the Confederacy's great defeat in the West. She remembered those days of decision in Richmond, when a choice had to be made between the East or the West. There would be no help here.

She said good-by to Joe and went back to Georgia. It occurred to her now that since she had been allowed to visit Vicksburg she might be permitted to go to Canada. She had not seen her children for almost a year.

This time her request was granted promptly and she hurried North. She found Polly bigger than ever and just as solemn, little

Jeff his usual lively self, and Billy still the quiet one. With them and her mother and Maggie, she laughed and cried. They all talked quickly, lovingly; but for the most part they avoided the subject that was closest to their minds—Jeff and his future. Still, there were good evenings in the Canadian spring, and the crisp clear air was a tonic for her.

This happy visit came to a sudden end. A friend went to their house one evening with shocking news.

"I don't know how to tell you," he began. "We've just heard. Mr. Davis is growing weaker again. They think he's—very sick this time."

As he finished she turned to her mother. "I'm leaving tonight. Is there a telegraph office in town?"

In a borrowed carriage they took her to the railroad station, and there she wired President Andrew Johnson: "Is it possible you will keep me from my dying husband?" The next day, on her way, she received the authority to visit Jeff in Fortress Monroe. After twelve months she would be seeing him again!

Holding little Winnie in her arms, she arrived at the dark fortress at four o'clock in the morning. She had to wait in a drafty hall until ten-thirty. Then she was taken to a casemate and told she must sign papers, see this official, then that official. Blindly she signed everything, promised everything.

"This way, if you please."

Her fingers quivered, and her palms were moist. A soldier stepped aside; bolts were drawn, keys were turned, the door swung open.

For a moment she stood speechless. Jeff was so old, so worn, his hair so white! He lay on his back, his head slightly raised. He lifted his hand to her, and it dropped back. He was crying, and so was she. Going to his side, she took him in her arms as she might a child. "Banny, what have they done to you? Banny . . ." His lips moved, but she could make out nothing he said. His eyes had gone to the child as she stood, frightened, in the doorway.

"Winnie . . ." His call to the little girl was a hoarse whisper. She did not recognize him, but slowly she came forward, until Varina reached out for her and brought her to her father's arms.

When the doctor came some time later she waited breathlessly for his report.

"Some improvement today," he admitted, "though he's still mighty sick. His nervous system has been injured, and his remaining eye"—he frowned—"it's weakened considerably."

Her eyes filled as she saw the shrunken hands and the thin body. She barely heard the doctor's words: "Nervous debility . . . sinking spells . . . disturbed by the loss of sight."

The doctor touched her arm. "But now he has the best tonic he could want—you and the baby." He pointed. Jeff was still holding the child, and on his tired face was an expression of serenity.

She made applications for an extension of her visit, and the doctor gave her discreet support. She would be allowed to stay at the fortress, but she could see Jeff only a few hours a day. Now she set out to make him more comfortable. His narrow bed was infested with bugs. She soon remedied that. When she first looked at his food she almost gagged, for the greasy, tasteless stuff was slopped into a dish and covered with a gray hospital towel. It took her several weeks, but she finally succeeded in getting permission to bring him some good food from outside which she purchased herself. Her funds, which had been so often augmented by friends and sympathizers, were dwindling rapidly, but these expenditures had to be made.

She saw that he rested for regular periods while she sat beside him. At those times she applied herself to a task no less important than the others.

"What do they say outside?" he would ask, doubt in his face.

She must reassure him, let him understand he was not forgotten, not altogether hated or despised.

The present room, though better than his first one, was underground, covered by fifteen feet of earth, badly ventilated, and damp. She had not been there a week before she caught a chill and fever. How much more dangerous it must be for Jeff!

Worse, for the immediate present, was the bright light that burned endlessly above his sensitive eye, and the tramp of the guard that was never out of his hearing.

"Winnie," he told her one day, "I've known nothing in my life like this sensation of being watched every moment of the day and night, the feeling that an eye is always on me, seeing the slightest thing I do. It's a kind of inquisition."

After a time Jeff's condition changed once more for the worse. Again he slowly declined. His eyes grew glassy, and even to cross the room made him pant. One day he could not get up, and the doctor shook his head.

"He's worse, a lot worse," he told her.

That afternoon she sent off a dozen letters to the most important friends she had in Washington and one to President Johnson himself, with a direct request for an interview. Without waiting for replies she left for the capital.

At first the President did not wish to see her. Through an intermediary he suggested that she apply to Congress, which had power over such matters as the disposition of Mr. Davis. Her friends persisted, and then late one afternoon she walked up the steps of the building she had never expected to visit again and set foot in the White House.

As she waited she looked around her, thinking of her visits during the Zachary Taylor days, during the years when Franklin Pierce lived there. She wondered if Mrs. Lincoln had suffered as much within these walls as she had in the Confederate capital. . . . A long time passed, and then she was admitted. Before her was the man who had once glared furiously at her in the House, with hate for her husband in his eyes. But a change had come over Andrew Johnson, and now there was no fire in his heavy face and no anger.

The words poured from her lips: "Unless you do something, my husband's going to die. The conditions, the constant light, the sentries——" She hardly paused for breath.

The man opposite her sat silent, yet his expression was almost benign. At the end he looked at her rather sadly.

"We have to wait. Our hope is to mollify the people."

"There'd be no need to mollify anybody," she cried, "if you hadn't made a proclamation that he schemed to kill Mr. Lincoln! I'm sure you knew better at the time."

He looked away and then said quietly: "I was in the hands of wildly excited men—and I had to show I was willing to act quickly to get to the truth."

"But"—her hands beat on the desk—"there never was the slightest connection between Mr. Davis and that man Booth."

Andrew Johnson cleared his throat. "Well, that's all over. It's now a matter of time."

"Still—you issued a proclamation based on perjury. And that's the reason he's there, and near death."

To her surprise the President shifted in his chair and cried out: "I have so many enemies in Congress. If they find any cause for impeachment, they'll degrade me. If I could do anything for you, I would——"

Suddenly the door opened and a man came in, without waiting to be announced, whom she recognized finally as Thaddeus Stevens, grimmest of the radical Republicans. Disregarding her, he spoke to Andrew Johnson as brusquely as if he were talking to a servant who had disobeyed. He even threatened him, and Varina listened to the tirade, all at once embarrassed for the President of the United States.

Thaddeus Stevens left, and Andrew Johnson turned to her.

"I'm glad you saw a little of what I have to contend with." He raised his eyes. "Trust me; I'll do everything I can to help him." He thought for a minute and then added: "Has Mr. Davis thought of asking for a pardon, the way others have?"

She put on her gloves. "No, and I suppose you didn't expect that he would."

The President nodded again, and with that she left, feeling strangely sorry for the man.

She wasn't too optimistic of the results of her visit to the President, and she was surprised when it bore fruit almost immediately. The attitude of the guards changed, the light was removed from Jeff's room, and his quarters were improved. Now she was permitted to send for the other children in Canada. Yet Jeff's spirit, like hers, suffered under the confinement, and his condition fluctuated, now good, now poor. Another fall came, and winter.

Then one evening she stood beside him, sudden new hope in her eyes. A grand jury in Virginia had brought an indictment against Jeff for treason. The other vague accusations—the assassination, mistreatment of prisoners, and the rest of it—had been dropped. At last there was a charge against him, a charge which she believed they could defend.

Yet, as before, nothing happened. The attorneys labored without result. Varina went to Washington and appealed to them: "What haven't we tried? What else can I do?"

One of them gave her a direct answer: "If only enough people with established reputations in the North will come forward to ask for his release on bail, then the government will listen."

"I'll see them, any of them, all of them!" she replied.

One by one she went to see the men whom her lawyers suggested. Most of them had been bitter opponents of slavery, but they signed the application for Jeff's release. Her lawyers told her that if she could get a man like Horace Greeley to sign, there would be no necessity of adding anyone else's name.

"But there are strong reasons why he might not agree," they warned her.

"I'll go to see him today," she replied.

Her knees shook as she walked up to Greeley's office to call on the man she had once thought the lowest of all their enemies, the erratic, peculiar, emotional man whom most people feared and very few knew. She weighed the facts as she knew them: Mr. Greeley was a candidate for Congress; friends were advising him strongly against any entanglement in this dangerous Davis matter. If he did anything to help Jeff Davis he might hurt his newspaper. On the other side of the ledger was the fact that Greeley had already written her several months ago expressing his annoyance over the way Jeff had been treated.

In his office Mr. Greeley remained silent, inscrutable, a plump, pink-faced man with a fringe of white hair on his crown. Her eyes burning with emotion, she talked of Jeff's condition, of the way the officials were shunting them about, of her children.

"Please," she ended. "Please . . ."

Mr. Greeley got up slowly and put out his hand. "I'll sign the paper."

Later that week she knew that the great editor had probably damaged himself irretrievably. His paper would lose circulation that he could never regain for it. But, having met this man who had been her enemy, she knew that no matter what happened he would not go back on his word.

Two years after he had gone to Fortress Monroe, on a May evening, Jeff Davis rode into Richmond to appear in court. As they rode along the streets Varina looked about her intently. There at the corner was the old, long-familiar home that had been the White House of the Confederacy. She glimpsed the white-pillared gallery facing the garden, and the gray walls, now a little dingy. She stared, then looked away. It was too much.

Under guard, they were taken quietly to the Spotswood Hotel, to the same rooms they had occupied during their first days in Richmond. There she waited while Jeff was taken to the court to see if he would be released. . . .

Even if he went free today, there would be many, some in the South as well as the North, who would condemn him and, doing so, charge him with things that were untrue. She shivered a little as she thought of it. . . .

She paced up and down the room, fearing that there must have been some last-minute change of heart, that in the end Jeff would be sent back to die in prison.

Then there was a loud knock on her door. She threw it open, and a friend shouted to her: "He's out! He's on his way back, and the people have gone crazy. Come look!"

Tears rose to her eyes as she was led to a window at the front of the hotel. Soon, however, she recovered her composure. Straightening herself, she stood there, a little apart from the others, a proud and determined figure in black. The gray strands had spread through her heavy black hair. Years of struggle and sorrow had left their imprint on her face, and in the wide brown eyes there was a new depth. Her mouth was the mouth of a woman trained to endless conflict. In spite of it all, she had retained much of her rich beauty, the softened loveliness of the mature woman. She lifted her head, and there was an air of triumph in the gesture.

She heard snatches of sentences: "They'll never bring him to trial now!" . . . "It's all over, all over." She learned that Jeff had insisted on his right to a hearing, the right to try to vindicate himself. But the main thing now was that he was free, and he was coming to her.

From a distance she made out the carriage moving forward slowly, surrounded by hundreds of people. She searched the faces of the crowd below her. There was love in them, and pity and sympathy. If there was hatred, too, it was hidden today. Men and women and children were shouting, crying, waving handkerchiefs, trying to get near Jeff to shake his hand, to kiss his sleeve, to touch him.

The carriage stopped, and they helped him out. He stood motionless for a minute or two, an intent look on his face, blinking in the sunlight. For the first time in many months no guards surrounded him. He moved toward the entranceway below her, and suddenly there was silence.

From somewhere back in the crowd a voice cried: "Hat's off, Virginians!"

First one, then another, then hundreds of men were standing bareheaded, facing her husband in the sun.

Slowly Jeff entered the hotel, and now he was at the head of the stairs. An old woman near him began to sob.

"Banny!" Varina cried.

He reached out and took her hand. His fingers trembled; his grasp was weak, so weak. . . . With a firm gesture she tightened her hand over his. Suddenly, then, she realized that from now on her strength must be his; she must give to him her resolution, her restless energy.

She had expected all along that with his release she would turn the burdens back to him. Now, when she saw the beloved face, so worn, so broken, as if for the first time, she knew what lay ahead. Their years together might be limited, but for her there would probably be many beyond. And her work for this man, and his memory, had only begun.